W9-CEC-347

Evil Eye

ALSO BY ETAF RUM

A Woman Is No Man

Evil Eye

A Novel

Etaf Rum

HARPER
An Imprint of HarperCollins*Publishers*

This is a work of fiction. Names, characters, places, and incidents are products of the author's imagination or are used fictitiously and are not to be construed as real. Any resemblance to actual events, locales, organizations, or persons, living or dead, is entirely coincidental.

ISBN 978-0-06-298790-7

FOR REYANN AND ISAH,

نور حياتي

كل الطرق تؤدي إليك، حتى تلك التي أخذتها لانساك.

—محمود درويش

All roads lead to you, even those I took to forget you.

—Mahmoud Darwish

Evil Eye

PROLOGUE

YARA'S JOURNAL

I don't know why I'm writing this. William said it would help me articulate myself to you, reconcile past and present. I need to go back there, need to find a way to reach you, but I don't know how.

I've never been good with words. There are some things language cannot communicate.

Instead, I paint pictures in my mind. I build a white house with a colorful garden and a tranquil lake covered in emerald-green lily pads, then I put myself inside of it. The rooms are bright and airy, with big windows through which I watch the world. Outside, birds chirp and flowers bloom and everything feels calm beneath the wide, open sky. I close my eyes and paint more images, one stroke at a time, of sunflowers and sunsets and rooms full of books so I don't have to be alone.

I'm trying to listen to William's advice, to close my eyes and quiet the voices in my head. But when I begin to write down memories, attempt to lay them out in clear sentences, the words won't connect. When I look back for you, my mind goes blank. I can't describe it, this feeling I cannot name, this wound I cannot see. I feel it, though, like every bone in my body is on fire.

William says that writing can transform the unspeakable into a story.

Only I don't want to tell a story, I want to break free.

YARA'S JOURNAL

For as long as you could remember, your mother, my teta, taught you to tread carefully through life. Teta said, in Arabic, "Bad luck lurks everywhere."

Growing up, you avoided walking under ladders or breaking mirrors. If you spilled something, you threw a pinch of salt over your left shoulder to protect yourself. You knew that scratching an itchy palm meant you were going to lose money and if you looked a black cat in the eye a jinn would possess you.

Teta's favorite superstition was tabseer: reading the leftover grounds of Turkish coffee at the bottom of a cup. Over the years, you watched her read grounds for family and neighbors and friends, all eager to learn their fortune. Teta would sit across the table from them on the rooftop balcony, her hands curled around a teacup intricately painted with flowers. It was small, only an inch or two in height and even less in diameter. She'd peer down into it, draw a breath through her nose, and nod. When she'd finally look up, there was a distinct air of knowing to her, a gleam in her eye.

You spent most of your time on the rooftop with Teta, planting and cleaning vegetables, baking bread, hanging laundry, singing and strumming your oud. Your shelter was small and cramped, and up on the spaciousness of the rooftop, in the wide-open air, you felt alive, free.

One morning, as she prepared the brew, Teta told you, "I was your age when my own mother taught me how to read the remnants on the bottom of a cup." The aroma of freshly ground beans was in the air. You sat close together on the rooftop of your cement shelter, in an overcrowded refugee camp in the occupied West Bank, as Teta began the practice that had been in the family for generations.

"Turkish coffee is first and foremost a tradition, a ritual," she began. "An art."

Cross-legged on the concrete floor, you watched Teta scoop two spoonfuls of finely ground coffee powder into a wide-bottomed copper ibrik, then fill it halfway with water. She held it over an open flame to get the best taste, whisking and stirring until the mixture reached a boiling point. As soon as the brew foamed over, she poured a stream of kahwa into two porcelain cups with saucers, then placed them on a matching serving tray. You thought the coffee set looked like a work of art, the intricate patterns hammered into the shiny copper by local artisans, the hand-painted tulips and blue-and-white hamsas, meant to ward off evil.

Your eyes fixed on Teta, you sipped the steaming, fragrant liquid. It tasted the way you imagined kawha would taste—strong and sweet, with a dark and bitter aftertaste.

"You need to drink slowly, Meriem," Teta said, pursing her lips around the porcelain rim. "After the last sip, you make a wish."

You followed her lead, drinking from the side so the sediments stayed loose, until your cup was empty.

When Teta finished her own cup, she placed a saucer over the rim and flipped it upside down. As you waited for the coffee dregs to dry, you sang and strummed your oud, your fingers plucking the strings of this ancient instrument while your mother hummed along. Eventually, she turned the cup upright and you both peered inside, studying the dark grainy streaks like reading a treasure map.

"You have to be careful," Teta said, her voice serious. "It's bad luck to read your own cup unless it's for practice."

Over the years, you and Teta spent many afternoons on the rooftop together like this, huddled over an empty cup, interpreting the swirls and streaks and symbols. With time, you learned to read the remnants yourself. Long trails meant the wish would come true, while short trails meant failure. Symbols near the rim predicted the future, while symbols on the bottom dealt with the past.

A ring meant marriage. Flowers meant happiness. Chunks of grounds on the saucer meant troubles were leaving you.

It wasn't until the night of your wedding that Teta agreed to read your cup for the first time.

Once again on the rooftop, Teta placed the coffee set in the same arrangement: the ibrik in the center of the tray, the well-worn cups on both sides. You sipped your kawha slowly, your fingers trembling, noticing a thin crack down the side of the cup. After the last sip, you swirled the sediments around the walls, then flipped the cup facedown on the saucer. Teta placed your wedding ring on the top of the cup, her hands fumbling at the fabric of her thob.

You watched her with great anticipation, wondering how you'd make it through the ten minutes it'd take the dregs to dry. Your mind wandered to a life beyond this camp, where you would spend your days doing something you loved, like singing, someplace where the neighbors wouldn't be watching your every move, waiting for you to get pregnant, chopping vegetables and gossiping, judging every decision you made. Someplace where you felt more free.

"It should be dry," Teta said, flipping the cup over at last.

You blinked your dreams away, inhaled a deep breath. This is it, you thought. A new beginning.

But when Teta glanced down at your cup, you knew instantly that something was wrong. She tilted it, frowned, then pulled the cup close to her face, uncharacteristically silent. She'd rarely needed more than a few seconds to interpret the symbols, and her seeming reluctance now filled you with dread.

"What do you see?" you asked. "Will I be a singer in America? Will I be happy?"

Teta's hands were shaking, and for several seconds she stared down at her lap, her face raked and twisted, before rearranging her expression and looking back at you.

"I see many nests," she finally said.

"Pregnancy?"

"Yes," Teta said. "Many children. You'll make a wonderful mother."

"Mother." You draw the word out, somehow, like a sad melody. Even though you didn't want children, even though you longed to be free, it must

have been inconceivable for you to imagine a life as a woman that didn't include motherhood.

"Great," you eventually said, frowning. "Like most women we know. What else?"

Teta swallowed, her eyes fixed on the cup. She shifted in her seat, tilting the cup to the side, her fingers unsteady. "There are mountains," she finally said. "Five, maybe six."

"What does that mean?"

Teta blinked, her expression hard. She knew you knew what this meant, but she obliged you. "Mountains symbolize hardships, obstacles." She shook her head, softening her features. "But it could just mean that you'll struggle adjusting to America."

"But what if it's a warning that something bad will happen to me?"

"No, no," Teta said, avoiding your eyes. "Everyone suffers hardships in this life, Meriem. Especially women."

You looked at her, unconvinced. "Do you see anything else?"

Teta opened her mouth then closed it. She shook her head, but tears welled in her eyes. "You don't have to go, ya binti. You can stay here with me, at home in your country."

"I wish I could, Yumma," you told her. "But Palestine is no longer ours, and there's nothing left for me here." Sitting there, wringing your hands in your lap, your body sinking toward the ground now, you felt an old darkness grow and spread through you, as if your soul were suffocating in tar. How could you tell Teta—you could not—that the fear of leaving her and starting anew could not compare to the gripping, sickening terror of staying behind? You looked up at her, struggling to keep your voice steady. "Please don't worry about me in America. I'll visit as often as I can, and the next time you see me, I'll be famous!"

Teta tried to smile, but she made a noise that sounded like a strangled laugh, then her tears streamed down her face and she started crying and couldn't stop. She set the cup down and buried her face in her hands. For a while you watched her, your hands clutched at your throat. And though you said nothing, your fingers pressed so hard into your neck that on your flight to America, your new husband would notice a blue bruise imprinted on your skin.

Eventually Teta caught her breath and wiped her face. She studied you for a moment, then she reached for the back of her neck to undo the clasp on her necklace. It was made of twenty-four-karat gold, and from it hung a blue-eyed hamsa charm that Teta's own mother had given her on her wedding night.

Teta brushed your hair to one side, kissed your forehead. Then she pulled you into her, your face pressed hard against her chest, then released you.

Slowly she hung the necklace around your neck, almost whispering. "Take this, ya binti. It will always protect you."

1

Yara was straining basmati rice in the kitchen sink when the doorbell rang. In a rush, she transferred the rice to a pot, adding garlic, allspice, turmeric, and a stick of cinnamon, wishing she'd had a red chili pepper on hand. Stealing a quick glance at the oven timer, she frowned. She tightened her fingers around the pot handle and listened to her husband's voice in the hall.

"Ahlan wa sahlan," Fadi said. "Come on in."

As she added warm water to the pot, Yara could hear Fadi kissing his parents on both cheeks, then the shuffle of shoes being taken off by the front door, then her two daughters' footsteps like drumbeats down the stairs. "Sitti! Seedo!" they called out.

On any other night, she would have peeked out of the kitchen to watch Mira and Jude descending the circular staircase to greet their father at the door, on his return home from work. Fadi would set down a box in the foyer, wiping his palms against his pants before his daughters clamped their arms around his legs. But on Sundays, Fadi took off work, and more often than not his parents came over for dinner. Yara always spent the day pacing around the house in preparation for their arrival, scrubbing the bathrooms and picking specks of dirt off the hardwood floors, before centering herself between the walls of her spice pantry, surrounded by olive oil, za'atar, nutmeg, and coriander, the aroma bringing her back to her grandmother's kitchen in Palestine.

She set the pot of rice on the stove and lit the burner. Looking up, she found Fadi filling the doorway with his tall, broad frame. "You've outdone yourself," he said. "Everything smells delicious."

Yara wiped her forehead with the bottom of her apron. In the foyer she could hear her daughters ushering their grandfather upstairs to play with them. "Thanks," she said, without meeting Fadi's eyes.

As soon as she grabbed a tall bottle of olive oil from the pantry, Yara felt another presence in the kitchen. When she looked up, her mother-in-law was standing next to Fadi.

"Marhaba," Nadia greeted her.

"Ahlan khalto," Yara said, forcing her mouth into a smile. She gripped the edge of her apron, breathing slowly.

"Try not to sound too excited now," Nadia said in Arabic as she peeled off her hijab, folded it neatly, and set it on the counter. Her short hair was henna-dyed a rich wine-red color, but tints of gray showed at her temples.

Fadi coughed, his face reddening. "I'm going to check on the girls."

Yara could feel her heart begin to race as he slipped out of the room. She unscrewed the olive oil, poured a splash into the rice.

"Shu? You're still cooking?" Nadia said, walking toward the stove. She was a plump woman with round cheeks and small, expectant eyes.

"I'm almost done," Yara said, her hands shaking. She put a glass lid on the rice, adjusting it so no steam would escape.

"Let's see what we have here," Nadia said. She walked over to the dining table, eyeing the Palestinian staples Yara had spread out on the sufra: olives and olive oil, hummus, pita, sliced tomatoes, pickles, lemons, and the chopped mint and parsley leaves that she'd picked from the potted plants on her windowsill.

"No salad?" Nadia said.

"There's tabbouleh in the fridge."

Nadia nodded to herself, hesitating for a second before walking back over to the stove. One by one, she lifted the aluminum wrapping off each covered dish, letting the steam escape from the shakshuka and fried kibbeh balls. Yara felt her ears get hot but kept her eyes on the water in front of her, almost at its boiling point. She added a teaspoon of salt and secured the lid.

"What else are we having?" Nadia said, eyeing the inside of the oven.

"Kufta kebabs with tzatziki and yellow rice."

"What about your father-in-law? You know he can't eat rice anymore with his blood sugar."

Yara swallowed, trying to remain calm, a state that was hard to access lately, especially in her mother-in-law's presence. "I know," she said, tilting her head toward the electric cooker. "I made bulgur for him."

"Good, good," Nadia said, running a hand through her hair as she circled the kitchen. She scanned the light oak floors and white granite countertops, which were spotless despite the three-course meal in progress. Seemingly disappointed, she went over to the eating area, where she picked at a spiderweb hanging from two light bulbs of the chandelier.

Yara sighed. "Sorry, I always forget to dust that thing."

"Clearly," Nadia said.

As usual, only a few minutes in her mother-in-law's presence and she was reminded of all the ways she was failing.

"You know what they say," Nadia said now, running her index finger against the windowsill, then bringing it to her face to examine it. "A messy house is a sign of a mess within."

Watching her mother-in-law survey the kitchen as the sun tucked itself behind the pine trees, Yara felt such a longing to be alone, away from the gaze of Nadia's judgmental eyes. Everything about Yara seemed to irritate her mother-in-law, especially lately. Maybe Yara was too defiant, too questioning. Maybe Nadia resented that she wasn't able to control her, or that Yara refused to be the kind of woman Nadia wanted her to be, even after all these years.

In the early years of her marriage, Yara had helped Nadia clean the same way she'd helped her own mother as a child: plunging her hands up to her elbows in dishwater, crouching under sofas and tables to retrieve crumbs of food left by Fadi's younger brothers, ironing and folding all their laundry, scrubbing bathroom floors, her head dizzy from the fumes as she wiped stray pubic hairs from the base of the toilet. Yara had hoped these acts of service would bring her and Nadia closer, but to her mother-in-law Yara was only doing what was expected of her.

When she thought about it, the tension between them began on the day of Yara's wedding, nine years ago, when Nadia had asked her to start wearing a hijab. Yara was nineteen then, a first-year in college, and she had flown to Fadi's hometown just days before the wedding—living there ever since. "No thanks," Yara had said without flinching. They were standing in the bathroom while Yara reapplied her eyeliner, having cried it off twice before. "Nothing against the hijab if that's what a woman chooses for herself," Yara had said. "The Quran clearly states it's my choice. But I'm not really religious."

Yara felt then the sudden weight of Nadia's gaze, so disapproving, it made Yara turn away from her own reflection. She swallowed, a soft ache beating inside her, like a bird unable to flutter its wings. Nadia shook her head slowly, her eyes assessing Yara—this was the sudden weight, her mother-in-law's judgment. "It's not just about religion," Nadia said, her lips curled in disapproval. "You wear it out of modesty, to prevent hakyelnas. We don't want people to start talking."

People, Yara had thought, swallowing hard. Of course.

Yara had been unsure about moving to the South, a place she'd known about only from her favorite southern writers: Flannery O'Connor, Alice Walker, Toni Morrison. From their books she'd gathered that southern culture was not so unlike her own: full of loud and large close-knit families where women married young and had many children, focused on conservative values with an emphasis on religion or tradition, with an adherence to recipes that were passed down through generations. Even the obsession with tea at every possible social gathering—though southerners preferred it iced while Arabs served it boiling—felt like a point of connection. The similarities filled her with both comfort and dread. What kind of life would she have in the suburbs? Would she fit in? Or would she feel like she'd felt all those years in Brooklyn: disconnected, unseen, alone?

She wished she had been able to voice her hesitation to her family back then. But she struggled to articulate her feelings, even to herself. Words diluted things, made them smaller. Growing up, she could not explain how it felt to look out the window every night, waiting for Baba to come home, or describe the fear that consumed her when his shouts echoed through the walls or the feeling of her face pressed against her pillow to drown out the noise, only to realize that it was coming from inside her.

Drawing, she soon learned, helped soothe the twisted feeling inside her, the dark pit of fear in the center of her chest, the certainty that something was constantly wrong. Alone in her cramped bedroom, she drew what she saw through the window: a row of red brick houses, the orange pink shimmer of a sunset, yellow dandelions dancing beneath the golden sun, the swirling dark turbulence of a night sky, a collection of vignettes, drawn in a frenzy, that left her in a strange state of emotional curiosity, as if her stiff heart had cracked open to the world. She hoped the pleasure she felt in these states would be enough to heal the darkness that rumbled through her, to cure the war inside her head. But these days, she felt very far from the person she wanted to be.

Now, as Nadia made her way toward the fridge, Yara slid in front of her and opened it first, scanning the glass shelves to make sure they were clean. With her back to her mother-in-law, she said, "It's been hard to keep up with everything lately."

"I can see that," Nadia said.

Yara's face went hot, despite the cold air from the fridge. She wanted to confess to Nadia that she really was trying her best, but lately there was this overwhelming darkness that seemed to stand beside her like a shadow.

"I know you've been struggling," Nadia went on, as if she could read Yara's mind. "But it's time you pulled yourself together, dear. For your family's sake."

Yara shut the fridge door and returned to the stove, where she lowered the heat on the rice. She leaned her hip against the counter and watched Nadia open the fridge, lift out one container after another, and scan the bottom for an expiration date, muttering to herself when she eventually found one to toss away.

"Why don't you come with me to the mosque this Friday?" her mother-in-law said, after pulling out the bright green tabbouleh and tasting it from a cupped palm. "A little socializing might cheer you up."

Yara frowned and opened a cupboard, pretending to look for something inside.

"You haven't been in a while," Nadia went on, her hand coated with olive oil and specks of fresh parsley and mint. "And the women have been asking about you. It would be good to show your face."

"Sorry, I can't. A new term starts tomorrow, and I'll have a lot of work to do."

"Right. But you're coming to Nisreen's baby shower next weekend, no? She would be so upset if you missed it."

Yara closed her eyes, her face hidden behind the cupboard door. Her mother-in-law knew she wasn't a lively person, preferring to be alone or with her immediate family, and yet she still insisted on inviting her to every Arab event in town. Their small town had an even smaller Palestinian community, with perhaps two dozen families, but Nadia knew mostly everyone, all the women coming together to form a little village of their own. Yara had accompanied her mother-in-law in the past despite her disinterest, smiling with perfect composure, even joining in on the gossip every now and then to show that she was a good sport. But lately these activities ceased to have any meaning, and she could no longer bring herself to pretend otherwise.

"Sorry," Yara said, turning the burner off under the rice. "I'm not in the mood to go anywhere."

Nadia was silent, reaching back into the bowl of tabbouleh.

"You can't keep avoiding everyone," she finally said, licking her fingers. "When was the last time you came with me to a wedding or had any of our friends over for dinner?"

Yara shrugged. Technically these women were Nadia's friends, not hers. She could easily go an entire week and only receive texts from Fadi, the only friend she had.

"It's unhealthy to keep to yourself all the time," Nadia continued. "Not to mention how important it is to maintain your social standing in the community. People will start talking if they don't see you."

Yes, of course, the people.

"What could they say? I'm not doing anything wrong."

"As if that's ever stopped anyone," Nadia said. "People don't hear from you for a while and they assume all sorts of things: you're up to no good, or afflicted with some disease, or God forbid, you're suffering from something mentally, an evil spirit."

Yara rolled her eyes. "A jinn, really? This isn't *Aladdin*."

"You act like I'm making this all up," Nadia said. "You clearly haven't been yourself, and we don't want to give anyone a reason to start rumors."

Nadia looked at her with those hard brown eyes, her expression so serious that Yara turned away. She lifted the bottom of her apron to wipe her forehead again.

"I've been worried about you, dear," Nadia went on. "Your eyes are sunken and your eyeliner is smudged. You look like you've aged ten years." She scanned Yara up and down. "And why are you always dressed in black and wearing leggings? You need to put in more effort. For Fadi's sake."

Yara leaned into the counter, wondering how long this would go on. She wanted to tell Nadia that she wished it were as simple as her appearance. She would rather have something wrong with her body, something fixable, than with her mind, which she suspected was the real problem. But she wouldn't dare admit that to her mother-in-law.

Instead Yara cracked her knuckles and looked at Nadia, at her slumped shoulders, and the way her body bent, as if life had weighed her down.

Yara willed herself to meet Nadia's eyes. "This is what I like to wear. Besides"—she hesitated—"why don't you ever tell your son to dress up for me?"

Nadia raised an eyebrow. "That's not how it works. Pleasing your husband is your duty."

"Is it?" Yara said. She was laughing now and finding it hard to stop. Of all the mothers-in-law she could've had, why did she have to end up with one who was intent on pressuring her to walk the same path she had vowed her whole life to escape? Not that it would've stopped her from marrying Fadi, even if she had known. She'd had other problems to worry about then.

"Oh, for goodness' *sake*," said Nadia, looking stricken. "I can't remember the last time I saw you crack a smile, and this is what you find funny? Is it too much to ask for you to put in a little effort, for your husband's sake? I've been trying to hold my tongue for some time now, but enough is enough. You can't continue on like this."

Yara stopped laughing and met her eyes. "Like what?"

"Moping around like you're on the verge of death yourself. You need to toughen up, dear. You have a family that depends on you."

Yara stepped away from the stove, adrenaline pouring through her veins. "You act like I'm spending my days in bed," she said. "I take care of the girls all by myself, go to work every day, keep up with all the housework, and have dinner ready for Fadi every night. Maybe if I had a little more help with the girls, I could worry about how I look. But that's the least of my problems right now."

"Your children are your responsibility," Nadia said, shaking her head. "You can't expect anyone else to raise them for you. If you're so overwhelmed, then you don't need to work."

"No way," Yara said too quickly. "My job is the only thing I do for myself. Why would I give that up?"

"Why not?" Nadia said. "Fadi makes good money, mashallah. He doesn't need your help."

It took considerable effort not to scream. Her mother-in-law rarely missed an opportunity to remind her that Fadi was the breadwinner, as if that wasn't the norm in her own family, too. Yara's parents had immigrated to America from Palestine shortly after they married, arriving in Brooklyn with a few hundred dollars in their pockets and no English. The Arab community in Bay Ridge and Baba working day and night to provide for them was how they'd survived.

In the early months of her own marriage, Fadi was still a cashier at his father's gas station, where he had worked since he was seventeen. Every night, Fadi came home to their cramped apartment complaining about Hasan, vowing the next shift would be his very last. "I don't see how a father can treat his own son like this," he would say. "Always looking down on me, never says thank you or nothing."

It wasn't until Yara became pregnant with Mira that Fadi thought seriously about his next steps. Without a college education, he decided he would be better off saving money to open his own business than trying to get another job. At the time, Yara was enrolled in a local college and qualified for financial aid and a full academic scholarship. Each semester, after her tuition was paid and her books bought secondhand, she received a substantial check in the mail, which Fadi had her sign over to him. When they'd finally saved enough, Fadi quit his job and started a wholesale company with his high school friend Ramy. Together they purchased large quantities of general merchandise—tobacco accessories, energy drinks and shots, pain relievers, sunglasses, gloves, batteries, and so on—directly from manufacturers, warehoused them, and sold them in smaller quantities to convenience stores all across the state. The business was financially solvent within six months and quite profitable within two years. "My father told me I would fail without him," Fadi said. "I've never seen a man hate this much on his own son, but I did it. I proved him wrong."

Yara was happy for him, but a part of her wished she had been able to do the same. Make something of herself beyond the confines of marriage and motherhood, outside other people's expectations. Create something from scratch, move with that kind of confidence and certainty, as if she'd grown up in a world where women could do that.

"It's not about the money," Yara said now, pressing her palms around the pot of rice until her skin burned. "I want to do something with my life."

Nadia let out a bemused laugh. "You *are* doing something, dear. You have a husband and children to look after."

"That shouldn't mean I can't do anything else."

"Except you can barely handle your responsibilities now." Nadia flicked her eyes back toward the chandelier. "It's time for you to take a break from work and focus on your family, your home." She paused, softening her voice. "You'll feel better with time, in the comfort of your home, you'll see."

Yara was silent. Giving up her work would not make her feel better. Not that she could expect Nadia to understand, considering the life she'd led. Much like Yara's own parents, Nadia had been born and raised in a refugee camp after her family had been evacuated from their seaside home in Yaffa during the Israeli occupation of Palestine in 1948. It was impossible for Yara not to feel deep and intense sorrow for her mother-in-law's loss, nor could she ignore the reality that her perception of the world was no fault of her own, but rather rooted in the world she came from. Of course Nadia believed that a woman belonged at home. Of course she valued the importance of preserving family, of keeping the family unit tight and intact with a father who worked long hours to provide and a mother who stayed behind, tending to the house and raising the children.

Her mother-in-law had been denied the privilege of a home, so now in this beautiful country, she would be insistent on preserving one.

Yara stared down at the yellow rice, almost finished resting.

These thoughts had always been a whisper in her ear, reminding her how good she had it, reminding her that the things she found unfair were nothing, *nothing*, compared to the struggles of her parents and grandparents. And yet there were days when her ability to empathize with her family's troubled history did not do what it had done for many years, which was to make her listen, submit, obey. Tonight, she felt as though she had lived her life carrying a weight she could not set down. She made sure to keep her eyes on the pot and not look Nadia in the eye or else she would drop to her knees and scream—the wail so loud and sharp like a dying animal. Why didn't Nadia understand that just because the women in her family had wholly dedicated their lives to their children, their husbands, that didn't mean Yara must? She felt the stain of an old sadness seeping into her now. Perhaps it was because of the sacrifices of these generations of women that the idea terrified her so deeply. Because she had seen what that kind of life had done to her own mother, had watched it suck the life out of her eyes, left her burning with resentment: wanting, reaching, incapable, afraid. All Yara wanted now was a life that was the opposite of that.

"You're quiet," Nadia said. "You must realize I have a point."

Yara shook her head, her face burning. "No, not really," she managed to say.

"Why not? Tell me, what could be more important than your family?"

Yara peered through the glass lid to the rice and reached for a fluffing fork from the drawer. She considered explaining to Nadia the consequences of their families having come to America, where women were capable of having careers *and* being mothers. She could tell Nadia that maybe she should ask her son to cut back on *his* work so that Yara could advance her own career. Or the thing she wanted to say most but could never muster the nerve: every time Nadia told her to stay at home with the children, it only heightened her resolve to keep working.

But she knew from nine years of being Nadia's daughter-in-law that none of this would be met with a receptive ear.

"There's no shame in admitting when things are too much for you," Nadia said, moving closer. "You're only hurting your daughters by pretending otherwise."

Fear came at the sound of the word *daughters*, arriving as a heavy sensation beneath her ribs. Yara gripped her fingers around the fork, her hands shaking.

"Think about your girls," Nadia said. "Think about how your behavior is affecting them."

She swallowed, unable to bear the thought of hurting her daughters. Didn't Nadia understand? She was always thinking about the girls, about her own past, about the sickening need she felt to put it all behind her. These days that's all she was able to think about.

A rush of steam hit her face as she lifted the glass lid off the rice. She touched her open palm to her cheek, her mouth. She stood very still, the heat leaching into her skin, and wondered why her life had unfolded in this way, despite all of her efforts, her sacrifices, her world now brimming with a deep sense of loss.

The rest of the evening progressed the same as it always did when her in-laws were over. The adults ate dinner around the sufra while Mira and Jude picked at chicken and yellow rice with their fingers in front of *Encanto* in the living room. Her father-in-law told a story about an argument he'd had with the neighbor. "He looks at me like I'm some sort of street rat," Hasan said. He was a loud, fumbling man who spoke with his hands, as though he were directing an orchestra. "I told him, 'Keep staring, and I'll poke that eye out.'"

Nadia made a face. "Is there anyone in town you haven't had a problem with?"

At the other end of the table, Fadi was shoveling food into his mouth, as if to prevent himself from having to engage in conversation. With a mouth full of tabbouleh, he turned to Yara. "Everything is delicious, babe," he said.

Yara nodded but couldn't manage to look him in the eye. Her mind was filled with the usual thoughts she had whenever she was around Fadi's family: her in-laws were there to keep her in line should she ever forget where she came from. Not that she ever could.

"Oh, for goodness' sake," said Nadia, when, in refilling Jude's plate with rice, Yara knocked it over, and the grains splattered like little insects across the sufra. Trying to clean up this mess, Yara tipped over her glass, and water spilled over the table, then onto the floor.

"This is exactly what I mean, Yara," Nadia said, standing up to grab a rag. "Another example of why you're not doing as well as you claim."

Yara sat back down, slumped in her seat, watching as her mother-in-law pushed the rag across the table.

"Enough is enough," Nadia said when she finished cleaning and plopped back into her chair. "You're clearly not in a good place, and it's time you did something about it." She turned to Fadi, who sat in his chair sideways, as though plotting an escape.

"Why don't you tell her, Fadi?" Nadia said, wiping sweat from her upper lip. "Say something."

His face flushed a deep red.

"Tell me what?" Yara said, an unexpected fury sprouting inside her.

Fadi swallowed, avoiding her eyes. "Nothing, nothing." Then he turned to Nadia. "Leave me out of this, Yumma," he said, his voice sharp. "I have my own shit to worry about."

"Do you?" Hasan said, setting down a skewer of kufta and turning to his son. "The last time I checked, you haven't stopped by the store in weeks. You still have a responsibility to me there."

Fadi was saying something back to him, but Yara couldn't hear him. She glanced over to Mira and Jude, afraid that they could hear the raised voices, but to her relief they were wrapped up in their show.

She touched her open palm to her cheek and sank farther into her seat. She turned to look out the window. Outside the soft light of sunset filtered through the branches of scarlet oaks and longleaf pines. Yara inhaled and wiped her palms on her napkin. The intensity in her body was very severe, like something was pressing down on her from all directions. For the rest of the dinner she said nothing, and heard only the tiny voice whispering, reminding her of all the things she could've done, should've done, all the ways she was failing. She stared at her plate, wondering what it would be like to feel nothing, to close her eyes and hear only silence inside her head.

2

Monday morning, a blaring alarm jolted Yara awake at twenty past six. She reached for her phone, her fingers mechanically tapping the glass, and shut it off. Twenty-two notifications: eleven emails, two calendar reminders, nine Instagram comments. Already her mind was racing like a browser with too many tabs open, brimming with everything and nothing at once. She stumbled out of bed and into the shower for a quick rinse, rocking herself back and forth under scalding hot water until the heat numbed her skin, loosened her shoulders.

She woke the girls—Mira first, then Jude—urging them to dress quickly. She brushed their hair, made them breakfast, and handed them the lunches she'd packed the night before, each with a note inside. Then she grabbed her work bag before rushing them out the door.

In the car, she clicked in her seat belt and made sure the girls did the same. She had twenty minutes until she had to be at work. If she hurried, she could just make it. Her eyes fixed on the rearview mirror, she backed out of the driveway. And then she was pulling into work, onto the college campus parking lot, only she didn't remember getting there.

She didn't remember dropping the girls off at school.

She didn't remember saying goodbye. Had they spoken to her during the drive? Had she responded?

She stared at the campus in front of her, Nadia's words in her ear. Too many of her days were passing this way, with whole blocks of time blurred or missing altogether. Her body moved through space and time without her knowledge or consent. Some days she couldn't remember putting on a particular outfit, or what had happened after retrieving the girls from school or extracurriculars. She'd pick up her camera in those moments and take pictures, one after another, just to be sure she was there.

She knew she was moving too fast, racing from one task to the next. The problem was, if she slowed down, everything only felt worse.

It was the first day of the new term, and the college was brimming with life. The sun golden against the brick buildings, students scurrying across campus to new classes, their schedules in front of them or staring at maps on their phones.

Pinewood College's three-hundred-acre campus was widely considered the focal point of their picturesque town. It was particularly beautiful in the southern autumn. Wide brick buildings were framed by trees—maples and oaks gone red and yellow, the cedars leaving splashes of green—and hiking trails wove through the campus, one of them leading to the lake, a popular gathering spot for students to swim and picnic.

Once in her office in the Humanities Building, a small room at the far end of the first-floor hall, Yara knew she wouldn't have to talk to anyone. There, she brewed coffee and made her to-do list: *reformat nursing website, print syllabus, photograph welding lab,* before tackling the first two items.

She'd come here to teach art, but she'd only been approved for one introductory course per semester: "Responding to Art: Form, Content, and Context." Otherwise, her real workload was as the college's graphic designer: inputting calendars, formatting websites, changing out images—all dull, repetitive tasks. Such a waste, she thought, then felt a jolt of panic, recalling Nadia trying to make her give up her work.

Jonathan, the director of the Humanities Department, had said three years ago that he would let her teach more art classes once a full-time instructor retired or left. Since then, budget cuts became his excuse whenever she checked in with him about opportunities. She knew she didn't look like what he thought an artist should, seeing it in his face the first time she applied for a faculty position. "I'm fully qualified for the job," Yara said when he blinked, defensiveness creeping into her tone.

During her first term teaching the intro course, Jonathan had sat in on her class and was stunned to see she was teaching the works of African American painter Philemona Williamson and Lebanese painter Helen Zughaib, that she was refusing to center whiteness as the custodian of high art. He'd given her "feedback" afterward, strongly encouraging her to bring back the lectures on Monet and Matisse, and only use unapproved works to add flavor rather than as part of the core canon.

Yara stacked the freshly printed syllabi on her desk and began to collate and staple them. Outside, kids flew by on skateboards, crossing the small green quad, so carefree. It was a feeling she'd rarely experienced in college, or ever, really. She'd been pregnant with Mira when she first enrolled here as a student, then with Jude, overloading her credits every semester and racing through back-to-back classes twice a week to minimize the time she spent away from home. Nadia's round eyes surfaced in her mind, and she shook them away. No, she had not worked this hard over the years—rushing through her degrees while raising two kids and maintaining a home and standing up to her mother-in-law and trying to succeed in a world that did not value her contributions—so she could stand in front of a classroom and perpetrate the very injustices that had colored her entire life. Her mother hadn't gone to college, and her father had only completed a semester in Palestine before they moved to America. Yara knew how privileged she was to be here and felt that she had a duty to spread awareness. But she also had dreams of making meaningful work, leaving her mark on the world. She felt certain, in the depths of her being, that something beautiful wanted to be created through her. How or what exactly, she wasn't sure.

Yara scanned the list again, reached for the camera, and headed toward the welding lab.

Outside, the sun was lifting over the buildings, warming the Carolina foliage, hints of hickory and pine in the air. A slight breeze swept through Yara's hair as she walked across campus, her camera dangling from her neck. She told herself, again, how lucky she was to simply be here.

When she was growing up, her parents were more interested in securing her in a marriage than in educating her. "It wouldn't hurt to get an education," her father had said. "But you can go to college when you're in your husband's house." But at the end of high school, she'd secured a full scholarship to a college in Brooklyn, and her father had allowed her to enroll as long as she promised to pursue marriage, too. A few months into her first semester, she'd returned home to find Baba sitting in the sala with three people she'd never seen before: a young man and his parents. Before Fadi, all her previous suitors had been too serious, too traditional. Fadi seemed like a breath of fresh air in comparison, and then it all happened so quickly. Within weeks, she'd moved to this small town in North Carolina and found herself married. She'd transferred her credits and classes to this local university, filled with hope at the promise of starting over with someone who wouldn't stand in the way of her dreams.

In her art classes, the other students dressed in bold colors and carried thick leather-bound sketch pads under their arms. In workshops, they expressed ideas about the intersection of history, philosophy, and art, articulating their opinions passionately and saying things like "Art does not need to address a public referendum beyond which the artist does not see past." They didn't worry about how the world perceived them, only about the impression they would leave on it. It was clear to her that they'd experienced enough of the world to have a solid sense of their place within it, that no one passing them on the street would ever give them a sideways glance. Listening to their discussions, an unrelenting sense of inadequacy grew within her.

She had assumed earning her degrees would move her beyond her limitations—her sheltered upbringing, her immigrant background, the fact that she had not had access to art—and the feeling that had stemmed from these limitations, that she did not have a right to create it. But her education had changed little inside of her. If anything, earning these degrees but still not producing anything herself only proved that she would never be the kind of woman she dreamed herself to be—creative, expressive, free—and that she hadn't escaped those barriers at all.

Still, in her increasingly rare free time, Yara painted in the sunroom of her home, on an easel she'd set up facing the windows. In those quiet moments, her thoughts became absorbed by the colorful loops, lulled by soothing sounds of brush against canvas. She was neither worried nor afraid at the easel. She had no thoughts about the past, no memories to mull over, no conversations with herself about everything she'd ever done—or had yet to do—in her life. Left to its own accord, her mind was unmanageable, frightening; but in that space, there was nothing to worry about, no buzzing in her ears, no reminders of her own inadequacy. How free she felt in those moments.

But outside of that room, the world darkened again, her mind filling with an onslaught of everything she wanted to forget. Nothing she could ever do would change that, it seemed. She would always be herself, and there was no escaping that.

In the welding lab now, where students in stainless steel masks operated high-end machinery, Yara brought the camera to her eye, checked the aperture, and focused the lens. Clicking away, she captured the yellow sparks that flew off all around them.

In the nursing hall, her next stop, a group of students in pale blue scrubs with stethoscopes hanging from their necks examined a drip machine.

In the garden maintained by the Culinary Arts Department, bushes of mint, sage, and basil gleamed in the afternoon light, their bright green leaves tender and dewy.

Yara tried to slip into each of these areas without the students noticing, hoping to capture a candid image to post to the college's Facebook and Instagram accounts. When she'd first started doing this work for the school, she'd focused on the campus's breathtaking views, images that inspired awe. But what interested her more now were the small details of everyday life, finding something intimate in the mundane, images that made her want to lean in and get a better look—street signs, peeling posters, a blade of glass.

Time softened, too, when she put the camera to her eye. The world went still and silent as she focused on the present: a single moment. Much like being in the sunroom painting, she felt for a short while that the world was not such a terrible place, that perhaps everything in her life had happened to bring her to this instant.

Inhaling a deep breath, she took a picture.

3

Welcome to 'Responding to Art.'" Yara stood in the center of the brightly lit, overly air-conditioned classroom and smiled at the new batch of twenty-one first-year students. "My name is Yara Murad, and I'll be your instructor. We'll meet here twice a week, on Mondays and Wednesdays."

She asked the students to take turns stating their name, what they planned to major in, and the last TV show they binge-watched, an icebreaker she did at the beginning of every term. With a smile, looking directly at each student as he or she spoke, she replied: "That sounds lovely. Glad to have you here."

"The last show I binge-watched was *Mo* on Netflix," Yara said when they'd finished going around the room. She'd grown up on shows like *I Love Lucy* and *Seinfeld*, relating to their everyday truths despite feeling like she came from a separate world. But *Mo* was the first time she'd watched a series that highlighted a Palestinian American family. "It's the closest I've ever come to seeing myself on the big screen," she said.

A few students nodded, but most of them looked at her blankly. She walked over to an empty student desk in the middle of the room to put herself on their level. As she lowered herself into the seat, she said: "I know most of you are here to fulfill the art elective, but my goal is for you to find something truly valuable in this class, regardless of your major or intended career."

They looked back at her, unmoved. She cleared her throat and went on. "You might be thinking: Why art? What can it possibly do for me? I get it. At one point, the humanities were a sacred endeavor where we were encouraged to seek and cultivate beauty in our every day, but that is no longer the case. Now we live in a world of mass media and technology, a world where everything must have a function, and maybe we've lost our appreciation for art, or for doing something for the sake of creativity and pleasure alone."

A few students shifted in their seats. Others looked down at their phones. Yara resisted the urge to get up and snatch their devices away. "Art is a window into the transcendent, into the divine," she continued. "And we need it in our lives in order to make a connection to something beyond the limited world we live in. My hope is by the end of the semester, you have made one beautiful thing, and by doing so, expanded your relationship with beauty in other parts of your life."

No one responded. This was a common occurrence, she'd found, teaching a humanities requirement in a school with few art majors. She couldn't blame the students. They were here to earn a specific degree in order to get a specific job so that they could contribute to society in a specific way. It followed that they viewed her class as a waste of time. Hadn't she felt the same her first year of college, racing through her prerequisite courses in an attempt to get to the finish line? And yet she hoped she could still change their minds about art, that they might leave her class prepared for the world in ways they hadn't known possible before. Some days she believed that teaching was her chance to do meaningful work in the world. Maybe, if she didn't have the ability to create something of her own, she could help her students do that for themselves. It was a thought that filled her with hope at the beginning of every term, briefly quieting the nagging whisper that she was settling, that she'd never make truly good or worthwhile work.

After going over the syllabus and class requirements and answering the same question about late assignments repeatedly, she at last turned to the projector. With the controller in one hand, and one eye on her students, she pulled up an image of the twelve-section color wheel.

"Ever wondered how artists and designers find their perfect combinations?" Yara began. "They use color theory. The color wheel was invented in 1666 by Isaac Newton, who mapped the color spectrum onto a circle. Knowing how to accurately combine colors, and understanding how they relate to one another, is critical for artists, designers, marketers, and brand developers, too."

A few students began to take notes. Others stared down into their laps, sneaking looks at their phones.

"Something else I wanted to say," Yara went on, and cleared her throat. "I wanted to say that often, when influential artists are discussed, it's always the usual suspects: Van Gogh, Monet, and so on. While we'll study some familiar paintings this semester, I'm also going to show you paintings by artists of color, artists I suspect you've never heard of, but who've made an indelible mark on the world. I hope this opens up some new doors to art movements and styles for you to explore." She waited. No one responded. "But for now, let's see if you can identify the ways in which color theory was used in these paintings."

On the whiteboard, she toggled forward through a series: Diego Rivera's *Street in Ávila,* with its gentle variations in red, orange, and yellow tones; Amrita Sher-Gil's *Hungarian Gypsy Girl*, a burst of intense greens, ochres, and browns, as well as her rigorous brushwork, like stepping inside a patch of grass; Safia Farhat's's tapestry *La Mariee,* a waterfall of colors—vibrant yellows, subdued blues, and deep pomegranate reds—inviting the viewer to lean in for a closer look. Inside the quiet classroom, clicking from one bright painting to the next, Yara moved through elation at their beauty to a sense that the walls were closing in on her. That everyone had turned to look and see what a fraud she was: teaching a class about art when she'd seen none of it firsthand and hadn't created anything substantial herself.

She stopped at *Café Terrace at Night* by Vincent van Gogh, a painting depicting a snapshot of a street in Arles. Tiny figures sat on the terrace, under the light cast by a yellow lantern shed that flickered on the cobblestones like loose change. Dark blue shadows of houses loomed in the background, and above them, a starry, shimmering sky.

"Do any of you recognize this painting?" she asked. A few students nodded. "It's a great example of using colors that sit opposite each other on the wheel to create contrast." Yara glanced around the room and then back at the board. "How can a painting depict night without any black in it? Here, Van Gogh creates light and intensity through the sharp contrast between the warm yellow, green, and orange colors under the terrace and the deep blue of the sky, which is reinforced by the dark blue houses in the background."

The students continued to sit with grave-looking expressions on their faces. Yara drew her brows together and exhaled. Were they already bored? Were they thinking about art, or about something else? Checking her watch to see there were about ten minutes left in class, she returned to her desk and asked them to free-write about a painting they found interesting. "Specifically, what about the painting moved you?"

"I've always been drawn to Edvard Munch's *The Scream*," Yara offered, typing the words on the keyboard. "It was first composed in 1893 and it's displayed in the National Museum of Art in Norway." She pulled up an image of the painting on the whiteboard, then took a step back to examine it. Whenever she saw this agonized face, she felt as though an infinite scream were passing through her, too, a scream she'd spent her entire life holding back. Yet despite its darkness, or perhaps because of it, the painting comforted her somehow, made her feel seen.

The students nodded in recognition at the iconic artwork but said nothing, though they all followed her instructions to flip to a blank page in their notebooks and began to write.

Relieved for the break from talking, she turned back to the whiteboard and stared at the piercing red sky, the long, unsettled face. Looking into those wide eyes, a warm ache filled her chest. The painting was a reminder of how she felt most days living in this world, her body tense as she completed assignments and chores, the hours speeding by, stacking against one another like beads on a string that would total her whole life. Only how much of her life would she remember living, anyway? How much of it would ever mean something?

A young woman in the front row raised her hand. Yara blinked to find herself back in the room, the light from the projector stinging her eyes.

"Yes?" said Yara. "It's Martha, right?"

Martha nodded, her face bright and energetic. "Is it okay if I don't know the painting's name?" she asked. "I see it everywhere but I don't know what it's called or who the artist is. But I think it's an Impressionist?"

"Of course. Do you want to try describing it?"

The young woman examined her fingernails, then said: "There's not much going on in it, really. There's a lake with boats and a tiny, bright sun in the distance. Do you know what I'm talking about?"

"I think so," Yara said, typing 'impression sunrise monet' on her keyboard. On the whiteboard, dull oranges, blues, and greens formed the backdrop for the dark green boats and vivid orange sunrise.

The young woman smiled. "That's the one."

"What a lovely choice," Yara said. "This painting is credited with inspiring the name for the Impressionist movement. *Impression, Sunrise* depicts the port of Le Havre, Monet's hometown. Instead of painting for accuracy, or re-creating the scene, like other artists of his time, Monet tried to paint the feelings brought on by the sunrise, his perception of the landscape, rather than the reality of the landscape itself."

Without removing her eyes from the screen, Martha nodded. Yara turned to the class. "Would anyone else like to share their choice?"

The others avoided her eyes, some shifting the paper in front of them.

Yara waited, her hand going to the gold charm dangling on a chain from her neck, a palm-shaped amulet that once belonged to Teta, her grandmother.

And then their time was up and the students were all rising and leaving, their energy again hurrying elsewhere, seemingly unchanged. Yara sighed. Not for the first time she wondered if art was something you could even teach, the same way you taught science or math. The rules of math were concrete, but with art, the locus of creation lived within the artist. The rules, "whys," critiques—they were all arbitrary. How could she begin to capture its essence, let alone transmit it to someone else?

Yara grabbed her things and walked out of the classroom with her head down, feeling a renewed heaviness in her body, the usual thoughts overwhelming her mind. Had she given up her own dream of making art to merely teach it to indifferent students?

College and master's degrees, she scoffed internally. Ha! She thought she'd been empowered. She thought she'd found the path, done all the right things. She thought she would be free.

Of course, she had also thought, planned, dreamed, that she would avoid marriage. It was an outlandish dream, but she'd painted it in her mind a thousand times: Yara, going to college, then traveling the world and painting. She'd make art out of living itself, never constricting herself to a man or a house or a soul-crushing job.

But, obviously, it hadn't worked out that way. A hundred times a day she reminded herself that this was her choice, her doing. She'd gotten on that plane. She'd married Fadi. Why hadn't she fought for what she wanted? Why had she surrendered to her parents' vision of her future?

As soon as these questions came, they were compounded by the one that followed: How could she feel this way, with the immense opportunities she'd been given, when there were women who were far less fortunate than her, women like Mama?

Mama understood what it was to have unfulfilled dreams. "When

I was younger, I wanted to be a singer," she'd told Yara once, offering her a rare glimpse of her inner life. "I wanted my voice to be recognized all over the world, like Fairuz." As a child, Mama had strummed her oud on their rooftop garden, singing into the open sky. Morning and night women would come out of their shelters, drawn by the soft sound of her voice, humming along as they hung clothes on laundry lines, watered their gardens, fed the chickens inside the coops. Yara imagined all their worries slipping away, as if Mama's melodies were medicine in the air. Teta would listen, too, as she watered her plants, then trace her fingers through Mama's long, dark hair and whisper: "Your voice has the ability to make us forget, ya binti."

It was Teta who shared the stories of Palestine with Yara: the flaming olive fields outside the home they were forced to leave behind, the harsh winters in the refugee camp, the glistening golden dome of the Aqsa mosque they could no longer visit freely, or at all. The rotting stench of feces outside the nylon tents, the hours-long lines to get food from the UN shelters, the pressure of the heavy water buckets on her shoulders as she hauled water back home. Mama never spoke of these things.

Sometimes Baba had spoken of his childhood in the refugee camp, though: plucking weeds in the fields with his father, kicking a soccer ball barefoot across the narrow dirt alleyways, or weaving around laundry lines on the rooftop of his home. Up on the rooftop, Baba could see the entirety of the overcrowded camp, a mash of concrete buildings stacked close together so that many streets were narrow alleys with barely enough space for people to pass. "I didn't own a pair of shoes until I was eleven years old," he would say, as if proud of this adversity, as though the suffering had made him a man.

Yara would turn to Mama then, eager to hear what she had to add, hoping Baba's stories had awakened a memory in her. But Mama would only look away, her voice trembling as she said, "The camps were a place to live, just like anywhere else. Why does everyone keep talking about them?"

Back at her desk, Yara checked a few items off her to-do list and heard her stomach growl. She hadn't had time to eat lunch. Not if she wanted to finish her work in time for pickup. She made another pot of coffee instead, scrolling through Instagram while she waited for it to brew, through photos of people she knew from her school days in Brooklyn, women in the community she'd met through Fadi and his mother, distant relatives in Palestine, her brothers, who were now scattered across the country; even her mother-in-law, who'd joined recently.

Yara also followed people she didn't know, celebrities and influencers displaying magazine-worthy images that filled her with envy. She refilled her mug, trying to keep her hands still, to not waste another minute mindlessly scrolling through endless content. But blinking up at her from the screen were foreign cities with cute canals and crisscrossed bridges, women contouring their faces with shades of concealer and bronzer, ads for products she didn't need but had been convinced she wanted. The thought that flashed through her mind wasn't *Why am I looking at all this?* but *What do people see when they look at me?* With every post Yara uploaded, she felt an unease wash over her, a desperate need to prove herself, prove that she was happy and thriving despite what had happened. Despite what they thought her life would look like.

Yara lifted her mug now, studied the ring it had left on the desk, her mind beginning to churn. Absently she took a sip and clicked onto her own profile. In one of her favorite posts, Mira and Jude were holding hands on their porch swing, begonias hanging from the bay window flower boxes beside them. Yara loved to photograph them in the waning part of the afternoon, as they played hopscotch or blew giant bubbles in the backyard, looking like the happiest kids in the world. Looking at her daughters' smiling faces now, Yara felt her shoulders relax. The way the light illuminated their skin filled her with warmth, as though she were sitting in the sun with them, a young girl herself.

She scrolled through her camera roll, to the most recent picture of them. Again, on the porch swing, but this time with Fadi in the middle, his arms around them. She uploaded the picture to Instagram, adding a quote by Nawal El Saadawi as the caption: "Love has made me a different person. It has made the world beautiful." A sting of deep embarrassment moved through her as she read the words. She put her phone away and returned to her desk to finish the rest of her work.

Focus, she told herself. But she couldn't focus.

Every few minutes, she stopped to check and see how many people had seen the photo, if they'd liked it, if any of them had written a comment. She looked at the photo within the grid of her other posts, to see if the colors complemented one another, and pulled it up again to inspect it.

Time passed. She refreshed the post. She thumbed through her other social media apps. On Facebook, the ice caps were melting. On Twitter, Elon Musk said free speech was essential to a functioning democracy. Back on Instagram, Beyoncé was releasing a teaser trailer for another song inspired by Jay-Z. Yara put her phone inside her pocket only to reach for it again, her eyes darting across the screen aimlessly. What was she searching for? She wasn't sure, but the more that was happening out there, the less was happening inside her, and that at least provided some relief.

Yara wished she could hear Mama singing now, wished her sweet voice could help her forget.

By three o'clock, she'd stared at the photo for so long she no longer saw Fadi and the girls smiling back at her. Instead she saw her own father, his face tight and glaring, and a younger version of herself, looking up at him pleadingly. She felt like a wet rag being squeezed too hard, her body remembering and trying to make her know. Her hand was a fist around the phone. Breathing hard, she pushed her scrambled thoughts aside and deleted the post.

4

Yara had just closed and locked her office door when she noticed two full-time instructors at the other end of the hallway and froze.

Shit. They'd seen her. And she had to pass them to leave the building.

"Heading out already?" Amanda said.

If Yara narrowed her eyes, she could blot out her colleague almost entirely. Amanda taught women's and gender studies at the college; "feminist studies," she said whenever someone asked. She had bright yellow hair and dull blue eyes. Walking toward them, Yara saw that Amanda had applied her eyeliner too thickly for her pale complexion.

"My work is done, and I'm heading to pick up my girls from school," Yara said.

"They have afterschool programs at the local schools, you know," Amanda said. "My kids love theirs."

This wasn't the first time Amanda had mentioned this. "Yes, well, I'd rather pick them up myself."

Michelle, who taught visual communication, looked up from her phone. "How do you get all your work done in time?"

Yara squeezed the strap of her handbag, forced a smile. "I guess I just want to, so I do."

"I could never finish my work by three every day," Amanda said, squinting through her smudged eyeliner. "You're such a good mother. Is that a cultural thing?"

"No, Amanda, it's not a cultural thing."

"Oh, right."

To this, Yara said nothing. She couldn't help but wonder what stereotypes might be going through Amanda's mind: how weak and domesticated Yara was, a good little housewife. Oppressed by marriage and motherhood. How very Arab. At work, whenever her colleagues asked about her background, Yara gave vague, noncommittal answers. If she told them she was from New York and they proceeded to ask about the city, she didn't mention that she hadn't seen much of it growing up. She didn't want to see the judgmental look in their eyes, as though she'd confirmed a suspicion they'd had all along.

Yara glanced down the hall now, trying to muster the courage to end the conversation and walk away, but just as she shifted her bag and opened her mouth to say goodbye, Michelle gasped. "Oh my goodness," she said, her eyes moving rapidly across the screen of her phone. "Did you get this email?"

Relieved at the change of subject, Yara reached into her pocket for her own phone and refreshed the screen. A few new emails appeared, the most recent: "Global Scholars Program Scandinavian Cruise."

"The college is putting out a call for chaperones for a Scandinavian cruise," Michelle continued. "Listen to this." She cleared her throat and began reading:

"'We are looking for faculty and staff members to accompany twenty-five students as the trip chaperones. This twelve-day spring cruise will include visiting the towering Norwegian fjords, learning fascinating Viking history, and seeing the opulent architectural wonders of Norway, Denmark, and Sweden. Students will also get to experience the vibrant city of Oslo, explore Copenhagen's whimsical Tivoli Gardens, and stroll along the narrow, cobblestone streets in Stockholm's historic district.'" Michelle paused, looking up. "How amazing is this?"

Yara's heart went beat-beat-beat, and she nodded slowly. This was the kind of trip she'd dreamed of as a young girl, traveling the world to explore unique arts and culture scenes. But, of course, she'd never dared ask her parents if they could travel anywhere besides

Palestine, a request she knew was as ludicrous as asking for a slap across the face. Just as Baba had said she could go to college when she was married, she knew travel was only possible then.

What would people think?

She wondered now what Fadi would think, if he would stand in her way.

"I went to Norway as a kid," Amanda was saying now. "Trolltunga is absolutely breathtaking. Have either of you ever been?"

Michelle frowned. "I've hardly left the South, let alone the country."

Amanda shook her head. "Are you serious? There's so much to see outside this old town." Glancing at Yara with apparent interest, she said, "What about you?"

"I've seen photos of Norway. On Instagram."

Amanda raised an eyebrow. "Wow. That's a shame."

Without looking at her, Yara nodded. The light in the hall flickered. "I've dreamed of visiting Oslo. There's a painting there I'd love to see. I was just discussing it in my class, actually."

"Really? Which one?" Michelle asked.

"The Scream. Edvard Munch—I'm sure you know it."

Michelle nodded. "You should definitely apply, then," she said. "The deadline is Friday."

"Are you two applying?" Yara asked.

"For a free trip to Europe?" Michelle laughed. "Obviously."

"Of course," Yara said, forcing her mouth to smile. "Who will watch your kids while you're gone?"

Amanda interrupted with a short laugh. "Seriously?" she said. "That's so sexist."

"Roger can watch them," Michelle said, unruffled. "If he can't, my mom could always drive down from Virginia to help out."

Yara took a step back, feeling her face burn. "That's nice of her."

"I don't understand why kids are automatically considered a woman's responsibility," Amanda said, trying to meet Yara's eyes. "Is that how it is for you?"

Yara swallowed. "What? Oh, I don't know."

"So you're applying, then?"

Yara wiped her forehead with her sleeve. "Yes. Of course." She pulled her handbag to her hip and pretended to look inside.

"Well, we'll all be in competition, then," Amanda said, giving them a playful smile. "May the best woman win."

Yara watched Michelle and Amanda turn and go, unable to move until they had turned the corner. She wanted to chase after Amanda, to tell her how she'd finished college despite being a new mother, that Fadi would support her career only if she worked during the girls' school hours. That she was trying to juggle work and motherhood and nightly homemade dinners. That all she wanted was to teach more, do more of the work she cared about, all while her mother-in-law constantly reminded her how she was failing to be the kind of woman she was supposed to be.

But how could Yara convey any of that without furthering the stereotype she knew Amanda believed her to be? No, she would rather pretend things were fine than be an object of ridicule or pity or, worse, validate their stereotypes. Who were they to take issue with her upbringing, anyway? It wasn't like mainstream, white-centering American culture was any better. It seemed to her that women were endlessly objectified, consumerism ruled their desires, and addictions were encouraged then stigmatized. Not to mention how we're all running around with our faces in our phones, constantly searching for something more, something better, something new. As a Palestinian woman, Yara knew she'd had to work twice as hard to catch up. Why didn't the world recognize that identity and privilege were accidents of birth? How much more empathy would people have if they understood that their position in life was decided not by goodness or merit or fault or need but by luck and chance, a toss of a coin?

Yara hurried across the campus parking lot now, her bag clenched to her side. Maybe chance had decided her starting point, but she felt some renewed determination now to defy the odds, to create her own destiny.

5

To get to Mira and Jude's elementary school, Yara drove down a two-lane farm road, past scattered houses encircled by trees. She rolled down the windows and inhaled the heady scent of fields ready to be harvested: soybeans, hay, corn, tobacco. Again, here were the reminders of how fortunate she was.

In the carpool lane, she shifted into neutral and leaned back against the headrest, feeling the sunlight warm her face. Outside, swallows soared across the brilliant blue sky and the elementary school building shimmered in the fall light. She rolled her window the rest of the way down.

Slowly the cars began to creep forward. Yara felt her earlier rush of intention leave her, replaced by a hollowness in the center of her body. She tried to understand where this feeling came from. Suddenly the person she wanted to be felt far away, and it seemed that she would always be out of reach. Frustration spread over her like a rash she couldn't stop itching. Would someone like her ever get a chance to see the world? She picked up her phone and reread the email calling for chaperones, her mind flicking through images and memories like it was shuffling through stations on the radio.

The only place she'd ever traveled to outside the United States was Palestine, where she'd gone most childhood summers to visit her extended family. She did not understand where they were going the first time they boarded the fourteen-hour flight to Jordan at JFK airport. As they approached Amman, a light rain drizzled over the

Dead Sea. Being Palestinian citizens, they weren't allowed to come into the country through Tel Aviv, so they disembarked at Queen Alia International Airport and took a bus to the Allenby/King Hussein Border Crossing to enter the West Bank. If they'd tried the direct way, through Tel Aviv Airport, they wouldn't be permitted into Israel and would have had to fly straight back to New York.

"We're the only people in the world who aren't allowed to enter our own country," Baba complained. At the border they waited in line for hours, going through one extensive check after another. The air smelled like sweat and cigarettes, and for a long time neither of her parents spoke, looking over their shoulders, their eyes dark, worried. Beside them Yara waited, holding hands with her brothers, all of them uncharacteristically silent, too. Long lines snaked around them, hundreds of people dragging suitcases, wiping sweat from their faces, praying to see the other side of the checkpoints. On that first trip, Yara heard a man near them in line tell the story of the time he had been strip-searched and made to wait naked in a cold room for six hours. She wondered if her family would be strip-searched, too. When she was older, she would learn that such extra questioning might have been because the man was traveling alone, or had an internet presence that suggested support of Palestine, or a passport with stamps from Muslim countries, or a name that sounded like it was of an Arab origin. Or it could have been merely because he looked like an Arab.

The sight of her grandmother's face always made Yara forget the wait. She spent those summer mornings on the rooftop with Teta, hovered over a taboon oven, slapping dough between their hands before throwing it on the hot clay to puff up. Above them, a trellis wrapped around the rooftop, covered in grapevines with green and purple fruit about to burst. Standing at the edge of the rooftop, Yara could see her brothers kicking a soccer ball with the neighborhood boys, and in the distance, golden hills scattered with olive trees.

Every time they arrived on the other side of customs back in New

York, Baba would tell Yara and her brothers, "We are so lucky to be in this beautiful country, in *Amreeka*. But it will never be home."

"Why did you come, then?" Yara asked once.

"We had no choice," Baba said, his voice cold. "We had to give our children a fighting chance."

Over the years, her father elaborated the reasons: Not wanting to raise a family in a war zone. Not wanting his children to live on land that had been stripped from them, a home that was no longer theirs. Not wanting the trauma of the past to define their future. Yara mouthed these words again now, waiting to spot her daughters' faces in the line of children emerging from the school. *Not wanting the trauma of the past to define their future.*

"It will if you keep talking about it," Mama always said, shaking her head.

Yara knew better than to question her parents' decision to leave Palestine, recognizing that they'd barely had a choice. But she wondered now if they had anticipated how their children would feel growing up in a place that would never be home. This sense that she belonged nowhere had hovered over her entire life: in Bay Ridge, as she boarded the bus for the conservative all-girls school where she was taught to keep her head down and obey; at home, sneaking glances of hypersexualized women in popular culture, confused until she realized that these norms belonged to a different world; and later in college, listening quietly as everyone around her flaunted their stories of drinking, smoking, having sex—a lifestyle that contradicted the conservative values she was raised on. But everywhere she went, every billboard, every magazine, every show on the television told her the Western way was how a life was well lived. The gold standard, the dream. It left her feeling alienated and detached, a stranger in her own body.

Yet, as the years passed, she had to acknowledge that her feelings of displacement were not specific to America. She felt the same sense of alienation when visiting Palestine, being an outsider there, too.

Her privilege as an American citizen stood in stark contrast to the poverty and powerlessness of the millions of Palestinians who lived in the crumbling camps, who faced staggering rates of joblessness and violence, who barely had access to clean water. It filled her with a deep sense of shame.

The car ahead of her jolted into motion and Yara shifted into drive. As she neared the main door, a teacher called the names of the departing students into a megaphone. Looking at Yara, she smiled and called out: "Mira and Jude Murad." Soon both girls were running toward the car.

Mira climbed quickly into the backseat, in the bright pink dress and sandals she'd picked out that morning, her long brown hair coming loose from the braid Yara had put it in. Behind her, Jude dragged her bag across the concrete, stopping to look up at a cardinal in a tree, her golden curls long since out of their bows. The girls were different as night and day. Mira was a bright sunny day of a child who loved neon clothes and bedazzled accessories, while Jude was quiet and inquisitive, and often lost in thought. Usually Jude was calm and curious, her eyes gleaming whenever she learned something new, but other times, she cried easily and for no clear reason. "A sensitive child," Nadia would say whenever she witnessed one of Jude's upsets, eyeing Yara critically. "But that shouldn't come as a surprise."

Jude shoved her bag into the backseat and climbed into the car, slamming the door shut. As Yara watched her click her seat belt, she spotted a large brown stain on the front of Jude's new white overalls.

"Your overalls," Yara said, reaching back to run her fingers over the stain.

"Ketchup," Jude said.

"But we just bought these, baby. You need to be more careful."

Jude frowned and crossed her arms. "Sorry."

Yara's chest tightened as she pulled out of the carpool lane and onto the main road. "It's okay. I'll put them in the wash when we get home."

Her eyes flicking back to see Jude in the rearview mirror, Yara shifted in her seat, taking deep breaths, an unintelligible whisper in her ear. During her parents' worst fights, Yara had imagined herself in a white room with big windows and yellow sunlight pouring through the trees outside. She paused for a long moment now, putting herself there again, feeling the sun against her skin until the dark whispers subsided.

Nobody had warned her of this as a girl, that the years would pass and she would still resort to this, that she would live in a body that was always on guard. Even now, with little girls of her own.

"So how was school today?" she finally said at a stoplight.

"It was great," said Mira. "We played soccer during recess and I scored two goals."

"Sounds like fun." Yara found Jude's eyes in the rearview mirror. "What about you, habibti? Did anything fun happen today?"

"No."

"Nothing at all?"

Jude shrugged. Her younger daughter looked so much like her, with her crescent-shaped eyes and honey-colored skin.

"Surely you must've done something," she said, but Jude just frowned and looked out the window.

At the next stoplight, Yara checked her phone again, but stopped when she noticed Jude watching her. Her daughter's eyes looked wet, but she wasn't crying, rather brimming with a nervous energy. The frown leaking off the ends of Jude's mouth filled Yara with nausea. Was she failing her daughters? Had the grief she carried in her bones rubbed off on them? Looking at the girls, she felt the shadow of her own childhood, reexperiencing it through their eyes, then an overwhelming tension inside her body, a panic she didn't know how to stop. Mothering was supposed to be the most natural thing in the world, but the sight of sadness on her children's faces made Yara ache, clawing at something deep inside her, an old wound unhealed, freshly open.

She met Jude's eyes in the mirror again. "What's wrong, habibti? Why are you frowning?"

"I don't know," Jude said, and the sound of defeat in her daughter's voice made Yara want to weep. How was she supposed to manage her daughters' emotions when she could barely manage her own?

"Please cheer up," Yara blurted out. "I don't like to see you sad. And really, there's nothing for us to frown about."

By the time they reached the library, Yara had a new mental checklist, hurrying the girls through the motions: first, homework and reading at the library, then gymnastics, then a quick trip to the grocery store for the red onions she'd forgotten to buy for tonight's mujadarra. If she didn't hurry, she'd have no time for the last stop. Yara steered the girls by the elbows across the parking lot, squinting into the afternoon sun. Mira stopped at the entrance, pointing at a pale pink flower. "Look, Mama! Isn't it pretty?"

"Yes, yes, but we don't have time," Yara said. "Let's go."

In the kids' section of the library, there were colorful bookshelves lining the walls, green tables arranged in the center, and purple beanbags scattered around. They settled on a red-and-yellow polka-dot rug in the quiet corner, just below a Dolly Parton book club poster. Yara crossed her legs while Mira and Jude lay on either side of her, propping up their heads with their elbows as they completed their homework. Mira filled out a math sheet on subtraction, while Jude practiced vocabulary by writing out definitions in her notebook, though she kept pausing between each word, her eyes wandering.

"Come on, Jude," Yara said, tapping her index finger on the vocabulary list. "Focus."

Jude moaned. "I don't want to do homework. What's the point?"

Mira looked up from her math sheet and said, "You have to. Don't you want to be really smart?"

"Not if it means doing pointless worksheets," Jude said.

Yara couldn't help but laugh. "What am I going to do with you, kid?"

Half-smiling, Jude shifted on the rug, her shoulders loosening. She turned to Yara. "Did you like school when you were young, Mama?"

It was better than being at home, Yara thought, a dropping sensation in her stomach. Avoiding Jude's eyes, she nodded. "Yeah, I did."

"What was your favorite subject?"

"I know!" Mira said. "I bet it was art."

Yara pulled her knees into her chest. "Actually, we didn't have art in my school," she said. "So probably English. I loved to read."

"Is that why you make us read every day?" asked Jude.

She laughed. "You got me, kid."

"You don't have to make me," Mira said, twirling her pencil. "I love books!"

Jude raised herself off her elbows and sat back on her knees. "What else did you like when you were little?"

Yara felt Jude's anticipation. "Well, I loved cooking with my grandmother, Teta."

In Palestine, she and Teta had baked bread together every morning, using the leftover dough to make fatayer, pies stuffed with spinach, meat, or cheese. Teta had taught her the basic dishes first: hummus served with a drizzle of fresh-pressed olive oil and a dash of sumac in the center; rolled grape leaves stuffed with rice and ground lamb; vegetables stuffed with spiced rice and simmered in a stew. Next, Yara learned to make musakhan, roasted chicken over warm taboon bread topped with pieces of fried sweet onions, sumac, allspice, and pine nuts; and maqluba, an upside-down meal of rice and vegetables that slid out of the pot like a glazed cake. Once she'd mastered those dishes, Teta showed her how to filet and cook fish, stuff it with cilantro, garlic, red peppers, and cumin, then marinate it in a mix of coriander and chopped lemons. "Then rummaniyeh, brown lentils gently simmered with peeled aubergines, fried garlic, lemon juice," Yara listed for the girls. "And the pomegranate molasses."

"What *else* did you like, Mama?" said Jude, still dissatisfied.

Yara rose to her feet, her face going hot. There wasn't more to tell Jude. If Yara's memories were a stack of photographs, most of the pictures were of Palestine with Teta. The two of them baking bread, Teta's smile wide and slightly yellow, her fingers patting the dough, Teta slicing open a ripe cactus pear, its ruby-red fruit glistening. Teta pruning the young olive trees she'd planted with her father in the camps after his family's olive fields had been burned.

Yara loved Teta like she loved the mulberry trees in Palestine, their sweet tear-dropped fruit a deep red, almost black. She loved her like she loved the black hawks gliding across the open Ramallah sky, like the sabra fruit in Mama's childhood garden, like the plump toot she snuck from the neighbor's mulberry trees. She loved her like she loved the vines hanging on the rooftop terrace, with their tart green grapes and mossy leaves, which they'd pluck to stuff warak dawali together.

In her stack of memories, there were a few images of Mama and Teta, too; Mama strumming her oud on the rooftop, singing so the neighbors could hear, her voice as sweet as the smell of fruit in the air. But the other photographs in Yara's pile were blank, moments she couldn't remember or didn't want to. Elbows at her sides now, Yara moved to the closest bookshelf. "That's it. The best times of my childhood were with Teta, back in Palestine."

"But you always tell us about her," said Jude. "What about New York?"

"I don't remember much."

"Why not?" asked Jude. "Baba always tells us stories about when he grew up."

Yara shifted her weight, wondering how to proceed. Her daughters were too young to understand that her childhood had been different from Fadi's, in ways that were difficult to explain. Fadi sometimes acknowledged that they'd both been raised in loveless homes. "My father treated my mother like shit," he'd say. "Still does, really. Cussing at her day and night, refusing to acknowledge all she did for us." Yara listened to him say this with some tenderness, not only because of the pain he had endured, but also because he recognized that his mother had suffered.

And yet he was quick to admit, with more than a little righteousness, that his experiences were nothing compared to what Yara had witnessed as a child. "Do people like that really exist?" he asked her once. "It seems like something out of a soap opera." Early in their marriage, Fadi had listened to her recall an incident between her parents. He seemed suspicious, as if looking for holes in her story. "Come on," he said. "There's no way anyone could be so cruel! It can't have been that bad."

"It was, though." She could say no more. She breathed in and out, trying to keep her face very still. As if he'd seen all that the conversation had triggered inside of her, he reached out to hold her hand. "Come here," he said, his voice low and gentle. "What happened is in the past, okay? You don't have to live that way anymore. I promise."

"You must remember some things, Mama," Jude said now, bringing Yara back to the room.

"Yes," Yara said. Trembling, she ran her hand across the shelf, searching for the crisp-cornered spine of a book they'd started reading together a few days before.

She felt Jude watching her, rocking back and forth, waiting for Yara to respond. How could she explain? Memories of Teta came to her with ease, as vivid as the vibrant colors of Palestine. But when she closed her eyes and thought of Brooklyn, the picture was murky and dark, swallowed by an unbearable loneliness.

"Who needs to hear my old stories when we have so many good ones right here?" She had found the book on the shelf, at last.

She pulled the girls to her again, on the polka-dot rug, and opened the book in her lap and read them the story of a thirty-story-tall high school accidentally built sideways. Mira and Jude laughed and leaned in closer each time she flipped the page. Yara paused at the end of each chapter, watching the anticipation on Jude's face.

"I thought you didn't like reading, Jude?" Yara said with a grin.

Her daughter blushed. "Well, this book is funny."

Yara loved huddling together with them, watching their eyes widen in excitement as she read, painting a story with words. Mira always chose mysteries, while Jude loved stories about animals. Yara had shared her childhood favorites with them: "Ali Baba and the Seven Thieves," "Sindbad," and *One Thousand and One Nights*. She had even recounted tales Teta had told her as a child, myths and legends about magic lamps and evil spirits, and, of course, stories about Palestine. In moments like this, her daughters' heads pressed to her, their skin warm against her own, Yara never felt happier. She wished she could capture this feeling, stretch it over her entire day for protection and comfort.

When they finished reading, she closed the book, reached in her bag for her camera, and asked the girls to smile for her.

"Not another picture." Jude groaned.

"Just one," Yara pleaded.

Mira said, "If you smile, it'll only take a second."

Jude slouched but looked at the camera. Yara had so few memories of her brothers growing up. Perhaps she'd have more of them, happy ones, if she had photographs to refer to. She stepped back and pulled the viewer to her eye.

"You'll be glad to have these when you get older," Yara said. "Good memories to look back on."

After a few clicks she got the shot, the composition and lighting right. She smiled and saved the photo to her gallery to post later. Wasn't this proof that she'd made it, of how far she'd come?

6

At eight thirty, Yara heard the sound of a key fiddling in the lock, then Fadi's voice calling out, "Lucy, I'm home!" She turned off the burner below the simmering pot of rice and lentils and walked down the hall to greet him.

"Why, hello there," she said.

"What a day," Fadi said as he took off his shoes and placed them by the door. Mira and Jude popped out of their bedroom shouting, "Baba's home!" They raced down the stairs toward him, lifting their arms to be picked up. They were always waiting, after she'd put them to bed, to greet him—though on some nights they drifted off before he made it back.

"How about you two carry me?" Fadi said with a grin. "I'm exhausted."

They burst with laughter, clinging to his legs.

Smoothing down her apron, Yara watched as they embraced him.

"Tell us a joke, Baba," the girls pleaded, collapsing into giggles when he agreed. Watching Fadi make silly expressions while reading them knock-knock jokes from his phone, Yara thought he held a special kind of charisma, like an actor onstage. His sense of humor was one of her favorite things about him, that and how almost nothing ever seemed to bother him. She couldn't understand how two people raised in the same culture could experience the world so differently.

Now, like a Polaroid, an image surfaced in her mind: the view from her window where she stayed up waiting for her own Baba to come home. She put her fingers to her eyes and found her hands were trembling. Fadi leaned in to kiss her cheek and she flinched.

"You okay?" he asked.

"Yeah," she said quickly. She felt the girls watching them. "Sorry," she added, still looking at Fadi.

He inhaled, his eyes drifting toward the kitchen. "What's that amazing smell?" he asked.

"Mujaddara." Yara cooked Palestinian dinners for Fadi most nights, using the recipes Teta had taught her.

"Yes!" Fadi said, making a fist in the air. He walked into the kitchen, the girls still attached to his legs, and Yara followed. He seemed to be in a good mood. Maybe he'd say yes to her going on the trip.

Fadi paused in the doorway, smiling at the sparkling tile and steaming pots on the stove. "Nothing like coming home to a clean house, a warm meal, and my three beautiful girls." He turned to look at her, his dark eyes shining under the lights.

Yara laughed and looked at the floor. "Thanks."

Lifting the lid from the pot of rice and lentils, he used the spatula to help himself to a bite. "This tastes like it did in Palestine, when I was a kid," he said, tilting his head to meet her eyes. "You're a magician."

"If you say so."

He turned to Mira and Jude. "Girls, your mother is the perfect woman, did you know that?"

Yara could feel her face flush. Looking up, she saw Fadi grinning at her and gave a nervous laugh.

Growing up, no one had taught Yara what to expect from men. She knew only what it was like to have little brothers to look after and Baba, of course. When she started sitting with suitors in her parents' sala, the first two had come and gone without an offer of marriage. Yara wasn't sure if this was because the suitors had heard the rumors about her family, or simply because they didn't like her resistance. Not many people in her community did. Fear and defiance had blended in her face as she insisted on finishing her education and pursuing her career, and both suitors had at once withdrawn their proposals. She could almost hear their thoughts: طب الجرة ع تمها بتطلع البنت لأمها

Flip a jar on its mouth, and the daughter comes out like her mother.

But things were different when Fadi and his parents came to ask for her hand in marriage. He had sat across from her on the leather sofa, and she'd found him charming and funny and felt a tingling in her fingers and uneven breath whenever their eyes met. She wondered how much Fadi knew.

Baba and Hasan, Fadi's father, had grown up together in the same refugee camp, plowing the fields and raising livestock, sheep, and other farm animals. By eighteen, Baba's family had saved enough money to send him to New York City. "Come with me," Baba had told Hasan. "You can start over. Have a better life."

But Hasan's parents didn't want him to go and refused to help pay his way there. "This land is who you are," his parents said. Hasan knew, though, that their country no longer belonged to them. After Baba left, Hasan took a side job selling fresh bread in the corner dukan to save money for his ticket to America. When he hadn't saved enough after a year, Baba sent him the remainder. "You're like a brother," Baba said. "You deserve a better life."

"I'll never forget what your father did for me," Hasan told Yara frequently. "He changed my life." Eventually Hasan moved to a suburb in North Carolina, preferring the gentle flow of creeks and rivers, homes surrounded by lush foliage. And he'd been here ever since, Nadia joining him a few years later after they met on one of his visits to Palestine and quickly married. When Fadi, the eldest of his three sons, turned twenty-five, he called Baba and asked if they could drive up to New York so that he could meet Yara. Baba had been relieved, as if Hasan were lifting a burden off his back, repaying a favor.

Through the open door, she and Fadi had heard their parents in the formal living room, giving them space to get to know one another with some illusion of privacy. "Yara will make an excellent homemaker," Baba was saying. "She's had plenty of practice, being the eldest."

"It sounds like he's selling off one of his goats," she said, rolling her eyes.

"A very pretty goat," Fadi said.

She blushed, and for a moment they sat in silence, looking at everything but each other. Eventually Fadi said: "Trust me, I'm not much better off."

"Yeah, I doubt that," Yara said, crossing her arms.

"It's true," he said. "I'm the eldest, too, so my father expects me to carry the family on my shoulders. It sounds like you know what that feels like, but at least you're a girl. Soon you'll get married and start a life of your own. But my responsibility as the eldest son doesn't end after marriage. Even with two brothers who can help out, my father says it's my duty."

"Is that why you work at your father's shop?"

He nodded. "Owning a gas station wasn't exactly my childhood dream," he said with a smirk. Then, finding her eyes, he said, "Someday, I'd like to start my own business."

Yara leaned in a couple of inches. "What kind of business?"

"I don't know yet, but it doesn't matter." Fadi paused, his voice softening. "As long as I'm successful enough to look after my family. As long as I don't have to depend on anyone but myself."

Sitting there, Yara felt Fadi's defiance pulsing off of his skin, as intense as her own. She studied him for a long moment, absently stroking the necklace Mama had given her not long before. She and Fadi shared the same ancestral history, both wanted to do things better than their parents had. Maybe they weren't so different at all. Maybe they would understand each other.

"What about you?" Fadi said, interrupting her thoughts. "What do you want?"

The question startled her and she sat back, her hands pressed together in her lap, her heart racing. Neither of the previous suitors had asked her that. What did she *want*? As if it mattered what she wanted. If it was up to her, she wouldn't have even been sitting here with Fadi to begin with, wouldn't even be living in her parents' house. If it was up to her, she'd finish college and spend a few years traveling the world with nothing but a backpack, a notebook and sketch pad tucked inside. She'd visit museums and libraries in every city, spend her days at cafés and parks with a warm drink in one hand and a pencil in another, exploring her place in the world by moving through it, experiencing it firsthand.

Eventually Yara set her cup on the coffee table, cleared her throat. She wanted to list her dreams to Fadi then, the way she'd painted them in her mind so many times growing up, but they felt impossible to describe with him watching her, his eyes moving discreetly over her face, her hair, her shoulders. She opened her mouth and considered telling him what she wanted most was to get rid of this terrible feeling inside of her, this darkness tainting everything. Instead, she swallowed and managed to say, "I want to be someone."

Fadi squinted at her. "What do you mean?"

"I want to be my own person," she said. "I want to be free."

He watched her in silence for several long seconds, his expression changing, as if recognizing something. "Yeah," he finally said. "Me, too."

She turned to look out the window then, feeling his eyes follow her face. For a moment, she could hear her parents' voices in her ear: *You can do what you want* after *marriage.* She glanced back at Fadi, and keeping her voice steady, she told him she was in her first semester of college and hoped to finish her studies after marriage. She watched his expression as she spoke, wondering if he would oppose her education as the other suitors had.

But Fadi only smiled and said, "That's cool."

Yara exhaled a sigh of relief.

After tucking the girls back into bed, Yara and Fadi went downstairs to shower. They showered together most nights, a routine that had started soon after their marriage and one that gave Yara fifteen minutes of uninterrupted time with him. In front of the large glass mirror propped on the bathroom wall, Yara considered the best time to bring up the trip. During their shower, when they usually spoke about their days, or later, over dinner? Behind her, she heard Fadi turn on the water and begin to undress. She busied herself with removing her own clothes, hoping the hot water would settle her nerves.

Fadi stepped into the shower, holding the glass door open, and she followed, closing it behind her. Steam filled the air so they couldn't see each other clearly.

Each night, standing beneath the running water, their bodies almost touching, Yara's shoulders would relax and the tension in her skin would ease. But tonight, her heart was swelling inside her chest, inching toward her throat.

"Man, what a day," Fadi said, squeezing a dollop of body wash onto his loofah. "Two employees didn't show up, so I was stuck doing their deliveries. I had to drive to Raleigh and back."

"I'm sorry," she said. "That sucks."

"It's fine," he said, meeting her eyes through the fog. "At least I'm home now."

The smile she gave him in response felt wide and childish, and she looked away. Would now be a good time to mention the cruise? Or was he in a bad mood? She wasn't sure. Despite nine years of marriage, she still had trouble deciphering Fadi. Or maybe she was afraid to say the wrong thing. There was something about their relationship that unsettled her, though she was never sure what it was. She often had a nagging suspicion that he was hiding something from her, as if only displaying what he thought looked best, presenting himself only in the best light. It didn't help that he was gone for most hours of the day, at the warehouse, or on the road, or on a trip somewhere for work.

Some nights, lying awake, she found herself wondering what Fadi was doing in all the hours he spent away from them. Was he really working, or was there something else, someone else? Fadi had never given her a reason to doubt him. If anything, he was the definition of a good husband, was arguably her closest friend. So why was it so hard for her to trust him?

To this question, she always settled on the same answer: something was wrong with her, her twisted view of things. She couldn't fault Fadi for her own defects, especially after all he'd done for her despite everything. Maybe he wasn't as present as she needed him to be, but he was working hard to provide for them. As much as she craved his attention, she couldn't bring herself to make the first move. The last thing she wanted was for a man to think she needed him. She'd seen enough to know how that would end.

Yara nervously turned up the hot water until the steam between them thickened. And then she was saying: "So I got an interesting email at work today."

"Yeah? About what?"

She hesitated, then shifted back to give him more of the water. "The college is sending a group of students on a Scandinavian cruise next semester." She opened the bottle of shampoo and massaged a dollop into her hair. "It's part of the Global Scholars Program."

Fadi said nothing, intently focused on scrubbing down his arms.

"They need volunteers to chaperone them." Yara stopped lathering her hair. "It's a twelve-day all-inclusive trip," she managed to add.

"Oh yeah? Sounds fun." He rubbed the loofah across his chest.

In a quiet voice she said: "I was wondering if maybe I could apply."

Fadi looked at her. "Travel to another country on your own? You're kidding, right?"

She swallowed. She felt the suds falling from her hair, down her back.

"Who would take care of the girls?"

"I was hoping maybe you could."

Fadi shifted back. "You know I can't take off work."

"I know," she said, her hands trembling as she wiped the soap from her face. "But you don't need to take off. You make your own schedule." Her eyes stung and she rubbed them hard. "Can't you ask Ramy or one of your employees to work in the early mornings and afternoons so you can do pickup and drop-off? Just this once?"

"Well, of course I could in an emergency, but not for twelve days straight."

Standing there, her heart racing and her hands clenched into fists at her sides, Yara felt her need to cry so sudden she had to close her eyes and look away. Of course he'd said no. What a surprise.

She tried to make her voice low and gentle. "Look, I know I'm asking a lot, but are you sure there's no way we can make this work? We could sign the girls up for an afterschool program?" But she could tell that nothing she said would change his mind. A prickling sensation shot up her spine, and she stepped back under the hot water, avoiding his eyes. In a quiet voice she said, "You've been promising for years that we would travel."

"I know, but things at work have been hectic. Ramy and I have so much to do and not enough hours in the day. Our business is still getting on its feet, Yara. I can't just let him do all the work while I stay home to babysit."

"Babysit? You sound like they're not your kids."

"Come on, you know what I mean. Stop trying to flip this on me." He glanced behind her, into the bathroom mirror, then rubbed his hands over his face. "You want to work? Sure. But we have a reputation. What will everyone say when they hear my wife is wandering the streets of another country without me?" He laughed to himself. "My mother would never let me hear the end of it. You'd be confirming all her fears. You know that."

Fadi stepped closer to her, as if daring her to say something, but her lungs fought for breath. She couldn't open her mouth. Again, she heard her father's voice. *You can do what you want after you're married.* Had she been a fool to believe him?

No, Yara told herself. She needed to stand up for herself.

"It's not fair," she finally said, meeting Fadi's eyes. "I've always done everything everyone expected of me, so why can't I do something for myself? Just this once?"

Fadi opened the glass door open and walked out. "You can do whatever you want, Yara, you know that. But you're being unreasonable now." He yanked the towel off the rack. "Anyway, what kind of mother leaves her kids behind for that long?"

The words were a slap to her face, and she might have lashed out at him if she hadn't forced herself to step back under the showerhead. She stood there, swaying back and forth, until the hot liquid numbed her skin. When she opened her eyes again, the bathroom was empty.

In the kitchen, Fadi was waiting for her. Without speaking, he grabbed two empty glasses from the cupboard and filled them with water while she fixed their dinner plates, which they carried back to their bedroom to eat in front of the television, a nightly routine these days.

Fadi cued up an episode of *Everybody Loves Raymond* that they'd seen many times before. Most of the shows they watched were classics and throwbacks, ones that were popular when they were growing up. Yara didn't know why they continued to watch these shows despite the endless new options available. Perhaps it was a bittersweet longing for old times, a desire to return to a simpler past, not that either of them had had idyllic childhoods. But the world was moving too fast, changing too quickly, and sometimes it felt like they couldn't quite catch up. Or at least that's how it felt to her.

As they ate in bed, backs against the headboard, Fadi laughed between mouthfuls of food. Yara tried to join in his laughter but couldn't, finding it difficult to focus. Though the volume was high, the only sound she could hear was coming from inside her—a swirl of scrambled, panicked thoughts. Should she wait until tomorrow and ask Fadi again, or had his decision been final? She chewed her food slowly and swallowed, trying to stop the ringing inside her body. Beside her, Fadi wouldn't stop laughing. She tried to loosen her shoulders and form her mouth into a smile. She breathed and breathed until the familiar throb of dread in her chest settled.

When they finished eating, Yara took the dishes to the kitchen, then brushed her teeth and got into bed. She unbuttoned her pajama dress, slipping it off her shoulders and folding it neatly on the nightstand, before pulling the covers over her nearly naked body. Fadi fluffed his pillow, and for a few minutes they were still and silent. Eventually she moved closer to him, laying her head on his shoulder, but his body felt stiff and he pulled away, as though remembering something. "I have to get up early tomorrow," he said, yawning as he kissed her face. "Good night."

"Good night," she said, pushing the words out.

The room was quiet except for the sound of her heart hammering in her chest. Breathing hard, she stared into the darkness and listened to the conversation in her head. The same thoughts went round and round: If she couldn't travel now, with a trip paid for by the college, then when?

Everything in her life had been a succession of things she hadn't really wanted to do, expectations she felt obliged to follow: getting married just so she was able to leave her father's house, moving to a small southern town because that's where her husband worked, having children because that's what the women in her life had all done, settling for a dull job because that was the practical thing to do for the kids' schedules. All this for no other reason other than to prove herself to the world, or was it to herself? To prove that she could make something of herself without giving up on tradition. That she could have both freedom and family, that she didn't have to sacrifice one for the other.

So why did it still feel like she had? And why had she allowed it?

As the answer revealed itself, Yara chewed on the inside of her cheek until the pain settled her nerves. It was because all her life she'd learned to feel safer in obedience than to be free.

She closed her eyes and lay there, focusing on her breathing and trying to calm her racing thoughts, until she experienced a moment of frightening clarity: there was more out there than the life she was living, she was sure of it.

But what would that life look like? another voice countered. What if it was worse than this one?

YARA'S JOURNAL

I cling to this rare memory of you, Mama, like a sweet cup of mint tea on a rainy day.

You spring out of bed bright-eyed and playful, your mouth stretched into a smile. You pull up the shades one by one, allowing the sun to spill through the house, the darkness receding like a shoreline. You bathe, then draw fresh kohl around your eyes and put on a new dress. A bright cherry red with ruffled sleeves that fall slightly off your shoulders. Your blue eyes, like the hamsa around your neck, flicker.

"Can you help me with this, Yara?" you ask, showing me the back of your dress. I zip it up and watch you twirl. "What do you think?" you say, turning your face to me eagerly.

You are a beautiful woman with the cheekbones of a movie star, especially beautiful on days like this when the corners of your mouth turn upward and your eyes squint into half-moons. "You look like Princess Badoura," I say, referencing a story Teta read to us recently, from One Thousand and One Nights, *about a woman who falls in love with a prince in her sleep.*

Then you let me comb your hair, which I love, my small fingers running through the long dark waves along your back. All done, I say, and you turn to look at me. Your eyes are soft and welcoming, your smile present. My heart leaps at the sight of you. I know it's going to be a good day. And it is.

You float around the house as you complete your chores, singing and dancing, making our cramped rooms feel enormous, endless, full of light. You sing as you mop the linoleum floor and rinse the rag in the sink. You sing as you chop vegetables for dinner. You even sing while my brothers bicker with one another, as if you are a balloon soaring and nothing can bring you down. "Go see what he's crying about," you tell me when Yazan shouts that he has peed himself. In the bathroom, I wash and rinse Yazan clean, then slip a clean shirt and fresh trousers on him. Quickly I return to you, eager to hear your voice again.

You are singing a Fairuz song now, one whose every word I've memorized. I watch you from the kitchen doorway, mesmerized.

Do you remember the last time I saw you? *you sing.* Do you remember the last word you said?

Noticing me standing in the doorway, you reach for my hands, cupping your painted fingers gently around mine. Together we twirl around the kitchen. A gust of happiness puffs through the room as your voice swirls around us, like a magic chant casting a spell.

While dinner is simmering on the stove, we bake a vanilla cake using Teta's recipe. I help you sift the flour, crack the eggs, and pour the thick batter into a wide aluminum pan. Then I lick the bowl clean as you wash the rest of the dishes and sing, the melody as sweet as the newly baked scent filling the room. Your voice envelops me, like I'm being pulled into your arms for a hug. Life seems so much brighter. Later, at the kitchen table, you sip chai while we eat slices of cake with our hands, the corners crispy at the edges, the sugar glistening on our fingertips. Though you never have much to say, sitting in your presence like this is a rare treat, sweeter than the cake against my tongue.

"This tastes as good as Teta's," I say, licking my fingers.

You smile and look toward the darkened window. "Vanilla is her favorite," you say, your voice fading. "Mine, too."

"And mine, too," I add.

You laugh, fingering the shiny pendant around your neck, that blue eye blinking on and off.

7

The week passed too quickly for Yara to register the details. She went through the motions—working, carpooling, grocery shopping, cooking, cleaning—each morning through sunset. On Wednesday, during the last fifteen minutes of class, she paced the room as she outlined an assignment to her students. They were required to research a work of art that represented their cultural identity and prepare to share it with the class on Monday. Yara had hoped they would find this assignment thought-provoking, maybe even fun. But they looked at her glumly as she spoke, sneaking glances at their phones, until it was time to go. Afterward she felt a sudden chill and stood by the window, one hand over her chest.

Outside a slight whisper of breeze was in the air, the pink-orange sun blazing like a small fire in the sky. She thought she might stop by the college's art gallery on the other side of campus, but she checked her calendar and saw that she had a faculty meeting.

She brought the camera along on her way to the meeting, snapping pictures in a rush as she went, as if the faster she moved, the further she would get from herself. It was, at least, a breathtaking day, the beginning of autumn creeping in. Nothing was more beautiful than the Carolina fall, when brick buildings peeked through the rows of crepe myrtle trees in shades of pink and red, just starting to shed their petals over paved walkways. Stopping to rest on a bench in the shade of an oak tree, she synced the photos to her phone, and uploaded one to her personal Instagram—the campus lake in August sunlight, its surface a shining mosaic.

"Drink your coffee, embrace the silence, do not take people seriously, do not take life upon yourself, do not exaggerate your emotions, and do not please anyone against your will," she wrote as a caption, quoting Mahmoud Darwish.

A heart popped up almost instantly from one of her brothers, though it took a second to register which one. Her parents had given all of her children names that began with the letter *Y.* Yousef, the eldest of the five boys and just a year younger than Yara, lived in Boston now and was married to a Palestinian girl he'd gone to college with. Yazan worked at a law firm in New York City and had recently gotten engaged to a Bosnian girl he met at a wedding. Yunus was in med school in the Dominican Republic, while Yassir managed an Apple store in Atlanta, or at least he had the last time she checked. She wasn't sure what Yaseen was up to now.

Since the last time she'd seen them, during the hot New York summer, they'd barely been in touch except on social media. She wondered if they knew that she resented how different their upbringings were. The only time she'd been allowed to leave the house without her parents was to go to her all-girls school, her face pressed against the same school bus window from kindergarten until senior year. She knew where all the shops were on a short stretch of Fifth Avenue in Bay Ridge, but everything beyond those few blocks was a mystery to her. She didn't know the difference between the R and N trains that ran past her house, or where the rail tracks led. She'd never visited any of the boroughs besides Manhattan, where Baba had taken them a few times to see his office, and it was only after she married Fadi that she got to see the Metropolitan Museum of Art for the first time.

And yet her brothers had no one telling them what to do. They came and went at any hour, no questions asked, and in their teens, they spent many evenings at the nearby hookah bar. At almost thirty, Yara had still never been inside a bar. Growing up, it had been impossible for her to imagine all the things they did when they were out, so she spent her time drawing and reading, avoiding thinking about what fun they might be having. It wasn't until the fall of her senior year, when Yousef was a junior and was considering applying to colleges across the country, that she dared to ask Baba if she could do the same. "Magnoona? Are you crazy?" Baba said. "No daughter of mine will live on her own before marriage. What will people think?"

What will people think? There was no point in arguing with him after that, as she knew nothing she could say would override Baba's regard for other people's opinions. And yet her brothers were able to follow their dreams without the same restraints. Yousef went off to study at Stanford and never came back to the East Coast, while Yazan headed to Ohio State to study finance. Shortly after the twins, Yunus and Yassir, left for college, Yaseen moved out, too, and soon had a child out of wedlock, one whose existence her entire family denied. She'd once mentioned the little boy to Baba, but all he did was sigh heavily and say, "What am I going to do with Yaseen?" Yara felt a sudden pain in her jaw but was so surprised by his reaction she started to laugh. "What's so funny?" Baba asked, but she was gasping for breath, unable to respond. All she could think was: what would her father have done had she been the one to have a child outside marriage?

Yara toggled over from Instagram to her inbox and reread the email, as she had at least once a day since it came in. She knew the details of the Scandinavian cruise by heart. Almost as well as she knew Baba's words in her ear. Well, he was wrong: she was married now and she still couldn't do what she wanted. And yet Fadi's travel was so regular she hadn't given it much thought until now. Last month he'd gone to Atlanta for the weekend for work, and a few months earlier, he'd gone to Miami for a convention, only telling her about it after he'd booked the flights. She'd been too distracted with work and the girls and homework and dinner to make it an issue. But why was it okay for him to travel and not her?

What will people think?

An image of Mama appeared in her mind: her face morbidly pale, her body tense as she scurried around the house like a mouse let loose. The memory shook Yara so badly that she leaped up from the bench, the camera strap going taut around her neck.

Maybe Amanda had a point.

She could hear her colleagues chatting now, coming around the path, only a few feet behind her. Yara turned and started walking, picking up her pace to stay ahead of them.

The faculty meeting was held in a large room with dark gray carpet and a podium in the center, and around it long tables were arranged in rows with silver-and-black monitors at each station. A couple dozen of her colleagues were already sitting toward the back of the room, talking about their weekend plans, their faces half-hidden behind screens. Yara scanned the room for a seat near the fewest number of people. She found it hard to talk to her colleagues—in fact, to most people. In the midst of a conversation, she'd find herself wondering: What should I say next? How should I arrange my face? Am I supposed to smile? She couldn't understand how everyone else did this freely, like the cord attaching their thoughts to their mouths ran smooth and uninterrupted.

She found a seat in a back corner of the room, then scanned the studio for Jonathan, her boss, but didn't see him.

From a few tables away, she heard Amanda saying, "I hope none of y'all applied to chaperone the cruise." Her colleague was leaning against the table, stroking the collar of her blue-and-yellow dress.

Yara pulled out her phone, pretending to study it. Of course, today was the deadline for the application. How had she let so many days pass her by?

"Turn down a free trip to Europe?" another teacher said, laughing. "Someone would have to be dying."

"Well, not everyone can just pick up and go abroad for two weeks," said another, a man in a white collared shirt that Yara didn't recognize. "I haven't been on a plane in years."

"So my chances are pretty good then?" Amanda asked him with a playful smile.

Before Yara could look away, Amanda met her eyes with a stare saying that they were this and she was that and that's how it would always be.

"Did you end up applying, Yara?" Michelle asked lightly, perhaps noticing the awkward moment.

Staring down at the keyboard on the desk, she said, "No."

"Oh, bless your heart," Amanda said. "You poor thing."

Yara looked up quickly. "Excuse me?"

Amanda cleared her throat. "Please don't take this the wrong way, but it's no secret that women from your country experience severe sexism and misogyny."

Yara's back stiffened. "My *country*?"

"Well, yeah. I mean, aren't most Arab women expected to stay at home and look after their children? Isn't that why you leave work early every day?"

Yara rose to her feet and reached for the desk to steady herself.

Mama's face appeared again in her mind, but she pushed it away and hoisted her bag and the camera back onto her shoulder, her fingers trembling. Then she heard herself saying, in a voice unlike her own, "I was born in Brooklyn, New York, you fucking racist."

Amanda gave a surprised little laugh as Yara stormed out of the room.

In the hall, bright white light fixtures buzzed overhead. Yara's forehead was warm and damp, and she felt a sharp pain in her chest and a tingling on her skin, like it was being peeled off. She must have exited the Humanities Building but didn't remember walking across the campus green, up the three flights of stairs, or into her office. Once there, though, she threw her laptop and the camera into her bag then left, hands still shaking.

Light seemed to shine all around her, color leaking from the sky to the ground as she drove the two miles to the girls' school. She was the first car in the carpool line. She was two hours early for pickup. She blinked rapidly and rubbed her temples, her mind racing with a loop of thoughts that felt impossible to escape.

She needed to talk to someone about this. Her mother.

"You should look on the bright side," Mama said, echoing something she'd said to Yara many times before. "At least you have a job. You're not stuck at home all day like I was."

Mama, Yara mouthed, looking at her empty hands. "I couldn't help it," she said aloud. "I just *lost it*."

Taking a deep breath, she heard herself describing Amanda's smug face, her ignorant comment, and how she'd snapped and stormed out of the room. "Everything went out of focus. Her words made me feel so small."

What Yara didn't tell Mama was that it wasn't just her own words that alarmed her, but also the severity of her reaction. One moment everything was fine, and the next she felt as if she were under attack. Recalling the incident now, the vein in her neck began to throb. She rubbed at her temples. Amanda's words whispered in her head: "women from your country."

Yara could hear the heavy sound of Mama's sigh, and picturing her shoulders slumped forward in defeat, she felt a deep and sudden pity. She looked out the window, toward the school, a tide of shame washing over her. Remembering Mama's sorrows never failed to remind Yara of her own advantages. That she was educated, that she had a job. That she had a husband who supported her right to work, earn her own money. Mama had never been so lucky.

"I'm sorry," Yara said. "It isn't fair."

Mama sighed. "Well, that's life," she said. "You think you can do something to change your fate, you think you're in control. But you're not. Especially if you're a woman."

"I know." Yara's eyes burned and she closed them. "I thought if I went to college and got a job, I'd finally feel powerful, in control of my destiny. But it seems like no matter what I do, there's something standing in the way."

"Something like what?" Mama challenged her.

Yara opened her mouth to explain, but she couldn't find the right words, had never been able to. Whenever she tried, the phrases seemed dull and meaningless. Sometimes the feeling appeared in her mind as a series of snapshots: blurred and grainy Polaroids, taken with trembling hands. A young version of herself curled up in a shadowy corner of a dark room, drawing or reading, unbearably lonely. Rain speckled against the window as she waited for Baba to come home after not having seen him in days, refusing to look at her. Mama scrubbing the kitchen floor, her knees pressed into the linoleum. All eight of them scrunched together in that house, yet somehow disconnected. Other times the feeling was more a murky sense of distrust or detachment, like she was looking at her life from far away, positioned where no one could reach or hurt her.

"Are you wearing your necklace?" Mama was saying now.

"What?" Yara said, jolted back into the car.

"The hamsa. Are you wearing it?"

Her mother had given it to her so many years ago, when suitors had started to come to the house. "Yes," Yara said. "I never take it off."

"Good, good," Mama said. "You can never be too safe, you know. This world is a dark and wicked place."

As a child, Yara had been surrounded by these sort of superstitious warnings: If she took a seat at the corner of a table, Mama would shout at her that it was a sign she would never get married. If she left a shoe upside down, it meant she was spitting at God. If she flaunted a good grade on a test, Mama would slap her knees, say a prayer in Arabic, and remind Yara not to share her good fortune out loud, lest she be cast with the evil eye, a curse that would bring continuous misfortune.

"The evil eye is nothing to balk at," Mama went on. "That's the reason my life turned out so badly, why I suffered this way."

"What do you mean?"

"Growing up, I was the envy of the neighborhood back home," Mama said. "The other girls were jealous because the elderly women used to call me Fairuz, convinced I would be a great star like her one day. And one of the girls cast a spell on me, I'm sure of it! As soon as I had a suitor from America. Why else did my life go downhill after that? A classic case of hasad."

Yara knew the story of Mama's wedding night, how Teta had read the bottom of her cup only to find bad news. You can't blame superstition, Yara had thought when Mama first told her the story. And now, the words were spilling from her: "You could've changed your fate if you'd tried, Mama. You could've been a singer if you'd stood up for yourself."

"Stood *up* for myself?"

Yara softened her tone. "I mean, maybe you didn't have to give up on your dreams."

She sat in silence, a familiar numbing feeling spreading through her. She shouldn't have said that, of course she shouldn't have.

"How was I to follow my dreams with six children to look after?" Mama's voice was sharp, cold.

Yara rubbed at her chest, feeling short of breath. She knew better, of course. Witnessing Mama struggle to raise six kids was precisely the reason Yara had refused to have more children herself, despite Nadia's endless attempts to guilt her into giving Fadi a son. Luckily, Fadi didn't pressure her. "I'm sorry," Yara said. "I wish you could've done both, like I do."

"Exactly. Like *you* do," Mama said. "You think your father would've been okay with that?" She paused, her voice cracking.

"Do you know what my life would've been like if I'd had a husband like Fadi?"

Yara wiped her tears on her sleeve. "I'm sorry you couldn't be a singer," she said softly. "It isn't fair for me to assume things could've been different for you. I can only imagine how hard they were." She heard Mama's long, exasperated sigh. "I really am sorry," Yara whispered, holding back new tears. "I wish you could start over, have a better life."

"Start over?" Mama was laughing now. Or maybe she was crying. "It's too late for me, habibti. That's it." She paused, then said, "But of course, you should know that more than anyone."

Yara flushed immediately and deeply. "I know, Mama. I'm sorry," she said, her words echoing in the empty car.

Then the school doors flung open and the next thing she knew, Mira and Jude were running toward her, waving at her from behind the glass. "I wish you were here," Yara said quietly. "I wish you could see them right now." She trembled as she unlocked the doors to let the girls in.

"Mama, Mama!" Mira said, bouncing in the backseat. "Guess what, guess what?"

Yara twisted around to look at her, heart thumping. "What?"

"I got a hundred on my reading test!"

"That's great," she managed to say as she turned back to face the windshield, her body feeling like a stretched rubber band.

"Me, too," Jude said. "I got a hundred on my math test."

Yara met her eyes in the rearview mirror. "Good job, habibti."

Mira said something else but Yara was already pulling out and didn't hear her. She stared ahead as she drove, her eyes flicking from one traffic light to the next, gripping the steering wheel to stop the trembling. She could still hear her mother's muffled voice, her crying, her pain. Cars buzzed past her, and she had the sudden urge to hit the brakes and walk out into the middle of traffic.

She pulled over to the shoulder of the road, stopping herself.

In the rearview, she caught a glimpse of Mira and Jude exchanging a look. The murmur of passing cars came through the window. Her body was shaking but inside she felt a kind of nothingness. She buried her face in her hands, tears creeping from her closed eyes. What if walking into the middle of the road was the only way to silence the thump thump thump in the center of her body? Or fix her brain?

"Mama," Jude said. "Why have we stopped?"

Yara sat, unspeaking, unmoving, unable to explain. It horrified her how far she would be willing to go to be rid of the darkness inside her, to quiet the voice in her head.

"Mama," Mira said. "Maybe if you play the Fairuz song for us?"

"Of course," Yara said, opening her eyes. She put the blinker on, pulled out onto the avenue. "That's what we need. A little music."

8

As they ate dinner together in bed that evening—falafel bowls loaded with hummus, tabbouleh, feta, olives, pickles, and warm pita—Fadi tilted his phone toward Yara to show her a video of a man falling out of a moving car onto the pavement. "Isn't it hilarious? I've rewatched it nearly a dozen times."

Yara, on the edge of the bed, leaned her face into her hands. "That's funny," she said, attempting a smile.

"What's wrong?" said Fadi.

"Nothing."

"You sure?"

She took a sip from the glass of water on her nightstand as she considered her response. He'd already made it clear the trip wasn't an option, and she hated the idea of letting him see just how much that had upset her. But saying nothing only left her feeling more alone, reminding her that she couldn't confide in the person she was supposed to trust most. She sank back against the headboard, panic and shame shooting through her chest.

"I got into it with Amanda today," she finally said.

Fadi laid down his fork and glanced at her. "Who's Amanda again?"

She raised an eyebrow. "My coworker? You know, the stuck-up white woman I told you about?"

"Oh, right. What happened?"

"She was saying things about women from 'our country.'" She paused, stabbing an olive with her fork. "So I snapped and called her a racist."

Fadi frowned. "Seriously? When did this happen?"

"At the start of our department meeting."

"You called her a racist in front of your entire department?"

"Well, yeah. But it's true."

"Wow," he said, shaking his head. "You can't go around calling people racists. You have to learn how to control your emotions. What will your boss think?"

Yara swallowed. This hadn't occurred to her yet. Jonathan paid a lot of lip service to "community building" on campus and probably was not going to be happy. "But she always talks down to me," Yara said, arguing with Jonathan now as much as she was explaining herself to Fadi.

"Does she, though?" Fadi put a spoonful of tabbouleh in his mouth, avoiding her eyes. "I mean, don't you think you're overreacting? You always assume everyone is out to get you."

She watched as he took a bite of his pita, his jaw clenching as he chewed. Did she? Maybe she did spend most of her days on the defensive.

Fadi put the pita down, picked up his phone, and began typing. "What made her say that stuff, anyway?" he asked distractedly.

"She thinks I'm an oppressed housewife because I didn't apply to chaperone the cruise."

"Wow. That's harsh."

She tried to meet his eyes, but he wouldn't look at her. The next thing she knew she was saying, "Well, actually, you are the reason I couldn't go."

Fadi turned to her and barked out a laugh. "Are you seriously claiming to be a stereotypical Arab housewife right now?"

"What's that supposed to mean?"

"I let you go to college and get a job."

"You *let* me?"

"You know what I mean," he said, his eyes back on his phone. "You're not a damsel in distress, Yara. You can do whatever you want."

"If that's the case, then why can't I go on the trip?"

When he looked up again, Yara saw irritation in his face. Calmly, sounding half-amused, he said, "Because I have bills to pay and a business to build. You can't possibly expect me to put all that on hold to watch the kids so you can go on vacation."

She had the sudden urge to fling her plate across the room but set it down carefully on the nightstand instead. "See, that's my point," she said. "Why do I always have to watch the kids? You travel all the time and you don't ask for permission. But the moment I want to go somewhere, not only do I have to ask you, but you can say no. It's a total double standard."

Fadi sighed. "It's not my fault we live in a world of double standards. It's not just an Arab thing, it's everywhere."

"Obviously," Yara said flatly. "But that doesn't make it okay."

He put the pita down and turned to her, softening his voice. "I'm a good husband and I've done my best to support you, Yara, but you know I have to work. I have bills to pay, this entire family to worry about. Between the mortgage, our cars, and providing for the girls, it's too much. And it's not like your job pays anything significant." He wiped his fingers with a napkin and looked at her. "What do you want me to do, quit my job so you can travel the world and take pretty pictures?"

"That's not what I'm saying."

"What are you saying, then?"

She shook her head, avoiding his eyes. "Nothing."

Silence fell between them. She could feel her face burn as she gripped her bowl and took a bite of falafel, the sound of her chewing ringing in her ears. Though she'd used fresh herbs and all the usual spices, the patty tasted bland, like she was eating rubber.

Fadi reached for the remote and turned on Netflix, queuing up an episode of *The Fresh Prince of Bel-Air.* Yara blinked at the screen, acutely aware of his body next to hers, their arms slightly grazing. She touched her necklace now, pressing the charm between her fingers, letting the pain seep down into her flesh.

"I don't want to fight," she said as soon as the episode finished.

"Neither do I," Fadi said without meeting her eyes. "I just want to relax. I had a long day, too."

She bit the inside of her cheek, wondering how to make him understand why she was so upset: that she had spent every night of her life in her parents' house before transferring to his and had never lived a day on her own. That most days it felt as if something was standing between her and the rest of the world. Anxiety bubbled beneath her ribs as she searched for the right words to explain the feeling to him, but all she could say was, "I'm sorry. I'm just stressed."

He looked at her then, like he was seeing her for the first time since they sat down together. "If you're so stressed, why don't you just quit? I make more than enough money for the both of us."

"What? No." She straightened, trying to combat the heavy feeling in her body, as if she were sinking into the mattress. "I didn't mean I was stressed because of work," she said. "If anything, my job keeps me busy. I like being busy."

"Then why are you going around making problems?" Fadi said, shaking his head. "Maybe if you appreciated how good you have it, you'd learn how to control your temper."

She felt her shoulders jerk upward and tried to hold herself very still. "Easy for you to say."

"What's that supposed to mean?"

"You get to do whatever you want, and I'm supposed to accept it with a smile? I want more for myself."

"Like what? You're one of the most independent Arab women I know."

"Exactly," Yara said, quietly gasping. "And I still have no independence compared to you or any man we know, and you know it. Just admit it."

Fadi sighed irritably. "This isn't some village back home," he finally said. "Stop pretending I'm some oppressor, just because you're unhappy with yourself."

"Excuse me?" She jumped out of bed, her heart swelling in her chest like a balloon about to burst. She reached for her glass of water again, her hands shaking as she tightened her grip. "What's that supposed to mean?"

"You heard what I said. Clearly you have your own issues that you're projecting on me."

Before she realized what was happening, she slammed the glass against the nightstand. It shattered, sending tiny pieces scattering everywhere and water gushing onto the floor.

"What the fuck, Yara!" Fadi said. "You'll wake the girls."

She brought her hands to her mouth, shaking her head quickly. The last thing she wanted was for her daughters to see her this way.

"This is exactly what I'm talking about," Fadi said. "What the hell is wrong with you?"

She opened her mouth but could think of nothing to say.

"You need help," he went on. "Can't you see that? My mother warned me this would happen again!"

Water dripped off the nightstand onto the carpet, but Yara could only stand there, her heart beating too fast. "I'm so sorry," she eventually said, heading toward the kitchen for the towels she needed to clean up the mess she'd made.

*She had done this before. The first time was a month into their mar*riage, when she and Fadi had gotten into a small argument, the subject of which she couldn't even remember now.

"I don't want to talk about it," Fadi had said, dismissing her with a wave of his hand. Her heart had begun pounding so loudly she could feel it in her throat, and the next thing she knew she'd stormed down the hall to the living room, where she spotted Fadi's favorite old mug on the coffee table, a Tar Heels souvenir. In a flash, before she could think, she'd picked it up and smashed it against the wall, and the ceramic shards went flying across the room.

When Fadi had come in, she'd been curled up on the floor next to the remains of the mug.

"What happened?" he'd said, staring down at her.

She'd buried her face in her knees, her body still shaking. "I don't know what came over me. I'm so sorry."

From the corner of her eyes she'd seen him back away, frowning and shaking his head. After she'd apologized repeatedly, she assured herself it was a fluke. She was a young bride—overly anxious and still naive in both life and relationships. This was normal, right? But then, a few months later, it happened again. One moment they'd been having a nice dinner and the next her plate had been in pieces on the floor. As soon as she'd realized what she'd done, she'd covered her face and burst into tears, overcome with shame.

Fadi had told her then she needed help, but it hadn't happened since the girls were born. Yara had made sure of it. She was terrified of her outbursts, the way the anger seemed to come over uncontrollably. But what had terrified her most was the possibility of hurting her daughters, and the realization that perhaps she was not so different from her parents after all. Eventually she'd learned to bury her feelings inside, making them smaller and smaller, pushing them further and further down until they disappeared.

Or at least, she thought they did.

9

On Saturday, Yara finished her housework in a frenzy, then, while the girls were playing upstairs, retreated to the sunroom, where she placed a fresh canvas on the easel, feeling a sickening need to let something out, only what she didn't know. One splotch of thick, dense paint after another, she mixed red and yellows and blues, lost in the soothing sound of brush against canvas, until the girls came storming in the room. She took a quick breath, startled, then put the painting away.

On Sunday, she busied herself with preparing for her in-laws' arrival—scrubbing, chopping, roasting—until it was time for dinner. Around the sufra, the air felt thick and hazy, then the slow feeling of things not feeling real, until the next thing she knew they were gone, the evening over.

Now Yara knocked on the half-open office door.

"Come in," Jonathan called.

He'd emailed her over the weekend:

Dear Yara,

We missed you at the department meeting yesterday. I heard about what happened. Please come by my office first thing Monday to discuss.

Have a good weekend,

Jonathan

Yara shifted her weight, looking at the floor. She couldn't tell from the tone of the message how much trouble she was in.

Jonathan gestured for her to sit before looking back at his computer. Behind him, a row of windows ran from the ceiling to the floor, and she couldn't help but notice that they were streaked with dirt. His office was a wreck, too: papers sprawled across his desk, empty coffee mugs on the file cabinet. She had the sudden urge to sweep it all into the trash and wipe down the surfaces, but instead she asked: "Is everything all right?"

"I want to talk about Friday," he said.

"Okay."

"I heard you called one of your colleagues a racist."

"Well, yes. But . . ."

"I'm afraid there's no excuse for raising your voice at someone in our community, or throwing around a term like that."

For a moment she sat there, looking at him. Then, quietly, she said: "I'm not making excuses, but she was acting like an ignorant white woman."

He winced. "Isn't that a pretty racist thing to call her?"

"Are you kidding me?" Yara felt her voice crack a little on the last word. "She assumed I was from another country and that my marriage is some kind of dictatorship. I've worked really hard to get here, and not so I can be stereotyped and dismissed by my colleagues."

"I see," Jonathan said, though she didn't think he did. He cleared his throat. "Perhaps there's more going on here."

"Like what?"

He paused, as though considering his response. "I just want to make sure everything is okay. I noticed you've been a bit withdrawn lately. I haven't seen much of you at the departmental meet and greets."

She raised an eyebrow. "They aren't mandatory."

"Or the professional development sessions?"

"Those aren't mandatory either, are they?"

Jonathan sighed, tapping his fingers against the desk. After a long moment of silence, he cleared his throat again. "Are you sure there's nothing wrong at home? Anything we can help you with?"

She jerked forward in her chair. "What are you talking about?"

He looked taken aback. "I'm sorry, I'm not trying to pry. But you seem a little distressed lately." He reached into his drawer and pulled out a file stuffed with papers. "Is everything okay?"

"Besides Amanda treating me disrespectfully, everything's fine."

He tapped the file folder. "Right. Well, my main concern is making sure you have the resources you need. We offer employee counseling here on campus, and I've enrolled you in the Employee Assistance Program so you can take advantage."

Yara stood up. "What?"

He flinched. "Please, calm down."

"I am calm," she said, sitting back in her seat, her heart pounding. *This* was her reward for all her hard work? "But you think I need counseling because I called Amanda a racist?"

He sighed. "The incident with Amanda might be the proximate reason you're here, but I've been concerned, too. I think counseling might help."

She shook her head. "No."

"Well, I can't make you go," he said. "But I strongly recommend it. We take mental health very seriously here, and we want to make sure our faculty and staff are equipped for success. It's in our students' best interest that their instructors are in the right mindset to teach, and after what happened, I'm not so sure you are." He paused, avoiding her eyes. "In the meantime, I've decided to reassign your class to another instructor."

"What?"

"Just for this semester, so you can take the time you need."

She stared at him, her mouth hanging open. "I can't believe you're punishing me for this. What about Amanda? Shouldn't she be in trouble for what she said to me?"

"Any disciplinary action regarding your colleague is confidential," Jonathan said. "As is this conversation, of course. And anything you say to a therapist is, too." He paused, making his voice softer.

"Please don't think of counseling as a punishment, Yara. We're offering you a chance to access extra resources to help you."

"I don't need your resources," she said, digging her nails into her palm. "Especially not ones forced on me."

"Nothing is being forced on you," Jonathan said, sliding a brochure from the file folder and offering it to her. "It's up to you whether you want to attend. Human Resources is very clear about that. But I'm afraid I have to reassign your class until I'm confident that you're ready to return to the classroom."

Yara wanted to open her mouth and scream and fling the brochure across his desk. Instead she grabbed it from his hand, teeth clenched, and walked out.

Back in her office, she pressed her forehead to her desk and shut her eyes. She couldn't lose this job. It wasn't perfect, or even fulfilling most days, but it gave her something to look forward to after she dropped her girls off at school, and it would be hard to find another job with the flexibility to be present for her daughters. Sitting there, her heart beating so fast, Mama's face surfaced in her mind, her blue eyes hollow and empty like a lantern with the lights flicked out. No. Yara couldn't let that happen to her. No matter what. Jonathan hadn't said he would fire her if she didn't go to therapy, but she knew all too well what would happen if she didn't fall in line.

10

In the shower that night, steam filled the air and made it hard for Yara to see Fadi, which was a relief. Things between them had been tense since her outburst on Friday. He'd barely spoken to her when he came home on Saturday, sharing nothing about his day at work and not even asking about the girls. The silence made her feel sick. She'd failed to make him forgive her, and now she needed to tell him that he'd been right.

She ran her face under the water, the sound crashing down around her ears as she rehearsed the words to make sure they would convey her exact meaning. But all she could say was, "I got into trouble today."

Fadi squinted at her through the steam. "What? Again?"

She reached for a bar of soap, avoiding his eyes. "Jonathan reassigned my art class and recommended that I start counseling."

He raised his eyebrows. "Because of what happened at your meeting?"

"Yeah. He says I need time off to work on my 'mental health.'"

"Well, obviously. You can't expect to go around losing your temper at work and not face the consequences."

Yara stared at the tile, feeling sick. He was right, of course. But why couldn't he be a bit gentler about it?

"You definitely need counseling," Fadi continued. "It's expensive, though."

She sighed. "They have it free at work."

"Then you'll go?"

"I think I have to at this point," she said. "I'm worried if I don't, he won't renew my contract next term."

"Well, I wouldn't worry about that. There are plenty of desk jobs out there."

Yara met his eyes. "I don't have a desk job," she said, raising her voice.

Fadi shrugged. "Right. But that's hardly the point."

The water was on full blast, but its sound was drowned out by the beating of blood in her eardrums. That was precisely the point! All those years cramming college courses in half the time and writing papers late at night and raising their daughters and having dinner ready every night—all that work and Fadi still couldn't see her for what she was? Someone who wanted to do something, *to be someone.* What had he thought she meant all those years ago?

She hadn't always wanted to teach art, which Fadi knew. Not having access to art classes in school, it had never occurred to her that she could one day major in art or make it into a real career. When she'd first started college in New York, she'd taken an introductory law course and liked the promise of power it offered. She imagined herself in a courtroom, standing up to her father, forcing him to treat her mother better, showing him that she could do the same things as her brothers, like Yazan, who'd said he would be a lawyer one day. But that was the only course she'd taken in law.

Soon after they'd married, she mentioned the possibility of continuing to study law to Fadi, and he'd said, "Don't lawyers work really long hours? That seems like a tough job to have with a family."

"Plenty of women practice law while raising kids," she said.

"Oh yes, of course." He looked back up at her, his voice softer. "It's not my place to decide for you. It just seems too stuffy for someone like you, with all your drawings and books. You seem more dreamy and creative to me."

She had nodded then, trying to contain her smile. She liked how he'd said that, how it made her feel like she was being seen for the first time. Maybe he was right, she'd thought. When she transferred her credits, she hadn't bothered to look beyond the art courses in the catalog.

In the shower now, Yara leaned back against the wet tile. "How can you say that's not the point?" she said. "You know how important my career is to me."

"Yeah, sure," he said. "I get that. But your boss recommended you go to counseling, and you're acting like he asked you to throw your life savings onto a bonfire or something." He let out a small laugh. "I've been telling you for years now that you should see a therapist. I mean, really." He sighed. "Maybe you can finally learn how to control your temper."

Standing there, Yara felt the impulse to spit in his face but stopped herself: that would just prove his point. Instead, she swallowed a knot of shame in her throat, then reached for the loofah and began to scrub her skin so hard it left red marks. Why did she leap to violence whenever she felt threatened? Why was she so volatile, teetering between extremes?

Swaying under the hot running water, she wondered if perhaps she'd made a mistake abandoning the idea of law school. The robotic memorization of statutes seemed somehow the easier thing now. As an art major she had always been encouraged to go off, experiment, create something that had never been made before. But how? she had wondered then. Was it possible for someone like her to find herself, to be her own person, when she had experienced so little of the world outside her home?

Fadi stepped out of the shower. "Come on, babe. I'm starving."

Through the fogged-up door, she watched him dry off, regarding himself in the mirror while he rubbed a towel against his broad shoulders and down his back. She tightened her fingers around the loofah, suppressing the urge to shove her fist through the glass. Part of her was ashamed of how foolish and pathetic she was, how she hoped he'd catch sight of her in the mirror and turn around, that he'd lean back inside the shower and kiss her. And yet another part of her was angry, not with Fadi, but with herself. Why had she allowed herself to be in this position, waiting for a man to give her permission to go after the things she wanted? Shouldn't she have known by now to depend on no one? Not a parent, not a brother, not a husband. That no one would soothe the pain in your heart. No one will rescue you.

11

To reach the Administrative Services Building on the north side of campus, Yara had to drive past the green quads and over a small river, where cypress knees poked from the mossy earth like gnome hoods. She rolled down the windows so she could hear the gentle sounds of lapping waves and trilling birds, and the luxuriously loamy riverbed reverberated through her senses.

On the fourth floor of the Administrative Services Building, inside the counselor's waiting room, Yara filled out an intake form she'd been sent that morning. She clenched her teeth as she flipped through the pages, her eyes struggling to register the words. One question asked whether she was of Hispanic, Latino, or Spanish origin. She circled no. The next asked about her race and included a list of options with checkboxes: American Indian or Alaska Native, Asian, Black or African American, Hispanic or Latino, Native Hawaiian or Pacific Islander, and white.

She sighed and reread the options. Her family had always been told to classify themselves as white because of their Middle Eastern origins. But Yara had never considered herself white or been viewed as white by anyone else, and marking herself as such felt inaccurate, as though she were being simmered down, reduced until she were invisible. She might as well be. Her Palestinian nationality had been erased by Israel, and here, in America, her Middle Eastern identity was erased, too. She felt a stiffness in her neck as she wrote "Other" underneath the list of options and made a checkmark next to it.

The last page of the form was a mental health questionnaire, a list of thirty questions glaring up at her. She bit the sides of her tongue as she scanned them, willing herself to focus. Words arranged in different ways, but all asking the same question: How do you feel?

How did she feel? She couldn't reduce the tingling in her body or the discomfort traveling from her spine down her fingertips to an exact emotion. Was it anger, anxiety, sadness, or something else? To her relief, though, she didn't have to describe it. All she had to do was circle "Yes" or "No."

She filled out the form quickly, then slipped her phone from her pocket. On Instagram, her latest post had been liked over two hundred times and had twenty comments. She scanned them: beautiful family mashallah, PERFECTION, #familygoals, and a dozen heart-eyed emojis. Then a small whisper, *What would people think?*

She tightened a fist around the phone. Was this the voice she was always answering to? Ashamed, she returned to the main grid. A collage of her life flashed before her: Mira's and Jude's rosy smiles as they tasted blueberries at the farmers market. Fadi's arm around her shoulder at a Tar Heels game. All four of them huddled close on a park bench, a loving family. The perfection of everything she'd achieved was captured in tiny squares across the screen, in full color, precisely as she'd intended. So why did it all feel so false?

Sliding the phone back into her pocket, she clutched the clipboard tightly and eyed the IN SESSION sign hanging from the knob of the counselor's closed door. She wondered who was inside. The only person she'd known to attend employee counseling was Julianna from the History Department, after she'd been diagnosed with cancer. Sitting there, Yara wished she was afflicted with some disease. At least then her anger would make sense. There would be a reason she snapped like that, a valid explanation to explain why she'd risk losing everything she'd worked for. What was worse than feeling bad was having no reason at all, at least none she could pin down and understand.

A few minutes later, the counselor's door opened and a man stood in the doorway. "See you next week," he was saying to the counselor. He was tall with a full beard and brown hair pulled back into a ponytail. Yara recognized him from the Culinary Arts Department, the smallest at the school. She'd photographed one of his classes for the website, distinctly remembering the dish he'd been making, that it smelled of brown sugar and sesame oil. She wondered why he was in counseling.

When the man didn't move, Yara realized he was holding the door open for her. Quickly she rose to her feet.

"Hi there," he said, smiling, a southern drawl to his voice.

"Uh, hi," Yara said, not knowing what to do with her body. Was she going to have to let someone in after her session, too? Shouldn't there be a back door where people could slip out unnoticed?

She hurried across the room, avoiding the man's eyes as she made her way toward him. But before she could reach the door, she tripped on the carpet. She righted herself, but not before the clipboard flew across the room, and her forms scattered everywhere.

"Shit," she said, picking them up in a rush. The ponytailed man let go of the door and leaned over to help her. She could feel her face burning as he squatted down beside her. "Thank you," she said.

"Don't worry about it," he said. Their eyes met as he handed her a couple of loose sheets without glancing down at them. Standing and opening the door again for her, he said, "I'm Silas."

Yara froze. She could see the counselor watching them from inside his office, leaning against his desk. Jonathan had promised that her sessions would be confidential, but could he have told the counselor anything about her, perhaps to warn him about lack of sociability? Or something else?

She tried to make her voice calm, even friendly. "I'm Yara."

"Yara . . ." Silas said slowly, and correctly, much to her surprise. "That's a beautiful name." Turning to leave, he added, "Have fun in there."

*The counselor was a middle-aged man, short and slim, with horn-*rimmed glasses and blond hair that looked too bright against his pale skin. He walked across the room and reached out his hand. "Yara Murad?"

She nodded and passed him the clipboard instead of her hand.

"I'm William Banks," he said and pulled the door closed behind them. "You can call me William. Would you like to have a seat?"

The room was more colorful than she'd expected, saturated in artificial light. A deep red sofa with navy pillows took up most of the space. Across from it, a mustard leather chair was propped at an angle, and behind that, potted plants filled both windowsills.

"You can sit wherever you like," William said, taking a seat on the leather chair. "I'll take a look at your forms."

Pushing one leg after the other, Yara decided to take the end of the sofa farthest from him, facing the window. Outside, she could see a skyline view of the campus grounds, patches of bright green grass then paved concrete, and beyond that, acres of longleaf pines surrounding the sprawling lake where students gathered. The sight reminded her of how much she wanted to keep this job, this time and place she had for herself.

When she finally tore her eyes from the glass, William was still reading through the forms. She had an urge to lean forward and snatch the file from his hands, but she couldn't move.

Eventually William looked up and said: "So, Yara, why don't you tell me a little bit about yourself? How long have you been in the States?"

"My whole life," she said quickly. "I was born and raised in Brooklyn."

"Right. Sorry for assuming." He paused, cleared his throat. "How was it like, growing up in New York? I'd like to learn more about your upbringing."

She frowned. Not even two minutes in and he was already attempting to go places she didn't want to take him. "I don't see what that has to do with anything."

"What makes you say that?"

"I'm here because of what happened with Amanda, and because I want my class back. My upbringing has nothing to do with that. I simply need to work on managing my emotions with colleagues." However ignorant they are, Yara thought.

William nodded. "Of course, of course. Sometimes it seems like the things happening now are the most significant," he said. "But many of our problems—especially when it comes to regulating our emotions—well, those are patterns that are rooted in our past. Therapy helps us explore the links between past and present so we can move forward and heal."

Yara slid her hands beneath her thighs, something Jude did sometimes when she was upset. "Well, there's nothing to explore."

For a long moment William studied her, as though she were a painting in a museum. Then he said: "All right. Why don't you tell me a little bit more about your life now, then?"

"Fine," Yara said, shifting her gaze out the window. She told him she was married with two daughters. That she'd moved here from Brooklyn nine years ago when she'd married Fadi, who'd lived here all his life. She looked back at William. "And I've been working at the college for four years, taking photos and updating website designs and doing everything Jonathan asks, because what I really want to do is teach full-time, but that hasn't happened yet."

"Has that been your goal since you started here?" William asked.

"Yes."

"What do you think the obstacles are?"

"I don't know. Maybe my schedule." She pulled her hands out

from under her legs. "Ever since Jonathan hired me, he's been conscious of the fact that I want to be with my daughters after school. That's very important to me. I started out as a part-time web designer because Mira and Jude were so young, but when Jude began preschool, he let me teach the morning art prerequisite course."

"So, time with your children is important to you," William said, trying to meet her eyes. "Why do you think that is?"

She shook her head and swallowed, looking away from him, at the ceiling. "I want to be a good mother to them, that's all."

"And you think working makes you a bad mother?"

"No, of course not, it's just . . ." She paused, her face burning. "I want to be present for them. As much as I want a career, it's not as important to me as being there for them, making sure they know they're my priority."

"I see," William said, pausing to write something down. They sat in silence for a moment before he asked, "Is there anyone who could help with childcare in the afternoon?"

"My mother-in-law, I suppose." Yara had thought of this before, but had quickly ruled it out. "She helps me out when she can but my husband's brothers are younger and still at home, and she has a lot to do there. And anyway, she thinks it's a mother's job to take care of her own kids."

William nodded. "What about your husband?"

"He has a wholesale business he's growing," Yara said, "and he still helps his father with his business as well. He works crazy-long hours, and his income provides for us." She paused. "I don't have to work, so I really can't expect him to stop what he's doing to help me."

With apparent interest, William said: "Does that bother you?"

"What?

"Having to put your career on hold for his?"

She raised an eyebrow. "I see where this is going. I share one thing with you and the first place you go is assuming that I'm held back." She shook her head. "Well, just so you know, I'm an educated, accomplished woman who's not oppressed by anyone."

William waited a beat, then replied: "I hadn't meant to suggest otherwise. I apologize."

Yara touched her necklace. "Fine," she said. "Thank you."

"Why don't we talk about what happened with your colleague, then?" he continued.

She realized her knee was shaking and pressed her palm against it. "I'm not proud of myself for snapping like that. It was not one of my finer moments."

"Yes, your altercation with Amanda, as I understand it, is the reason this session was suggested," he said. "But there's something that worries me more."

"What do you mean?"

He looked down at the clipboard, flipping through the pages until the last one. Watching him, Yara wished he would hurry up and say whatever it was he was going to say.

"Have you ever been to therapy before?" he finally asked.

"Why?"

"I'm trying to get to know you," William said. "That's part of the process here in counseling. To understand all the aspects of your past and present, and ultimately help you."

"I don't know that therapy helps anything," Yara said.

William uncrossed his legs and crossed them again. "That's a strong opinion. Has that been your experience in the past?"

Yara shrugged and jammed her hands into the pockets of her sweater. Eight years ago, during her six-week checkup, after baby Mira had been born, Yara's gynecologist had asked her a few questions about her emotional state. Afterward, she had quickly scheduled an appointment for Yara to see the psychiatrist in her practice. The following week, she rocked Mira nervously in her lap as the psychiatrist, a white woman in her late forties, told Yara that she was experiencing symptoms of postpartum depression. Staring at the screen of her laptop as she spoke, she told Yara that it was common, and that there were medicines to help with many kinds of depression, including postpartum. Some were not safe to take if Yara was planning to continue breastfeeding, she said, and others had potential side effects, like violent behavior, mania, aggression, or an increased risk of suicidal ideation.

The whole time the woman was talking, Yara kept swaying Mira back and forth while swallowing a thick lump in her throat. She wanted to snatch the doctor's computer and break it against the edge of the chair. Instead, she closed her eyes and clenched her teeth until the impulse faded. Yara thought about telling her how sometimes she smashed things and didn't know why, but that it hadn't happened since becoming a mother. That she must be mistaken, that Yara was doing better now than ever before. But the doctor seemed focused on the challenges of new motherhood, and Yara couldn't bring herself to tell her otherwise. How could she possibly explain to this woman the utter confusion and helplessness she was experiencing as a young married woman and mother, still feeling like a child herself? At the end of their brief session, the psychiatrist wrote her a prescription for an antidepressant, which Yara never filled. She didn't mention the appointment to Fadi.

Now Yara turned to William and said, "I just don't see how western therapy could help someone like me."

"I see. Do you know anyone who might have had a different experience? Anyone in your family, perhaps?"

She laughed suddenly. "Definitely not."

"That's a shame." He paused to make another note on the clipboard, and Yara felt her skin burn. "What happens when someone has a problem or needs help?"

"They definitely don't talk to a stranger about it."

"What do they do instead?"

She sighed, feeling defeated. *Idiot.* Why had she mentioned her family at all?

"My grandmother liked to do Turkish coffee readings," she offered. Her eyes itched and she rubbed them. "I guess it was a form of therapy, if you think about it."

"Do you believe those readings were helpful?" asked William.

"Yes, to her. I guess." Yara went to touch her necklace again, then quickly stopped, worried William might ask about it.

"Then, possibly, might conventional therapy be useful, too?"

Yara shrugged. "I mean, it could be, in the right circumstances."

"But you don't think these are the right circumstances?"

She stared out the window, at the skinny spruce trees along the edge of the lake, her heart beginning to race. "No, they're not," Yara said. "I'm sorry, but you don't know anything about me or where I come from, and the things you do know are probably caricatures or misrepresentations. I'm not trying to be rude, but I don't want to waste my time talking to you about things you'll never understand, though I'm sure you mean well."

She put her hand to her cheek, and her face was flushed. She hadn't anticipated saying any of this, but it was as pure a distillation of her feelings as she'd had in some time.

"You're right," William said. "Unfortunately, my understanding of your culture is very limited. But that doesn't mean I can't help you." He rubbed the edge of the file with his thumb. "And I do think you need some help. I don't mean to alarm you, Yara, but some of your answers here are very concerning to me."

She chewed the edge of her nail. "Look, the questions were confusing. I didn't even know what I was circling half the time." This came out more defensive than she'd intended, her voice unsteady.

"I can understand how difficult this must feel for you," William said. "From what I see here, it seems likely you're struggling from depression and you might want to consider medication."

Sweat pooled above her upper lip, and she wiped her palms on her knees as William went on about treatment options, his voice becoming just a loud buzz in the room.

"Yara? Would you like me to refer you to a psychiatrist, too?" William said, and she was finally able to discern the words.

She blinked. "No. I'm not depressed, and I don't need medication. Why are drugs the first thing you people think of?"

"We can hold off on a referral if you feel strongly against it," he said. "But if you want to improve your mental health and work on the triggers that cause you to react in anger, you need to give me a chance to help you."

Yara frowned, looking at the floor.

"It would mean us meeting here once a week. Every Friday afternoon, at two P.M.? Does that work? For your schedule, I mean?"

"Yes," Yara said, standing up to leave.

"Great. I'll see you on Friday, then?"

"Okay," she said as she rushed out of the room, not sure that she would return.

12

Think of what Kahlil Gibran wrote," Mama said. "'Travel and tell no one, live a true love story and tell no one, live happily and tell no one. People ruin beautiful things.'"

"I don't know what you mean, Mama," Yara said, turning down Jefferson Road.

"Yes, you do," Mama said.

"It's not like I wanted to see a counselor," Yara said. "I barely had a choice." Having fewer tasks at the college now, Yara was early to pick up the girls again and had decided to drive around until it was time. "He thinks I might have depression," she added.

"Depression?" Mama said. "That's ridiculous!" She let out a harsh laugh. "What reason could you possibly have to be depressed? At your age, I was raising half a dozen kids and spending my days cooking and cleaning."

A sting of deep embarrassment shot through Yara, and she bit on her lip for a moment, thinking back to Mama then, how she had been like a ticking time bomb, especially after Teta died, and even worse after she went to see the fortune teller.

In a low voice, Yara asked, "Do you think it's possible you were depressed, Mama?"

"Ha!" Mama laughed, a sharp sound. "Was I angry and tired and sick of some things? Yes, but that's not depression. Leave it to Americans to make a sickness out of being sad. Don't they know that everyone in the world suffers? Just remember that the longer you pay them to listen to your problems, the worse you'll feel."

"I don't think I have a choice, Mama, not really. I want to have my job back next term. I want to teach again." Yara pressed her back against the seat, a small wave of fear passing through her at the thought of their failing to renew her contract. "I can't lose my job and be only a housewife, depending on a man for survival. I won't do it."

In a tight voice Mama said, "You mean, like me?"

Yara felt a bead of sweat on her forehead. "I'm sorry. I didn't mean it like that."

For a moment neither of them spoke, and Yara felt like she was sinking into wet concrete. She straightened and checked the clock on her dash. Still twenty minutes until she had to pick up the girls.

"I think it's obvious what's happening here," Mama finally said.

"What?"

"You're cursed."

Yara blinked, rubbing her eyes. "What do you mean, *cursed*?"

"With the evil eye, of course."

"Why would anyone curse me?"

"Why wouldn't they?" Mama said. "You're educated and successful. You're married to a wonderful man, and you have two beautiful children. That's a recipe for envy, habibti. But you should already know this by now."

Yara felt her face go hot, the sun beating through her windshield. She cracked her window, inhaled the cool air.

"How are you feeling right now?" Mama asked. "Do you have a fever or headache? Is there a green tinge to your skin? What about your eyes, are they yellow?"

Yara glanced at herself in the rearview mirror and saw the usual reflection: deep black eyes and wild dark hair tucked behind her ears, her face the color of burnt sugar. Amhiyeh, Teta had always described her complexion. "Like golden wheat."

"I look normal," Yara said. "A little tired, but nothing out of the ordinary. What does my appearance have to do with anything?"

"Sometimes the evil eye manifests itself physically," Mama said. "Unexpected illness or sudden discomfort could be a sign of it. Do you remember my mother's garden back home?"

"Yes, of course," Yara said too quickly, eager to hear Mama speak of Teta. She'd rarely spoken of her after she'd passed, and Yara had kept her memory alone, repeating the recipes Teta had taught her, cooking for Mama and her brothers when she was only fourteen, desperate to keep her grandmother's spirit alive. "What about Teta's garden?"

"One summer when I was a young girl, it wilted overnight," Mama said. "Her figs and blueberries all fell to the ground and turned brown. She was convinced that our jealous neighbor had cursed it, and after that she never invited her over for chai again."

Yara pictured Teta in her garden, which was the most bountiful in the neighborhood. She could see her grandmother squatting over the boxes she had built on her rooftop, plucking tomatoes and squash for dinner, mint and sage for tea. It was conceivable to her that someone could envy her grandmother's garden enough to curse it, but this kind of superstition was inseparable from the beliefs Yara had grown up with.

"If a small garden in a refugee camp is enough to bring about the evil eye," Mama continued, "what can be said about your life? All those fancy photos you put on the internet for everyone to fawn over?"

Yara gave an embarrassed laugh. "I didn't realize the evil eye applied online."

"Of course it does when you put your private life there for the world to see!" Mama clucked her tongue, then lowered her voice to a tight whisper. "Displaying your blessings too proudly will only bring you hasad. You know how dangerous envy can be."

Yara paused for a long moment, staring out the windshield, her body on fire. Overhead the sky was a perfect blue, fading white clouds scattered across it. "Those pictures," she finally said. "They don't even feel true."

"True or not, you can't be so reckless when it comes to these things. One moment your life is fine, and the next a terrible misfortune befalls you. You have to be more careful."

Approaching a red light, Yara slowed the car to a stop. Closing her eyes, she tried to steady her racing heart.

"What?" Mama said when Yara didn't reply. "You don't like what I'm saying? I'm telling you this for your own good. Believe me, I would know." She made a noise that sounded like a small cry. "Don't you remember?"

"I don't know what you mean," Yara said.

"Why, of course you do. Have you forgotten what the fortune teller said?"

Yara's fingers went tight around the steering wheel, the realization washing over her. She remembered all too clearly when Mama had visited the strange woman, how changed she'd been afterward, as if a jinn had entered her body and sucked all the light out. "No," Yara said, shaking her head. "Of course not."

She watched the tips of maple branches flying by outside her car. Two more turns, ten more minutes, she'd be with her girls again.

"I was never the same after that," Mama said, her voice quieter now.

"I know," Yara croaked.

"One bad thing happened after another. It seems similar to what's happening to you, habibti. Maybe we're not so different after all. Maybe—"

"No!" Yara said before Mama could go on. "My life is completely different from yours. I'm completely different from you."

"You think so," Mama said. "But an evil eye is an evil eye, and you know what happens once you're cursed."

YARA'S JOURNAL

In my memory of that day, when you took us to visit the fortune teller, it was as if you were cast under a spell.

"Never mind where," you say, when I ask where we are going. You push the double stroller down Fifth Avenue tight-lipped, staring ahead in a flat, unblinking way. My brothers and I stuff our hands in our pockets as we struggle to keep up with you. The wind whips my hair across my face and sends a chill down my spine. We walk along the noisy, crowded, tree-lined blocks in silence, shoving through a stream of pedestrians as we cross a wide intersection. You stop suddenly when we arrive at our destination, and we breathe out puffs of air, our legs stiff. Sparrows circle overhead, dipping behind the quivering trees. I look up at the old building, with its crumbling red brick and rusted fire escapes, wondering why on earth you've bought us here.

Inside the building, you take off your coat and roll up the sleeves of your blouse to your elbows. Then you begin to shove the stroller up the stairs before stopping to ask if I can lift the end. I do, and we continue up two narrow flights of stairs, panting. You are still catching your breath when you knock on the door and a tall and lean woman appears. I stare up at the fortune teller, awed by the sight of her. In a long, flowy blue kaftan and a matching shawl wrapped around her hair, she looks majestic, like a character in one of the fables we read. Her green eyes are heavily rimmed with kohl, and her hands are covered with henna patterns in a stain the color of blood.

"Meriem?" the fortune teller says, and you nod. "Come in."

You look over at us nervously, then push the stroller into the dim apartment. My brothers follow you, and I inch behind them, inhaling the strong scent of sage as I step through the front door. With wonder, I glance around at the darkened room, still confused about why we are here. Everywhere I turn, there are crystals: smoky, black marble stones, purple and rose-colored pendulums, large clusters of clear quartz so radiant they must have come from a magic cave. A large curtain made of crystal beads divides the room in half. On the other side of it, an old wooden table sits next to a flickering lamp, and in the center, a palmistry hand with an all-seeing eye. It looks just like the charm you wear around your neck.

On the far end of the room, a small TV is playing Tom and Jerry. *You position the stroller in front of the screen, then turn to me. "Stay here and watch your brothers," you say before disappearing through the beads.*

I try to do as you say. I watch the boys and distract myself by drawing a bird in the fibers of the carpet with my index finger. But the next thing I know, I've risen and I'm peeking through the slits in the beads.

"Take a seat," the woman is saying now, pointing to a prayer rug on the floor.

You pause, gazing down and rubbing your eyes. I can tell that you are nervous. Is it because of the rug? Are you afraid of what God would think about your visit? The only times I've seen you sit on a prayer rug are during Eid, when we kneel together in the back of the mosque, in a section designated for women, while Baba and the boys pray in the main room. I wouldn't describe you as a religious person, but lately you seem more resistant to prayer than usual, and your eyes seem electric, intense. I wonder what's wrong, and if it has anything to do with why you brought us here.

Eventually you take a seat on the rug, keeping your gaze down. The fortune teller picks up a stick of white chalk and proceeds to draw a large circle on the ground around you, writing Arabic words on the perimeter. Her long ornate letters are ones I learned in school but can't make out now. After she finishes writing, she enters the circle and begins to recite mantras and incantations as she places iron stones around the outer perimeter.

"The jinn fear iron," the woman says.

You look at her, running your fingers along the edges of the rug, but say nothing.

The fortune teller keeps going. "We summoned you for a ruqyah," she says, and suddenly the hair on the back of my neck stands up.

Shakily, I scan the room, wondering who the fortune teller is speaking to, but all I see are my brothers in the corner, glued to the cartoons. I start to return to them, but the woman's voice, low and thick, keeps me rooted to the spot.

"Tell us, what does Meriem's future hold?"

A long pause. The woman is focused, her eyes fixed on something in the distance, seemingly communicating with someone.

"Strange," she says at last. "What else?"

You sway back and forth in your seat, clenching and unclenching your fists. I can hardly believe that this is happening. Watching you, I can hear only my heart throbbing in my chest. Finally, the woman blows out the candles.

"I'm sorry, Meriem," she says. "I'm afraid it's out of my hands."

You sit up, fixing your eyes on the woman. "What do you mean?"

"You've been cursed."

A look of confusion crosses your face. Then, a flash of recognition. You open your mouth, but all that comes forth is a single, painful moan. Eventually you bring yourself to your feet unsteadily, as though the ground is shifting beneath you.

"I'm sorry, there's nothing I can do," the fortune teller says, then sweeps the beaded curtain open. I scuttle back to my brothers just in time.

You walk over to us, seemingly in a trance, not hiding the helplessness on your face. I try to meet your eyes as we carry the stroller down the staircase, but you won't look at me. When we reach the bottom of the staircase and put down the stroller, you stop. You stand there with your hands shaking at your sides, breathing hard. Then, in a blink, you drop to your knees, your face in your hands, and scream.

13

In the kitchen the next morning, Yara traced the outline of her hamsa charm as she handed Mira and Jude their school lunches. Their mouths were moving but she couldn't hear what they were saying. Her eyes kept wandering from their pink and purple lunch boxes to her own tired reflection in the microwave door. The memory of the visit to the fortune teller had played on repeat in her mind all night. Numbness covered her like a blanket as she ushered the girls out of the house, and she had the sensation that she'd moved back in time. It was as if she had never actually escaped that moment, as if her body had remembered all along. She had one hand on the wheel all the way to work, and kept the other on her necklace.

She didn't remember much of what happened after that visit, only how much had changed. In the schoolyard, Yara heard whispers about her parents, about Mama. Baba said they were a disgrace, that their family was shamed. They stopped attending community functions, stopped visiting Palestine. Yara didn't understand what was happening, but a feeling of dirt she couldn't rinse off clung to her skin. That same feeling returned on the day Fadi and his parents came to ask for her hand in marriage, and she overheard Nadia whispering to Fadi in the hall, "Are you sure, son? It's not too late to back out. You know what they say: 'like mother, like daughter.'" Hearing this, Yara felt an unendurable sense of shame pour over her soul. She had vowed to herself then to prove Nadia wrong. She would be nothing like her mother.

At work, Yara drifted across campus, clutching her camera against her chest. The ease with which she normally completed her to-do list had evaporated, and she found herself unable to concentrate on cropping a simple photo or doing a basic web page update. She missed teaching, the way it helped her take her students to other worlds. And yet she was grateful for the solitude, this time alone to reflect on her life and take inventory of all the things that had happened, memories she'd spent most of her days outrunning.

She decided to take the camera out for a walk around campus—she could return to her to-do list later. Outside, on the tree trail past the main buildings, along a brick paved walkway shaded by maples, the scenery was quiet, empty, peaceful. Pushing the fortune teller out of her mind, Yara replayed the recent past instead: the incident with Amanda, her first counseling session, the way she'd flung her glass across the room like a crazy person. How had so many things gone wrong in such a short period of time? And how could she have let them happen, after how hard she'd worked to get her life to this place? It doesn't matter, she thought, as she stopped to watch a bright red cardinal perched on a branch. All she could do now was fight to keep her job. Without it, she would be nothing more than an Americanized version of Mama, a woman circumscribed by marriage and motherhood. It shamed her to feel this way, but it was true.

She pulled the camera to her eye, mesmerized by the cardinal's brilliant color, the warm reddish tinges in its wings, tail, and crest. But as she peered through the narrow viewfinder, the beauty of the bird seemed diminished somehow. As Yara brought the camera down to adjust the aperture, she felt someone watching her from across the courtyard: Jonathan. He did not wave or offer a smile. Quickly she snapped a photo and hurried with her head down in the opposite direction until she was certain he couldn't see her anymore. Did she look as ashamed as she felt?

Back in the Humanities Building, she caught sight of herself in a darkened window and flinched, horror-struck: it was as if she were looking at her mother's face. She took a step back and closed her eyes. She didn't want to remember, but the memory defied her now.

Without her consent, a movie projected itself in her mind: There was her mother, standing at the kitchen sink, moving a sponge over a dish for what seemed like the hundredth time. She'd been sullen all week. Yara could not recall the last time Mama had sung to any of them. It seemed years since she'd danced around the house or shown any signs of happiness.

"You have a beautiful voice," Yara offered from the spot where she was drawing at the kitchen table.

Mama looked up from the sink. "Thank you," she said.

"You could have been a famous singer, Mama." Yara had been trying not to look too hard at Mama, but now she saw her mother frown.

"That was my dream when I was your age."

"Really?" Yara said. "Why didn't you?"

Mama turned and stared at Yara then, a sudden coldness in her blue eyes. "My dreams died the day you were born."

For a few seconds Yara heard nothing. Not the water running in the sink, not the cartoons her brothers were watching in the other room, not even her own breath. The words exhausted her so entirely that her bones began to sink into the floor. In that moment, for the first time, she wished herself dead.

To Yara's relief, the rest of the week passed in a blur. She reasoned that the busier she stayed, the less room she'd have for memories to invade her mind.

Each day, after she picked up the girls from school, she resumed the daily routine that kept her body moving and her mind asleep: they finished homework at the library, then gymnastics, then hurried home, where Yara cooked elaborate dinners, then mopped the floors, wiped down the kitchen counters, and got the girls showered, fed, and ready for bed.

She made her own spice blends and organized them in her pantry in clear plastic containers and with labels she'd ordered online.

She cleaned up the sunroom, stacking her dried canvases, throwing away old paints, making room for the items Fadi said he needed somewhere to store.

She even suggested having his parents over for a weeknight dinner, much to his surprise.

When they came, Nadia looked at her from across the table, over the cabbage rolls that Yara had come home early to prepare, seeming quite pleased. "Everything is delicious," Nadia said, smiling.

Yara even agreed to accompany Nadia to a family friend's bridal shower. When she did, Nadia gave her a puzzled look and then leaned in and hugged her tight, as if finally satisfied that Yara was being a proper wife.

But staying busy did not stop the memories from rising up, creating a sinking feeling inside her as they did.

On Saturday, she made a fresh batch of za'atar, combining wild thyme and toasted sesame seeds, just like Teta had. The sumac filled the room with a citrus smell, and the marjoram added a hint of sweetness, taking her right back to Mama's kitchen in Bay Ridge.

On Sunday, when she rolled up her sleeves and scrubbed down every surface of the house even though it was already clean, her mind was back there, with Mama. Kneeling on the floor, she remembered her mother's hands and feet, always pruned from cleaning, and the eternal smell of bleach on her skin, as if she'd bathed in Clorox. She remembered the dusty smell of those dark, claustrophobic rooms, Baba away at work, and Mama alone with six children, all seven of them scrunched together like pennies in a pocket, and her mother always squirming to break free.

Some days, when Yara and the boys were occupied with the TV, Mama would put Arabic music on the cassette player and sing along, her voice low and fractured now. She'd squat down on the linoleum to pick up specks of food so Baba wouldn't feel them under his stocking feet when he came home, wouldn't shout about the filth. Yara would watch Mama, struck by the beauty of her face when she sang, the way she swept her long black hair off her shoulder when she leaned down into the sink. Those moments when Mama sang, it was like she wasn't there with them. As though the music had suspended time, had taken her out of her body. As though she'd forgotten that she was dressed in a bleach-stained nightgown, tracing a rag along a dirty linoleum floor, cooking endless meals for endless hungry mouths. It was as though she were dancing in her mind, with someone else, somewhere else. As though each new day wouldn't mimic the one before it, the rest of her life stretched out before her, already determined.

After the visit to the fortune teller, Mama stopped playing music altogether.

Now, pacing around the kitchen as she waited for a pot of water to boil, Yara caught sight of her reflection in the darkened window and looked away, ashamed. The whispers in her ears were even louder in the stillness: *You know what they say: like mother, like daughter. An evil eye is an evil eye. What would people say? My dreams died the day you were born.*

Would this be the rest of her life, too? Confined to the four walls of this house, to the whispers of other people's fears, scrubbing away, while another world was happening out there, happening without her?

14

That Friday at two o'clock in the afternoon, Yara returned to the counseling center. Again, Silas the culinary teacher held the door for her, this time just nodding his head in greeting as she passed.

Once inside William's office, she took the same seat by the window. Outside, the fall had painted the peaks and valleys in brilliant color. William greeted her from his desk, then got up and moved to the armchair facing the couch. "Yara, today I'd like to hear more about the incident with your colleague, if you don't mind. What do you think made you react that way to her?"

Yara pressed her fingers onto the tops of her thighs and turned to look out the window. "I already told you," she said. "Amanda was stereotyping me and my culture and I snapped."

"You snapped," William repeated. "Understandable. I mean, no one wants to be stereotyped. Was there anything about her words that you found particularly triggering?"

"No, I—" There was a box of tissues on the table, and Yara reached for one, crumpling it up in her hand. "I mean . . . it wasn't just what she said." William nodded, waiting for her to continue. "I really wanted to apply to chaperone the trip. I wish I could see more of the world. I love early-twentieth-century art, and there are so many paintings and so many important buildings I haven't gotten to see."

He cocked his head. "You're young. You still could."

William spoke as if picking up and traveling the world was as simple as packing a suitcase. She wondered if he had children.

Calmly she said, "It's not realistic. I can't just hop on a flight to Italy when the mood strikes. I have children who depend on me."

"Perhaps you can travel once the girls are out of the house?"

"Perhaps," she repeated, frowning.

William met her eyes. "Did I upset you?"

She looked up at the ceiling. With Fadi's business aspirations, she suspected he would continue to find an excuse to delay traveling. The girls would have to be in college before she could have the freedom to go anywhere. But hadn't freedom been the reason she'd gotten married to begin with? She'd been so desperate to leave home and start anew with Fadi. She'd chosen this life. She wasn't like Mama, stuck in a foreign country with no income or education, denied the luxury of self-determination. This was all her choice, her doing. Lately, she wondered, though: Had she decided on this particular path for herself, or had there been an invisible hand alongside her the whole time, steering her toward it?

Each time she tried to articulate these thoughts to William, she stopped, afraid of how meaningless the sentences might sound. Words simplified situations and emotions, robbed them of their complexity. Could her words portray how powerless she felt, how torn? Never fitting in, unable to truly belong. Or would they convey another message, validating Amanda's assumptions: How insular her community was, how limiting?

She wished she hadn't stopped at calling Amanda a racist. She should've told Amanda that misogyny and sexism were hardly exclusive to the Middle East, that the oppression of women in the West looked a little different, a little less explicit, but it was still happening all around them: everywhere she turned she was bombarded with hypersexualized images of women, messages so blatant they became invisible, encouraging the normalization of female objectification and amplifying age-old pressures for young girls to conform to certain sexualized narratives. Not to mention the psychological risks (shame, anxiety, depression) faced by women in a toxic culture that was constantly looking at, evaluating, and objectifying their bodies. How could she explain this to William now? She knew the minute she opened her mouth, her words would only convey a blurry fraction of what she'd intended. Language was often a bridge, but sometimes a barrier. No matter how she chose her words, they would likely come out a bit distorted, inadequate. So she said nothing for a while. Silence was better than being misunderstood, erased, unseen for who you really were.

"It's not that simple," Yara eventually managed. "Not everyone gets to do what they want. We're all held back in some way or another, aren't we? That's just life. If anything, I have it better than most people."

William raised his eyebrows. "How so?"

"I have a good husband, wonderful kids, and a career I worked really hard for. I'm extremely privileged, really. Just because I couldn't go on this one trip doesn't mean Amanda was correct," she said. "Trust me, I know what oppression looks like, and this isn't it."

William leaned forward. "What does it look like to you?"

She fixed her eyes on the window.

"Is oppression something you saw growing up?"

"No." The word left her lips more quickly than she'd intended. She had Mama's voice in her ear, the words of Kahlil Gibran again: *tell no one.* William was probably sitting there with his clipboard imagining the kind of life she might have had so that he could pretend to understand her. She didn't need his pity.

"If that's the case, why don't we talk about it?" he said. "I know it's only our second session together, but I'd love to know more about your childhood—your parents, your siblings, your experience at school."

"There's nothing to talk about. My parents may have been immigrants, but their struggles were just like everyone else's. My dad worked a lot, and my mom stayed at home to look after me and my brothers. They did the best they could."

"Can you tell me a little more about your parents?"

She shook her head, avoiding his eyes. "They have nothing to do with why I'm here."

"Maybe not," William said. "But in order for me to help you, we need to talk about the past, even if it feels unrelated to the present."

Yara turned to look out the window. She didn't think William understood. A thing repressed was buried so deep you couldn't feel it anymore. You might even forget it was there. But once you dug it up to the surface, you were forced to feel it again, like a throbbing tooth every time your tongue grazed it. And she couldn't do that. It made the everyday task of living unbearable.

"I'm not here to talk about them," she finally said, looking back at him. "I just want to get my class back. I won't be going to Oslo, but I'd like to at least speak of such places with my students again."

William sighed, rubbing his hands over his face. "I know this must be difficult for you, but I'm afraid I can't help you if you refuse to let me. You might not think it's necessary to explore your past, but until you are ready to do that, I'm not sure how much you'll benefit from our sessions."

Yara crossed her arms and for the rest of the session she sat there in silence, turned to face the window. She'd snapped at Amanda because of her colleague's condescension, not her own upbringing. Amanda's ignorance was what was relevant. And even if the past had had any bearing on Yara's reaction, why would she ever want to talk about it with William, who would barely be able to comprehend what a childhood like hers looked like, much less felt like?

People ruin beautiful things.

Back inside her office, she closed her eyes and let her tears flow. Even if William was right, what difference would it make now? She tried to picture herself back in her childhood home. She tried to envision opening up to Mama, the only person who could understand how she really felt, who could possibly help her get rid of this cursed feeling. But she couldn't do it, and the tears continued to stream down her cheeks.

15

Yara had planned on taking the girls straight home after gymnastics, but Jude was bouncing with excitement when Yara picked them up from school. "We painted in art class today," she told Yara as she climbed into the backseat, a gap-toothed smile filling her face. "The teacher liked my painting so much she hung it in the hallway!"

"That's really special," Yara said. "I hope I can see it soon. What did you paint?"

Jude beamed. "A picture of me, you, and Mira having a picnic at the park."

"Aww, that's sweet," Yara said. "Where was Baba?"

Frowning, Jude looked down at her hands. In a small voice, she said, "He was at work. He's always at work."

Catching a glance of her daughter's face in the rearview mirror, Yara swallowed and tried to focus on the road, her eyes skimming over the orange-red trees. How often she had felt that as a child, her Baba's absence.

At a red light, she met Jude's eyes again. "I have an idea. How about a quick stop at the park before we head home?"

As they pulled into the playground parking lot, Yara said, "We have twenty minutes." The girls jumped out of the car and raced to the swings.

The jungle gym was shining in the afternoon sun, and Yara

grabbed her camera and a spot on a bench beneath the shade of a red maple tree. The air was crisp and smelled sweet. All around her, the rolling landscapes were illuminated with countless shades of crimson and gold, and the bright blue sky sliced through the branches. At the other end of the playground, a woman sat on a bench, looking down at her phone. A boy who might've been her son chased Mira and Jude around the swing set, laughing. Yara studied the three children, her heart racing, moved by the joyous expressions on their faces, the sound of innocence in the air. But the other woman didn't look up. Eventually she collected the boy and left, and the girls moved on to the jungle gym.

Circling the playground, Yara took a picture of Jude hanging off the blue monkey bars, then another of Mira at the top of a yellow slide.

Watching them, she wondered what they would remember about their childhoods. Perhaps the vibrant colors of the Carolina fall, or the sound of leaves crunching beneath their feet, or the smell of bonfires and roasted marshmallows in the air. Whatever their memories were, though, she hoped they would be good. She was always working to give them stability and happiness. Even taking a job, she felt, made her a better mother to them.

The camera still tight between her fingers, Yara's mind wandered to her own childhood, to the times Mama had taken her and her brothers to McKinley Park to pass the long hours until Baba returned from work. But Mama had only watched them from a bench, her eyes vacant and body slumped over, until it was time to go. Yara remembered their long walks back home, the sound of Mama's breath as she pushed the heavy stroller, her lips quivering, her eyes far away.

Now, Yara felt a different sensation on her arm and glanced down to find Mira tugging on it. "Mama, Mama, Mama," Mira was saying. Something about the way her daughter said those words took her back, breaking the last string holding back the memory—

"Mama, Mama, Mama!"

Only it wasn't Mira repeating the word, it was young Yara. And she wasn't in a park in North Carolina on a warm fall day, she was on a Brooklyn sidewalk in the dead of winter, the cold air sharp against her skin.

Mama had taken them from Bay Ridge to nearby Dyker Heights to see the extravagant Christmas lights displayed there, an annual activity even though they didn't celebrate the holiday. Yara and the older boys flanked Mama, who pushed a double stroller holding the younger ones. All around them the neighborhood was ablaze with holiday decorations spilling out over homes, roofs, and gardens. Christmas trees as tall as streetlamps, glinting with tinsel. Inflatable life-sized Santas on lawns. Brightly lit Rudolphs on rooftops. Glittery candy cane soldiers. Houses flickering with twinkling ornaments, windows bright. The cheerful sounds of children's laughter and the smell of hot cocoa in the air. It was as if they'd entered another world.

Yara held Yunus's hand and followed Yousef's and Yazan's gazes to a long line of children waiting for peppermint candy canes that were being dispensed in front of a house. Yara looked up to her mother, who was searching in the bottom of the stroller for something to make Yaseen stop crying.

"Mama," Yara said, but her mother didn't look up. "Mama," she said more insistently. "Can we go get some candy canes?"

"One second," Mama said distractedly. She grabbed her bag and snapped open the clasp.

Yara watched as more children joined the line. "Mama, Mama," she said impatiently, tugging on her coat. But her mother was silent as she poured two scoops of powder into a baby bottle filled with water and handed it to her son. At last, Yaseen stopped crying.

"Mama—" Yara started again, but at once Mama's palm was hot against her face.

"How many times do I have to tell you?" she snapped. "Stop calling for me endlessly!"

Horrified, Yara took a step back, tripping over the edge of the sidewalk then righting herself in the street. She rubbed her tongue hard against the roof of her mouth, holding back tears.

"All I ever do is mother you," Mama said through clenched teeth. "It's all I ever do!"

Now Yara felt another tug on her own sleeve and realized that Mira was standing and staring at her, Jude by her side. She tried to push the memory out of her mind, but it seemed as though she was still on the Dyker Heights sidewalk, her bones going numb under the weight of her body, closing her eyes to block out the holiday lights.

"Can you push me on the swing?" Mira was saying.

For a moment Yara was unable to speak, Mama's slap still stinging against her skin, so sharp all those years later. Eventually she managed to say, "I think I need to sit down for a moment."

"But I can't go across the monkey bars without you," Jude said. "I need you to hold me up."

Yara felt a ladybug crawling up her arm and shook it off. "Not now. Maybe in a few minutes. Why don't you two play together?"

"But we want to play with *you,*" said Mira, a whine creeping into her voice.

"Please, Mama," Jude said, frowning. "Just carry me across one time?"

"In a minute."

Mira stomped and said: "You *never* play with us."

"Play with you?" Yara stood up, her cheeks quivering. "After everything I do for you, every day, you're complaining about me not playing with you?" She was shouting now. "Do you understand how hard I'm trying? You have no idea how good you have it!"

Mira and Jude both took a step back, horror spilling across their faces.

At once Yara jerked her hand up to her mouth, breathing hard. The look in their eyes made shame wash over her, dissipating her anger instantly. How could she have lost her temper so quickly over such a small request? "I'm so sorry, babies," she said. "I shouldn't have yelled at you like that. Come here. I'm sorry. I'll play with you."

In a trance she followed the girls to the jungle gym, holding back what felt like an ocean of tears. She held their little hands and reminded herself to breathe, but her body strained and tightened. She was there in the playground, pushing Mira on the swing, then holding Jude up off the ground as she swung from bar to bar, but her mind was someplace else.

16

That night Yara undressed with her back to Fadi as he turned on the water to start the shower. As he stepped inside, his feet made a soft clapping noise on the tile. Still out of sorts after the park, she hadn't said much since he returned home.

"How was your day?" Fadi asked when she joined him.

"It was fine." Her mouth felt tight and she struggled to push out the words. "Yours?"

"Busy as hell. I'm exhausted."

She nodded, avoiding his eyes. The warm water against her skin calmed her, but she continued looking up at the steam, swallowing, worried that he could make out her expression, or worse, discover the kind of mother she'd turned out to be. She considered telling him why she'd snapped at the girls, thinking it might relieve some of the debilitating shame she felt, but quickly decided against it. There was no need to add to his list of the ways in which she was unable to control herself.

For a few seconds, Fadi said nothing. Yara was attuned to his movements beside her, the brisk way he lathered his hair with the new shampoo she'd bought him this past week. The smell of citrus filled the air, and then she heard him talking about his father, about something Hasan had said to him that morning. She made an effort to look up at him.

"My brothers always get to do whatever they want, while he still expects me to manage all of the finances at the shop, as if I haven't started my own business." He was frowning to himself. "It's not fair. Nothing I ever do will be good enough for him."

"I'm sorry he makes you feel this way," she said, trying to meet his eyes. "You're doing the best you can. It doesn't matter what he thinks."

Fadi shrugged. "It doesn't feel that way. I'm nothing more than a himar to him, just a donkey."

A shiver ran along her jaw, and she tried to make her voice soft. "I'm really sorry," she said again, but he only shook his head and rubbed his hands over his face.

Fadi had only grown more and more resentful over the years. He'd wanted to go to college in Tennessee after high school but couldn't because Hasan relied on him to look after the gas station, and now it was the finances, blaming him for their struggling, while his brothers seemed to have no responsibilities. Yara often listened to these complaints and tried to soothe him, saying things like: "I understand how unfair this must feel." And when she saw the heartbreak in his eyes, she felt a constricting pain in her chest and throat that made it difficult to breathe. In those moments, she was certain that she understood Fadi more than anyone else. And it was his vulnerability that most attracted her to him. Perhaps she saw herself in his pain. Fadi knew some things about her family's past, about her mother—some things were impossible to keep secret in their community—and he had accepted her anyway. That had to mean something.

She closed her eyes and put her face under the running water, standing very still as the heat numbed her skin. She looked back on all the things that had happened in their lives, struggles that shaped who they were and perhaps had even brought them to this very moment. She had been keeping the very darkest parts of her past not just from herself, but also from him. But who else would understand her, if not Fadi? Perhaps revealing more of herself would even bring them closer.

"Do you ever think about things that happened when you were

young?" Yara asked him after they got out of the shower, as she buttoned up a knee-length cotton nightgown. Outside the window, the moon gleamed, almost full in the blue-black sky.

Fadi leaned in to study himself in the bathroom mirror, water from his hair dripping down the back of his neck. "What do you mean?" he said.

She glanced at his reflection in the mirror, but he wouldn't meet her eyes, and at once she felt a certain weakening in her body. Maybe if Fadi knew how scared she was, he would help her. Maybe he was afraid of the past, too. Maybe he, too, struggled to be a better parent and partner.

"I've been remembering things lately," Yara said, taking a step closer to him. "About my parents. How things were when I was younger." Her breath quickened. "Do you ever wonder if we're becoming like them?"

"What? No way. We're nothing like them."

There was a heavy quiet as Fadi walked into the bedroom and reached for his phone on the nightstand. She debated whether to tell him what Jude had said about her painting. She knew that even hinting at the idea that he wasn't a present father would only make him defensive, but it was a chance to make him see that her fears were not unfounded. And that if they weren't careful, they'd become just like their parents, lost in the hustle and unaware of their daughter's worries.

"Jude made a comment today that concerned me," Yara managed, fiddling with the sleeve of her nightgown.

Fadi looked up from his phone. "What did she say?"

"She told me about a picture she painted of me and her and Mira. She said you weren't in it because you're always working."

He frowned, raising an eyebrow. "Are you trying to make me feel guilty?"

"No, no," she whispered. "But when she said that, I couldn't help but think of my own dad."

"So now you're comparing me to your dad?"

"That's not what I meant," she said, her voice shaking. "But I guess a part of me is afraid of repeating their mistakes."

"What are you talking about? I'm nothing like my father. Or yours."

"I know," she said quietly. "But sometimes I worry . . ." She paused, looked at him. "Sometimes I worry that I'm like my mother."

Fadi took a step back. "Like her how?"

"Not in the way you're thinking," she said quickly, feeling her face burn. "Only as a mother."

He just looked at her.

"Lately I've been thinking about how she was when we were young," Yara said. "She was so vacant and agitated and sad—and I can't help but worry that I'm like that with the girls." Embarrassed, she lowered her eyes. "Do you think I am?"

"I don't know," Fadi said, sounding looser now that the focus wasn't on him. "I don't see you with them during the day."

She glanced back out the window, then looked at him. "Sometimes when I'm with them I feel like I can't relax."

"Yeah, well, you can be a little uptight. But that hardly makes you like your mother." He paused. "Then again, you know better than me what she was like when you were little."

"Some things are hard to remember."

"Maybe you should ask your brothers?"

She took a deep breath and realized she didn't remember the last time she'd picked up the phone and called one of them. She had never felt like their sibling, only another caretaker for them. What would she even say? That she was afraid of the type of person she had become? As if they cared. They seemed to be living their lives, free and unencumbered, as though they'd been unaffected by their past. Even if she managed to swallow her anger at this injustice and reach out to them, what good would it do? It would only bring up all the things she wanted to forget.

"If you're worried, then don't just sit around complaining. Do something about it," Fadi was saying on their way to the kitchen. "That's what I did. My worst fear was turning into my father, so I made it a point to be nothing like him."

She half-listened as he went on about how he couldn't imitate Hasan even if he tried, her hands shaking as she plated their meals. Fadi had plenty in common with his father and hers, she thought, though she would never tell him this. Just like Hasan, Fadi was regimented and work-obsessed. He didn't seem to have any interests or aspirations besides providing for his family, and when he was home with them, his mind was often elsewhere, in his phone, or fretting over bills and finding new accounts. Even Jude could see that. And while Yara would never point it out, she saw the way Nadia looked at Hasan at dinner, as if he were a stranger to her—after thirty years of marriage.

But maybe Fadi was talking about other things. Maybe he meant he was different on the inside. He did make them all laugh. Hasan certainly never cracked a joke. She'd rarely ever seen him smile, walking around so serious most days, as if he was tugging the world on his back. It reminded her of her own father.

Fadi handed her a glass of water. "Did you hear what I said?"

Yara looked around, remembering the dinner plates, and felt disoriented suddenly. "What? No. I'm sorry."

"Are you okay?" He gave her a puzzled look. "You've been acting weird lately."

"Sorry. I'm not trying to be. What were you saying?"

"You can control the way you respond to things," Fadi said. "You can change, if you want to."

She nodded. It seemed like everyone in her life wanted her to change. Changing certain things was easy, she saw it in advertising every day. She could decide what foods to eat or what kind of shoes she wore or how she organized her cupboards. But what of her insides, all the things you couldn't see?

"I want to—" she started to say. But Fadi had already grabbed his plate and walked away, and in the darkened kitchen window, she watched him inching down the hall, the steam of his warm meal trailing behind him. In her own reflection, all that glimmered was the blue-eyed hamsa around her neck, the charm that was meant to ward off the evil eye. "I want to be different, I really do," she whispered. "More than anything. But I don't know how."

Mama's warning was the only response: *once you're cursed, you're cursed.*

17

When she got to campus Monday morning, the Humanities Building was already humming with activity. Jonathan had organized yet another meet and greet for faculty and staff. They were encouraged to stop by before the regular workday started, to eat and chat with one another. The last thing she wanted was to go through the motions of conversation with the people she hadn't seen since her incident with Amanda, but she now understood it was expected of her.

Inside the hall, artificial yellow lights hummed overhead. Yara scanned the room for an empty table before remembering that she was here to socialize, to prove that she was trying. Around her people sat in groups and chatted so loudly it felt like the noise was happening inside her skull. She straightened and walked toward a table in the back of the room, where coffee and pastries were on offer.

There, at the front of the line, in a white chef's coat, was Silas. Yara watched him take a bite from a mini–blueberry muffin, then wipe his mouth with the back of his hand. She was glad to take a spot at the end of the line and avoid him, but he turned and saw her.

"Hey, Yara," he said, waving. He stepped out of the way, allowing others to the front of the table and walked toward her. "I've never seen you at one of these things," he said, looking at her intently.

She glanced around the room, shaking her head slowly. "It wasn't exactly by choice."

He followed her eyes to land on Jonathan. "Ah, I see." He moved closer, standing beside her as she waited in line. She nodded, resisting the urge to walk away, then she took her phone from her pocket and refreshed her inbox, trying to look busy.

When she looked up, Silas was watching her, suppressing a smile. "You don't like being around people, do you?"

"What?" She met his eyes. "Did William tell you that?"

He laughed. "Of course not. But it's pretty obvious."

"And why's that?"

"Well, I almost never see you at school functions, and when I do, you're always sitting alone."

She flushed at the realization that he had noticed her before. Staring straight ahead, she said, "That doesn't mean anything."

"Also, you've barely made eye contact with me."

"That's not true," she said, turning and looking at him purposefully.

He grinned. "There's nothing wrong with wanting to be alone sometimes."

"Tell that to Jonathan. Or William."

"I'm guessing you haven't warmed to William yet?"

She shrugged. "He's okay."

"I've been going to him since last semester," Silas said. "It gets better, I promise."

Yara returned her attention to the line but felt her skin getting hot. Her left leg began to shake, and once it started, she couldn't get it to stop. She stepped out of the line abruptly. "I need to get some air," she told him.

"Mind if I join you?" Silas asked.

She wanted to say no but didn't want to hurt his feelings. "What about all the meeting and greeting you need to do?"

"It'll be here when we get back," Silas said, putting down his plate on a nearby table.

Without speaking, they walked down a dimly lit hallway and out the front doors of the building. It was a bright fall day, glowing with crisp golden light. Yara's eyes were still adjusting to the brightness when she heard herself asking, "So, why are you in counseling?"

"I'm trying to get joint custody of my daughter, and it's been a little tough," Silas said. "The college wanted to make sure I had help during the process."

"Oh." She hadn't been expecting such a forthright answer. "I'm sorry to hear that."

He shrugged, shoving his hands into his pockets. "It's okay. Everything happens for a reason."

"Really? That would mean there's a reason for all the suffering in the world, and that's just terrible," she said.

Silas stopped midstep and rubbed the back of his neck. "I never thought of it like that." He looked at her for a long moment before asking, "What about you? Why do you see William?"

"Jonathan *strongly* recommended it after I called one of my colleagues a—well—a fucking racist," Yara said, regretting the admission as soon as it left her mouth.

"Ouch," he said. "Which colleague?"

"Amanda Richardson."

He chuckled. "Oh yeah, I know Amanda. I can see that. She comes up to our kitchen on the first Friday of the month, when we host lunch for the staff? Have you ever been?" Yara shook her head. "Yeah, she always has some snarky comment. The other week I made *coq au vin*, and you know what she said?"

"What?"

He held up his hands in an attempt to imitate her: "'This isn't an authentic French recipe, of course. Traditional coq au vin is made with a Burgundy wine, like pinot noir.'"

Yara laughed suddenly, the sound loud and vibrant, then covered her mouth. "I thought she was only like that with me because—" She stopped.

"Because of what?"

She rubbed her palm on the hem of her shirt. "You know, because I'm Arab."

"Oh," Silas said. "I don't know. She's kind of a pain in the ass with everyone."

Yara nodded, feeling relieved of something, though she wasn't sure what. She glanced ahead, across the freshly manicured campus fields, and inhaled a deep breath. With the sun against her skin and the smell of freshly cut grass in the air, the first leaves of fall cartwheeling down the paths, Yara wished she could lay a blanket out and take it all in—with no work, no phones, no distraction or deadline to pick up the girls.

As if reading her mind, Silas said: "It's a beautiful day, isn't it?"

"Yeah. My kids will want to go to the park again."

"You have kids?"

She nodded. "Two daughters, eight and six. And how old is yours?"

"Olivia is three."

"Aww. That's a sweet age."

Running his hand over his beard, Silas said, "I have to say, you look too young to have kids in school."

"Yes, I get that a lot. But I started young."

"What, at sixteen?" He laughed, and she realized he was trying to make a joke.

"No, twenty."

"Oh."

She shrugged. "My mother had me at eighteen. My grandmother had her first child at fifteen."

"Really? That's crazy." He rubbed the back of his neck. "Is that common where you're from?"

"Where I'm from?"

He was quiet for a moment. "Sorry. That didn't come out quite as I'd intended."

For a few seconds she continued looking at him, and then she said: "I'm from Brooklyn. Born and raised."

"Right." He nodded, his cheeks flushed. "I guess I meant, where is your family from?"

"A country that doesn't exist."

Silas looked at her. "How's that?"

She sighed, not wanting to get into the politics. After a moment she said, "They live a few miles outside Jerusalem."

"You're Israeli, then?"

"No," she said abruptly. "I'm Palestinian."

"I'm sorry," Silas said, frowning. "I wasn't trying to offend you. I don't really understand the politics of it all."

"Most people don't."

He rubbed at the back of his neck again.

"What about you?" she said. "Where is your family from?"

"Here?" he tried, blinking at her. "Or do you mean, like, their origin?"

"Yes, their origin."

"Uh, I'm not really sure," Silas said. "Maybe the UK? My family has been here for so long, no one's really sure."

She started to laugh.

"What's so funny?"

"Every day people ask me where I'm from like I have an imported stamp on my forehead. But why do you all want to know, when you don't even know where you're from?"

"I'm sorry," Silas said. "I really didn't mean to—"

She cut him off. "You know, I've heard half the people in this college's administration refer to me as 'the foreign girl,' as if I don't have a name. I mean, if you want to be technical about it, unless you're indigenous, then we're all foreigners. We're all immigrants."

"I'm so sorry," he said again, trying to meet her eyes. "It wasn't my intention to insult you."

Yara laughed again and found this time she couldn't stop. "Wow. Sorry," she said, composing herself. "I don't know where all that came from."

Silas's hazel eyes sparkled, and Yara was surprised by the warmth she saw in his face now, how it opened up, looking at her. It was an unfamiliar sight. "Don't apologize," he said. "You said what's on your mind. I'm the one who was being an idiot."

"If I went around verbalizing my thoughts all day, I'd be in even bigger trouble than I am," Yara said.

"But look at that smile," he said. "Maybe you should speak your mind more often."

She nodded and turned her face away, feeling it burn beneath the sunshine. Was he flirting with her? The thought that he might find her attractive popped into her head, and Yara felt a sudden disorientation, as if someone had shoved her hard and she was struggling to find her footing. She felt an almost desperate urge to escape, and yet she couldn't move.

For a moment they stood there without speaking, looking out at the crepe myrtles swaying in the breeze. Their conversation had had an effect on her, though she wasn't sure exactly what it was. Finally, Yara turned to look at him, and he smiled again, his kind eyes almost translucent in the sunlight. Had anyone ever looked at her this way?

"I should get going," she said, taking a step back. "I have to show my face in there so I don't get fired."

"Well, maybe I'll see you around?" Silas said, gesturing in the direction of the building holding the Culinary Arts Department.

"Maybe," she said, pushing out the word. It seemed like the appropriate thing to say.

18

For the next few days, Yara worked until it was time to pick up the girls from school, then sped through the usual afterschool ritual with them. At home she continued to cook elaborate meals every evening, without a single night off, in order to avoid the memories that crept up on her when she was still, the panicky, dismal feeling that came over her whenever she slowed down. She helped Fadi move a few more boxes into the sunroom, pushing her paintings into the far corner.

On Friday morning, before her alarm went off, Yara awoke to the sound of her phone ringing. Groggily she reached out and grabbed the phone off the nightstand, answering it without looking at the screen. When she heard the voice on the other line, she wondered if she was still asleep, having a bad dream.

"Salaam, Yara," Baba said.

In a frenzy, she sat up in bed and swung her legs off the side. Her father almost never called her, and when he did, there was usually something wrong. Like when her brother Yassir dropped out of engineering school and Baba had her talk him into reenrolling. Or when Yaseen got arrested for selling weed and Baba told Yara to find out why he was throwing his life away. Yara didn't know why he asked for her help. She held no sway over them. She was not Mama. The last time she'd spoken to Baba, he'd said: "I don't even know why I tell you about them, I know they'll never listen." But Yara guessed he liked having someone to complain to.

"Yara, are you there?"

"I'm here," she said, rubbing her eyes. She looked around the room, disoriented. Fadi's side of the bed was empty—he'd left for work already. "Is everything okay?" she asked.

"Yes, I just wanted to check in."

Baba's voice sounded raspy, like he'd started smoking again. She wanted to ask him, but as soon as she opened her mouth, she knew why he had. She thought of Mama nagging him to stop, then pushed the thought out of her head.

"How are you?" Baba said.

"Alhamdulillah. I'm fine."

"And the girls?"

She stood, feeling her body stiffen. "They're doing well. Growing fast."

"Good, good."

Tucking the phone under one ear, she made the bed in silence. She couldn't remember what Baba's most recent request for her intervention had been. "You're such a good listener," he always told her.

"Mira asked about you the other day," Yara said now, feeling her face burn as she thought of the girls asking for childhood stories. She wanted to say, I had nothing good to tell them, Baba. Instead, she added, "So did Jude."

"That's sweet," Baba said. "How old are they now?"

"Eight and six."

"Mashallah, they're getting so big."

She moved her mouth around uncertainly for a moment, then swallowed. "They miss you," she said.

"I miss them, too," he said. "But you know how busy work is."

"Yeah, I know." She smoothed the comforter and rearranged the pillows, tugged on the bedsheet to get it into place.

Baba cleared his throat. "So tell me, how are things with Fadi?"

"Everything's fine. Why do you ask?"

"That's not what I've been hearing."

She stopped, adjusted the phone under her ear. "What do you mean?"

"I'm not trying to get in the middle of your marriage," Baba said with a sigh. "But Fadi's telling me that you had some trouble at work and that you've been acting out at home ever since. What's going on?"

"Nothing."

"Are you sure?" Baba said. "Fadi says you've been picking fights with him, too, complaining about his hours at work, even being physical. Is that true?"

Yara leaned against the mattress, her knees shaking. "What? When did he say this?"

"Never mind when," Baba said. "You know how much that man works to look after you and your children. Why are you giving him a hard time?"

"I'm not. I just wanted his help with the girls, that's all. They're his kids, too."

"I know, yaaba. But you have to be reasonable. Is it fair for him to work so hard to pay the bills and help with your responsibilities, too? I've always known you to be a very sensible person, Yara. Deep down you know what I'm saying is true, don't you?"

Something came over her now, she didn't know what it was, but she found herself sinking to the floor on her knees. She bit her lip hard, her mouth stinging.

"Instead of making him feel guilty about his schedule," Baba went on, "why don't you try to be a source of comfort for him? Have a nice meal ready when he comes home, maybe put on something nice. Men are visual creatures. It doesn't take much to make them happy."

Almost inaudibly Yara murmured: "Dress up for him? Is that what Fadi wants?"

She closed her eyes for a moment, searching for the words to make her father understand. How could she explain that every decision in her life had been an attempt to overcome the powerlessness she had felt growing up, to prove herself to her parents, her community, to Fadi—as capable, as faithful, as dedicated—only she'd gotten nowhere? Nowhere near where she actually wanted to be, anyway.

"What about me?" she finally said, breathless with disbelief. "Does it matter whether or not I'm happy?"

"What's not to be happy about, yaaba?" Baba said. "You have so many blessings to be grateful for. All I'm asking is that you try and make peace in your home."

Those last words made Yara feel as if he'd pushed his arm through the phone and was gripping her heart with his fist. She leaned back against the edge of the bed and stared at her knees, breathing in and out slowly. Before she knew it, she was saying: "Just like you made peace for us?"

She could hear her heart thumping in her chest as she waited for him to respond.

"That was different," Baba finally said. "Your mother made things difficult when you were all very young. We could've been happy if not for her lack of respect."

Yara pushed herself to her feet. "So everything was her fault, then?" she said, gripping the phone. "And you did nothing wrong?"

"Lower your voice," Baba said. "Your problems are your own making. They have nothing to do with me and your mother."

"It has everything to do with you," Yara said, realizing that this was the first time she'd said those words aloud. "You two are all I ever think about."

"Really?" Baba said dismissively. "If that's true, then why haven't you learned from your mother's mistakes, huh? I shouldn't have to tell you to take care of your husband and put some effort into your marriage. You know how lucky you are to have such a good marriage. If I hadn't known Hasan—"

"Stop—" Yara shouted. She took a step back and collapsed on the bed, dizzy with shame. "Please, just stop."

"I don't know what's gotten into you, Yara, but you need to get it together. The last thing this family needs is another museeba. No more disgrace. Fahmeh?" Baba commanded. "Understood?"

"Yes," she croaked, but the word rang hollow.

"Good girl," Baba said, letting out a deep breath. "I'm counting on you."

"I know."

As soon as Baba hung up, Yara started to call Fadi but stopped herself, knowing it wouldn't solve anything, that he hadn't been listening to her at all. Anything she told him would only be relayed to her father. Her hands were shaking, and she wanted to crush the phone between her fist. How could Fadi betray her like this?

She could imagine how Baba and Fadi must have talked about her: Fadi saying, I work so hard to provide for our family and take care of her. I don't know what she's complaining about. Her father dismissing her, just like he'd done to her mother.

Her heart was racing. She didn't know if she felt more embarrassed or enraged. She wasn't proud of her behavior. But, she thought, heading to the girls' room to wake them up for school, something had to change.

Tears burned in her throat as she looked at Mira's and Jude's innocent, sleeping faces from the doorway. A rush of love filled her heart. It seemed to her now that no single moment of her life had prepared her to be the kind of person her daughters needed her to be. Nobody had warned her of this, how much of her own childhood she would relive through her children, how much of her pain she would pass along. It was up to her to protect her daughters, to give them a good life. She couldn't let Baba or Fadi get in her head. What she needed to do instead was prove them both wrong, get her act together. Mira and Jude would not grow up in a cold, loveless home. They would not become like her, staring blankly into the distance, constantly afraid, constantly trying to stop the memories from rising up.

She was strong enough to do this. If not for herself, then for them.

She closed her eyes now and imagined she was being cleansed, her past washing off her skin, as she finally became the person she was supposed to be. Or the person she wanted to be. She wasn't sure what the difference was. All she knew was that she wanted to be better. A better wife, a better mother, a better human.

The thing was, hadn't she been trying to do that all along? Wasn't that why she'd married Fadi and had kids and gone to college and gotten a job and cooked and cleaned her house and done what was expected of her? So why did it still feel like everything was wrong? Why was happiness still eluding her?

These questions played on a loop as she got ready for work. Studying herself in the mirror, Yara couldn't remember the last time she'd dressed up, done her nails, or put on any makeup. She couldn't even remember her last haircut. Maybe Baba was right, maybe she had let herself go lately. The realization made her feel sick, sour heat all over her skin. What did Fadi think? What did he see when he looked at her? Did he even love her?

Impulsively, she called Nadia to see if she could watch the girls that afternoon. A few small changes wouldn't hurt her marriage. Maybe if she put in a little more effort in her appearance, maybe then she could get Fadi to see her, to listen. Maybe then he would understand why she'd been so unsettled, why she still hadn't moved on. Maybe then he would understand why she needed to see the world, could maybe even help her to see it, too.

Yara inhaled, letting the possibilities calm her. "Ready, girls?" she called.

19

Yara fingered a dry strand of hair as she pulled into the parking lot of the salon, checking her reflection in the mirror before climbing out of the car. At the front desk, a redheaded woman informed her that her stylist was just finishing up with another client. "Make yourself comfortable," she said warmly.

She took a seat in the waiting area and looked around at the marble-and-gold interior, feeling out of place, with her unstyled curly hair more than halfway down her back. She couldn't think of the last time she'd treated herself to a cut anywhere but a chain salon. Was it shortly after Jude was born? Spending money on herself seemed frivolous. Though Fadi rarely scrutinized how much money she spent from their shared checking account, she tried to be as frugal as possible to make up for her inability to contribute to their finances in a meaningful way. She'd make up for this indulgence by cutting back on this month's grocery bills.

A young woman with short brown hair and wide eyes approached her, and Yara rose from her seat. "I'm Rebecca, I'll be your stylist," she said, then led Yara toward a seat facing a row of tall, lighted mirrors.

"Now then," she said to Yara's reflection in the mirror once she was seated. "What kind of style are you looking for?"

"I'm not sure," Yara told her. "What do you think?"

Rebecca paused and pursed her lips, running her fingers through Yara's long, unruly hair. Her hands, soft and gentle, felt warm against the back of her neck. "You definitely need a good cut," she said. "I see about six inches of split ends. How much change are you looking for?"

Not much, Yara wanted to say, but realized that was the wrong answer. Change was good. Change was precisely why she was here. "Do whatever you think would look nice."

"Really?" Rebecca said, delighted. "This will be fun. Any preferences on color?"

Yara shook her head. "Just nothing too crazy."

"How about a long, soft bob, slightly below the collarbone, with a few golden highlights to frame your face?"

"Oh, I don't know," she said, suddenly second-guessing herself. "I've never gone that short before or colored my hair at all."

"You'll look gorgeous, I promise."

She felt a stab of shame slice through her at the sound of the word. "I highly doubt that."

"Nonsense," Rebecca said, studying her, as if to make sure she was only joking. "You're beautiful no matter how you wear your hair."

Yara nodded, but there in the salon mirror was young Yara, young Yara looking in the bathroom mirror of her Brooklyn home, trying not to cry as Mama pointed out all the ways she resembled Baba: from her dark skin to her curly hair to her prominent nose, which seemed to irritate her mother the most.

"Hang tight for a second," Rebecca said.

Yara swallowed, shoving the memory down.

Rebecca returned with a cart filled with color tubes, foil, and other supplies. "I'll apply the color first, then cut it," she said, sweeping Yara's hair behind her shoulders and out of her face. She grabbed a wide-toothed brush and gently combed out the tangles, then proceeded to paint various strands of hair with thick globs of paste. She worked slowly, folding the painted hair into squares of foil. After thirty minutes and nearly two dozen squares of tinfoil later, Rebecca went to the back and returned with a hot lamp on a stand, which she placed over Yara's head.

"The color needs about twenty minutes to develop," she said. "Hang tight."

Yara busied herself with her phone, trying to avoid her reflection. But when she finally glanced up and saw her face, the memories were overwhelming, like poison tainting everything. All the times her mother looked at her with revulsion. How Yara averted her eyes with humiliation whenever Mama told her how much she looked like Baba. The shame that sprouted inside her at the realization that she was difficult to look at and hard to love. And then the crushing thought that followed: perhaps her ugliness was to blame for her mother's inability to forgive her.

And yet, daring to look at her face in the mirror now, all Yara could see was Mama's face. Her sharp jaw and fig-colored lips. The deep intensity in her eyes. The quiet sorrow. It made Yara want to cry.

"All done," Rebecca said, her voice bringing Yara back to the room.

She removed the heat lamp and led Yara to a sink in the back, where she unwrapped the tinfoil and began to shampoo her hair. The steady noise of the running water was soothing, and the firmness of Rebecca's fingers against Yara's scalp made her shoulders relax and a warm sensation run down her spine.

"Ready?" Rebecca said, with Yara back in the chair and a shiny pair of sharp scissors in her hand.

Yara nodded, then heard slicing, then felt the hair falling away. Lots of it.

"Not too short," she said, trying not to panic as she saw the strands hitting the floor from the corners of her eyes.

"Don't worry," said Rebecca. "You're going to love it."

When she'd finished cutting and blowing Yara's hair dry, Rebecca spun the chair around and smiled broadly. "What do you think?"

Yara was startled by the face looking back at her in the mirror. She appeared so unlike herself. Her hair, resting below her shoulders now, was full and bouncy, and the honey-colored highlights made her skin look bright and dewy, framing her face in a way that made her seem sophisticated, even beautiful. That didn't seem right. A deep discomfort flushed through her, as though she had slipped into a body that wasn't her own. It felt inappropriate. Again, she saw Mama's face in the mirror, her cold, judgmental eyes, the curl of her upper lip. Yara ripped her eyes away, fighting back tears, and looked down at her hands.

"Thank you," she said, avoiding Rebecca's eyes.

She paid the bill without catching her reflection on the way out.

When Yara picked up the girls from her in-laws' house, Nadia greeted her at the front door with an amused expression. "Wow, you look stunning," she said. "Zay el amar. As beautiful as the moon."

Yara took a step back, unable to hide her surprise. "Thank you."

Nadia grinned. "Now, this is good. This is how I like to see you."

Mira and Jude squealed in delight at the sight of her new style, and on the ride home they studied her, mesmerized. At a red light, Mira reached out and touched a strand. "You look so pretty, Mama," she said. "Can you cut my hair like that, too?" Smiling, Yara said she could. Jude leaned closer, her seat belt stretching, and said: "You look like Princess Belle from *Beauty and Beast.*"

"I love Belle," Yara said.

"Your hair," Fadi said when he entered the kitchen later that evening. Yara wiped her palms against her apron and swallowed, looking down at her hands. "You cut it," he said flatly.

"I got some highlights put in, too. Do you like it?"

"It's nice. But why did you cut so much off?"

She frowned, tugging on a golden strand. "I thought a change would be good. I thought you'd like it."

"I do," he said quietly.

She looked away, trying to focus on the positive. Even though he was only pretending to like her hair, he was making an effort to compliment her.

"I wish you would've told me first," he said. "I really did love your long hair."

"Oh. I'm sorry," she heard herself say. For what exactly, she wasn't sure. For starting problems lately, for cutting her hair, for standing there pathetically—for apologizing for all of it. Ridiculous.

"Don't be sorry," Fadi said, looking at her now. "It'll grow back soon."

Stiffly, she followed him upstairs to tuck the girls into bed. So this was how Fadi saw her? As someone who needed permission to cut her own hair, as though her every movement required his approval? And yet she'd gone to the salon for him. To make him see her, to fix things, to break the curse that had plagued her whole life—this unsettled feeling that something was deeply wrong and that something even worse was coming.

Fadi ascended the stairs with his head down, reading something on his phone. Behind him, Yara pushed one foot in front of the other with effort, replaying Mama's warning about the evil eye. She wondered if Fadi was aware of how often his eyes were on the screen instead of on hers. The entire world must be cursed, she thought, to spend so much of our days walking around with our eyes glued to a device that only left us feeling more alone. She had stopped posting. Stopped pretending, online at least. But that hadn't changed anything, had it?

Inside the girls' room, he finally slipped the phone into his pocket and leaned over to kiss Mira and Jude good night. Even in the near darkness, she could see how tender he was with them, how genuine his smile seemed. When was the last time he'd smiled at her like that? Watching him, she wanted to throw herself into his arms and confess how much she needed him, how scared she was, but she only stood there, clenching her teeth. The words were too vulnerable. He couldn't see her as weak. Eventually she swallowed a lump in her throat and closed her eyes, holding back tears. All these years she'd prided herself on her strength and independence, but she could no longer deny that what she wanted most was Fadi's love. Or at least some reassurance that she wasn't alone, that he would be there to comfort her, to love her despite how hard it was to love herself. But in moments like this, his love felt so far away, like love was a country she would never hold claim to.

Had she ever felt truly loved? Even as a child, she'd yearned to be loved and had believed that if she only tried hard enough, she'd someday feel it. But she'd gone without it, the coldness in the house so severe it made her bones ache. The thoughts crept up to her now until it was impossible to look away from them: What if *this* was actually her curse? Not losing her job or failing at marriage, but simply being unlovable, unwanted, no matter what she did.

Frowning, she turned toward the window, her daughters' sleepy voices getting quieter and quieter. Outside, she saw the soft glow of streetlights against the pavement, the sky dimming and darkening, and she stood there, silent, scanning the row of brick houses, her chest rising and falling in the darkness.

YARA'S JOURNAL

Those summers, when we are in Palestine, that is when you come alive. Like a bright campfire in a darkened field. You have a ritual there, every morning: waking at dawn to the rooster crow and the call of the adhan from the nearby mosque. "To look at the sky," you say. "Every day is a new painting." Is this where my love of drawing began?

Afterward you take long walks in the hakoora, a small field near the camp, returning home with a basket spilling with fruit. "To clear my mind," you explain. "To help me feel connected."

"To what?" I ask.

"The trees," you say. "The land of my home."

I beg you to take me with you, and one morning, you do. We walk hand in hand, each carrying an empty basket. Summer coats the hills and valleys with fresh grass and wildflowers, scattered wherever we look. We stop at every fig bush and almond tree, their delicate fruit supple and sweet. We stretch our hands and pick what's hanging close, filling our baskets. We climb the branches and stuff our pockets, lifting the ends of our garments to hold the rest. Then we walk home, eager to show Teta what we've collected.

"Baraka," Teta says as she grinds the fruit into jam. "A blessing."

On our last trip there, I watch you and Teta stand over the simmering pots and pans, your shoulders pressed together with hers, your lips settled into a smile, as if happiness is painted on your face.

Through the open kitchen window, I see my brothers, dressed in American clothes, running with a flock of neighborhood kids. The kids' shirts are patched, their pants too big, their sandals held on with ragged straps. They all play together with sticks and old bicycle tires, laughing as if they've found a treasure.

On this bright summer day, the sky is a crisp light blue. Laundry lines all around us, sheets fluttering in the wind. The women laugh and gossip while they sip Turkish coffee and dip warm bread in zeit-o-za'atar, while the men sit inside, playing cards and smoking hookahs packed with tobacco and filled with rosewater and lemon.

That last evening there, you strum your oud and sing, as if you are far away, as if you had slipped into the music.

Eventually the women begin to dance, slipping off their headscarves and veils. They form a circle around you, clapping and singing, one after another entering the middle of the circle, rolling their hips, their bodies radiant with freedom. I watch, hypnotized by the unfamiliar sights and sounds, the uproarious laughter, and the lyrics of Umm Kulthum, the melodies of Fairuz. The rasp of your oud still echoes inside me—igniting a longing to return to those sweet, lovely days, a time that seems now like a flicker of magic moving through you, rolling over everything, illuminating the hand-painted coffee set, the embroidered shawls, the lush green hills in the distance. And you, the voice that seems to be orchestrating all of this, the music rooted in my body, settled in my bones. You, Mama, you also showed me another way to be.

20

By October, the roads were covered in wet leaves and the smell of cedarwood and pine lingered in the cool air. Lately, Yara walked around in a state of furtive urgency, her parents' voices in her ear as she tried to bring order to days that seemed like a deck of cards scattered across the floor. At home, she attempted to get Fadi's attention as they ate their dinners in bed, but failed.

Baba had been wrong. If anything, the sudden change to her appearance had backfired on her, only heightening the insecurities she felt within. Glancing at Fadi one evening as they ate in bed, she wondered what he saw in her, if he even saw her at all. She was struck by his profile as he shoveled food into his mouth, only moving his eyes from the screen on the wall to look at the screen of his phone. In the silence that followed, her anger spread and grew, swelling like an ocean around her.

"Do you actually think this is normal?" Yara snapped one evening after he queued up yet another episode of a sitcom. "Zoning out in front of the TV every single night? It's the only thing we ever do."

"Why do you talk to me like this?" Fadi said. "Do you think that makes me want to talk to you? Relax, woman."

But she couldn't relax. She felt disoriented, like she'd opened her spice cabinet to find all her containers rearranged, as if her life had suddenly become unfamiliar to her.

At work, she completed her tasks with a concerted effort, hoping to make up for the failure she felt like at home. She redesigned the college's home page and edited the typography on each digital platform. She went back and rephotographed each building on campus, including the clock tower. Jonathan organized two new professional development sessions, and though she dreaded going, she attended both.

She worked slowly, editing the school's social media postings multiple times before she shared them online, carefully checking her captions for typos. Sometimes, on a particularly slow day, she found herself going to Instagram, as if on autopilot.

Quickly, she'd close the application before she could post anything, Mama's warning hovering in the air. She hadn't posted a single photo since her mother's admonishment, but nothing significant seemed to have changed in the way she felt, her body still as heavy as if a boulder were pressed against her chest. The piercing glare of the evil eye seemed to stand beside her like a shadow that wouldn't go away.

And yet she was pleased with her own composure when, during the next department meeting, Jonathan announced that Amanda had been chosen to chaperone the cruise. From the back of the room, Yara examined her fingers and let out a low breath, suppressing the bubbling sensation beneath her ribs like she was closing the lid on a pot of boiling water. Amanda smiled and thanked Jonathan, a surprised, innocent expression on her face.

When the meeting was over, Amanda turned to face her and said, "I'll bring you back a souvenir from that museum you told me about."

Yara didn't want to meet her colleague's eyes, but Jonathan was looking at her expectantly. "Thank you," she replied. "That's very kind of you."

At the end of every week, Yara sat on the red sofa in William's office, looking out the window. He always sat across from her on the mustard chair, a pencil tight between his fingers, taking notes. Each week, he would begin with a question that was supposed to nudge her toward opening up and allowing him in. But she left each session feeling more closed off than when she'd started. She stared at the clock with her arms crossed, tapping her feet. Every minute wasted with him was time she could be working, doing something, anything, else.

"We're already halfway through the term," William said now, clicking the pen against his notebook. "I want to help you, Yara. But I'm afraid I can't if you continue refusing to open up with me here."

"If you're worried about what happened with Amanda, you have my word that I would never act that way with a student," she said. "Or ever again with a colleague. I had a perfectly civilized interaction with Amanda just the other day. You have to know by now that getting back in the classroom means everything to me. I won't jeopardize that."

William nodded. "Why is it so important for you to teach, do you think?"

"What do you mean, why? It's what I've been working toward for so many years. I've barely been allowed to do it as is."

"Allowed? Allowed by who?"

She shook her head. "I mean by Jonathan. You know, because of my schedule."

"I see. But why is teaching so important to you?"

She sighed. "Isn't it obvious?"

"No, I'm afraid not."

Yara wanted to scream into the throw pillow next to her until she lost her voice, or storm out of the room and slam the door shut behind her. Instead, she closed her eyes and thought back to the days she spent sitting by the windowsill of her bedroom in Brooklyn, drawing. Paper, a pencil, markers when they hadn't dried out. Outside, she could see a row of brownstones across the street, which she sketched into the cheap ruled notebook paper. Sunlight came in through the glass, warming her face, and the sound of her pencil against the paper soothed her. She drew until she saw things more and more clearly, until she'd replaced the familiar images in her head with ones of escape, of happiness: a father holding his daughter's hand at the park; a young girl smiling up at her mother; a family sitting around the dinner table, laughing, talking about their days. Between the pages of her sketch pad, she didn't feel so alone.

Finally she looked up at William and said, "I wanted to be an artist. I wanted to do something meaningful. Art, drawing, painting, they've always made me happy. They've taken me places."

"How is that related to teaching? You taught the art prerequisite course, isn't that right?"

Yara nodded. "It's hard to explain," she managed to say. "I might not be able to create anything for myself—I mean, not everyone can be an artist—but maybe I can teach someone to make something beautiful? Maybe I can help them find their own light? That's what I love most about teaching, the possibility of helping others create art, even if I'm incapable of creating it myself." She pressed her thumb against the top of her thigh, shaking her head.

"I've seen your pictures," William said. "On the website. Your graphic design."

"I didn't go to art school for that," Yara said, waving a hand in front of her.

"But that is art." He uncrossed and recrossed his legs. "You've got a very good eye."

Yara felt a wave of confusion. What was he suggesting? Did he know something she did not? Was she not going to be able to teach again? Had she been coming here for no reason at all?

"I'm afraid our time is up," William said, standing to show her out.

21

On Saturday, Fadi brought Yara and the girls to his business partner Ramy's home for dinner. Ramy's wife, Hadeel, had just returned from Palestine with two jugs of olive oil and freshly picked grape leaves, so they'd invited the Murads over, along with another high school friend of Fadi's, Nader, and his wife, Yasmin. Yara wasn't close with either of the wives, and stared out the living room window at the velvet-blue sky as everyone else chatted before dinner.

"Itfadalu, help yourselves," Hadeel said when the food was ready, inviting them to have a seat around the sufra. Hadeel had stuffed the grape leaves with rice and minced lamb, which she was serving alongside an assortment of Palestinian sides: kufta skewers, hummus, falafel, tabouleh, red lentil soup, and warm pita.

All the adults gathered around the sufra while the girls ate at the coffee table in the living room, watching *Vivo* with Ramy and Hadeel's three-year-old son. From across the table, Fadi passed Yara an empty plate without meeting her eyes and said: "I'll have everything except soup, please."

She nodded and filled his plate, adding an extra spoonful of hummus and dash of olive oil.

Beside him, Ramy popped a grape leaf in his mouth, turned to his wife, and said: "Habibti, this is delicious."

Hadeel slapped his wrist playfully and said, "You need to wait for our guests."

"Sorry babe, I can't help it, your food is so good."

His wife blushed, but her face erupted in a smile.

Glancing back and forth between them, Yara shifted in her chair, feeling out of place. She swallowed a mouthful of water and tried to catch Fadi's eye, but he wouldn't look at her. Instead, she poured herself a bowl of red lentil soup and took a sip, then busied herself by adding a squeeze of lemon to offset the strong cumin flavor.

As a child, Yara had struggled to form close friendships, despite attending school with the same group of girls most of her life. She wasn't a bright and bubbly child, the way her Mira was, and always preferred to sit alone at lunch, her nose pressed into the pages of a sketch pad or a paperback novel instead of chatting with her classmates.

Sitting around the sufra with Fadi and his childhood friends and their wives, Yara felt like she was back in her school cafeteria. She resisted the impulse to excuse herself to the restroom, a tactic she'd often employed at school, hiding in a stall and taking long, slow breaths until the tension in her body settled.

Moving to Pinewood, she had wondered if meeting new people would allow her to also meet another version of herself, a livelier one, someone open and energetic who thrived in social gatherings and didn't shut people out. But it had remained hard for her to connect with others, to let her guard down. It was only in front of class, speaking about art, about something she knew and believed in, where she felt comfortable talking and sharing. That was what she had needed to say to William! She realized it now. As if she could make him understand how she felt here, even in this house.

She wasn't the only person at the table who'd had to start over. Hadeel had come here from Palestine to marry Ramy after sitting with him a few times in her parents' sala. Yasmin grew up in Ohio, met Nader at a wedding there, and moved here after he'd flown back up to ask her parents' hand for marriage. Both women had left their families behind, too, yet they seemed to have handled the transition much better than Yara had. They'd transferred to new colleges, made new friends, and blended into the local Arab community as though they'd been part of it all along. Yara still didn't understand why she hadn't been able to do the same, to assimilate, to fit in, to be herself—not even here.

How had Mama done it? Marrying Baba and moving to America at only seventeen, adding a language barrier to the list of limitations she already faced. How had she felt? With six children to look after, her long days at home, and barely any friends. How had she managed the loneliness? Yara felt sick at the thought. Of course, Yara realized, the memory creeping in. Yara excused herself to the bathroom, closing the toilet seat and sitting on it with her face in her knees. How could she have blamed her mother? She was barely handling it better than Mama had.

After dinner, the adults gathered in the living room while the kids went upstairs to play. "Is everyone ready for chai and knafeh?" Hadeel asked.

After a wave of *yeses,* Ramy stood up and said, "Let me help."

From the living room, Yara watched as Hadeel brewed a pot of tea in the kitchen with Ramy beside her, their shoulders touching. He sliced and plated the knafeh, sprinkling the thin red crust with ground pistachio, while she filled glass cups with sugar. Watching them work side by side gave Yara a strange feeling. Eventually Ramy circled the room, passing out slices, and when he served her, she thanked him without meeting his eyes.

Ramy reached his wife last. "I saved you the biggest slice," he said with a smile. Then he sat on the floor beside her, leaning back against her legs, kissing her knees every now and then when he thought no one was looking.

Yara could feel her skin burning. For a few moments she tried to meet Fadi's eyes, but he didn't look her way. As soon as they finished the knafeh, she said it was getting late for the girls and they should go.

On the drive home, Yara stared out the window in silence,

one hand pressed to her mouth. Fadi sighed, his hands clenched around the steering wheel. She thought back to the early days of their marriage, how she'd waited for him to come home from work each night, pacing anxiously around the kitchen until she heard the sound of his keys at the door. He'd greet her with his charming grin, but she had still felt so afraid. She'd straighten as he approached her, commanding her body to relax, but her bones would feel as heavy as if she were sinking toward the center of the earth.

Looking at him each night, and particularly at the uncanny way in which he was starting to resemble her own father, she had wanted to hide her face in both hands and disappear. But she couldn't move. Eventually she would follow him to the bedroom, her head aching, her body tight like one big fist. Breathing hard, she'd try to imagine their future together: taking evening walks, Fadi wrapping his arms around her, kissing her face softly, his lips warm against her cheek. Or regarding each other across a candlelit table or sharing an ice-cream cone in the park on a warm afternoon. But all she had been able to call up were the usual dreary snapshots: Baba gritting his teeth when he came in the door from work, yelling at Mama for oversalting the rice or calling her a sharmouta, grabbing a fistful of her hair and slamming her head against the wall.

Even then, in those early days, when Fadi held her in a loving embrace, she could feel herself as a child, sobbing on the floor, her face buried in her hands, and it was Fadi's body looming over her, his eyes flashing, instead of Baba. She'd spent years looking for Fadi's love, learning to paint it in her mind with warm, bright colors, but all she could see now was gray.

"You awake?" Yara asked Fadi in bed later that night, their backs to each other. Moonlight filtered through the window, filling the room with soft blue light.

"Yeah," he said, but didn't move.

A prickle ran down her spine. In the darkness, she pulled the covers up to her neck, hoping to soothe the nagging sensation in her body. Or perhaps to silently communicate her need for comfort to Fadi. But his inability to understand her without words triggered a hollow ache inside her.

"Tonight was nice," she said.

"Yeah, it was." Fadi sounded annoyed.

"Ramy was all over Hadeel," she continued, unable to stop herself. "How come we're not like that?"

He scoffed. "Like what? Practically making out in public?"

"Not just that," she said. "He was being so sweet, helping Hadeel serve everyone."

Fadi let out a sharp laugh and turned over to face her. "Are you seriously picking a fight with me over dessert? You always do this."

"Do what?"

"You always find a way to ruin a good time," he said. "Why do you have to act like this whenever we hang out with friends?"

She felt a tingling in her hands. "Act like what?"

"Like you don't want to be around them, like you're better than them or something."

"What?" she said, pushing the quilt off her body. "I don't think I'm better than anyone."

"Then why were you acting so weird tonight?"

"I don't know. I wasn't doing it on purpose." Her voice sounded weak and small to her. "You're the one who was acting like I didn't exist."

"Bullshit. You always do this when things don't go your way. We haven't hung out with our friends in months. Am I not allowed to talk to them? Why is everything always about you?"

"I never said you can't talk to your friends. But you didn't even look at me all night. The least you could've done was try to make me feel included."

"Fuck, Yara! You've known these people for years. Don't attack me because of your own insecurity."

"I'm sorry, I'm not trying to attack you." The vein in her neck was throbbing, and she rubbed her palms on the quilt. "I just wanted you to talk to me. Why are you making me feel like I'm crazy?"

"I'm not *making* you feel anything," Fadi said. "You feel that way on your own."

For a few seconds she heard nothing, not even the sound of her breath, then she touched her face and realized she was crying.

"This was supposed to be a fun night with our friends," he went on. "But again, you've made the entire night about you. You're so selfish."

"I'm sorry," she whispered.

"You're always sorry, Yara," Fadi said with a sigh. "How long do you expect me to keep putting up with this? It's starting to get old." Then he turned over without saying good night.

An uneasy feeling struck Yara then, sharp like a warning, but she pushed it away.

In the darkness, her heart was racing. She thought back to the night that Fadi had asked for her hand in marriage, the shock she'd felt, that this man wanted to marry her despite the whispers about her family, their poor reputation. Baba had told her how lucky they were then, too, urging her to be grateful. She'd felt indebted to Fadi then, for looking past the shame. And now, for how hard he worked to provide for her and her girls.

So why was she giving him a hard time, forgetting all that he'd done for her? Why couldn't she be happy?

Fadi could've kept her up all night, fighting. It was what she deserved. He could've called her a sharmouta. Or so much worse. He could have been the kind of husband who slammed her face against the wall, who grabbed her by the throat until she couldn't breathe. The kind she'd feared he might be—but he hadn't been. And now here she was, as he said, making up problems. He was a good man. He wasn't a cheater, gambler, or an alcoholic. He didn't prevent her from exploring her own ambitions, not the most important ones at least. Why couldn't she just believe that he loved her? Why was it impossible for her to feel wanted, safe? It wasn't his fault she couldn't be happy. She couldn't keep punishing him for all the pain she'd seen in her life.

Her mind was unable to stop now. No marriage was perfect. Everyone had problems, and hers weren't so bad. Fadi's withdrawals weren't his fault, really. He was probably loving her the best way he knew how. It's not like he'd seen what a healthy marriage looked like, either. Maybe that was why he couldn't love her the way she wanted, for the same reason she found it hard to believe in his love. It wasn't that he wanted to hurt her, or didn't care. He just didn't know how. And that was understandable. She could forgive him for this. If anyone could feel his pain, it was her.

22

As the Thanksgiving break approached, Yara wandered across the cold campus with her camera bag wrapped tightly around her body. The sun hung low in the sky while she went through the motions at her desk, shuffling papers, checking off items on her agenda. Maybe it was because of the colder weather, but she had no desire to work. She scrolled through the site, updated a few calendar items, but she couldn't bring herself to do the requested page updates for the various departments or post announcements to the college's social media. The thought alone fatigued her.

At home, she moved through the motions of cooking the recipes she knew by heart, but every dish was bland to her.

"No, no," Fadi assured her. "It tastes just like the last time you made it."

In bed each night, she closed her eyes and saw Mama's face, her eyes filled with anger and fear. Sorrow and guilt. Or were these her own eyes? She couldn't be sure.

On the last day before the break, Yara found herself in her office with the blinds drawn, without the necessary motivation to go shoot pictures or respond to emails, only waiting for the day to pass, when there was a knock at the door.

"Just wanted to drop this off," Silas said. He was standing in the brightly lit hallway holding up a covered dish and silverware wrapped in a napkin. "I made it for you."

"Oh," Yara said. "That was nice of you." She felt acutely aware of her own body, blocking the doorway. When she stepped aside, Silas took this as an invitation to come in, handing the dish to her as he entered.

"It's coq au vin," he said.

A small smile betrayed her. "The same dish Amanda took issue with?" she asked, peeling back the wrapping to have a look: chicken and vegetables, a rich dark sauce.

"Yeah, I thought you could try it and tell me if it tastes like the real deal," he said, taking a seat in the empty chair where students sat on the rare times they came to her office.

Yara hadn't yet eaten, having only watched the girls eat their breakfasts. Returning to her seat, she set the plate on her desk and unwrapped the cutlery, then sliced a bite-size piece of chicken, smothered it in sauce, and popped it into her mouth. "Oh, wow," she said, already eager for another bite. "Brings me back to my summers in France."

Silas laughed, and Yara couldn't help but laugh, too. "Thank you," she said, covering her mouth as she finished the bite. "This is very good."

"Thanks," he said, moving to the door. "I'm glad you like it."

She held the door open for him, and as he slid past he turned and looked at her. "Your hair looks great, by the way. I wanted to tell you at William's last week, but it's been harder to catch your eye lately."

Her face burned, and she stared at the floor.

"The highlights, they really suit you," he said. "You look beautiful."

With great effort, she managed to look him in the eye. "Thank you," she said. "That's nice of you."

At home, Yara sliced red onions into paper-thin slivers and seasoned chicken drumsticks and thighs with cumin and allspice for Fadi's favorite meal, musakhan. Traditionally the dish was made by roasting a bone-in chicken, but tonight she was taking a shortcut.

Outside the sky was darkening, but a sliver of the sun was visible among the empty tree branches. Mira and Jude were playing in the backyard, and the sound of their laughter came through the open kitchen window. Yara hummed an Arabic melody as she poured a splash of olive oil into a large skillet. She seared the chicken until the skin was golden brown on both sides before transferring it to the oven. In the same pan, she sauteed the onions in sumac, the bright, lemony ground berry spice staining the onions a deeper red. In a separate pan she stirred pine nuts constantly until they were a golden brown. Finally, she arranged a few pieces of warmed flatbread on a large platter, topped it with half of the onions followed by the chicken, then spooned the remaining onions over the top before sprinkling the dish with pine nuts and parsley. As she stood there, adding a final drizzle of olive oil, she wondered if Silas had ever tried musakhan.

Maybe she would bring him some by the Culinary Arts Department, as a thank-you.

But what would Fadi say if he knew she was making friends with another man? And that the man had complimented her, too? Panic began to set in, and Yara leaned into the counter, trying to catch her breath, gripping her necklace, trying to resist an old memory that seemed intent on coming up. Tonight it arrived with a sharp pang: she was in the kitchen with her mother, but Mama wouldn't look at her. And why would she, after what Yara had done? She felt a pain in the back of her throat and closed her eyes, the memory of her mother's face as she realized that Yara had told Baba. That Baba knew. How long ago that was, and how little she'd been, how she hadn't really understood what it was she had confirmed for Baba. How that day would change everything between her and Mama for years to come.

Fadi slammed the front door shut when he came home a few hours later. The girls were already sound asleep, and Yara was painting in the sunroom, where she flinched at the sound, startled.

"Is everything okay?" she said when she walked into the hall to greet him.

"Yeah, it's just been a rough day."

She started to ask what had happened, but he was already moving toward the bathroom. Yara followed him and they showered in silence, Fadi moving more quickly, gruffly. She kept her distance as she dried off, stealing glances of her husband in the bedroom mirror as he dressed. Angst filled his face, and he was shaking as he slipped on a pair of green plaid pajama pants. As Yara looked down at her hands, an absurd thought popped into her head: Had Fadi somehow found out about her friendship with Silas?

"Are you sure there's nothing wrong?" she asked gently once her nightclothes were on.

"Nothing's wrong," he said. "I've had a long day, that's all."

He brushed past her and headed toward the kitchen, and she followed, her stomach twisting.

"I made musakhan," she said.

Fadi nodded but said nothing. The silence, roaring between them, was giving her a headache.

Back in the bedroom with their dishes, Fadi chose an episode of *Law & Order.*

Yara sat with her plate warming her lap, unable to eat. Fadi's forehead was furrowed as he stared at the screen, chewing.

When the episode ended and he queued up another one, she managed to say: "Can we turn off the TV?"

He pressed pause. "Really?" he said. "This is the only time I have to unwind."

"I know," she said, then hesitated. "But you seem upset, and I want to make sure you're okay."

Fadi sighed. "I'm fine. I just had a rough day with my dad, going over some paperwork. He's screwed up his books and is behind on his taxes. It's not my fault, though he thinks it is."

She exhaled, relieved it wasn't about her, but saddened that his relationship with his father could make him feel so small. "How much does he owe?"

"Ten thousand."

"Ten thousand dollars?" she said, unable to keep the strain from her voice. "Does he want you to pay? That doesn't seem fair."

"When has Hasan ever cared about fair?"

"Oh, Fadi. I'm sorry."

He gazed off into the distance, then reached for a glass of water on the nightstand. "Look, I don't want to talk about this," he said. "I just want to relax and watch my show."

Without waiting for her to respond, he unpaused the TV.

Later, when they'd gone to bed, Yara tried to reach him again. "I'm sorry this happened with your father," she said. "If you want to talk—"

"I don't," Fadi said, then turned over and switched off his bedside lamp.

Instinctively, she nestled up against him, pressing her face against his neck and inhaling the citrus and clove scent of his skin. He looked back at her, seeming surprised, but didn't pull away. "I'm sorry he treats you like this," Yara said.

The only light in the room was coming from the full moon filtering through the blinds, and the darkness made her feel safe. Slowly she placed her hands on Fadi's chest. In a small voice she said, "You're a good son. A good man." He made a low noise in his throat, and she couldn't help but notice how defeated he looked, his eyes shining.

"It's fine," he eventually said. "We can cover it. And it's not like I ever expected anything different from him."

Yara imagined Fadi as a young boy, stocking aisles and counting twenties at his father's gas station, desperate to please him, and her body ached with tenderness for his sorrow. She leaned in even closer to him now, kissed his neck. Softly she said: "I don't like to see you upset. I just want us to be happy."

"I know," Fadi said. "Me, too."

In the total darkness, Fadi pulled her in toward him and she could feel her body relax. He kissed her, his face warm, and she was moving her hand over the back of his neck, leading him closer, an overwhelming sensation filling her. His skin pressed against hers, everything hurt a little less, felt a little lighter. Afterward she lay in his arms for a while, breathless, feeling his fingers moving through her hair, wondering if he was still wishing that she hadn't cut so much away.

23

During the Thanksgiving break, Yara spent most of the day at home with Mira and Jude, cuddled up together in front of the fireplace, reading, or watching them build castles with LEGOs on the living room floor while she sipped coffee on the sofa, her mind far away, unable to stop racing. Sitting on the sofa, she could hear her thoughts, could feel them pulsing inside her skull. They seemed to be warning her, with their endless chatter, that she needed to listen, that something bad would happen if she didn't. "Come play with us," the girls would say whenever they sensed her attention slip away, and Yara felt a rush of anxiety, wanting nothing more than to sit there and dissect the voice in her head. But the sudden loneliness she saw in their eyes, the pleading way they looked up at her, made Yara set her cup down, her hands shaking, and join them. It was as though they could hear the tormentor inside her head, as though they knew what Yara didn't yet understand, that her greatest enemy lived between her two ears.

"I need your help," said a voice from the doorway of her office on the first day back from break, and Yara looked up from her desk to see Silas looming in it again.

She sat back in her chair, slightly startled. It was almost 1:00 P.M., and she had finished her work in a breathless rush, pausing only to brew another pot of coffee.

"Didn't mean to interrupt anything," Silas said.

Yara blinked at him. "Not at all," she said, rubbing her temples. "I've been staring at a screen all day. What can I do for you?"

Silas helped himself to the empty chair. "I'm trying to create a photo tutorial for one of my classes, but I'm not really sure how I can shoot it and bake at the same time, if that makes sense?" He took out his phone and showed her a YouTube video he'd been watching. "I'm not that great when it comes to technology, and I thought maybe you might know how to do something like this?"

"Of course," Yara said. "I have the camera tripod you need and can help you set it up. It's much simpler than it looks."

He glanced at his phone, seeming to consider something, then back up at her. "Actually, do you think maybe you can shoot the tutorial? You'd do a much better job, and I'm sure the students would really love your professional touch."

"Sure," she said. "Did you want to do this right now?"

"Is that possible?" he asked, scratching his beard. "I'd set everything up before I realized I didn't know how to shoot it."

Yara looked back at her desk. "Well, you'd be saving me from that glaring screen."

He smiled, an easy smile. Yara grabbed the tripod and followed him to the campus kitchen, her camera around her neck.

Stepping through the black double doors, she paused, startled by the display. Devoid of other people and state-of-the-art, the campus kitchen looked like something out of a high-end home magazine. A large stainless steel island took up most of the room, glistening pots and pans hung from the ceiling, and plump fruits sat brightly in baskets.

"This is lovely," Yara said, snapping open the tripod next to the stainless steel countertop. "You'll do most of the cooking here?"

Silas nodded.

"We'll put your phone on the tripod, shooting the video with that here," she told him. "And I'll use my still camera as you work, so that you can cut in inserts of still images later. Does that sound good?"

"Sounds like you know what you're doing!"

Yara found she was smiling again and covered her mouth. "Well, you're the one who has to do the cooking."

As Silas moved toward the walk-in, she hit record on his phone. "We're recording now," she said, moving away from the tripod.

"Okay, great," Silas said, coming back out with eggs and butter in hand. "Hey, class, Chef Silas here. Today we will be making French macarons."

Staying out of frame, Yara shot each new ingredient on the back counter after he'd used it: almond flour, powdered sugar, vanilla extract, cream of tartar. Finally, Silas grabbed a tube of pink gel from the pantry and returned to his station.

Then he paused, looking up for a moment. "Yara, why don't you get a little closer?" he said. "I promise I won't bite."

She blushed and waved him off, pointing at the video that was still rolling. "Class, this is Yara Murad, an art teacher here and also the source of all the incredible images on our website."

She stepped into the picture to wave and smile, feeling briefly as if she were back in front of the classroom. He'd called her an art teacher. Still in the frame, she lifted her own camera and took a few more pictures as he folded the egg whites into the batter. With each snap she attempted to capture the ease with which he moved, whisking together ingredients in strong, decisive moments. It reminded her of watching Mama strum her oud. Of Teta's confidence in the kitchen.

"How did you learn to do this?" Yara asked when she paused the recording briefly to readjust the tripod.

Silas wiped his fingers across his apron. "I grew up eating country ham and grits, not having much access to foods outside of southern cuisine, so I was drawn to learning about culturally diverse foods when I went to culinary school." He lined a baking tray with parchment paper. "Don't get me wrong, though. Nothing beats southern food."

Yara shrugged. "I wouldn't know."

Silas looked up from the tray, raising his eyebrows. "Seriously?" he started, but Yara quickly resumed the recording. He cleared his throat. "All right, kids, so now these need to go into the oven for fifteen minutes." He slid the pan into the oven and motioned to the tripod. Yara moved over to it and stopped the recording again.

"How long have you been down here?" Silas asked.

"Almost ten years," Yara said. "But we almost always eat at home."

"What about southern barbecue?"

"No, never tried it."

"Fried green tomatoes, collard greens, creamy grits?"

She shook her head. "Sorry."

Silas blinked at her. "How about pimento cheese? We take our pimento cheese very seriously around here."

"Don't kill me, but I don't even know what that is."

"Wow," he said, shaking his head slowly. "We need to do something about this."

Yara laughed. "I see you have some pretty strong feelings about your local cuisine," she said. "Not that I blame you. I cooked with my grandmother growing up and it gave me this obsession with Arab food." She paused, finding it hard to keep her voice from breaking. "My teta meant a lot to me, I'm sorry. I was fourteen when we lost her. She lived in Palestine. We didn't—" Yara caught herself. "We couldn't go back for the funeral. I think I cook her food as often as I do to keep her memory with me." She looked down at her hands, at the camera, wondering why she had just shared all of this with him.

"I think that's sweet," Silas said. "That you've found a way to keep her close. I used to cook with my grandmother, too."

"Really?"

He nodded, returning his attention to wiping down the counter. "My best memories from childhood are of being in the kitchen with her, even though I was always teased for it."

"For cooking?"

"No, not just that." He paused, reaching inside a drawer for a clear plastic piping bag. Without looking at her, he said, "I mean, it's not a very manly activity, cooking with your grandmother, is it? I think my nana knew I was gay before I did. The neighborhood kids who teased me certainly knew."

Silas laughed, but Yara felt frozen. She had never known someone who was openly gay. Quickly, she tucked her hair behind one ear, trying to hide her surprise. Or was it disappointment?

For a few seconds she was silent as he continued to work, opening the clear bag and filling it with batter. She wasn't sure what startled her more: it never occurring to her that Silas might be gay, or that she secretly wished he wasn't. Or that he was sharing something so intimate with her, someone he barely knew. Did he consider her a friend?

"I'm going to make extras to give a few to each of my students. Is that crazy?" he asked.

Yara shook her head and set her camera down. "That must've been hard," she said. "I mean, growing up, being teased."

Silas filled the bag with batter, then leaned over the baking tray, positioning the piping tip over the parchment. "It was. I mean, especially before I even knew who I was. It's terribly difficult to feel like there's something wrong with you, that everyone knows it, without you knowing exactly what that is. Does that make sense?"

Perfect sense, Yara thought. "Yeah," she said. "I can understand that feeling."

He looked at her again. "When I think about those days, all I remember is how afraid I was of disappointing my family. My parents cared a lot about traditional values. We had dinner together every night and went to church every Sunday. Marriage was between a man and a woman. That's all I knew."

She nodded to encourage him to continue.

"My parents meant well, I'm sure. But I struggled to find myself, and I went far off the path they wanted for me. I was still trying to figure things out when my daughter was conceived. And then I felt like it was the right thing to do—to marry her mom—" He broke off, shaking his head, then fixed his attention again on the piping bag, squeezing the batter into silky pink circles, about an inch and a half in diameter. "Am I saying too much?" he asked, looking up at Yara now.

"No, no," she said. "It's not too much at all."

As Silas filled the tray with row after row of circles, it wasn't hard for her to picture him as a young boy, huddled beside his grandmother in the kitchen instead of playing outside with other boys. She imagined how lonely he must have felt trying to figure out who he was, and wondered if the more he was teased, the more he pinned down parts of himself, getting smaller and smaller, until eventually he lost sight of who he truly was.

Hadn't she felt this way her whole life, too? She'd never been sure of who she was. She'd never belonged anywhere—not in Brooklyn, not in Palestine, and certainly not here. Her soul had always been cracked in the center, her body split in two, her feet stretched so wide between opposite sides of the globe that she couldn't stand straight. She was American but un-American; Arab, but not entirely. It comforted her to know that Silas seemed to have worked out who he was eventually. She didn't know if she could do the same.

"Did you know that you were gay?" Yara ventured. "When you married Olivia's mom?"

He nodded, avoiding her eyes. "It's not something I'm proud of. I still feel really bad about that most days." He looked as if he might cry.

"I'm sorry," Yara said. "None of this makes you a bad person."

"I know," Silas said. "William's been helping me see that. I'm a better father now, being myself. It's what's best for Olivia, too."

He cleared off his station, returning the unused ingredients to the pantry. When the timer went off, Yara started recording again. Silas looked pleased as he removed the first round of shells from the oven.

Yara caught more images of Silas, as he whipped together a vanilla buttercream frosting, then spread it with a piping tip on one side of each shell. And finally, the end result: a beautiful plate of delicate macarons that looked like they came from the finest patisserie in Paris.

Yara stepped closer to get a shot of the final product. "Wow. Those are too pretty to eat," she said.

"See that, class? These macarons are sure to impress."

She turned off the camera. "That was perfect. You're a professional."

"So are you," Silas said.

Yara blushed. "Thank you."

"But now you have to try my too-pretty-to-eat macarons."

"I'd be crazy if I didn't," she said, reaching for one. Her teeth sank into the soft, airy cookie, and a warm tingling spread through her body. "Even better than I'd imagined."

He met her eyes, his expression soft. "Thank you."

She took a halting step forward. "May I ask you one more thing?"

"Sure."

She looked down at the floor, then forced herself to meet his eyes. "How are you able to share such personal things with me?" Instead of stopping to let him answer the question, more words leaped off her tongue. "You make it seem so easy, talking about your life. About, well, about being teased. But I can't even open up to William—someone who I'm supposed to tell things to—and I've been talking to him for more than two months now. It's embarrassing. Most days it feels like I'm terrible at being a person."

"I'm so sorry you feel this way," Silas said softly. "If it helps you, I struggled with opening up, too. But seeing William helped me learn how to understand my feelings and communicate them better."

"It feels so hard to do."

"Maybe you should share that with William?"

Yes, she thought. Maybe just talking to William about her inability to express herself was a start. Maybe he could help her find the words. Yet she'd just spoken her mind so freely just now, with Silas.

She couldn't remember the last time she'd had a conversation where she was able to say exactly what was on her mind, or even any exchange that didn't feel stilted. Maybe she could keep going with him, right now.

She inhaled, pressing a hand across her collarbone. "I can relate to how you felt growing up," she confessed.

Silas met her eyes. "How so?"

"I never felt like I fit in either," she said. "In my family, women are supposed to be a certain way, and, well, I just never wanted to be that way. I wanted to do things differently."

He was quiet for a long moment then said, "And did you?"

She stared down at the little shell-like pastries, feeling exposed.

All these years she thought she'd carved her own path, but now she wondered if she'd just taken the easy way out by marrying a man who was only less conventional on the surface. She had once believed she would break the curse of generations of women before her and start anew. Maybe in a way she had. There was no denying her progress. And yet she couldn't help but feel that she hadn't truly changed anything.

She looked at Silas. "I'm not so sure anymore."

24

On Friday, as Yara headed into William's office, she smiled back at Silas and thanked him for holding the door. She wasn't sure what she would share with William today, but she felt now their sessions might help her feel better. Silas had let her in without fear of judgment, so perhaps she could do the same with her counselor.

There was a stillness in the room as Yara took her seat, and she set her hands in her lap and looked down at them. From his usual seat, William adjusted his glasses and regarded her. He was wearing a light blue tie that made his eyes seem more intense than usual, almost violet.

"Let's get started, shall we?" he said, beginning the session with a few general questions: How were things at work? How was she sleeping? How did she feel today? Yara answered as plainly as possible, choosing her words with great care to make sure there was no room for misinterpretation. Back and forth they went, their exchange shallow, until she quickly said: "I think I'm ready to really talk now."

William paused midsentence and looked at her carefully. "That's great, Yara. Where would you like to start?"

She swallowed. "What do you want to know?"

"We haven't talked about your family. Are you on good terms with them?"

"Not really." Yara reached for a navy throw pillow and hugged it toward her chest. "I have five younger brothers, but they're scattered across the country and we're not that close. My parents, well—" She paused, cleared her throat. This was much harder than she'd anticipated. She took a deep breath and pictured Silas—thinking of how open he'd been the other day in the kitchen. Releasing the pillow onto her lap, she said, "To be honest, I don't really get along with my dad."

William nodded, allowing her to continue.

"I mean, we talk from time to time but he's . . ." She trailed off.

"Why don't you get along with him?"

"There's no specific reason," she said. "Maybe some things from when I was younger, the way he treated my mom." She felt tears forming in her eyes and quickly wiped them away, surprised at how difficult it was for her to say the words aloud. "Sorry, this is really hard to talk about."

"Please don't apologize," William said. "It's very brave of you to share this with me."

She looked toward the window. "I don't know why I'm still so upset. It was all a long time ago. I guess I keep hoping that he'll try to make amends. But he never has."

"It's natural to feel this way," William said. "It sounds like you were hurt by someone you relied on for your safety and well-being. That's going to have an impact."

She nodded, keeping her eyes fixed on the window.

"Family relationships can be very complex," he continued. "Even the best of them can leave scars on the ones they love, and they have a powerful influence on who you are as an adult." He paused, trying to meet her eyes, but she couldn't bring herself to look at him. "How are things with you and your mother?"

Yara shook her head, feeling suddenly sick. "I'm sorry, but I don't want to talk about her."

When she looked back at William, something in his expression had changed. After a moment he asked, "Have you ever talked to your parents about how you feel?"

"No, never."

"You might find healing by doing so."

The room was suddenly cold.

"I can't," Yara said. "It's complicated. Besides, half the time I'm not even sure what I feel, let alone how to express it."

"Why do you think that is?"

She fingered the edge of the pillow in her lap but said nothing.

"Trauma, in our childhoods, can make our emotions—even as adults—feel very disorganized. It's sometimes incomprehensible to us, why we react the way we do—" He went on. Yara watched as he spoke, could hear the words coming out of his mouth, but she wasn't listening. She was realizing that whatever she shared with William wouldn't fix what happened. It would only force her to relive those moments, bringing on the same pain all over again. She hadn't been strong enough to endure it then; why would she be now?

"Is there?" William was saying, trying to meet her eyes. "Something in your childhood that you feel afraid of today?"

"Afraid?" Yara repeated. Mama's face came to her mind, and she squeezed her eyes shut. When she opened them, William was looking at her empathetically.

"I can see this is painful for you," he said. "This is a safe space, Yara. Whatever you say in here, it's in confidence. I only mean to be helpful."

"I want to explain it, I do. But it's hard."

"I understand," William said. "But it can be helpful to put our past into words. Verbalizing our emotions can help us navigate the world we're in now and give us more resources in the long term."

"What if I can't find the words?"

"It's very normal to find it difficult to articulate deeply distressing events without feeling overwhelmed. Is that how you feel?"

Yara nodded.

"There are several things that can help with that." He walked over to his desk, reaching inside the drawer and pulling out a black leather notebook. "Some people find it easier to process certain events by writing about them. Have you ever tried journaling?"

She shook her head. "No, I haven't."

"Would you like to?" William reached out, offering her the notebook.

"What do I do?" She took the notebook and opened it. "I just write down my thoughts?"

"Yes, more or less," he said. "But you may want to focus on your memories, on the things that feel overwhelming when you say them out loud. Try to recall them, notice how they make you feel, and write that down."

Yara raised an eyebrow. "Remembering bad things will only make me feel worse, not better."

"I know it seems counterintuitive," William said. "But repressing undesirable thoughts and feelings can give them more power over us. Once you're able to identify and work through them, you may find that you're better able to regulate your emotions when those memories come up, or even when current events resemble those memories. You'll be able to separate the feelings more easily."

"I don't know," Yara said, closing the journal.

Across the room, William folded both hands in his lap. "Perhaps it would be useful to write a letter that you will never send."

"A letter?" Yara said, confused. "What would I put in it?"

"Think of the things you would like to say to your father or mother, perhaps, but feel you can't. Just the process of expressing yourself to them can be healing."

Yara stared at the leather notebook in her lap, imagining her handwriting inside. She didn't know if William was right, if finding the words would relieve her of this feeling she couldn't name, if writing a letter would help finally let go of the pain. Either way, she couldn't go on as she was.

"I know that accessing these memories can be frightening,"

William said as Yara stood to leave. "But closing off the past will only keep you feeling imprisoned. Wouldn't you rather be free?"

As Yara walked out of the office, she replayed his last question in her mind. *Wouldn't you rather be free?* That was the thing, she didn't know if she wanted freedom as much as relief. To stop feeling entirely. Her body had carried her pain for so long that all she wanted now was to set it down. To stop feeling it in her bones.

25

By early December, the mountains around campus were a gloomy gray, the trees bare, and the fields, once blooming with cotton, sugar-cane, and rice, were covered in frost. Every morning, Yara bundled up Mira and Jude in long-sleeved thermals, thick overcoats, and heavy rain boots before dropping them off at school. Their breath rose in a mist as they waved goodbye to her and hurried inside.

At work one of those bleak mornings, sitting in her office, Yara pulled out the notebook from a desk drawer. She had yet to bring it home with her, feeling funny about leaving it lying around. So far, she'd written down only some of her better memories. Memories of Teta, of Palestine. Of the few times she remembered Mama being happy at home in Brooklyn. She'd only written down what she wanted to remember, but she still felt a weight pressing down on her. Without thinking, she slipped her phone out of her pocket and unlocked it. There were no new notifications. Of course not. She'd stopped posting weeks ago. Scrolling through her social media accounts, she saw now that she was two separate people. Online, she looked and sounded strong and self-assured, with a perfect family, a well-respected job, and a life that seemed bright and full. Looking at her, people would say she had done well for herself. But the other version of herself, the one she was tapping into now, couldn't regulate her emotions and kept secrets even from herself. The falsity of it, and how easy it had been to pretend, made her nauseous.

Yara looked down at the notebook, at the fresh blank page in front of her. She wanted to believe she could be strong and self-assured in real life. That she could stop fearing her past. That she could muster up the courage to face that time in her life head-on, confront all she'd done. But the truth was, she was still afraid.

As she was picking up a pen, a knock at the door startled her. She touched her heart and said, "Come in."

It was Silas. "Hey there," he said. "Do you have a minute?"

"Sure."

"I wanted to thank you for helping with the tutorial the other day." He stood there as she closed the journal and slid it back into the drawer. "My mom made chicken pastry for lunch."

"That sounds nice."

"Good, because I was hoping you'd join me at her place today. If you're free, of course."

Yara froze, unable to hide her discomfort. Was she really going to go to a stranger's home? Would Fadi be uncomfortable if he found out she'd had lunch with another man?

"It's time you had some authentic southern food," he said gently. "Please?"

Looking up at him, the memory started to rise, but quickly she pushed it away. It was just lunch, and Silas's mother would be there, too. Fadi didn't have to know. Did Fadi tell her whenever he went to lunch with someone? She doubted it.

"Okay then," Yara said, and retrieved her coat.

Yara followed Silas's car to his mother's house, which was on several acres of land just a few miles from campus. It was a large white house with a wraparound porch and a steeply pitched roof that gave it a cottage feel. Silas led her through a garden in the back, where he told her his mother grew all sorts of vegetables in season. Then he pushed open the back door and ushered her into the kitchen, calling out, "Mama! We're here!" They were greeted by a comforting fragrance coming from the large pot on the stove. The counters were clean and a stack of *Southern Living* cookbooks was arranged neatly on the corner shelf. An array of houseplants filled one windowsill, and on the kitchen table sat a vase of yellow tulips.

"This is my mother, Josephine," Silas said to Yara when his mother appeared in the kitchen doorway.

From the side she looked a little like Mama: bright blue eyes, high cheekbones and button nose, a similar thin-shouldered build, but Josephine's hair was a honey blond instead of Mama's ink black.

Yara stepped forward and held out her hand, but Josephine pulled her in for a hug. "It's so nice to meet you, dear," she said, holding Yara tight.

Yara's arms hung at her sides, her eyes open and fixed on Silas's face. "It's nice to meet you, too," she said when Josephine let go.

"Silas tells me you've never had southern food before," Josephine said. "Is that true?"

Yara laughed. "Yes, unfortunately."

"And why haven't you remedied that yet, Chef?" she asked Silas, a twinkle in her eye. "She can't possibly appreciate the South until she's tasted our food."

"Mama, please," he said.

"Relax, honey. I'm just teasing," Josephine said, then ushered Yara into the living room. "Please, dear, make yourself at home. Would you like some sweet tea?"

"I would love some," Yara said, settling into a leather recliner.

"I'll get it," Silas said.

"Bring the pimento cheese biscuits, too," his mother told him. "They just came out of the oven." As soon as he walked away, Josephine leaned in toward Yara. "He's a big teddy bear, isn't he?"

Yara smiled, shifting in her seat. "He's great."

"So do you teach, too?"

"Yes, I—" She paused. "Well, not at the moment. Mostly I manage the college's web design and social media profiles."

"Oh, that sounds interesting," Josephine said. "Are you enjoying the work?"

No, Yara thought. She swallowed. "Not as much lately. I'm eager to get back in the classroom. "

"I'm sorry to hear that," Josephine said. "I've had a fair share of unenjoyable jobs in my life, and I've learned that nothing is more important than loving what you do. It's when all the magic happens." Perhaps sensing Yara's discomfort, she added, "But you're still young, dear. You have plenty of time to find your spark."

"I hope so," Yara said, and Josephine smiled.

Silas returned with the tray of biscuits and a pitcher of tea. Yara grabbed a biscuit and watched him pour the amber liquid into her cup.

"Plastic cups, really?" Josephine was saying.

"It's fine," Silas said. "Yara's not a stranger."

"Really, I don't mind," Yara said. She smiled and took a bite of her biscuit. "Wow, this is delicious."

"Why, thank you, dear," Josephine said. "Silas is not the only chef in the family. They were his favorite when he was a little boy."

"I can see why," Yara said. "My girls would love them."

"I'll pack you a couple to take home, then."

Yara thanked her, sipped her tea, and looked around the room. Family photos were everywhere: the mantel, the walls, the coffee table. On a built-in shelf near the TV was a framed picture of Silas holding a young girl, both of them grinning at the camera. Yara rose and walked over to get a better look.

"That's Olivia," Silas said.

"She's beautiful," Yara said, looking at the girl's wide eyes and wider smile.

"She is," Josephine said, her voice softening. "It's a shame she has to grow up in a broken home." She turned to her son. "But Silas tells me it's for the best, don't you, son?"

His eyes remained trained on the photograph. "It is, Mama."

"I hope you're right, honey," Josephine said. "Doesn't mean it's not sad for that little girl."

Yara took a seat again and discreetly scanned the room for a photograph that included Olivia's mother. Though she knew she probably wouldn't find one, she was curious to see an image that told another story.

"How old was Olivia when you and her mother separated?" Yara said.

"Just two," said Silas.

Yara nodded. "She won't remember much then, and hopefully won't know any different. A loving family is a loving family in any form, I think."

Silas and his mother both looked at her, then he said, "I hope so."

"Me, too," Josephine said, reaching out and touching her son's knee, her eyes shining with tears. "You're a good father."

Josephine was staring at her son with so much love and compassion that Yara couldn't quite bear it. She thought for a second about getting up and leaving but didn't want to alarm them. Instead, she slipped her hands beneath her thighs and squeezed tight.

"Come on," Josephine said now, standing up. "Let's eat."

They gathered around the kitchen table. The chicken pastry was thick and warm, and Josephine served it with fried, thin corn bread and more sweet tea. "I made the dumplings from scratch," she said when Yara asked her about the recipe. "But you could use store-bought pastry strips if you're in a hurry."

Yara studied the thick beige-colored stew in her bowl before eventually taking a spoonful. The broth was luscious and full-bodied, and for a few seconds she closed her eyes to feel the warmth filling her body.

"It tastes much better than it looks, doesn't it?" Josephine said.

She nodded. "It's delicious. Thanks for having me."

"You're welcome anytime, dear."

As they ate, Josephine chatted about her work at a community development organization, where she did fundraising to develop programs that served the underresourced neighborhoods in the county. She touched Yara's arm a couple of times as she spoke, and Yara felt her shoulders loosen, fall away from her ears.

"So tell me, dear," Josephine said. "Do you like it here? This little old town must be so different from New York City."

"It's pretty different," Yara said, looking up from her bowl. "But it doesn't feel that way to me. I grew up in Bay Ridge, which is a very tight-knit Arab community in Brooklyn, and I never really experienced much of the city, anyway."

"Why not?"

Yara paused, considering her response. To her surprise she said, "My parents were immigrants, and, well, they were very protective of us. I had a sheltered upbringing."

Josephine nodded slowly, and Yara suddenly felt something like car sickness as she wondered what the other woman must be thinking. Maybe her childhood would've been less restrained had she been raised back home, in Palestine, protected by a village of familiar people. But here, in America, corruptness threatened to disrupt all the values her parents held dear to their heart: family, loyalty, modesty, hard work. All her parents could do was shelter them from this new world and pray they remained untouched by its sickness, pray they remained pure, honorable, a united family front.

"Do you have family near?" Josephine asked.

"No." Yara looked down at the cup, then took a sip of tea. "Well, my husband's family lives here and we see them often, but we're not all that close."

"That's unfortunate," Josephine said. "Did something happen?"

"Mom! Stop being so nosy," Silas interjected.

"Forgive me, dear," his mother said, placing a hand on Yara's arm again. "I was only trying to make sure you were okay. Having family support is very important."

"Please don't apologize," Yara said. And then suddenly tears were streaming down her face. "I'm so sorry," she heard herself say. "I don't know what's gotten into me." The next thing she knew she was standing up and saying that she had to be going, that she was so sorry, but she had to leave. She was out the door and back in her car before she realized she hadn't said a proper goodbye or thank-you and still had an hour before it would be time to get the girls, but she couldn't go back to her office, where Silas might track her down to ask her what had happened.

She took two wrong turns on the way to the girls' school, but that was where she went, waiting across the street, trying to catch her breath, her hands clenched around the steering wheel. She had the urge to yank her car back onto the road and drive straight into a tree.

What kind of life was this? What was the point of being alive if she couldn't escape the feelings that overwhelmed her body and made ordinary life impossible? She had to do better than this, *be* better than this.

After a few long breaths, she pulled up Silas's information on the college website, thinking she'd write him an email to thank him for having her over and apologize for leaving in a rush. Then she wondered if it was more polite to mail a thank-you card. Eventually, she began typing an email. Then deleted it. Then composed it again, staring at her phone until it was just a big white blur in her hands. Why was it so hard for her to do things most people could do without a second thought? A normal person would just send the email. She inhaled and continued to type, then without reading over the message, quickly pressed send.

A few minutes later, Silas responded: "It's okay, there's nothing to be sorry for. We should do it again, if you're up for it. My mom loved meeting you and wanted you to try her warm banana pudding."

She wasn't sure what to reply, so she put her phone down, shut her eyes, and pressed her face against the steering wheel until the other cars began pulling in for pickup time.

26

For days afterward, Yara dreamed of her mother, imagining things they'd never done. Sometimes they were huddled together in her childhood bedroom while Mama braided her hair. Other times they were holding hands as they strolled around Bay Ridge, Mama stopping at a corner ice cream truck to get her a cone. In one dream, Mama was tucking her into bed while singing one of her favorite Fairuz songs, her voice enveloping her like a soft blanket. Yara hummed along sleepily, reaching up to trace her fingers across her mother's cheek. But it seemed like the farther she stretched out her hand, the farther Mama drifted away, until she eventually disappeared.

Things weren't any better between her and Fadi. He was quieter than usual and had become increasingly irritable when he returned from work, seldom making it in time for bedtime stories with the girls. Within seconds of showering and then flopping in front of the television, he'd zone out, and there was nothing for Yara to do but eat beside him in silence before retreating to the kitchen. Once there, she'd scrub their plates clean with trembling fists, staring at the outline of her reflection in the window with loathing. Then she'd busy herself with wiping the counters, wondering what was wrong with Fadi. Perhaps something had happened at his work, or his father had upset him again. Or perhaps he had somehow found out about her lunch with Silas.

She'd tried asking if he was okay, terrified of the possibility and simmering with guilt, but he'd snapped at her: "Everything's fine, why do you keep asking?"

"Nothing," she said, red faced. "Sorry."

Tonight, they ate maftoul while watching a rerun of **The Bernie Mac** *Show*. Fadi was slurping the savory tomato broth, which she'd made with cumin and allspice. "This is so good," he told her, the most he'd said in a while.

"Thank you," Yara said.

At the end of the episode, he turned to her and asked, "How's counseling?"

She put down her spoon, surprised he'd asked. "It's fine," she said. "I think it's helping me."

Fadi reached for his glass of water and took a gulp. "You don't seem to be getting better, though."

"I don't?" she asked. She didn't feel better exactly, but she did feel different.

"You seem the same, that's all. I thought counseling was going to help."

She paused. "It's been harder than I thought."

"How's it hard?"

Looking down at her plate, she said, "It has me thinking a lot about my childhood and . . . I don't know. It's hard to explain. I want to get better, I really do."

"So why don't you?"

She swallowed, pressing her fingers against her neck, then shook her head. "It feels like there's something in the way."

"Like what?"

"That's the thing, I don't really know."

"I don't get it," he said, shaking his head. "Why do you keep using your childhood as an excuse for your behavior? Some people still have to deal with their families as grown adults, you know. At least you got to move away."

"Only it feels like I'm still there," she said, her heart beating too fast, her hand clutched around her throat. But when Fadi didn't reply, she realized the words hadn't left her mouth.

27

On the last day of the term, Yara received an email from Jonathan asking her to stop by his office.

The air felt crisp and sharp against her skin as she walked across campus, and she rehearsed her argument as to why he should allow her to teach again. That had to be the reason he wanted to see her, to discuss her contract for the next term, to offer her the course back. She'd gone to all the social coffee and department meetings and hadn't missed a single session with William, even if she had only begun to make use of them. Relax, everything will be okay, she told herself as she took a deep breath and knocked on the half-open door.

"Come in, Yara. Have a seat," Jonathan said from behind his desk.

She did as he said, anxiously studying her short bare nails in her lap while Jonathan cleared his throat.

"I've called you here to talk about the next term," he said.

"Yes," Yara said, looking up now, her argument ready.

Before she could speak he said, "Unfortunately, enrollment has declined and we've had to make a few budget cuts. This is to say, we're unable to renew your teaching contract, and I want you to know that has nothing to do with anything other than our operating expenses on the rise—"

She felt disoriented suddenly, the room spinning. "What about the website, my photographs?" she said, her voice shaking. "What if instead—"

"Yes, about that. The college has decided to outsource this work to a company that can make the site updates on an as-needed basis."

"But my photographs?"

"Yes, they're wonderful. They'll stay—"

"But no new images?"

"I'm sorry, Yara, but the position is no longer one we can afford. You haven't been fired, but your position, it's been—"

"Terminated," Yara finished for him, swallowing a lump in her throat. She wanted to weep.

He reached into his desk drawer and took out a manila file folder. She stared at it, biting her lip and trying to restrain herself from dropping to the floor and curling up in a ball.

"I'm sorry we won't be able to continue working together," Jonathan said, arranging a stack of papers into the file. "If you have any questions, they should be covered in this packet."

She couldn't bring herself to open her mouth as he rubbed the edge of each sheet of paper with his thumb, avoiding her eyes. Finally she said: "I do have one question."

Without looking up, he said: "Sure."

"Were you ever going to let me teach full-time? Or was I just spinning my wheels here for the past four years?"

Jonathan raised his head, cocking it to one side. "Needless to say, academia is a hard place to be right now, especially in a field like yours." He handed her the file, which she snatched from his grasp, without his having answered the question. "This might be overstepping, but I hope you continue to talk to someone. In counseling, I mean."

"I won't be able to see William anymore," Yara said, not asking, but realizing it as fact.

Not wanting to hear him reply—or worse, apologize—she stood and left, pulling the door shut on her way out.

In her office, she gathered her things into a file box. She turned off her camera and slipped it in her bag. She unplugged the coffeemaker, placed it in the box, too, and hoisted the box to her hip. Her books and paintings were too heavy to carry on her own—she'd have to return for those.

On the way to her car, she kept her eyes on the ground, hoping no one would see she was crying. She managed to open her car door and get inside, but her right hand refused to start the ignition. Instead, she sat there listening to the thoughts hammering in her ears. Maybe she should've been content with having a warm bed to sleep in, a roof over her head, a husband who gladly provided for her, who didn't beat her. Maybe Fadi would love her more if she wasn't always trying to prove herself. Maybe she would've had more time to focus on her daughters if she wasn't so obsessed with her accomplishments, making something of herself. What kind of mark on the world was a person like her supposed to leave, anyway? And who did she think she was? She wasn't an artist. She hadn't painted in weeks, months maybe. And she certainly wasn't a professor. She'd only been a part-time instructor. She wasn't even a web designer anymore. And whose fault was that? Was Fadi right? Had she been making excuses?

Something was very wrong, there was no denying it any longer. She had no idea how to be a wife, or how to keep a job. For the first time in her adult life, she felt as scared and powerless as she'd been as a child. And yet she was no longer a child who could be sustained by the possibility of a better life. This was it. This was her life. Her chance to do better. And she was failing.

Tears spilled down her face and she wiped them away quickly, but more came. The colors of the campus all blurred together. It felt as if she was in the middle of a tunnel, one that was blocked on both sides. All these years she'd convinced herself that she was in control of her own life. Yet was she? She'd thought she'd find freedom once she left her parents' home, but she'd been following the prescribed path of all the women before her. Steered by the same fears, confined by the same shame. Except she'd deluded herself into thinking that her life was somehow better than theirs. But it wasn't, and why would it be? She didn't deserve to be happy.

The journal! She looked through the box on the seat beside her. How had she forgotten it? She leaped from the car and ran back toward her office, unlocking it and retrieving the journal from the bottom drawer of her desk. She understood now, wiping at her face, her head down as she speed-walked back to her car.

Her mistake had been to think she could dismiss her family's superstitions, ignore her history. But the past had finally caught up to her.

It was Mama who she needed to talk to most, Mama who could show her the truth.

YARA'S JOURNAL

The phone rings. I peek from the kitchen doorway and watch as you pick up the receiver. Your body stiffens and you take a step back. Your face is white and getting whiter, then you are screaming and screaming and pulling at your hair.

For days after the call from Palestine bringing you the news of Teta's death, you refuse to leave your room. You stay in bed most of every day, crying. The curtains are pulled shut and the room smells like sweat and dirty linen. The boys and I crawl to the foot of your bed, waiting for you to settle. But you only cry and cry, stuffing your face in your pillow and pulling the sheets over your head. I take my brothers back to the kitchen, pour them each a bowl of cereal, and turn on the television, hoping the cartoons will drown out the sound of your suffering.

I'm drawing in my sketch pad at the kitchen table when you finally emerge from your room. It has been a week, maybe more. The house is not clean, but the boys have been fed.

Quietly you slip into the kitchen and fill a bucket with water, a faraway look in your eyes. Sun seeps through the window and fills the room with a harsh yellow light, making your face look gray. You twist a wet rag in the bucket then drop to the floor, squatting as you collect bits of food and dirt in the center of the linoleum. I try to figure out when was the last time you showered, or even washed your face. Your face is stained with kohl and tears, your hair is greasy, and you've been wearing the same bleach-stained nightgown ever since the phone rang. I miss Teta, too, but someone had to care for everyone.

I watch as you crawl across the floor and wipe the linoleum again, then stand and wring out the rag at the sink. Your face is flushed and your eyes swollen and red. I stare at your puffy eyelids, the deep lines that frame your mouth, the look of resignation on your face. The last time I saw you like this was after Baba came back from his trip. A sick feeling passes through me, and I pull myself away from the kitchen table, wanting to wrap my arms around you. To apologize for what I'd done that day. I was so young then, it was as if I were another girl altogether and I am sorry for ever having been that little girl, for not having always taken care of everyone. Of you. But you flinch now at the sight of my face.

"Stay back," you say, sticking your hand out. "The floor is still wet."

I settle back into my seat, afraid. It's the first time I let myself feel how enormous this loss is: my teta, your mama. Our summers in Palestine. We will never go back again. I don't know this then, but I feel it, feel that old world ripped away from us. I rub my eyes at the thought, wiping loose tears.

Still by the sink, you stare blankly into your hands, the running water the only sound in the room. It startles me how much weight you've lost. Your eyes are hollow and your cheeks drawn, making your face look almost skeletal. Just like a painting I've seen somewhere, in one of the art books I used to check out from the school library.

When you finally look up, your eyes are brimming with tears.

"Are you okay, Mama?"

"Marvelous," you say, your voice cracking. Eventually you turn off the faucet and drag a chair across the room and climb it. Only the back of your head is visible to me as you open the cabinet and reach inside. This, I realize, is where you keep the coffee set, the blue-and-white copper one that Teta had given you the last time we were with her.

As if she knew we would never see her again, I think now.

I watch as you take down the intricately painted pieces and stack them on their matching tray. You fill the ibrik with water and set it on the stove, the curve of the pot's spout shining beneath the kitchen's harsh yellow light. As soon as the water comes to a boil, you scoop two spoonfuls of ground coffee from a container on the countertop and place them inside the ibrik, then whisk and stir until the coffee rises and foams over. Watching you, I notice how much your movements are like Teta's, and I wonder if this is your attempt to reach her again, one last time.

At the kitchen table, you pour yourself a cup of coffee, your eyes trained on the steaming liquid. You look down at the cup, your hands shaking, then lift it to your lips and take a sip.

Yunus and Yassir race through the kitchen, shouting at each other, and you flinch again. Your eyes meet mine for the first time in days. "Go stop your brothers' fighting," you snap. As if this is all I am good for.

I do what I am told, as I have for the last four years, desperate to atone for what I did. But you will always blame me. When I return to the kitchen a few minutes later, I find you slumped in your chair, studying the bottom of your empty cup as if in a trance, your fingers clenching and unclenching.

"What's wrong?" I ask, but you don't respond, your eyes fixed on the cup in a flat, unblinking way.

I have seen enough of Teta's readings to know that something is off. What do you see now, what new troubles have been foretold? It was not so long ago that the fortune teller confirmed your curse, and now we have lost Teta and I fear that I have lost you as well. I wonder if I should get you out of the house, get you some fresh air, but I dread a possible confrontation. A shiver runs along my jaw when I open my mouth, but I try to keep my voice soft. "Mama," I say. "Do you want to go to the park?"

"No."

"Then how about a walk around the neighborhood?"

Slowly you reach for the ibrik, your fingers trembling as you pour yourself another serving of coffee. "I don't feel like going anywhere," you snap.

I try to keep my voice low and gentle. "But you've been home for days, Mama. We need to do something."

You set the cup down and stand, snapping your eyes at me. "Do something?" you say, your upper lip quivering. "Look around, Yara. What exactly do you expect me to do here?"

I inch back, unable to look away from the electricity in your eyes, the thick blue vein bulging in your forehead.

"My mother is dead and I couldn't be with her," you continue, your voice growing angrier. "I was stuck here with you, like always. Mama, Mama, Mama, I need this, Mama, do this. Do something? Why? When I do anything, you complain. When I am happy . . ." You trail off, falling back into the chair. "When I was happy, you ruined everything. Why can't you just be grateful?"

"I am grateful," I whisper, stumbling backward, my back now pinned against a wall. "I am."

You stare at me, your eyes on fire. "Then act like it."

"I'm sorry," I say, looking up at you, afraid. I know this anger, the way it simmers before it explodes. I have seen it before, in Baba, in you. As if you have sensed my thoughts, you sweep your arm forward in one smooth motion, sending the coffee cups—Teta's beautiful cups—tumbling from the table, and one, still full with hot liquid, at my chest. The coffee strikes my throat, my shoulder, it runs down my skin, but in this moment I feel nothing but regret. Oh, how I want you back, the happy you, the Mama I can barely remember anymore.

That is when you drop to your knees with a thud and stick out your hands, palms turned upward, as though you are praying. Your body is trembling as you scream at God, "What did I do to deserve a selfish, ungrateful daughter? She ruined my life. I wish she was never born."

I am shaking my head, bending toward you, knowing what you are doing, how you are blaming me for everything now. "No, Mama! Please don't say that. Please!"

But you won't stop. You hold your palms up to the ceiling and recite: "Allah yighdab aleki." You say these words again and again, drawing them out like a dark melody. "May God curse you with a terrible life, a punishment for being a terrible, terrible daughter."

28

After the girls had gone to bed, Yara wrapped herself in a coat and retreated to the back deck. Moving lightly on the wooden swing, she stared blankly into a dark sea of empty trees. She couldn't bear to hear a human sound: not the shuffle of Fadi's shoes by the front door, or the rumble of her daughters' footsteps if they got out of bed and ran to greet him, or their pleading for him to tuck them in again. But she was grateful for the winter hum of trees moving in the howling wind, their thick rustling loud enough to drown her thoughts. She was lost in these sounds when Fadi opened the back door.

Around them the sky had gone dark, the warm milky glow of the full moon shining bright. He walked over and leaned down to kiss her cheek. "Hey, how was your day?"

"It was okay," she said slowly. "How was yours?"

"Good. Glad to finally be home."

She said nothing, staring ahead. Was she hearing the yips and howls of coyotes or the pounding of her heart?

"Are the girls asleep already?" he said.

"I just put them down."

"Oh, okay." He took a step back, rubbing his neck, as if he was confused that she hadn't gotten up. "Dinner smells delicious," he said. "I could smell it as soon as I walked in."

She nodded and closed her eyes. "Thanks."

"What did you make?"

"Lentil soup."

"Great, I can't wait."

She looked up at the moon, big and bright in the dark sky. "It's beautiful," she said. "A full one tonight."

Fadi looked up. "I hadn't noticed." He turned back to her. "You okay?"

"I'm fine." She kept her eyes fixed above. "I'm always in such a rush that I never stop to appreciate it."

"Can you appreciate it tomorrow? I've had a long day and I'm starving. There's a new episode of *Chicago P.D.* tonight."

Her heart sank, and she turned to him. "That's all we do, isn't it? Work and watch our shows."

He shrugged. "I guess so. Are you sure you're okay?"

It was quiet, and their voices sliced through the thick air. "Jonathan didn't renew my contract for next term for my teaching," she said, as quietly as she could. "And he's going to outsource the design work."

"Oh," Fadi said. "I'm sorry. But look at the bright side. It's not like they paid you much for all the time you put in."

She managed to meet his eyes. "It wasn't really about the money."

"Then what was it about?"

She sighed. Even if she found a way to articulate it to Fadi, what difference would it make? "Nothing. It doesn't matter anymore."

"Seriously. Don't worry about it," he said. "You don't need that stupid job anyway. I'm here. Besides, there are plenty of things to keep you busy at home," he said. "Taking care of the girls, all the meals, not to mention the house. My mother will be pleased," he added playfully. "You'll be able to do more with her now."

He grinned at her, but she exhaled, clenching her teeth. "Is that what you want? More cooking and cleaning? More time with your mother?"

"Relax," Fadi said. "I was only kidding. I just meant you do a lot already, and I really appreciate it."

Without looking up at him, she asked, "You appreciate me? Or the things I do?"

Out of the corner of her eye, she could see him shaking his head slowly. "Why do you always twist my words?"

When she said nothing, he turned to leave, mumbling, "I don't have time for your bullshit right now."

The air had turned cooler and she started to shiver as she stared past the whispering pines and into the inky darkness. All these years she had succeeded in keeping herself remote from most people, distant enough that no one could hurt her. But she had let Fadi close enough to see her pain, and here he was, incapable of seeing her.

29

The next morning, on the ride to school, Mira and Jude bickered in the backseat over a Barbie doll. Mira wanted to dress her in a gown. Jude said she liked her better in overalls. Yara gritted her teeth, her hands cramping on the steering wheel, before making eye contact with Jude in the rearview mirror and quickly softening her expression. It occurred to her that both girls were constantly watching her: every move she made, every reaction, every word she said and didn't say. They were studying her the same way she had studied Mama, observing and learning by example. What had Yara taught them over the years? What kind of example had she set? Embarrassed, she refocused her gaze on the road.

After she dropped them off, she drove to campus to pack up the rest of her belongings, which Jonathan had said she could do anytime that week. Inside her office, she emptied the drawers and boxed up the books on the shelves, then took down her paintings from the wall. She'd messaged Silas that morning telling him what had happened, and he'd said he'd stop by to help her move her things.

"I'm sorry, Yara," Silas said now. "I wish there was something I could do." He had just finished loading the last of the boxes of books into her car, and he was standing in the cleared-out office looking at her.

"Being here is more than enough," Yara said. "Thank you."

"Of course." He was quiet for a moment, then said, "Do you need help looking for another job?"

She shrugged. "I don't really know what I want to do next. To be honest, I never really cared for anything I did here besides teaching."

"I never would've guessed. You were so good at all the photo and video stuff," he said. "So would you try to find another teaching job?"

"I'm not sure. I loved a lot about teaching, especially introducing students to new worlds, but I think I was mostly drawn to it because it made sense for me as a mom, and not because it was my dream."

The words surprised her as they came out of her mouth, but they rang true. She wasn't truly utilizing her imagination and creative impulses at her job, hadn't been using art for self-expression, vulnerability, and growth. And maybe that was her problem: she'd abandoned what she really loved in the first place.

"So what *are* you passionate about?" said Silas. "If you could have any job in the world, what would it be?"

Yara frowned. "That kind of wishful thinking has never gotten me anywhere," she said, then, changing the subject, "But what about you? What would *you* do?"

"Easy," Silas said. "If I didn't have my daughter here and bills to pay, I would travel the world and eat."

"That's an actual job?"

"Sure it is. Food critic for a magazine or newspaper."

"Seriously? That's what I would do, too, then."

He laughed. "Come on. You can't copy my answer."

"Traveling the world and eating the finest food in every country? It's like a dream come true."

"Okay, fine. But what would you *really* want to do, Yara?"

"Right," she said. "Hmm, let's see."

She didn't know, except that she wanted to do work that made a significant difference, that left the world a better place. The thought sounded too foolish and naive to articulate aloud, but Yara was clear that she didn't want to waste her limited years on this earth in an endless, self-defeating pursuit of money and status, that what she wanted wasn't only work but a meaningful existence. To live a life that was inspired, creative, free. Maybe that was why she felt a need to travel, to find out what she was supposed to be doing, to discover what else was out there.

"During my first year of college, I briefly considered becoming a lawyer," she finally told Silas. "I didn't have access to art growing up, had never seriously considered it as a career, and so when I was deciding on majors I thought being a lawyer would help me feel more powerful and safe in the world." Perhaps she would've looked different on the outside, with shiny hair and a well-tailored skirt or pantsuit. But her insides would've been the same, unable to alleviate the emptiness she felt within. "I don't think I would've found it fulfilling, though."

"Why not?" Silas asked.

For a moment, she considered telling Silas about Mama's curse, how it had tainted everything for her, all her life, that no job or career would undo that. But instead she said, "To be honest, I've been thinking a lot about what my purpose is. For years I was fixated on landing a successful career and proving myself to my family and community. But now I'm beginning to wonder if I've been focusing on the wrong thing."

Silas nodded. "It's not too late to shift your focus, if that's how you feel."

"Except I have no idea how. Or to what."

He stared at her, and she looked away, feeling exposed.

"Will you continue seeing someone?" Silas asked. "Sorry, I know it's not my place to ask, but it might be helpful as you figure things out."

Yara stood by the window, stared up at the cloudy sky. "I'm not sure if it would," she said. "I've been meeting with William all semester, and so little has changed."

Silas moved to the window, turning to look at her. "It can take a while to see the benefits of therapy, and that's perfectly normal. I can help you look for a new therapist, if you'd like."

She felt a sharp pain in her chest and rubbed her palm against it. "I know I have to do something," she said, meeting his eyes. "But the last thing I need is another stranger judging me."

"I know this feels like a lot," Silas said. "There's always other things to do if you're not ready for more therapy. Meditation, journaling . . . even just talking to a friend. I'll be here."

"Thank you," Yara said.

She smiled at him, then glanced over his shoulder at the gray clouds suspended over the horizon. Maybe journaling would help. Even if going back there wouldn't make her feel better, it couldn't possibly make her feel worse than she had during the past few months, trying to resist the memories as they bubbled up. Maybe writing about those dark places was the first step.

As she said goodbye to Silas in the parking lot, she felt her chest expanding with hope—or was it fear? The choices in her life felt like roads, all looping back to the same destination. But it was in her hands to steer the wheel, her decision alone how far she could go.

30

Back at home, the house was unnaturally still. Inside her sunroom, sunlight streamed through the windows, but the room had been filled with more of Fadi's boxes from work.

Yara had unpacked her office things—her paintings, her camera, a few boxes of her books—by stacking them in the corner, moving a few of Fadi's boxes outside the doorway to make room. She walked in and out of the sunroom, pacing from box to box, feeling a lump in her throat. This had been her space, but she'd let it go because she'd had the office at school. She hadn't noticed him taking over her room.

Later, as she waited inside her car for dismissal, she picked up her phone and opened Instagram, desperate to relieve the pounding in her head. On the home grid, images and videos were arranged neatly on the screen in squares and rectangles: striped gondoliers floating beneath spectacular arched bridges, crystal blue waters and white pebble beaches, a marble courtyard covered in mosaics of flowers. For a while she sat scrolling, her eyes dimming and widening at images from around the world, stopping every now and then to examine one in detail.

She pulled on her sweater, shivering inside the car. Closing her eyes, she pictured herself in Palestine, between hillsides scattered with red slanted roofs, hundreds of olive trees, and the glistening Dead Sea in the distance. With her eyes still shut, she transported herself to Egypt, imagining the heat of the sun on her face as she stood before the great Pyramids, the yellow limestone beneath her fingertips as she explored narrow corridors and hidden chambers. Then in Spain, picking fruit in the terraced vineyards and cliffside lemon groves, then Italy, overlooking the rugged shoreline dotted with charming beaches and pastel-colored fishing villages. As she pictured a small, old town and placed herself inside it, she heard a soft rapping noise. Opening her eyes, she realized it had begun to rain. Water trickled against the window and slid down the glass, clearing all her dreams as it went. She sighed. There was so much out there she wanted to see, so much of herself she had yet to discover.

Then something occurred to her. What if there was a bigger reason that she'd lost her job? What if it was for her to go somewhere, finally?

That night, Fadi came home as Mira and Jude were brushing their teeth, preparing for bed. After they read the girls a bedtime story, Yara paced around the kitchen as she considered how best to approach the subject. Using another of Teta's recipes, she'd made fried kibbeh—balls of glistening ground beef stuffed with bulgur, pine nuts, and warm spices. She plated the kibbeh with dollops of tzatziki on the side, her hands shaking. Breathing in and out, she pictured herself roaming the mazelike alleyways of Morocco until she felt her body relax.

Maybe she should set the table tonight, she thought, and make their meal special. It wouldn't hurt to try something new. When she finished drying off from their shower, though, Fadi was already in bed, sitting up as he fiddled with the remote. His hair was still wet, his beard freshly trimmed.

"Do you want to have dinner at the table tonight?" Yara said, raising her voice so as to be heard over the television.

"I really just want to watch our show," Fadi said. "Do you mind?"

She shook her head and went back to the kitchen, where she grabbed their plates and returned to the bedroom. Forcing her mouth into a smile, she handed him his dinner and took a seat on the bed beside him.

"This smells amazing," Fadi said. With his fingers, he lifted a kibbeh to his mouth and took a bite. "Wow, it tastes even better." He set his plate on his lap for a moment, then flicked through the seasons for the most recent episode.

Yara took a quick sip of water, wiped her palms against her thighs, and cleared her throat. "It felt weird not having to go to work today," she said.

"Lucky you," Fadi said, setting down the remote. "I can't remember the last time I had a whole day with nothing to do."

She ignored the dig. "You know, I was pretty bummed out about losing my job, but after having a little time to clear my head, I realized you have a point."

"Oh yeah?"

"I couldn't picture myself as someone who stayed at home, but I started thinking: maybe this is a chance for me to learn more about myself, you know?"

Fadi nodded, then set his fork down and took a sip of water. Swallowing, he said, "I'm glad you're finally seeing that. I told you, you don't need to worry about making money. And besides, you do a lot for this family. I don't ever want you to feel like you're not valuable." He bit into another kibbeh. "Your cooking alone is out of this world."

"That's nice of you to say," Yara said. "Thank you."

He picked up the remote again, but before he could start the episode, she reached over and placed a hand on his arm. "I've been thinking, though," she said. "Our tenth anniversary is in May. Maybe we should do something special?"

Fadi whistled. "Ten years already? That was fast."

"Time does seem to get away from us with everything we have going on," she said, "which got me thinking: Why don't we take a trip somewhere to celebrate? The weather in May is perfect almost everywhere."

"Maybe we can go to New York," Fadi said. "We can see your family."

"I think we can do better than that."

"What do you mean?"

Yara had been mulling it over all afternoon. She didn't want to lose out on another chance to travel. And it didn't seem right not to celebrate this milestone with something special. Besides, Fadi had promised they would.

"Let's have an adventure, go someplace new," Yara said. "Italy, maybe? We could visit the ruins in Rome, and see the Sistine Chapel. Or France? I've always wanted to go to the Louvre."

Fadi took another sip of water. After a pause, he said: "That sounds really nice, but we're not in a place to take a trip like that right now, you know?"

"I know," Yara said, too quickly. "Flights can be expensive, but hear me out. I can take on some freelance photography work, or sell a few paintings, or something. With all this free time I have, there's plenty I can do to chip in."

He shook his head. "Trust me, I make more than enough to take you anywhere you want to go."

Yara looked at him. "If it's not about the money, then what is it?"

"The warehouse gets really busy in May," he said. "And I'm not at a place where I can just leave it behind and jet off to Europe. I'm sorry, I know this means a lot to you, but it might not be a good time."

"But it's still five months away. You might be in a better place by then, don't you think?"

"I don't know."

"Please, don't say no just yet," Yara said. "We need this trip. I know you think this is all about me, and it's true that I've dreamed of traveling since I was a little girl. But it's about us, too. We could use this time to just be together and reconnect. Just think about it, please?" She tried to meet his eyes, touching her hand to his. "That's all I'm asking."

Looking over at her at last, Fadi smiled. "Okay, I'll think about it."

YARA'S JOURNAL

In the last memory I have of Teta, we are sitting together on the rooftop. Around us, fabric on laundry lines dances in the cool breeze and sunshine slices through the rows of vegetable patches. Teta is watering her plants and telling me about the nakba. I walk behind her, one hand up to my face to block out the sun. Though she's told me the story many times before, I lean closer, hungry to hear it anew. I do not yet understand my grandmother's need to retell the events of the day, her obsession with speaking the words aloud, as though desperate for someone to validate her experience. I have not yet learned what she has, that refusing to acknowledge a pain endured hurts worse than the pain itself.

"After the Israeli planes bombed the olive trees," Teta began, "the soldiers gave us thirty minutes to leave our home. I remember watching my mother turn off the stove before leaving the house. My father locked the front door and clutched the house key, as if certain we would return soon. It seems so foolish now, looking back. But what we were experiencing was unfathomable." She frowns, pushing out the words slowly. "Can you imagine someone breaking into your home, on land you've lived on for generations, and forcing you to leave?"

I look at her in disbelief. Even thinking about her loss fills me with so much sorrow, I can't bear to imagine how she might have felt living through it.

"What happened after that?" I ask, though I already know.

"Our family came here, to Balata," Teta says, waving her hands around

them. "The camp was overcrowded and cramped. Our tent was the size of a small room, barely large enough to fit the seven of us. But when winter came, I was thankful to be huddled close with my brothers and sisters in the freezing cold. Outside thousands of tents were stacked up against one another like a deck of cards. You could see them stretched out into the distance. Laundry lines connected each tent to the next. Children walked on the earth barefoot. The winters were harsh, the summers blazing. We barely had enough food and water, never mind electricity, roads, or sewers. We stood in lines for hours at the UN getting rice and blankets. The smell of rot surrounded us and it felt as though we were living inside a dead body.

"By the time I was fifteen, most of the tents in our camp had been replaced with huts made from concrete blocks, like this one," Teta continues, gesturing to the space around them. "We're still crammed together, but it's better than the tents. When they built these shelters, they also built water sources, schools, clinics, and centers. I remember feeling so happy at the possibility of a new house, not having to carry water buckets over my head, even someday going to school. But my father only cried. He knew it meant we would never return home."

"Wait a minute," I say. I look around, scanning the graffitied buildings, narrow alleyways, and lines covered in drying laundry. Some of the windows are covered with plastic, and cigarette butts litter the ground. "This is where the tents were?"

"Yes," she said, holding back tears. "Though the tents are long gone, it's still the same place."

"Why haven't you ever left?" I ask.

"I used to wonder the same thing," Teta says. "My father said that if we gave up on the camp, it meant we'd given up on our right of return. He wanted to go back to Yaffa, where his grandparents and great-grandparents were born. He was right, you know. Even after he died, I couldn't give up and leave. We could never belong anywhere else. Yaffa is who we are."

Back inside, Teta reaches into her drawer and pulls out a rusted wrought iron key. Slowly she hands it to me.

It's much heavier than it looks and feels cold between my fingers. "What is this?" I ask.

"The key to our home."

"Wow, I can't believe you still have this."

"My father held on to it for so many years, hoping we would someday return," Teta says. "When he passed away I kept it, too, in case he was right. He wouldn't have wanted me to lose hope. I don't even remember what Yaffa looks like. When I close my eyes, I can barely picture the sparkle of the Dead Sea, the fig-colored rooftops, the wild orange trees. I try to think of better days, but all I can seem to remember is rot and mud and, all around us, the smell of death."

I look at her but do not know what to say. For a few seconds we just sit there in stillness, the sound of chirping birds all around us. I wonder if I will ever understand what it means to experience this kind of suffering and loss.

"Do you think you can ever go back?" I ask.

Teta covers her face, avoiding my eyes. Quietly she says: "Even though I've lived in this camp for over fifty years now, I was raised with the hope of returning to my homeland, and I still have that hope. And if I don't, maybe my children will return, maybe my grandchildren, maybe you. That's why I've kept this key all these years."

Her eyes glaze over, as though slipping into a bad dream. Watching her miserable expression, I feel a certain pressure in my temples and my eyes blur. I swallow and look away, chewing my lower lip.

"Teta," I say.

"Yes, habibti."

"Do you think one day you can give the key to Mama, so that she can pass it along to me?" I feel my face screwing up, then the warmth of tears slipping down my cheeks.

"Oh, habibti, don't cry. Come here," Teta says too quickly, pulling me into her lap. She smells like sage and mint, a hint of cumin. "Of course I will. That's why I held on to the past so strongly. I want our identity—who we are—to live on. It's already enough that our people are homeless and nameless. But our history runs through our veins. We can't let them take that away from us, too. And they won't. As long as we continue to share our stories, our history will be remembered."

31

What do you want to do today?" Yara asked Mira and Jude on the first day of Christmas break, as they were finishing breakfast at the kitchen table. Their winter vacation was twelve days long this year. Fadi had to work his regular schedule, so Yara spent most of this time with them alone, as she did most years. This was another reason why working at the college had been so convenient: her breaks usually coincided with theirs.

At once Mira and Jude began shouting suggestions. Movie theater. Bowling. Shopping (Mira's idea, which Jude protested).

"Can we go to the library?" Mira asked, looking up at her with hopeful eyes.

"The library? Seriously?" said Jude, crossing her arms. "Let's do something fun."

"That is fun."

Yara smiled as she watched them bicker with each other: Mira bouncing up and down in her grass-stained sneakers, and Jude standing there with her eyebrows scrunched, as though she were trying to solve a mystery.

"What about ice-skating?" Jude finally said.

"Yes!" Mira said, round-eyed, and in the next breath she turned to Yara. "Can we go ice- skating, Mama? Please?"

Looking at her daughters' eager faces, she felt a rush of desire to make them happy. "Sure, why not?" she said. "Let's go."

They threw their arms around her, squealing in delight, and as Yara held them tight, a warm comfort spread through her.

Outside the weather was cold and gray, but her small town came alive in the winter. The sights, sounds, and smells of the season were all around them, in the brisk chill of winter swirls, the cheery lights and glowing shingles and shrubbery, the pine and cinnamon perfuming the air. After two hours of skating, they had lunch together at the local bakery, where they ordered cheese biscuits and hot cocoa to warm them up. Afterward, Yara pushed a cart through the bright aisles of her local grocery store, gathering all the ingredients to make the girls' favorite holiday snacks: rice pudding, gingerbread men, and maamoul—buttery shortbread cookies filled with dates and nuts.

It wasn't difficult for Yara to find things to do with the girls for the next twelve days. All week they watched movies, rode carousels, and strolled through quaint shops selling everything from gifts, paintings, and sculptures to housewares. On the weekend before Christmas Eve, they went to see the festive lights downtown, and afterward they watched fireworks and an accompanying tree-lighting ceremony with cups of hot cocoa and fresh-baked gingerbread cookies in hand. On the drive home, Yara played their favorite songs, and they all sang along loudly, not wanting the day to end. She tucked them in that night feeling lighter than usual, as though this time with them had brought them closer together, recharged them.

One sunny morning soon after the break ended, Yara dropped the girls off at school and drove to Josephine's house. Silas had texted her, asking if she wanted to try out one of his new recipes, and when she arrived, he was pulling a pie out of the oven.

"It smells so good in here," Yara said, walking over to the sink to wash her hands. "What are you making?"

"A sweet potato and onion tart. It's my grandmother's recipe."

"I can't wait to try it. Thanks for inviting me."

Silas smiled. "Of course. I hope you'll stay for lunch after the taste test. I'm making shrimp and grits."

Yara looked around the kitchen, remembering that Josephine was at work. "Are you sure Josephine's okay with that? I don't want to impose."

"Impose?" he said. "I haven't seen you in a couple of weeks and you turn polite on me?"

Yara laughed, blushing. "Fine, I'll stay."

"This looks amazing," she said as Silas plated two slices of tart and carried them to the table. "I feel like I haven't seen you in ages. What's going on with the case?"

"It's good so far," he said, pulling out a chair for her. "My court date is at the end of the month, and I'm a little nervous."

"Of course you are. I would be, too," Yara said. "But you're a good dad. The judge will see that."

"You think so?"

"I know so. You got this."

"Thanks," he said, smiling. "So, what do you think?" he asked after they'd taken a bite of the tart. "Any good?"

"It's delicious. The Gruyère adds a lot of depth. By the way," she said, reaching into her bag, "I made this for Josephine."

She set a clear Tupperware container on the table, and he pulled it up to eye level and peered inside. Glancing up at her, he said playfully: "Nothing for me?"

She laughed, pulling out another container. "I made some for you, too, don't worry."

"You better have," he said, lifting the lid to release the scent of cinnamon and rosewater. He met her eyes. "Oh my God, is this baklava?"

Yara nodded. "I hope she likes it."

He took out a piece and popped it in his mouth. Licking his fingers, he said, "That's if I decide to give it to her." She laughed. "You have to teach me how to make this," he said.

"Sure. I have loads of time now."

"What have you been up to?"

"The girls have been on break for a couple of weeks, but besides that, I've been painting, reading, and spending time with them. Nothing major, but it feels good to slow down a little."

Each morning, after the girls returned to school, Yara couldn't get over the weird feeling that she had nothing to do until pickup. Some mornings she drove to a bakery, where she sat by the window eating a warm croissant and sipping a cappuccino. She'd spend the rest of the morning sketching or reading, head bowed, looking up only when it was time to go. Other days she stayed at home and painted before heading to the grocery store, buying supplies for dinner, and returning home to do a load of laundry before she had to get the girls.

"Sounds nice," Silas said.

"It is," Yara said, tucking a strand of hair behind her ear. "I've also been journaling."

"Really? That's great," he said, biting into another piece of baklava. "What about?"

The question would have been intrusive coming from anyone else, yet Yara felt completely at ease with Silas. "Stuff from the past, memories mostly. William had suggested that maybe I should write a letter, but . . ." She paused. "Remembering certain things is much harder than I thought."

"I'm so sorry," Silas said. "I had no idea."

Yara nodded but said nothing. Silas seemed to take this as permission to continue. "I remember the times I tried to tell my family I was gay," he said, now staring fixedly ahead. "I was so terrified. I couldn't let go of this picture of my life as they wanted it for me."

"What made you finally do it?"

"One day I woke up and looked in the mirror and thought: how many more years of my life am I going to waste running away from myself? That night, I sat my parents down and told them."

"What happened?"

"They were shocked and confused at first. I mean, I'd married a woman and had a daughter, and even though I was teased as a kid, it had never crossed their minds that I might be gay. But we kept talking. It wasn't easy for them at first, but eventually they were supportive. I honestly don't know what I would've done without them the last few years."

Yara shifted in her seat, a heaviness coming over her body. "That's really nice," she heard herself say, but she felt tears streaming down her face.

"Oh, Yara. I'm sorry. I didn't mean to make you cry."

"No, please." She wiped her cheeks. "It's not your fault. Really. Apparently I love crying at Josephine's house."

He laughed, then slowly reached out to take her hand. She started to pull back, but then stopped and let him. A warm tingling started in her chest and spread outward, infusing her body with an unfamiliar comfort. For a moment, glancing up to meet his eyes, Yara felt like a little girl again, reaching for one of her brothers and holding on tight.

"That was really brave of you," she eventually said. "Coming out to your parents. I wish I was that brave."

"But you are," Silas said. "We all are. Sometimes the fear just takes over and we lose sight of what matters most."

"That's the thing. I'm not sure what exactly I'm so afraid of."

"Understanding yourself is the hardest part," Silas said. "But maybe now that you're journaling, it won't feel so scary. Maybe getting your feelings out on paper will help."

Yara started laughing.

"What's so funny?" he said, turning pink.

"You sound just like William."

When Yara got home, she pulled out her journal and flipped to a new page. A jolt ran through her body. Silas was right. She had to be brave. The memories were incredibly painful, but if she continued living as she had, running in place, avoiding them, she would always feel this way, as if she'd been trapped under a curse from which she could never escape.

Trembling, she reached for the journal again and opened it. Slowly she picked up the pencil, bringing it to the paper. Her heart raced as she wrote one word, then another, then another, her fingers tightening with each loop. She paused to catch her breath, looking down at the page. The letter, to Mama. At the top, it said:

I don't know why I'm writing this.

For a second, she wanted to stop and rip the page from the journal, then tear it to shreds. But she took a deep breath instead. She had to go back there, even if it hurt. Maybe if she pushed through the pain, she'd reach the other side, a place where she didn't feel so afraid. Maybe if she learned how to express herself to Mama, she'd be able to articulate what it was she was running from. Maybe then she'd finally be able to forgive her mother. Maybe she could even forgive herself.

She put her pencil to paper, ready to begin.

YARA'S JOURNAL

Dear Mama,

This is my attempt to make sense of my childhood relationship with you, and how it's affected all the years that followed, staining every thought I ever had about marriage and motherhood and children and love, about grief and regret, about isolation and despair, about all the ways we close ourselves up from the world because we are afraid, about this feeling I have had since I was a little girl, one that I have carried with me into adulthood, into motherhood. How freeing would it be to finally release it? To have it fall away? To live my life without it?

In my first memory of how this feeling started, I am nine years old and I am in bed, wishing that I was dead. I can still feel the damp cotton pillowcase against my face, the salty taste of tears running down my cheeks, the throb in the center of my head. I didn't want to hurt myself, nor would I have. But the thought of being alive felt more painful than death could be.

As I got older, I imagined all the ways I could stop feeling. I would lie in bed, you and Baba's voices booming on the other side of the door, and I would dream up the ways it could happen. Cancer, the kind that spreads in days. A stroke while I was asleep. A fatal car crash.

I never managed to die, though. I made it out of that house, started a new life, put it all behind me.

Or at least this is what I've been telling myself all these years.

32

For most of January, it rained and rained. Yara spent her mornings cleaning and running errands with her sweatshirt hood pulled over her head, her skin smelling of cold weather and Clorox. As soon as she was done, she'd retreat to the sunroom with her journal until it was time for pickup. She had pushed Fadi's work supplies to one side to make room for a chair, then propped her feet up on one of the shorter stacks of boxes. Rain rapped against the window as she stared down at the page, unable to fully surrender to her memories. Purposefully dwelling on and dissecting old scenes made her feel raw, like tugging at a scab that hadn't fully healed. Still, she had the sense that perhaps she could trap all her sadness inside her notebook and finally be free of it.

One afternoon, she took the girls to the library for their usual afterschool routine. In the reading section, they leaned in close to her on the rug, warming her like a soft sweater. Jude wanted to read a funny story, but the book they'd ended up with was more sad than funny. In it, a young girl spends her summer searching for her mother, but because of her dog (who's named after a supermarket), and the new friends she makes along the way, she learns to let go and forgive. As Yara read the words aloud, her eyes burned, but she was grateful that Mira and Jude were too absorbed in the story to notice. They moved even closer to her as she turned the pages, their hair grazing her skin.

On the drive home, she played a Fairuz song through the speakers, hoping she could feel Mama's touch through the melody. The girls were in a cheerful mood, singing along and dancing in their seats. At a traffic light, Yara turned to see Mira twisting her braids and Jude swaying from side to side, smiling to show her new front teeth coming through. Listening to the refrain, Yara was transported back to her days at home with Mama, who'd spent every moment singing until her voice got smaller and smaller. In the last times Mama had sung, Yara had wondered why she sounded so sad. She'd been afraid to speak, to interrupt, not wanting her to stop. But she had stopped anyway. It was as if her sorrow had sucked the melody out of her slowly, very slowly, until eventually she had no music left.

Tears slipped down Yara's face. She could no longer ignore the ache Mama had left inside of her, all the ways in which she'd never recovered. The next thing she knew, the girls were saying, "Why are you crying, Mama?"

They were talking to her, of course, but the way they said *Mama* made her insides burn.

"I'm sorry, babies," Yara said, quickly wiping her face. "I'm just having a sad day."

They both looked at her, their eyebrows knotted, and she felt a tightness in her chest that wouldn't loosen. Pulling up the memories was painful, but in the process something was becoming very clear to Yara: she didn't want her daughters to feel an ounce of this hurt, and if facing her past would help her find a way out of it, then she would keep doing it, no matter what.

When she finally pulled into the driveway, Yara unfastened her seat belt and turned to face them. "I love you," she said, holding back new tears. "You know that, don't you? I love you so much."

Mira and Jude nodded and said they loved her, too, and Yara started to cry again because it was the sweetest sound she'd ever heard.

Later that night, after she put the girls to bed and had dinner with Fadi, she wished him good night and retreated to the sunroom, desperate to pick up where she'd left off in her journal.

But standing in the doorway, seeing how Fadi's boxes were taking up more than half the room, an unsettled feeling washed over her. It swept her up, tossed her upside down. She rolled up the sleeves to her nightgown and squatted down by one of the boxes. She tried to pick it up, but her hands were shaking too badly. She attempted a few deep breaths, then caught sight of her pale reflection in the darkened glass and looked away.

Then she managed to lift the box and carry it into the living room, setting it down with a loud thud.

YARA'S JOURNAL

I'm in bed, the way I often am on nights like this: crunched up into a tight ball, the covers pulled up to my shoulders, my heart beating so fast. The room is small and dark, only a sliver of moonlight streaming through the window, and a thin slice of yellow light peeking from the slightly open bedroom door. Behind it, a steady rise of voices gets louder.

You and Baba are fighting again. Ever since what I'd done, your fights have gotten louder, more intense. I can see your silhouettes through the crack in the door and hear your voices crashing. I wonder if my brothers are able to sleep. The twins' bed is in your room, but the four of us big kids share this room with two bunk beds: Yousef and I on one side; Yunus and Yassir the other. I have the top bunk because I like to look out the window as I fall asleep. It's beautiful, and also a bit sad for me to see the inky blue darkness, like a painting, and so many stars stretched out in the distance, seemingly endless.

Looking out there, I am reminded that there is so much I'll never get the chance to see. I know that when I get older, my life won't be much different than yours. I'll be expected to cook and clean for my brothers, and later, my husband. I can go to college, possibly—I've seen some women do that. I can be a teacher or a nurse, maybe even open a small business. But I know I can't be a surgeon, or a CEO, or a world-famous painter with exhibits around the globe, or anything that interferes with my duties as a wife and mother.

I close my eyes now and hear other sounds: a loud thud, a crash against the wall, then a strangled cough, like someone is choking, holding on to a last breath. I stuff my head beneath my pillow to drown them out. But it's as if the sounds have crawled into bed with me, found their way beneath my skin.

Another thud, louder this time, then I hear you wailing. I want to help you, but I can't lift my body off the mattress. My skin tingles and my face burns, as though someone has set me on fire. Breathing hard, I attempt my usual routine on nights like this: I fix my eyes on the room's pale wallpaper—white irises with green stems, metallic glimmers across the borders, tiny blue birds—until I float up into a cloud and everything goes white.

But before I reach the cloud, as I watch my brothers sound asleep beside me and the open sky shimmering through the window, I hear your screams and see your face and wonder if I can ever be free.

33

Yara was surprised to find that she started slipping her notebook into her bag and carrying it with her everywhere. She found herself pulling it out whenever her mind raced: in the waiting room at the doctor's office, in the carpool line, evenings when Fadi was still at work and the girls were playing happily upstairs. But mostly she wrote in her sunroom, where she settled behind her desk and opened her notebook—trying to ignore the boxes scattered all around the room, the baggage of her life strewn all around her. With enormous effort she willed herself to look away, planning to remove more boxes later.

In the privacy of the pages, she tried to recall as many memories as she could. Some were scary to put down, like they might leap off the page and come after her. Others were scattered and blurry, and she couldn't be totally sure they had happened. But she pushed through the pain, writing until she found herself depleted. She needed to keep getting back there.

Two years ago, even two months ago, she would not have allowed herself to sit there, open to attack. But she was surprised to find that the act of writing filled her with a certain validation and sense of relief. At her desk, pieces of the past rushed through her head like loose photographs: A sweaty day at McKinley Park, Mama sitting on a bench, the sun dancing on her face. A basketball dribbling against the asphalt, the noise pounding in her ears. Her brothers laughing as they descended the slide. Mama's face turned away from them, her eyes fixed on someone in the distance.

She recorded the images diligently in her notebook, determined to find a way for a set of words to sum up unbearable feelings. Every time she filled a new page, she felt as if a vessel had been emptied, followed by a sense of safety, knowing that her memories were contained. Writing had the effect of a spell, taking her out of her usual dread. She drove her girls to school with a small smile on her face, and when she picked them up, it was still there. The motions of everyday life seemed more manageable. It wasn't as difficult to speak to the girls, touch them, put her phone down and look them in the eyes, repeat *I love you.* When they complained to her or bickered with each other, it wasn't as hard to pause, take a breath, and control her impulse to snap at them. She could tell they noticed and were relieved by her unusual calmness.

As she wrote and wrote, it became clear to her how much energy she'd expended suppressing her inner chaos over the years. Her mind and body had been locked in that fight, and it had kept her from being fully present in the world. She had organized her life as if her past was still happening, as if she was still anticipating an attack.

But through her writing, she was beginning to feel a new agency. She'd spent her life running from her memories and now she was running toward them. It was painful, yes, but she had more control now. The memories were no longer knocking on her door uninvited. She had opened the door and let them in.

YARA'S JOURNAL

The night after we go to see the fortune teller, you cook dinner without any music playing. I watch you standing silently by the sink in your faded nightgown while a pot of okra stew simmers on the stovetop. I'm not sure why you are making bamya again. Last week, Baba took one bite of it and flung his plate across the table. I was shocked, not at the bright red sauce splattered across the linoleum, but at your reaction. You stood there with your arms crossed, seeming amused. When Baba started shouting, his eyes flashing as he called you all sorts of names, I thought you would retreat to the kitchen sink to grab a rag. But instead you spat at him, and a shiny thick glob of saliva landed smack in the middle of his cheek. I stared at you with my heart beating in my throat. Baba rose and took a step forward, curling his fists, before catching my eyes from across the room. Quickly he grabbed his keys and stormed out of the house. He didn't come back till morning.

In the kitchen now, you cover the steaming pot with a glass lid, then turn your tired gaze to the window.

"Why did that woman say you were cursed?" I ask.

You flinch at the sound of my voice. "Were you eavesdropping on me?"

"I'm sorry," I say, too quickly. "I didn't mean to. But I heard her say something about a curse." I pause, lowering my voice. "Is it true?"

You look away, toward the window. "Yes," you finally say. "But I should've known. I've been cursed most of my life, ever since I left Palestine."

"What do you mean?"

You turn to look at me, and I see the kohl smeared all around your eyelids. "I left my family and my home behind, thinking I would have a better life in this country," you tell me. "But I've been cursed since the moment I came here. I wish I could return home, wish I could spend time with my mother again, before it's too late. She won't live forever, you know. But I'm stuck here, now, with all six of you kids, living like this."

I feel myself go numb. It's not that I don't know you aren't happy here. I hear it in the sound of your voice; I see it in the way you look at Baba. But your confession feels like a chain around my heart, adding a new layer of pain inside of me. How this is even possible, I'm not sure.

I move closer, trying to get a better view of your face, but your head droops over your chest, your eyes pinch shut. "I don't want to live like this anymore," you whisper.

I bite my lip as a sick feeling passes over me.

"You're upset," you say when I don't respond. Your voice is suddenly sharp, cold.

"No," I say, my hands floating to my chest.

"You think it's my fault, don't you?

"No, no. I just don't understand, that's all."

Your eyes are wide. "Why not? You see the way I live. You should be on my side."

I take another step forward, reaching for your hand. Your fingers are clammy, and you're shaking. "I am on your side, Mama. I am."

"No, you're not," you say, snatching your hand back. "I can tell by the way you look at me. You think I'm a bad mother."

"I don't think that."

"I'm not a fool. I know you do."

Ashamed, I look down, wondering if you can actually see this. I know how much you've been through, and I'm ashamed of myself for not being more understanding. For adding to your pain. A bubble of guilt swells up in me now, and I swallow hard. In a small voice I hear myself say: "So why don't you leave, then?"

"I can't," you say, shaking your head.

I force myself to face you. "Why not? Because of a curse?"

"Yes," you say. "A curse." I stare at you in silence, waiting for you to say more. "I don't expect you to understand now," you finally add, your voice fading. "But someday you will."

34

In February, Silas messaged Yara and asked if she could teach him some of her grandmother's recipes. One whole afternoon was consumed this way in Josephine's kitchen, Silas standing over Yara's shoulder while she showed him how to make hummus like Teta's. Afterward she taught him her method for stuffed grape leaves.

"Start by tucking in the bottom corners," Yara instructed. "Then tuck in the sides and continue rolling it, almost like it's a cigar."

Silas laughed. "Have you ever rolled a cigar?"

"Well, no," she said, tapping him playfully on the arm. "But I'm sure it would look just like this."

She could've easily spent all her free moments cooking with Silas, but she needed time to write. If a couple of days passed without her having the opportunity, she found herself itching to be alone, desperate to get back to her sunroom and get her racing thoughts down on paper.

"You seem antsy lately, like you'd rather be somewhere else," Silas said the following week in his mother's kitchen, where he was showing her how to make buttermilk biscuits. "Is everything okay?"

"I'm sorry," Yara said, seeing no reason to lie. "I don't mean to be rude. I've just been a bit distracted since I started journaling."

It was the kind of response that Fadi might have rolled his eyes at. But Silas just leaned back in his seat and took a sip of Diet Coke. "Oh yeah," he said. "How's that going?"

"Good," she said, relieved. "Great, actually."

His silence gave her the impression that he was expecting her to say more, and she looked away, blushing. In a gentle tone, Silas said: "Are you still having trouble remembering things?"

"No, not really. I've been writing a lot about the past, more than I ever thought I could."

"That's great. I'm so glad to hear that," he said, placing a spoonful of rice and minced meat in the center of the grape leaf before rolling it. "Tell me about them. Your childhood, your family, that kind of stuff."

"It's not really a pleasant topic for conversation," Yara said.

He pressed on. "Are you on good terms with them?"

She shrugged. "I guess."

Lately Silas had been sharing increasingly personal and even intimate details about his past, like telling her about the first time he'd been with a man. He asked her questions about her childhood with the same liberty, and though she'd gotten more comfortable with accessing her memories on her own, she couldn't bring herself to talk about them with him. At the end of their get-togethers, she was always left wondering how he found it so easy to open up, and why she couldn't do the same.

Now Silas smiled at her with a twinkle in his eye. "I don't know how you do it."

"Do what?"

"Reveal so little about yourself."

She fixed her eyes on the grape leaves. "I've never had much luck opening up to people, maybe because I don't have a lot of friends, especially here. Relationships have always been hard for me to navigate."

"Why is that, do you think?"

She felt her chest tighten. "My parents were pretty closed off to us when we were kids, and I imagine it's a result of that."

"What about Fadi?"

"Well, I mean, we talk. But not like you and I do."

"What about when you started dating?"

"We didn't date, really." She paused, avoiding his eyes. "I went to an all-girls school, and we weren't even supposed to talk to boys we weren't related to."

"So how did you even meet Fadi? Or decide to marry him?"

She laughed, trying to mask her embarrassment. "Well, our fathers introduced us, he asked for my hand in marriage, and then we got to know each other. I guess it was like dating, just backward."

Silas blinked at her, touching the base of his neck.

"It might sound strange to you, but it's what many people I know do."

He shook his head, his ears red. "No judgment here," he said. "Out of curiosity, how does that usually work out?"

Yara shrugged. "Okay, I guess. To be honest, I don't know many divorced people in my community. It pains me to admit it, but unfortunately, some stereotypes are true. Divorce is very taboo, and in the rare cases it happens, people don't talk about it."

"I see," Silas said. "I guess it's like that in some Christian circles, too. Is it a religious thing?"

She considered it for a moment, then shook her head. "No, it has nothing to do with Islam. The Quran grants women the freedom and right to seek divorce. It's more cultural, or maybe regional. The importance of family values and keeping the family together, that sort of thing."

"So what happens if you want to get a divorce?"

"Well, I wouldn't," she said quickly.

Silas tilted his head to one side. "I meant hypothetically. Would your family be okay with it?"

"Oh, right." She swallowed, trying to imagine the scenario. But all she could see was Baba's face in her head, his eyebrows pinched together in disappointment and shame, his mouth open but no words coming forth. Tears pooled in her eyes and she swallowed, felt them burning down the back of her throat. "No," she finally said. "They wouldn't."

"I'm so sorry," Silas said in a low voice. He paused, reaching for her hand. She could tell that he didn't want to say the wrong thing.

She willed herself to meet his eyes. "Can I ask you something?" she said.

"Always."

"Do you think the fact that I can talk to you in a way I can't with my own husband makes me a bad wife?"

"No. Of course not."

"But sometimes I wonder why Fadi and I can't connect like that. And then once I start thinking about that, my mind goes all sorts of places and I remember how my mother—" She stopped, her cheeks on fire.

"What about her?" he asked gently.

Yara shook her head, avoiding his eyes. "Nothing."

Silas looked at her for another moment, then said, "I'm sorry you're feeling this way, Yara. I hope you're able to deepen your relationship with Fadi. I've always felt that life's greatest opportunities and gifts are found in my connection with others. It's when I feel most happy."

"You can't rely on other people for your own happiness," Yara said, frowning. "The only person you can trust is yourself, and sometimes even that's not easy."

Silas looked at her as though seeing her for the first time. "I understand why it might be really hard for you," he said. "But forming safe connections is necessary for a meaningful and satisfying life."

However obvious that sentiment was to her now, hearing it aloud made it hurt so much more. But pushing down the pain, she laughed and said: "William has definitely gotten into your head."

35

I feel like we've barely talked lately," Yara told Fadi one Sunday afternoon in March. They were in the car with the girls on the way to see Disney on Ice, an hour away in Raleigh, to celebrate Mira's ninth birthday. In the backseat, Mira and Jude were listening to a story on their headphones, oblivious to their parents' conversation.

"What do you mean?" Fadi said. "We talk all the time."

She looked down at her broken cuticles. "Well, yeah, but only about the girls or what's for dinner."

"Well, what else is there to talk about?" He met her eyes briefly before returning his attention to the road. "We're parents. We have kids, commitments, responsibilities."

"I know. But sometimes I feel like you're so far away."

"Why? I'm right here."

She searched for the right words, but her mouth felt stiff. She rolled down the window, feeling her shoulders relax as the cool air hit her face. Things between them hadn't improved lately, despite her attempts to bridge the distance. Fadi went through the motions when he came home each night, kissing her by the front door and commenting on the smell of spices in the air. Afterward they showered and ate together and watched TV in the same manner they'd done for nine, almost ten, years.

And yet she felt as if everything had changed. Or maybe it was only she who had changed. She never seemed to come fully awake until the moment each day when she sat at her desk and turned to a new page in her notebook, but most nights she was less than present. Sitting next to Fadi in bed, she blinked at the TV screen while dissecting the thoughts running through her head, mapping them out before she wrote them down.

"Fine," Fadi was saying as the inside of the car came back into focus for Yara. "What do you want to talk about?"

What *did* she want to talk about? The list had gotten so long she'd lost track. She wanted to tell him that ever since she started writing in her journal, she'd been thinking *about* her thoughts. Did he do the same? Had he ever stopped to notice the endless stream running through his head, seemingly uncontrollable? A voice that just wouldn't stop talking, observing, judging? Maybe he didn't have it. But once Yara had registered it was there, it was impossible for her to ignore the nonstop chatter. Why couldn't she turn it off?

She wanted to tell him she'd become grateful for this time off work, because it had allowed her to pause, to notice. Because it had allowed her to see how dysfunctional she'd been before, living in a constant state of anxiety, always feeling unwell and exhausted. She wanted to tell him that he could use some time to slow down, too, that maybe it would help him think about what he wanted out of life. Because this couldn't possibly be it, could it? Working all day, then coming home to zone out in front of a screen, only to do it all again? Was she the only one who noticed how they stared blankly at the television most nights, their bodies present but their minds so far away? That they would much rather stare into the eye of a glaring screen than at each other?

But saying all this to him would only make him think she'd gone mad. Instead, she turned to look at his profile and said, "I've been thinking a lot about Palestine lately."

Fadi kept his eyes on the road. "Oh yeah. What about it?"

"I haven't been back in so long, you know, not since before my grandmother died." She paused, feeling short of breath, then shook her head. "I was wondering if maybe for our anniversary trip we can go there—with the girls, of course. It would be good for them to learn more about their history, not only so they can appreciate their privilege, but also to get a fuller picture of the world."

Without changing his tone of voice, Fadi said, "That sounds nice, but like I said, I'm not even sure I can take off work."

"But you promised you would try, right?"

"I know," he said, clenching his hands around the steering wheel. "And I will try. But I have so much going on right now."

Yara sighed. Did Fadi realize that he always had something going on? That as long as he continued living this way, racing desperately from one accomplishment to the next in an effort to get ahead, there would always be a new goal in his life to distract him? Perhaps he wanted the same things she wanted—a better marriage, a bright future for his family, a deeper connection with his children than the one he shared with his parents—but he seemed addicted to getting ahead. If he dared to look inward, would he see that he would always be running? She doubted it. Hadn't she been the same way only months ago? She wished she could tell him about the changes she was going through, but she didn't think he'd understand.

"What do you want?" Yara said now.

Fadi exhaled through his nose. "I don't understand what you mean."

"What do you want out of this life?"

"I don't know," he said, rubbing his temples. "I want to make enough money so I don't have to worry. I want to retire young knowing that my kids are set and college is paid for and our future is secure."

"That's it?"

"Yeah. You know that's all that matters to me, right? Making sure you're all taken care of."

She nodded. For a few seconds they sat there in silence, and she stared out the windshield at the cars ahead. Fadi worked so hard for them, but was this how he wanted to spend his life?

The question left her lips before she could stop it: "But are you happy?"

Fadi snorted. "Of course," he said. "My business is doing well. I have a beautiful family. What more could I ask for?" He shook his head lightly, as if he found the question amusing.

She was envious, suddenly, of her husband's optimism. Was this how Baba had felt, too, working seven days a week? She wondered how he felt coming home at night, his children already in bed, to find Mama glaring at him, her face imbued with sorrow, like that figure in the Munch painting.

"Is there anything you wish was different?" she said, trying to keep her voice light.

Fadi laughed. "Is this one of your counseling exercises?"

"No. I'm trying to get beneath the surface, that's all."

"Well, sometimes I wish I didn't have to work so much" he said, his expression softening. "But I know it's for the best."

"How do you know that?"

"Because one day the business will be worth millions," Fadi said. "And I can just sit back and relax. It'll all be worth it someday. You'll see."

Would it? Weren't they just waiting to enjoy life? Why not now, in these precious present moments? Yara shook her head as Baba's face came to her again, sweat pooling at his temples after a long day, his thin lips curled into a frown. In a voice she didn't recognize, she said: "My dad used to say that to my mom a lot when we were growing up. That he was working hard for our future, that eventually he wouldn't have to work so much and the struggles Mama faced as a result would be worth it. But he spent most of his life away from us, and she was so lonely and . . ." She paused, softening her voice. "I think what I'm trying to say is, What's the point of working for the future if it means forgetting to live?"

Fadi sighed again, more irritably this time. "Are you seriously comparing me to your father now, after everything I've done for you?"

"No. Of course not." Her head throbbed, and she felt more like Mama than ever before. "I'm just afraid, that's all."

"Of what?"

"We've both been working toward some imaginary finish line for almost a decade now, trying to get ahead. But what if we look up one day to realize that we've missed out on all this time together and with our kids? I know it's really important to you to build a future for us, and I'm really grateful for that and I want to help you. But sometimes I also just want to slow down and spend time with you and live, really live."

"Fuck," Fadi said, and Yara felt her body stiffen. She glanced over her shoulder and was relieved to find the girls blinking at their screens, still absorbed in their stories. "All you do is question everything. What if this, what if that. Everyone works, Yara. That's life. We can't just ignore our responsibilities. I wake up every morning with a plan: go to work, pay the bills, come home to my family, and do it all again until we get to where we need to be. I don't have time to dwell on anything else."

She wasn't sure whether she heard courage or cowardice in his words. "But don't you want more?"

"I have everything I want."

"But don't you want to *feel* something?"

"Feel something? What are you even talking about?"

Her face burned. No, that wasn't it. She didn't want to feel anything, quite the opposite. She wanted to unfeel.

She swallowed, took a deep breath. This was her chance to be honest with him. If she couldn't do that, then how could she blame him for not understanding her?

She exhaled. "To be honest, Fadi, I feel like there's something wrong."

"Like what?"

"It's hard to explain. Something is out of place and I can't quite express it, but it doesn't feel right to me."

He looked at her from the corner of one eye. "You're right," he said sharply. "Something is wrong. You're starting to sound just like your mother."

The words felt like a hot palm against her face. "What? No."

"Then why are you always complaining? Our life is fine. You're the one who's too blind and ungrateful to see it. But that shouldn't come as a surprise. I should've known."

Yara turned toward the window, her face crumpled.

"We have a good life, and it's about time you started appreciating it," Fadi went on. "Tell me, what's there to complain about?"

Only a few months ago, Yara might have said everything was fine, too. She had been living on autopilot for so long, plugged into everything but herself. But after everything that had happened that fall, and having time away from work, she'd slowed down and noticed how disconnected she'd been from the woman she wanted to be. She wanted to explain all this to Fadi, but it was clear that all he saw when he looked at her was Mama. She couldn't talk to him without feeling foolish, judged, ashamed.

"Nothing," she finally said. "Never mind, you're right."

YARA'S JOURNAL

"Make sure you don't turn out like your mother," Baba tells me once. I must've been fifteen, maybe older. The years have passed, but nothing has changed.

Baba is home early, and we are sitting together at the kitchen table while he eats dinner. I curl my fingers around a carton of apple juice and watch him, his sleeves rolled up to the elbows and his fingers stained with yellow yogurt sauce, pleased to have this time alone with him. My brothers are playing outside, in the small space behind our building, and I can hear them laughing through the window you'd opened to air out the house. "It's stuffy in here," you'd said. "I feel like I'm trapped inside a glass jar."

Maybe you didn't say that exactly. Maybe I'd come across those words in one of my books and thought of you.

Outside the sky is a deep golden color, and inside Baba slurps down the cauliflower stew, wiping his mouth with the back of his hand. Every now and then he takes a bite of rice, chewing irritably, before spitting it into his palm.

"You see, this is exactly what I mean," he says, pushing his bowl away. "She can't even cook a decent bowl of rice. She's exactly the type of woman you don't want to be."

I look over my shoulder nervously, hoping you didn't hear him, but you're nowhere in sight. I turn back to meet his eyes. "Why not?"

"Isn't it obvious?" he says, frowning. "She thinks too much of herself, expects the world to treat her like she's special, and acts crazy when it doesn't."

He pauses, shoving a spoonful of stew in his mouth. "She thinks she's a man or something."

I sip my apple juice, considering his words. You have been acting strange lately, more defiant. Ever since Teta's death, nothing seems to matter to you anymore. And Baba's temper has gotten worse, too. The fights that used to happen while we were asleep now rage anytime he's home. It's as if neither of you care if we're watching, as if you've both given up on concealing your unhappiness from us. Still, I feel sorry for you, alone all day with all six of us, the meals and chores seemingly endless. How could Baba not feel sorry for you, too?

"Maybe she's tired," I say, the words hitting the air before I can stop them. "Or sad. We can be a handful sometimes."

"Sad? What's there to be sad about?" Baba is shaking his head now, his eyebrows drawn. "She forgets that she was raised in a filthy old camp, and instead of being grateful for an apartment with food and electricity, halal markets down the street, Palestinian neighbors—she walks around wanting more, like this life's not good enough for her. No, no, no," he says, his index finger twitching. "The woman has lost her damn mind, I tell you."

"What do you mean, lost her mind?"

"She's sick in the head," Baba says. "Magnoona."

"Magnoona?"

Baba nods. "She's crazy. Rakibha jinn or something."

"A jinn?"

"What else could explain it?" he says. "A normal person doesn't act like that."

I crush the juice carton between my fingers, considering his words.

I knew, even then, that possession by a jinn was a shame that families went to great lengths to hide. I'd overheard women telling stories of how the jinn would enter a person's body and take charge of it. The person would be unable to speak from his or her own will, becoming aggressive, restless, even violent. Some might see or hear strange things, talk to other jinns, even speak in an incomprehensible language.

But could you be possessed? Is that what the fortune teller told you? And why you have been so defiant lately? Do you need a spiritual intervention to make it leave your body, and if so, why haven't you gotten one?

As I watch Baba finish his meal, I can't get an image out of my mind. You standing with your hands on your hips one moment, then collapsing to your knees and slapping your own face the next, a switch so sudden it seemed like a magic trick. There's clearly something wrong with you. Even I can see that. Maybe Baba is right. Another woman wouldn't make him so angry he hit her. She wouldn't float around the house and then turn in an instant, fury in her eyes, the veins on her neck bulging. Maybe it is a jinn.

36

Congratulations," Yara told Silas as he lowered the tailgate of his truck. "Or as we say in Arabic, Alf mabrouk."

It was a beautiful April day, with damp scents rising from the grass. They were standing together on the grass, overlooking the lake, where Silas had invited her for a picnic to celebrate that he had just won joint custody of his daughter. Initially Yara had been reluctant to return to campus, afraid of encountering Jonathan or Amanda, but recently she'd been worrying much less about what anyone thought of her. Surveying the students sprawled out nearby on picnic blankets, she found her mind sliding into the fear of running into someone she knew, before it occurred to her: she had nothing to be afraid of, no hard feelings left. If she hadn't lost her job, she never would've been able to slow down, pay attention to what was happening inside her.

"It's the perfect weather for a picnic," Silas was saying.

The sun was slightly warm, and everywhere she looked flowers were starting to bloom, with the fragrant scents of snapdragons and azaleas in the air. Around them people were fishing and picnicking, gathering around metal tables or outdoor blankets. Silas reached into his truck to break out a cooler of chicken salad and pimento cheese, plus two sleeves of club crackers. He opened a can of Diet Coke, beaming as he narrated the morning's hearing. Silas had only been able to visit with Olivia up until the ruling, wanting her to feel as stable as she could while all of this was being decided. But now he couldn't wait to have her stay with him again, he said. He and his ex hadn't yet decided how they would organize Olivia's time, he explained, but they would likely end up rotating weeks with her.

Silas smeared a cracker with pimento cheese and passed it to Yara. "All things considered, I'm lucky," he said. "Most of the divorced dads I know only see their kids every other weekend. I was preparing myself for the worst."

"I'm so glad things worked out," Yara said. "Olivia is so lucky to have you."

"I hope so."

She had met Olivia earlier that month, during one of her visits to Josephine's house. They'd been in the middle of a halva-making lesson when Josephine came home with the girl after an early school close. She was quiet, carrying a doll in one hand with her thumb in her mouth. "Nice to meet you," Yara said, watching her suck her thumb, searching her face for hints of her own daughters' personalities. But Olivia wouldn't look up. Her fingers wrapped tightly around her doll, she then buried her face in Josephine's lap and started to cry. "I'm sorry," Silas had said. "She hasn't been herself lately."

As she listened to Silas debate the merits of various custody arrangements, Yara ran her finger along the edge of a club cracker. She pictured Olivia's face, imagining how hard this must be for the little girl. Her mind wandered to her own daughters, and whether they could feel the tension between her and Fadi. Nothing had changed on the surface. They exchanged all the usual pleasantries when he came home in the evenings: How was your day? Great, yours? Fine. And the girls? Good. Great. She had hoped their conversation in the car might've had an effect on Fadi, but it did not. He still left the house before sunrise each morning and returned home in darkness, reaching for the remote as soon as he collapsed on the bed. Still, each night she wondered if maybe she should bring up the idea of a trip again. But she could never find the right moment. Studying him as he stared at the screen, Yara thought that his eyes were bright with what looked like a momentary relief from himself.

In bed the previous night, before Fadi had had a chance to grab the remote, Yara had managed to push out the words: "Our anniversary is only a month away. How are things looking at work?" Quietly, without looking up, he'd said: "Not promising." She'd gone on watching him while he avoided her eyes. "But if now's not a good time, when is?" she'd asked. "I don't know what you want from me," Fadi replied, frowning. "I'm trying my best here."

"What do you think, Yara?" Silas was saying now.

She looked up. "Sorry, what?"

"Do you think it would be better to alternate weeks or split the week in half?"

"Hm, I don't know." As she sat there gripping the cracker, she imagined having joint custody of Mira and Jude. Forcing them to live in two homes, sleep in two beds, divide themselves and their belongings between two parents. They were already split between cultures, and breaking their lives in half again seemed unfair, almost cruel.

"What do you think that'll be like for Olivia?" Yara finally said.

"I know it's not ideal," Silas said. "But I think it's better than her watching her parents live a lie. I'm just going to try to be the best dad I can be."

"Of course," she said. "You already are."

In front of them, the lake was large and brilliantly blue, and students circled it on the footpath. She barely recognized her own voice when she continued: "To be honest, I'd be a mess in your situation. I can't even seem to decide how I feel each day, let alone go through something as major as divorce. You're really brave."

"Thank you," Silas said, but he was looking past her, seeming to consider something. Feeling nervous, Yara reached into the cooler for a bottle of water. She pressed her fingers hard around the cap, the plastic digging into her skin until eventually she loosened her grip and twisted it open.

"Would you ever get a divorce?" Silas asked.

She looked up at him quickly. "What?"

"I'm sorry," he said. "It's none of my business, really. But it's been on my mind ever since you told me how your family felt about divorce." He paused, frowning. "I want to make sure you could leave, you know, if you wanted to."

She set the bottle down, feeling short of breath. "I'm not some helpless prisoner," Yara said.

He shook his head. "That's not what I meant."

"I know." She turned to look back at the lake, the mountains' reflection like a painting on the water. It wasn't his question that startled her as much as his ability to sense her concerns about her marriage. It was something she'd never experienced before, a relationship with someone who understood her without words. She looked back at Silas and said, "Even if I wanted a divorce, I'd find a way to make my marriage work."

"Even if you weren't happy in it?"

She nodded. "It wouldn't be worth it to get disowned from my family or forced to give up my girls. I wouldn't put them through that." A picture of Mama came to her, how her eyes lit up like a candle in a dark room when she saw the man from the park, how desperately she had wanted to start a new life with him. Looking at Silas, Yara suspected that she wasn't all that different from her mother. She swallowed a lump in her throat and said: "Sometimes I wonder how differently my life would've turned out if my mother had been able to get a divorce."

"What do you mean?" He tried to meet her eyes, but she stared out toward the water.

"My mother wanted to leave my father but couldn't," Yara said, the words burning in her throat. She swallowed. "She didn't have close friends the way other mothers did. She spent most of her days with us, which made her feel worse. Eventually she had an affair. I was really young when it happened, maybe nine or so. It was a really bad time for my family."

"I'm sorry to hear that," Silas said.

She imagined what he was thinking. A battered housewife, sure. Depressed, distant, withdrawn? Typical. But this?

Yara turned to him. "You didn't expect me to say that, did you?"

He shook his head. "You never really talk about her."

"It's not the easiest topic of conversation," she said. "And I hadn't allowed myself to think about it for years. To be honest, I've been feeling a little guilty about our friendship because of it, and I haven't yet mentioned you to Fadi. I know we're not having an affair or anything, but after everything that happened with my mother—" She stopped, horrified.

"Oh, wow," Silas said. "I didn't realize our friendship was making you feel this way. I'm sorry you're going through this. Maybe if you're honest with Fadi, it'll relieve some of your guilt?"

"I know, but things have been tense lately. I don't want to give him any more reason to be upset with me."

"Why would he be upset with you?"

She could feel the tears coming, and she closed her eyes. "Nothing, it's nothing. I'm sorry. I don't even know why I'm telling you all this."

When she opened them, Silas nodded slowly, like he was thinking about what she'd shared, trying to make sense of it. "I know what happened with your mother must be very painful for you," he finally said. "But regardless of what she did, *you're* not doing anything wrong. I'm sure Fadi will understand."

"Yeah," she said. "You're right. I guess I should just tell him."

When Fadi came home that evening, he seemed irritable. He frowned to himself as he slipped his shoes off by the door, then avoided her eyes when they put the girls to bed. While he peeled off his clothes to shower, looking lost in thought, she studied him for a moment. He was absently rubbing his hand over the back of his neck and shaking his head.

"You all right?" she asked. "You seem like you're someplace else."

He glanced at her. "I'm fine, just a rough day."

As they showered in silence, she wondered if his strange behavior was a projection of her own guilt, or if there really was something wrong. It was obvious he wasn't sharing everything about his life with her, but how could she blame him? She was keeping things from him, too: a close friendship with another man, haunting memories from her past, and lately, the burning desire to change her life.

In bed, they chewed their dinner in silence and watched an episode of *Chicago Fire*. More than once, Yara considered grabbing the remote and hitting pause, getting Fadi's attention and telling him about Silas. She wanted to confess that she wished their marriage was more like the relationship she had with Silas. That their friendship only intensified her nagging suspicion that something was wrong between her and Fadi.

But she couldn't bring herself to articulate any of these thoughts because she knew what Fadi would say. He would tell her, in ascending order, that she always said things weren't okay. That just because she felt like something was wrong doesn't mean it actually was. Are you sure you don't need to see someone, Yara? he'd ask. Here we go again with your feelings, Yara. You have some serious issues, Yara. Why do you always overthink things?

Maybe Fadi was right, a voice inside her head answered. Why did she always think something was wrong when nothing in her life indicated that, when she couldn't even explain what that something wrong was?

As soon as Fadi fell asleep that night, Yara retreated to the sunroom to check if her latest painting was dry yet. The room smelled metallic, like turpentine and linseed oil, and the dusty boxes still lingered on the floor. Through the glass, the sky was vast and almost black, the night stars shining everywhere. Yara stepped toward the painting, her heart beating fast and loud. She stood there in the cold quiet, breathing it in. Then she ran her fingers along the canvas, her palette a sea of glorious blues, the eye in the center glaring.

YARA'S JOURNAL

That cursed summer, when I was nine years old, Baba booked a work trip to Palestine for two weeks. You did not beg and plead for us to join him. Whenever Baba planned these trips, you'd spend days trying to convince him to take us along. But this time, I ask him more than you do, and when Baba calls to tell you he's arrived safely, you grin from ear to ear.

After making a quick phone call, you summon me into your bedroom and tell me we're taking a day trip to Coney Island. The man from the park is driving us there. This is not the first time we have met him in secret, but it's the first time we'll have been in his car.

"But what if Baba finds out?" I ask as you rummage through your closet, deciding what to wear.

"He won't."

"But what if he does? What if one of the boys tells him?"

You don't respond. You choose a long, flowery dress, slip it on, and call my brothers into the room. "Listen up," you say. "My friend is coming with us to the beach. But you can't tell your father. Do you understand?"

They nod.

"Good." You turn to me. "See? Nothing to worry about."

The man arrives at our house an hour later with a blue Jansport bag hanging from one shoulder. In the van, he fastens the boys' seat belts and asks if they need anything before we hit the road. Seeming to sense my unease, the man smiles at me from the driver's seat, and I feel my ears go hot.

I keep my face pressed against the car window, trying to tune out the sight of you, sitting in the passenger seat and singing along to Arabic songs. This is as happy as I've ever seen you, a sudden rush of life in your face, your voice. He says something I do not hear and you laugh so hard you start coughing. You trace your fingers against the back of his neck so tenderly.

The beach is gray, nothing like the picture I'd painted in my head. The sand is too hot and the water is murky and the women are barely wearing any clothes. I don't understand how they're able to walk around so exposed. Some of them even lie on their stomachs to tan and undo the tops of their bathing suits! Watching them, I want to dig my feet into the sand until I disappear into the center of the earth. In my capris and long T-shirt, I feel like the world can see right through me, like I need even a few more layers to be safe. Yet these women seem like they are protected by an invisible layer. I wonder what it is and if I can ever have it.

"Why don't you go play with your brothers," you say now, looking radiant in your sundress. You and the man are lying down on a beach towel, watching the boys build sandcastles a few yards away, toward the water.

"I don't want to play," I say. "I want to sit with you."

"Well, the adults are talking now, so run along. Yallah. Go."

I march toward my brothers with my arms crossed. As soon as I reach them, I'm overcome with a destructive impulse, and before I can stop myself I kick in their sandcastle and storm off as it crumbles.

"Yara!" you say as soon as my brothers begin to cry and shout. "Come back here now."

I drag my feet across the sand until I reach you. I shut my eyes and sigh, defeated.

"Why did you do that?" you ask.

"I don't know," I say, my body shaking.

"Look at me." You lift my chin. "Do you want me to slap you in front of all these people?"

"No."

"Then go apologize and help your brothers rebuild the sandcastle."

As slowly as I can, I walk back over to my brothers and sink to my knees beside them.

They're still upset, looking back at me reproachfully. I'm sorry, I want to say, but my face begins to twitch and I turn away. The ocean is roaring in the distance. With shaky hands, I grab a bucket and fill it with sand. Every now and then I look back to see you laughing with the man, and I want to scream. I imagine you staring absently out the kitchen window. I hear Baba yelling, his bowl of food hitting the wall. Tears slide down my face as I make a tower. It falls over. I wipe my eyes and try again, stealing another quick glance at you, now running your fingers through the man's brown hair, smiling so wide. How, I am wondering, are you so happy to be with him but not with us?

Keeping my body very still, I watch you. Then I turn back to face the ocean and think, for the very first time, that maybe you deserved to get beaten after all.

37

Yara painted. She wrote. She sorted through her memories as if she'd been seeing them all wrong, looking through a contorted lens, as if she'd been an unreliable narrator of her own life.

Every morning after dropping the girls off at school, she slipped into the sunroom. She'd carved out enough room to move more freely in the space, having stacked up Fadi's boxes outside the door. She pulled out her paints, laid a canvas on the easel. Water on her brush. Then bold layers of color, stroke after stroke, until the walls of the room softened and her mind went blank, as if under a spell.

But as she painted, examining the same image day after day—the eyelid that sagged in tired folds, the sharp, piercing blue gaze—all Yara could see were Mama's eyes. Would this be her own face, she wondered, twenty years from now?

The painting unsettled her, but she could not rip her eyes away. Eventually she reached for her notebook and turned to a new page. She wrote about Baba's fingers around Mama's neck. She wrote about Teta flipping a coffee saucer on its head, reading the grounds. She wrote about her great-grandfather's olive trees on fire, their history forgotten. She wrote about how her ancestral trauma had trickled down to her, leaking from her body to her marriage to her motherhood.

She put down her pen, catching sight of her painting. How could she have judged Mama so harshly, considering all her struggles? She wished desperately for a way to go back to that moment and apologize, to confess that she finally understood her pain. But all she could do was flip to a new page, hoping the words could make up for the agony her mother had endured, repay her for all she'd lost. Or at the very least, provide a testimony that acknowledged all she'd been through.

Back in front of her easel, Yara stood for a long time, mixing blue colors with her palette knife. Her mind wandered to a blue afternoon in Palestine, to sitting under the shade of an olive tree, Teta telling her another story about the nakba, her words attempting to paint a picture: a chlorine-blue sky. Men heaving burlap bags stuffed with their family's belongings over their shoulders. Women balancing baskets on their heads. Children weeping in the summer heat, clinging to their mothers as they fled their land for Lebanon, Jordan, and the West Bank. Hundreds of thousands of people marching down the road like tiny insects, rusted iron keys dangling from their necks.

Yara added daubs of blue color to the painting, working them in carefully.

"'All the earth is a hotel,'" Teta had said, quoting Edward Said. "'And my home is Jerusalem.'"

38

On the morning of her tenth wedding anniversary, Yara sat up in bed, rubbing sleep from her eyes. Fadi had left for work at sunrise, and the girls were still asleep upstairs. Through the window, white clouds glided across a spotless blue sky. The flowers had bloomed in their neighborhood, and sweeping beds of azaleas surrounded the terrace of every home. Yara reached for the phone on her nightstand before slipping back under the covers and scrolling through her photo gallery. She and Fadi had taken so many photos together over the years, she thought as she searched for the perfect one to post—though perfect in what way, she wasn't quite sure.

She paused on a photo of them from the night of their engagement. They were sitting together on the sofa in her parents' living room, Fadi handsome in a white button-down shirt, his arm around her waist. She was wearing a light blue dress and a nervous smile that masked her inner trepidation and excitement about how much of her life had passed in her father's house, and how much of it was about to begin.

Scrolling on, she found another photo of them, this time in Mexico for their honeymoon. Yara had been wearing a cream sundress and an oversized hat, lying on the beach even though she hated sand and felt out of place, covered up while everyone was naked. Beside her, Fadi was shirtless, grinning wide at the stranger who took their photo.

Then another image of them on a ferry to the Statue of Liberty while she was pregnant with Mira, standing close together as cold air blew at their faces, and Yara feeling a low ache inside her that she didn't know would only worsen over the years.

Then one they'd taken on her birthday a couple of years ago, in the restaurant of a bed-and-breakfast they'd visited while Nadia watched the girls for the weekend. Face this way, their waiter had said while he took their photo. Yara in a satin red dress, her hair loose and blowing in the breeze, the full moon shining in the darkness behind them, and Fadi looking lovingly at her instead of at the camera. Afterward they'd watched the sunset together, something they'd never done before, and Fadi talked about his parents, how they made him feel so unseen. She'd understood him more deeply in that moment than ever before, and she told him more about her father and her brothers, how alone she felt in her family, too. Her eyes were shining and she could feel tears about to come, but then he took her by the hand, led her inside, and made love to her. In the pitch blackness of the room, his body pressed tight against hers, she didn't feel so lonely anymore.

Yes, she thought. The photo from that evening was the one she would post.

With a few taps of her thumb, she uploaded the picture to Instagram, biting the inside of her cheek as she typed out the caption: Happy ten years to my number one. I'm so grateful for you. I love you so much.

Reading over the caption, she wondered why her message was addressed to her husband, as though only he would see it. In fact, Fadi wasn't even on Instagram. Who was she writing this for, then? Why did she feel the need to share her feelings on a public platform? Would declaring her love publicly somehow make it more real? It wouldn't. And yet it seemed like she had come to depend on this performance, as if it was necessary for her to believe it herself. She felt a low ache in her core as she reread the words. Then she pressed her thumb against the backspace key until the draft was deleted and put her phone away.

After she dropped the girls off at school, she treated herself with a trip to the coffee shop, where she ordered an oat milk latte and grabbed a seat by the window. When her phone buzzed, she slipped it from her pocket to see it was a text from Fadi. She flicked the notification with her thumb to read it.

Happy anniversary, habibti. I can't believe it's been ten years. I've planned a little surprise for you later. My mom will pick the girls up at five, and I'll be home shortly after. I love you.

Happy anniversary, I love you too, can't wait to see you, she responded, then put down the phone and gazed out the window. She wondered what kind of surprise Fadi had planned. Maybe he would surprise her with tickets to Rome, where she could finally see the Sistine Chapel, or Mexico City, where they could visit the largest collection of Frida Kahlos in the world. Yara laughed at herself now, feeling foolish. It was unlikely, she knew, and yet a part of her hoped Fadi was capable of such a romantic gesture. Maybe she'd misjudged him all along, and their relationship wasn't so bad after all.

She finished her coffee and went home, where she searched her closet for an outfit, picking out an emerald-green dress she knew Fadi loved. Afterward she tidied up the house, packed an overnight bag for each of the girls, sealed the envelope to Fadi's card, and wrapped his gift: tickets for a Tar Heels game.

Later, after Nadia had come by to pick up the girls, Fadi arrived home with a bouquet of two dozen red roses, a small white gift bag, and a card. Yara had heard his car in the driveway and stood in the hallway to greet him. She'd made an extra effort tonight: her hair was pulled back loosely, a few wavy strands framing her face, and she was wearing a rich, burgundy lipstick and shimmering eye shadow. Around her neck, her thin gold necklace gleamed.

"Wow," Fadi said, leaning in to kiss her. "You look stunning."

He handed her the roses, and she lifted them to her nose, inhaling. "They're beautiful."

"You can open this at dinner," he said, gesturing to the bag in his hands. "I'm going to go shower and change really quick."

"I can't peek while I wait?"

"Only if you want to ruin the surprise."

"Fine," she said, unable to contain her smile. "I'll try and behave myself."

An hour later, they were seated in a dimly lit steakhouse at a table draped in white cloth, at the center of which was a tiny candle floating beside chrysanthemums and sliced citrus. In the background, other diners' conversations simmered.

"This restaurant is beautiful," Yara said. "Thank you."

"Of course," Fadi said. "I know a night out isn't the same as a trip across the ocean. But hopefully we'll be ready for that before you know it. Thank you for being so patient."

She nodded, her eyes darting to the chair beside him.

"Oh yeah, I almost forgot," he said, and passed her the bag holding her gift. "Open it."

Her face burning, she said: "You go first."

"You sure?"

She nodded. Fadi reached inside his gift bag and lifted out the envelope, gasping at the sight of the tickets. "No way," he said, glancing up at her then back down at them. "Thank you. You're the best."

She took a sip of water and swallowed. "It was nothing."

He gestured toward her gift. "Your turn."

Her heart racing, she pulled the bag close. It was heavier than she expected, but she hoped there could still be boarding passes inside. She spread the bag open to see a large black jewelry box, which she removed slowly, confirming there was nothing else in the bag and feeling stupid for having considered it. And yet her mind was unwilling to let go of a small hope, that perhaps he'd folded up a set of boarding passes and placed them inside. When she finally lifted the lid and saw the contents, she looked up at him.

"What, you don't like it?" Fadi said.

"No," she said, shaking her head, then nodding. "Of course I do. I love it."

Gently she detached the bracelet from the velvet backing. It was a dainty gold chain with a small hamsa pendant, and in the center of the hand, a blue eye.

"I thought you'd like it, seeing how you're always wearing the same necklace. Go on, then," he urged. "Put it on."

She nodded and extended her arm, and Fadi reached across the table to attach the clasp around her wrist. He didn't notice the shadow of blue paint that now lived around the edges of her nails.

"You don't seem like you like it," Fadi said, and she looked away, taking another sip of water. "What is it?"

"Nothing, I'm so sorry," she said, keeping her eyes on the flickering candle. "I guess I just hoped you would surprise me with a trip somewhere. It sounds more foolish now than it did in my head, if that's even possible."

Fadi shook his head slowly. "I didn't mean to get your hopes up. I thought I was clear when I said it wasn't a good time."

"You were," she said, her eyes stinging. "It was my fault for assuming."

He frowned. "I guess this is disappointing, then?"

"No, I really appreciate it, I do."

"It doesn't seem like it. I thought I was doing something nice," he said. "Buying you that bracelet and planning this dinner. But no matter what I do, you always find fault."

"I'm sorry. It's not that I don't love it. It's beautiful." She fingered the bracelet, unable to hide her nerves. "A part of me just hoped you'd find a way for us to travel because you knew how much it meant to me. I thought you'd find a way to do this for me."

Fadi raised an eyebrow. "So now I don't do enough for you?"

She opened her mouth, but he cut her off: "Look around, Yara. You live a tremendously privileged life. Can't you see how selfish you're being?"

She tried to swallow but her throat felt dry. "I'm sorry," she said.

For a long moment they were still, then Fadi returned his attention to his food. She swallowed back tears, though a faint trickle was slipping down one side of her face, and reached for her fork and knife. They were silent until their main courses were finished, and Fadi asked for the check as soon as they were cleared.

Only when they got home did they speak again. Fadi was standing in the doorway of their bedroom, looking down at his phone as he typed. Then, hesitating, he told her that he'd had to book a flight to Vegas for a convention and that he would be gone for five days.

Yara took a step back, dumbfounded. It felt like he had shoved his fist down her throat and cracked her heart in half. "Can I come with you?" she asked once she'd composed herself. "I've always wondered what Vegas was like."

He frowned. "It's a work trip, and Ramy will be joining me. What would I look like if I told him I'm bringing my wife?" He laughed, seeming to find the scenario amusing.

"I won't interfere with your work. You won't even know I'm there."

He was back to typing again. "I'm sorry," he finally said. "Besides, you wouldn't really like it, anyway."

She didn't say anything after that, slipping quietly under the covers. She was too worn out to argue, too tired to articulate that it felt as if for her whole life the rules had been different for her because she was a woman. She could feel her heart hardening as she tossed and turned in the darkness, shimmering with rage. She could no longer pretend she wasn't angry, and she desperately wanted to release the feeling. When Fadi finally fell asleep, she got out of bed and went to her studio, where she opened her notebook and turned to an empty page, picking up where she'd left off.

39

After the night of their anniversary, Yara felt like someone had crawled inside her mind and flipped a switch. Every old thought was suddenly turned on its head. She walked around the house in a daze, her eyes puffy and swollen, finding her life unbearable in a completely new way. It didn't matter how hard she'd tried to get close to Fadi. It didn't matter how desperately she wanted to make her own choices. The fact was that she would never be granted the same freedoms as him and nothing, *nothing*, she could ever do would change that.

On the night before Fadi left for Vegas, they ate in bed while watching an episode of *Everybody Loves Raymond*. Fadi was laughing so hard he was almost choking on his food, even though they'd seen the episode a dozen times. Yara pressed her dinner plate into her thighs as she stared at the television, her body shaking. Ray and Debra were having a three-week-long fight over who would put the suitcase away. Debra refused, desperate to prove a point. She said, "Why does the woman have to do everything? And besides, isn't lifting a heavy suitcase the 'manly' thing to do?" Ray tried to get Debra to move it by hiding a block of cheese inside and letting it rot. Fadi laughed between shoveling mouthfuls of rice and said, "Isn't this hilarious?" Yara cracked her knuckles and said, "Yes, very."

After Fadi left for the airport the next morning, Yara paced slowly around and around the house wiping down the windows until each room gleamed to an industrial perfection, as though the act of cleaning would somehow remove the dirty feeling that clung to her body. But it did not. She had spent so much time over the years scrubbing and tidying, compulsively keeping everything in order so she could feel in control. And yet an unbearable chaos brimmed beneath her skin as she blinked stupidly at the streak-free glass, unable to take in the smell of Windex without a sense of humiliation. As she stumbled over to the kitchen, returning the spray bottle to its spot beneath the sink, she became faintly aware of a change taking place within herself. She began to understand for the first time that she could no longer go on deluding herself: these external things—her house, her career, her degrees—would never remove the unworthiness she felt within. But how else was she supposed to get rid of it?

For the next several days, she went through the motions, racing frantically from one task to the next, caught in a spiral.

At home with the girls, she wanted to peel herself out of her skin. She made eye contact with Mira and Jude while they spoke so they could see she was paying attention. But she was not paying attention. The meals she made were flavorless, and she couldn't bring herself to do any basic cleanup. Instead she walked around the kitchen, opening and closing cabinets, picking things up only to set them down again. Everywhere she looked, there were tasks to do, places where her services were needed. The dishes in the sink, the laundry piles, the entire house was now a reminder of what she stood for. "Mama, look. Mama, look," the girls kept saying, but she couldn't bring herself to meet their eyes. When at last she did, they looked so much like the little girl she once was that she was ashamed of herself.

Afterward Mira and Jude went off quietly by themselves and lay silently by the television. Slipping into the sunroom, she sensed a glint of knowledge in her daughters' eyes: we know you can't see us, they seemed to say. But what are you looking at in there?

• • •

"Can you cook bamya tonight?" Fadi texted her on the day he was coming home. She'd been keeping up only the most basic communication with him while he was away. "I've been missing your delicious dinners."

She put her phone down without responding. Instead she split open a warm pita for a hummus sandwich for Mira and Jude, who were watching an episode of *SpongeBob* in the living room. They were lying on their stomachs, hands under their chins, staring unblinking at the screen. The sight suddenly made her nauseated. Was this how the habit started? She swallowed a lump in her throat as she smeared the pita with hummus, then told the girls it was time to turn off the TV, to a chorus of protests.

She didn't cook *bamya* for Fadi that night. In fact, she went to bed right after the girls did and barely registered his presence in their bed. When Fadi texted her the next morning from work asking why she hadn't stayed up to greet him, she told him that she'd been tired. If he didn't see how unfair it was for her to be confined to their home while he roamed the country at a moment's notice, then nothing she could do or say would change that.

"What's for dinner?" Fadi asked the next night when he came home to find Yara reading an art history book in the living room. Without looking up from the pages, she said: "Nothing."

"Nothing?"

Yara shrugged. "I didn't feel like cooking."

She could feel him staring at her, but she wouldn't look at him.

"What am I supposed to eat, then?"

"There's hummus in the fridge, if you want to make yourself a sandwich."

"Are you serious?"

She glanced up from her book. "What?"

"Why are you acting so weird?"

"Because I'm not cooking?"

"Not just that," he said. "The house is a mess. It's unlike you. What's going on?"

"I'm tired."

For a long moment Fadi just looked at her. "Tired?" he finally said, laughing. "I'm the one who's been working all day. What have you been doing?"

"Nothing," Yara said calmly. "I'm just tired of you."

When Fadi stormed out of the room to shower, she didn't follow him. Somehow the idea of standing naked in the shower with him made her feel sick. All these years she had thought that revealing herself to him in that intimate way—every inch of her body exposed to him each night—would help him truly see her. But all it had done was leave her desperate for his approval, unable to see herself. She gave a small shake of the head before returning her attention to the chapter she was reading, then headed to the sunroom. She'd managed to move most of his boxes to the garage, but the ones that remained were now stained with smears of paint all over the cardboard. Settling in front of the easel, she went back to the same painting, the blue eye in the center so intense now. She added more color to the canvas, blues and whites and blacks, in frenzied loops and swirls.

As she painted she pondered what her life would be like if she stayed on this path with Fadi. She was certain now, in a way she'd never been before, that she couldn't become the person she wanted to be if she remained with him. No matter what job she found or which goals she set, she'd never have the freedom to chase her dreams the way he did. He'd always depend on her to look after the girls, prioritizing his own career because he'd make more money. Not to mention the amount of energy she wasted trying to win his love and attention, waiting for him to come home every night just like she'd waited for Baba all those years. Did she want to spend her life as Mama had, waiting for a man to give her what she wanted and feeling worthless when he didn't? Was that the woman she wanted to be, the example she wanted to set for her daughters?

She reached for her notebook now, flipped to a blank page. How could she achieve what she wanted if she couldn't even figure out what that was? She'd spent her life trying to be the type of woman everyone wanted her to be, but who was she truly?

She started to make a list of all the things she would do if she had no limits: she would see the world and visit all the museums containing her favorite artists. She'd visit Palestine again, bringing the girls there, too. She'd open her own studio. She'd paint. She'd write. She'd live every moment fully here, alive and present. But most of all, she wouldn't let herself be confined, simmered down, erased. For once in her life, she would make a choice that was fully her own.

40

In the sunroom one morning, as Yara stood in front of her easel with her mind in a faraway place, a sharp ringing brought her back to the room. She looked down at the screen of her phone to see Baba's name. She set the brush down on the palette, then took a deep breath and answered. "Hello?"

"Yara?" Baba said, his voice urgent. "Are you alone? I need to talk to you."

She inhaled, wiping her hands on her apron. "What's going on?"

"You tell me."

He paused to clear his throat, and Yara swallowed, feeling a twist in her stomach, a slight chill on the back of her neck. "What are you talking about?"

"Fadi called me again," Baba said. "He says you're giving him a hard time. Is it true?" Before she could respond, he went on. "Why am I getting calls every day about how selfish you're acting, huh? What's going on?"

Her heart was beating faster, and she looked down at her hand to see it balled into a fist. She looked up at the canvas, the blue eye electric now. In a sharp voice she said, "Since when do you care?"

"Excuse me?"

"You only call me when it's about one of my brothers," she said, beginning to pace. "Or lately, Fadi. When have you ever called to ask about me?"

Baba paused for a moment. "What does that have to do with

anything, Yara? This is about your behavior. I've always prided myself on how well you were doing, mashallah. You've always done what's expected of you, so what's changed now?"

She paced around the room, anger flaring through her veins. For a moment she searched for the words to tell him what she was feeling, to explain the changes happening inside of her. But instead she shook her head and said: "It doesn't matter what changed. But I'm not doing what you and Fadi want anymore."

"Shu? Why are you acting like this?"

Calmly, she said, "I'm not acting."

"No wonder Fadi is upset," Baba said after a pause. "You're starting to sound just like your mother, only thinking of yourself, ruining everything."

Her mother *was the one who ruined everything?* The room fell into complete darkness. She held the phone to her ear, listening to the shallow rise and fall of her chest until she managed, "What about all those times you beat her?"

"Excuse me? What did you just say to me?"

"You heard what I said." She inhaled, forcing herself to continue. "When are you going to acknowledge the pain you put *her* through? You're the reason she was so miserable. It was your fault."

"My fault?" Baba said, indignant. "Don't you remember the shame your mother brought us, the harm to our family's name?" He was shouting now, breathing heavily into the phone. "Don't you dare blame me. She deserved everything she got."

Yara closed her eyes, feeling exhausted. Hadn't the years taught him anything about shame? That there was only so far we could push it down, that it was only by acknowledging the truth that we could ever be free.

"No," she finally said. "She didn't deserve that. Maybe you can't admit it to yourself, but deep down we both know the truth."

41

When Yara heard Fadi's car in the driveway that night, it took a considerable effort for her to refrain from rushing outside and making a scene. She wanted to smash the flower vases on the front steps and shout until her throat was sore and the neighbors were peering out their front windows. But instead she went up to the girls' room, where she busied herself with bedtime stories, letting her torment dissolve at the sight of their eager faces as she flipped the pages. Again she didn't shower with Fadi and barely said a word to him as they ate dinner in bed, though he seemed pleased she'd cooked bazella. As the *Law & Order* theme song thundered through the speakers, she tightened her fingers around her spoon and stirred the pea and carrot stew, unable to lift it to her mouth.

Fadi turned to her, but she kept her eyes on the television. She sat very straight and feigned great interest in the case unfolding on the screen.

"You're quiet tonight," Fadi said. "Everything okay?"

She nodded, feeling stiff. Did he know that Baba had called her today? Was he waiting for her to bring it up first? There were so many things she wanted to say, but she didn't know where to begin.

Eventually, the episode ended and Fadi turned out the lights. She dragged herself to the bathroom and brushed her teeth but felt like vomiting as she hunched over the sink. Catching her reflection in the mirror, she wanted to smash her fist into the glass. What was it about her face that revolted her so much? She stared into her own eyes for a long moment, trying to figure it out. Was it that she was the reason Mama couldn't live a happy life at home, why she had to go and love another man? Or that Yara herself couldn't escape this feeling of being unloved and unwanted, of belonging nowhere? Or that, despite having everything, her marriage was crumbling before her eyes?

Though she'd tried so hard to be better than Mama, she was limited in the same ways, disconnected from the people she was supposed to love and be loved by, searching for happiness in all the wrong places. She'd tried to learn from Mama's mistakes, do things differently. What would Mama do now, at this very moment? Whatever it was, Yara needed to do the opposite.

She slipped into bed silently, and then, before Fadi could turn off the light, she heard her own voice: "My father called me today."

For a moment Fadi didn't respond, just blinked at her from the doorway. She took a deep breath and continued. "But you already knew that. Why did you involve him? You know how I feel about him."

There was a long silence before Fadi finally said, "Look, I was upset and thought he'd be able to get through to you. I mean, you're not acting like yourself."

"And your solution is to go running to my father, of all people?"

"I'm sorry," he said, his voice faltering. "I was worried about you, and I didn't know who else to call."

She was quiet for a moment, staring up at the ceiling. "Do you actually care, though?"

"What? Of course."

"It doesn't feel like it."

She must have not turned off the bathroom faucet all the way, and the loud drips punctuated the silence. Fadi stood at the edge of the bed and faced her. "What are you talking about?"

"Sometimes I feel like you love me because you're supposed to—because I'm your wife and the mother of your kids. Not because of me or who I am on the inside."

He flopped his hands in the air. "Here we go with this again. Act normal, will you?"

She said nothing for several seconds, watching the rise and fall of her own chest. "I don't know much about love," she finally said. "But I'm starting to feel like this isn't it. It's as if we're going through the motions, as if we're only together because I'm some woman you sat with a few times and decided to marry, and you had some kids, and now you're trying to make it work so you don't look bad." She paused. "Maybe that kind of love was enough for me back then. I probably deluded myself into believing our marriage wasn't some sort of transaction, so I felt like I had some control over my own life. But now I want something better. I deserve better."

For a minute Fadi didn't say anything, just rubbed his brow, as if to ward off a headache. "I don't know what's going on with you," he said. "But you're wrong. We didn't have to marry each other. We chose each other."

"Bullshit," she said through her teeth. "We didn't even know each other. We both just needed to start new lives, and here we are. Except our new life feels exactly the same."

Fadi let out a short laugh. "Are you delusional? How can you even say that?"

"It's true. You're just not paying attention. Most days it feels like you're not really here. Even when we're together, I feel alone."

"Alone?" he said. "I come home every night. I'm right next to you. What the hell do you want from me?"

The words felt like bricks on her tongue. "I want to feel connected to you."

"Are we back to this again? Who do you think I work so hard for?"

"Yourself."

"Myself?"

She sat up in bed, surprised at how she could suddenly articulate her thoughts and how badly she wanted to express them.

"I appreciate that you work hard," Yara said. "But you've been working like this since before we met. It's who you are. You're not doing this for me. And if you are, then stop. It's not what I want."

"Then what do you want?"

"I want to feel connected to you," she repeated, but as the words left her mouth, she realized that the person she had most wanted to connect to was herself. "I thought maybe going away together someplace might help us reconnect, but it doesn't seem like you care about that at all. Do you?"

"I do."

She waited for him to go on, but he didn't, sighing and switching off the light instead. In the darkness, she could see him nod to himself, but it was impossible to tell whether he was finally beginning to understand what she was trying to tell him.

The room was cold, and she could feel her hands begin to shake. "I understand that you can't take time off work to travel right now. But do you think we could spend more time together, maybe see each other during the day, when the girls are in school?"

He nodded. "Yeah, I guess. I don't know."

"You know that bakery next to your work? Maybe we could meet up for lunch there during the week. Or even just a quick cup of coffee. It would be nice to see you."

"I have deliveries during lunch. Most days, I eat on the road."

"Well, it doesn't have to be then. It can be anytime you're free."

Fadi shifted beneath the covers. "I'm sorry, but I don't think I can get away during the day at work. I have a lot to do."

She opened her mouth, but there were no words left. Her eyes burned, and she could feel tears rush down her cheeks.

"Please don't do this," Fadi said. "Why are you crying? This is exactly why I called your dad, Yara. I'm worried about you."

She closed her eyes and searched for the precise moment that led her here. Was it the curse? Or was this payback for what she'd done to Mama, or for what she hadn't done, failing to understand her mother all these years?

In a dull, flat voice she said, "Is it because I'm a bad person? Is that why you don't love me?"

"You're not a bad person." Fadi sighed. "Look, I know you've been through a lot, but I don't think it's fair for you to keep blaming me or our marriage for whatever you're going through. I'm not your parents. I'm not the one who hurt you."

She felt a pain settle behind her eyes. "This isn't about them."

"Of course it is," Fadi said. "Stop lying to yourself. I've been here for you through all your bullshit because I felt bad for you, but enough is enough. I've given you so many chances to get your shit together, and I'm not going to stand here and be your punching bag." He grabbed the covers and pulled them over his chest then said, "But you know what? It's my fault. I should've known. My mother warned me this would happen, and I didn't listen. But she was right. You need some serious help, can't you see that?"

He turned over, and it was clear the conversation was over. He was right, of course he was. She opened her eyes and stared into the darkness, filled with the sense that she was a bad person, unworthy of being alive. Her whole life she'd tried to get further from this feeling, but it was still there, like a thick, dark stain on her skin.

Outside the rain tapped against the window, again and again, until eventually it drowned out the endless stream of thoughts whispering how wicked she was. Her eyelids were getting heavy, and she didn't know what to make of this realization, which was old and new at once.

42

The next morning, after dropping the girls off at school, Yara drove aimlessly around town, her hands tightening around the steering wheel. She'd tossed and turned the night before, replaying Baba's and Fadi's words, unable to silence the thoughts in her head. Both of them seemed intent on minimizing her concerns, on insisting that the only thing wrong was her. She stared out the windshield now as panic set in. She couldn't go on like this, pretending things were fine. She had to do something.

"Of course," Silas said when Yara texted him to ask if they could meet. "I'll meet you after my noon class. Just let me know where to go."

A couple of hours later, they were sitting across from one another in the coffee shop, each sipping a golden milk latte. The sunlight streaming from the window was so strong it made Yara's head hurt.

"Thanks for taking the time to come see me," she said. "I didn't know who else to call."

"Of course," Silas said. "That's what I'm here for." He set his cup on the table and reached for the cookies he'd bought. "The barista said these were fresh out of the oven," he said, handing one to her. She thanked him and took a bite. It was thick with barely crisp edges, flecked with dark chocolate chips. After biting into his own cookie, he said: "So what's going on?"

Coming from him, this simple question felt more honest and true. Looking across the table at him, she was overwhelmed by the thought of the kind of person she would've been, the kind of life she would've had, if she'd ever felt safe with another person the way she felt with Silas. And then another thought came: What would she have done if Silas hadn't been gay? Would she have done what Mama had—run into the arms of a man who wasn't her husband?

She took another bite of the cookie, which was buttery and chewy with a hint of sea salt. Without looking up, she said, "Fadi and I have been fighting."

"I'm sorry to hear that," he said. "Do you want to talk about it?"

She nodded. In the back of the coffee shop, their drinks on the table between them, she told him what had happened on their anniversary, and how things had only worsened since. Silas said nothing, just nodded and traced a finger around the rim of his mug as she spoke. When she finished, he said: "So what are you going to do now?"

She stared out the window. "I don't know," she said. "First, I lost my job; now my marriage is on the verge of collapse. It's hard not to feel like I deserve all this."

Silas shook his head, frowning. "What makes you think that?"

"It's hard to explain, really."

"Want to try?" he said gently.

She could feel the tears coming, and she kept her eyes on her drink. "Things with Fadi have always been difficult. I don't know why I can't make him love me—what's so wrong with me that I can't be loved?"

"What are you talking about?" Silas said. "I don't know about Fadi, but plenty of people love you—your children, your parents—"

"You don't know that."

"Of course they love you. Why wouldn't they? You're amazing." Silas reached across the table to touch her hand, and she quickly pulled it back.

"You don't know anything about my family," she told him. "Or me."

Her eyes burned, and she rubbed her lids, pressing her fingers very hard. In a quiet voice she said, "I didn't really see a lot of love growing up. My dad used to hit my mom, and well, she did a lot of things as a reaction to that."

She opened her eyes, and for a few seconds Silas said nothing, frowning. Then he said, "I'm so sorry. I had no idea."

"It's okay," she said.

He looked down into his cup, breathing slowly. "Is that why you think you deserve bad things to happen to you?"

She shrugged, staring at her fingers. "No, not just that."

He waited for her to continue, but when she didn't say anything, he asked, "Is it because of your mother's affair? Did you feel that by loving another man, she didn't love you?"

She nodded and stared down at her lap, trying to keep very still as tears started leaking out of her eyes.

"It's all right to be upset, you know," Silas said. "This must be so painful. I can see why you might have felt abandoned watching your mother with another man, but I'm sure she loves you."

She felt short of breath. "You don't know anything about her."

"Maybe not," Silas said. "But maybe talking to her about your experience would help you feel better?"

Yara shook her head, her hands forming fists in her lap. She couldn't ask Mama. It was Mama who did all the judging, Mama who brought out all the shame. "She can't help me," she finally said.

"I know you may feel that way," Silas said softly. "But why not give it a try? She's your mother."

Something about the way he said this made Yara feel so disgusted with herself. She stared down at her hands, ashamed of what he must be thinking, about how foolish and pathetic and unlovable she was.

The next thing she knew, she could hear herself bursting into sobs, then the heavy sound of her voice saying: "Because she's dead, okay? She's gone. Please, I don't want to talk about her anymore."

43

Raindrops sprayed the windshield as Yara drove to pick up the girls from school. Her stomach hardened as she replayed the way she'd just rushed out of the coffee shop, unable to look Silas in the eye after her confession, and a new wave of shame flooded her as she pulled into the first spot in the carpool lane. As soon as the rain stopped, she opened the window and heard the bright, chirping sounds of birds, taking in the pungent scent of the rain-washed earth. For a long time she sat, gazing out at the trees and the sky until her phone beeped. She looked down to see that Silas had sent her a long message.

I'm so sorry for being insensitive, Yara. I had no idea about your mother, and I feel like a jerk for assuming. I can't possibly understand what you're going through, but I'm here for you. If you feel uncomfortable talking to me, perhaps you could consider another therapist? I know William wasn't the best, but there are good ones out there. It's none of my business really, and I won't say another word about it unless you want me to, but I care about you and want to make sure you're okay.

Minutes later, he sent a follow-up message saying: I forgot to tell you, I made baklava for my class earlier. Needless to say, it tasted nothing like yours. You think you can teach me sometime? Please say yes.

Reading his messages, Yara smiled, then took a deep and cleansing breath. Her chest expanded with relief at the thought of having Silas in her life—how much safety and comfort he gave her, how much hope. His friendship was a gift, one she didn't feel worthy of receiving, but had anyway.

She wiped her face with her sleeve and typed out a reply. "You have nothing to be sorry for," she wrote. "You're a good friend, and I'm so lucky to have you."

"Are you having another sad day, Mama?" Jude asked her later that day.

Yara had decided to spend the afternoon with Mira and Jude in the backyard, hoping the sunshine would make her feel better. Outside the air still smelled earthy and damp, and she watched Mira and Jude kick a soccer ball from one end of the fence to the other, trying to see who could propel it the farthest. But now Mira was plucking dandelions at the end of the yard, and Jude was wiping her nose with the back of her hand, waiting for Yara to answer.

"No," Yara said, trying to sound normal. But she felt a sudden bead of sweat on her forehead. "Why do you ask?"

"You seem sad."

"Oh, habibti." She squatted down to her daughter's level. "How could I be sad when I have a kid like you?"

Jude looked at her through eyelashes as thick as butterfly wings. "Then how come you don't smile often?" she asked, unconvinced.

Sweat was now rolling down Yara's face, and she looked down at her feet. In moments like these, she had the sense that her daughters were able to see right through her in the same way she had seen through Mama. She had hoped she could spare them from the feeling that something was deeply wrong, and she was being reminded now that she hadn't. "I'm sorry, baby," she managed to say. "I'll try to be better."

Jude ran across the yard to join her sister, and the tears Yara had been holding back were now sliding out of the corners of her eyes as she remembered feeling the sorrow of Mama's life, and the dreariness of one day having to grow up and live it herself. This was not what she'd wanted to teach her daughters about the world. And then Yara felt something unexpected: a desire to hold out her hand and ask for help.

Maybe Silas was right. It wouldn't hurt to try therapy on her own terms. What did she have to lose at this point? She'd already lost her career, her marriage was in free fall, and all the things she'd feared were staring her hard in the face. She'd spent her entire adult life trying to escape her childhood, but she hadn't succeeded. And now the pattern was repeating itself with her daughters.

In bed that night, she googled therapists near her zip code, then filtered the results to see which ones accepted her health insurance. She read through dozens of bios until she found one she liked, from a holistic psychologist named Esther. Frustrated by the limitations of traditional psychotherapy, Esther said, she offered a type of therapy that addressed the "whole person," integrating spiritual, mental, and emotional well-being in order to awaken one's authentic self. Yara wasn't totally sure what that meant, but she liked the promise of developing a deeper understanding of herself on all these levels and figuring out: Who was she, really?

The question went straight to the tender root of everything, taking her back to a time when she'd wanted desperately to prove her worthiness, making decisions she'd thought were hers but that were guided by the beliefs that others had put upon her. She thought back to a sculpting class she'd taken in college, where she studied Michelangelo's *David.* When he was carving the structure, Michelangelo was rumored to have said that he was only bringing out of the marble the figure that was already there. Maybe that was how she would uncover her true self, too, by chipping away at the person her ego had built, uncovering what had been buried beneath the layers, and eliminating beliefs that no longer served her. Yara wasn't sure whether the sudden hope she felt was a sign, but she made an appointment for the following week.

44

Esther's office was located on the seventh floor of an old brick building downtown. To get there, Yara drove past the college campus then continued for miles down a one-way road until she reached the town's main street. As she passed streetlamps with flower baskets hung on their poles and shop windows blinking with OPEN signs, she wondered how her experience with Esther would compare to her time with William. Would Yara finally open herself fully to another person, or even just to herself? She exhaled as she stepped into the building, reminding herself that she was here by choice, that she didn't need to book another session if things didn't feel right.

The waiting room was plain with light gray walls and neutral furniture, but there was a large, colorful poster on the wall detailing the seven chakras, and on the coffee table she saw a selection of brochures about alternative treatments: reiki, yoga, breath work, and meditation.

A middle-aged woman came out to the waiting room and smiled warmly. "Yara? I'm Esther. Why don't you come in?" Yara blinked and stared at her. Esther was beautiful, her dark hair loosely pinned back, and there was something in the tilt of her head, the openness of her brown eyes, that reminded Yara of Mama. Back in those rare happy days, before Yara ruined everything.

"You can sit down wherever you like," Esther said.

Yara chose a plump leather chair, unable to take her eyes off the older woman's face as she settled on the other end of the sofa. When she eventually managed to look away, she noticed how serene the office felt, sunshine pouring through the gauzy white curtains. In the back of the room was a large framed copy of a quote that read: "We are not human beings having a spiritual experience. We are spiritual beings having a human experience."

As Yara reread the words, she thought she felt a vibration in her chest that felt like certainty. Something about this claim rang true to her, or at least she wanted it to.

She turned to Esther. "What does it mean?"

Something in her face became determined, and her eyes were bright. "The physical world is constantly reminding us that we're having a human experience," Esther said, "with our five senses telling us what we hear, see, feel, smell, and taste. But something in us, deep in our heart, knows that we are made up of more than the sum total of our thoughts and feelings. We come into this world with an innate knowledge of our infinite spiritual nature, but through our human conditioning we forget who we really are, the true magnificence of our being."

Yara listened to her in silence, trying to process her words. She'd felt small and uncertain most of her life. Was it possible that she could be more than that?

"Have you ever had a feeling you couldn't quite explain?" Esther asked. "A sudden and unexplainable urge, a knowing in your gut?"

Yara nodded. "All the time."

"That's your intuition, your spirit, guiding you."

Yara nodded, her shoulders loosening. The possibility of being vaster than her ego felt relieving, even if she couldn't access the knowing of it directly.

The soft white walls of the office seemed to expand as Yara continued to scan the room. On the wall facing her was a painting of a bridge on a foggy day, a city skyline blurry in the distance. She leaned forward in her seat to look at it, fixing on the vivid brushstrokes, the swirl of colors coming together.

Esther folded her hands in her lap. "Why have you come to see me today?" she said.

"Not a specific reason, exactly," Yara said, thinking back to everything that had happened since her altercation with Amanda. "I guess I've been feeling bad for a while now. I was seeing a counselor at my old job, but I no longer work there, and I figured it was time to try again."

"Well, I'm glad you're here," Esther said. "When did you start feeling this way?"

Yara thought back to how all this started, last summer, when she first learned the news of Mama's death. How one thing had led to another, until her emotions were so intense and jumbled she couldn't differentiate among them. But the seed of her discontent had been planted long before her mother had passed, Yara realized now, and it had been growing inside her for years, waiting for the tiniest rupture to burst wide open.

"For as long as I can remember," Yara said.

Esther nodded. "I see. Why don't we start from the beginning, then?"

Yara kept her eyes on the painting of the bridge the whole time she spoke. She told Esther about her childhood, leaving home to get married, her life with the girls and at work, and how she'd lost her job. She talked about Mama and Baba, how they'd come to this country in search of a better life, or perhaps to try to heal from their own damaged pasts. She described her childhood visits to Palestine and her feeling of helplessness listening to Teta's stories about the nakba, picturing the tragedies her family endured. How Mama had wanted to be a singer but had instead spent her days at home with six children, cooking and cleaning until Baba came home late at night. How Yara had watched from behind her bedroom door as Mama got beaten, how she could still hear her choking sounds and screams when she closed her eyes at night. She told Esther how Baba had called her one day with news of Mama's sudden death, and how he'd continued on with his life as if nothing had happened, as if Mama had been little more than an appliance that had stopped running on him. Yara backtracked then, to how invisible she felt as a child, watching her brothers do things she wasn't allowed to do. How she'd married Fadi and moved far away, desperate to start over. To prove there was nothing wrong with her, that she wasn't weak, that it was possible for her to be someone, even as a woman. That it was possible to feel safe in her body. To get rid of this feeling.

Only she couldn't. She told Esther about getting pregnant so soon after the wedding and being so afraid. How she didn't want to repeat Mama's life, trapped by marriage and motherhood, so she finished undergrad and got a master's despite her mother-in-law's disapproval. How Fadi had been mostly supportive, yet she still felt like something wasn't right between them. How she couldn't be a good wife even though he was so much better to her than Baba had been to Mama.

As the words fell out of her, she felt as if something heavy was lifting. She looked away from the painting and met Esther's eyes. "I thought I could be a better woman than Mama, but I was wrong. I'm worse. I've had things so much better than she did and I'm still so miserable."

"I'm sorry you're feeling this way." Esther spoke quietly, squeezing her hands in her lap. "You've been through a lot."

Yara nodded. The relief of releasing these words gave way to an overpowering sense of sorrow in her. Swaying and twisting in her seat, gripping the insides of her thighs with both hands, she stared at her knees until the urge to cry passed. How could she tell Esther that all her years of feeling guilty about Mama were actually amplified now, sitting there in her plush leather chair, with the privilege of being listened to, being heard?

"How did your mother die?" Esther said.

She was silent. Her longing to stand up and leave the room was like a throbbing wound, but she forced herself to remain seated, her lungs fighting for breath.

Yara didn't know what she was thinking when she first heard the news of Mama's death. In fact, she couldn't seem to remember much of it. The funeral was held in a dark mosque with stained glass windows, and an imam in a layered white robe recited verses from the Quran. The casket was closed and remained shut as they lowered it into the center of the earth. Yara could still feel the heavy feeling in her body as she stood there, immobilized by grief. Then the rage simmering in her throat watching Baba and her brothers moving on so easily while Mama's body disintegrated beneath them. The guilty feeling she swallowed was sharp, intolerable.

"My mother died in her sleep from a pulmonary embolism last summer," Yara said finally. She realized it was the first time she'd let the words leave her mouth. "It was unexpected. I wish I would've had the chance to say goodbye."

"I'm sorry to hear that," Esther said gently. "It seems like your mother's death, as well as your relationship with her, have had a big impact on your life."

Feeling exhausted, Yara shut her eyes, shoved down the burn of tears in her throat. She wanted the session to be over, and yet she was grateful that Esther was giving her the freedom to share only as much as she was ready to.

After a moment, she said, "I blocked out so much of my childhood, including how much she hurt me. I think maybe it was easier for me to remember her as the victim than to remember her making me feel like I was nothing." She shook her head. "I have so many conflicting feelings. I'm upset at her for not showing me love, for having an affair, for not standing up to Baba. But she was a victim, too, you know? My dad made her suffer so much. How could I be upset at her after everything she went through? It just feels so selfish and cruel, especially when I—" Her voice cracked, and tears rushed down her face.

Esther handed her a box of tissues from the coffee table. "Take your time," she said gently. "I can see this isn't easy. You're doing really well."

Yara looked back at the painting, the outline of the bridge against the night sky, the seemingly endless layers of deep violet-blue brushstrokes, the scattered disks of stars glowing a warm yellow. She thought of Mama, how she wished she was still here, how badly she wanted to say goodbye. It was a strange feeling—to go from being angry at her mother to wondering why she'd waited until she was gone to reach out to her, why she hadn't tried to forgive her sooner.

Without looking at Esther, she said, "I think what hurts the most—what's been hardest to accept—is that I'm not all that different from her." She stared down into her lap while Esther waited for her to continue. "It's hard for me to be present with my girls. I'm not a good mother. I'm not a good wife. When I stop to think about the woman I am, I'm so disgusted with myself for failing, just like Mama said I would. She was right."

"I know these feelings must be extremely isolating for you," Esther said. "But what you're describing is a typical complex trauma response. It sounds like your mother endured a great deal of suffering as a young girl in Palestine and also as a young wife and mother in America. She may not have been able to help passing along some unhealed trauma to you. Did she have any kind of support?"

Yara shook her head. "No, and I think she was struggling with a mental illness," she said. "She was never diagnosed, though. Never saw a therapist or anything. Mental health care is stigmatized in our community."

"Unfortunately, it's very common for unhealed trauma to be passed down in families, and it can be particularly strong in ethnic minorities, who often deal with more stigma and discrimination, and can receive compromised care," Esther said. "Your mother was a victim, of course, but she was also a perpetrator. She might not have even been aware of this, and her behaviors may have simply mirrored what she saw in her own family. More and more research shows now that behavior patterns that reinforce trauma are not only passed down in a family, but they can also be transmitted through DNA."

Yara sat in silence. She thought about what Teta said, how the tragedy of the nakba had sucked the color from their lives. She thought about Mama coming to America to escape the powerlessness she'd felt in Palestine, but being unable to do so. How Yara herself had tried to escape her own pain but couldn't either.

"But Mama and Teta had *reasons* to be that way," she eventually said. "Teta grew up in the middle of a war. Mama was surrounded by poverty and violence before she came to this country and had a hard load to carry when she got here. My struggles are nothing in comparison."

"There is no hierarchy of pain when it comes to traumatic experiences," Esther said. "I know it's hard to accept that your suffering is legitimate, too, but I promise you it is."

Yara gripped the edge of the sofa. She rubbed her eye and looked away, controlling the urge to put her face in her hands and sob like a child. "Or maybe Mama was right about me. Maybe I'm just a bad person."

"What makes you think that's true?"

Yara opened her mouth to tell Esther about Mama's curse, but she couldn't bear to call up the words, much less say them aloud. Instead, with a nervous laugh, she told Esther about the time she smashed Fadi's Tar Heels mug. She told her about flinging her phone across the room, the times she'd broken dishes in anger, how she'd collapsed to her knees like a child and refused to get up afterward, not only because she was so ashamed of what she'd done, but also because her body physically couldn't move, so heavy with disgust and self-loathing.

"Have you always had trouble regulating your emotions?" Esther said softly.

Yara nodded. "For a long time, I assumed I was overwhelmed or struggling to adjust to getting married young and moving far from home. But after my incident at work, the counselor wanted me to see a doctor for antidepressants."

"Did you decide to do that?"

"No."

"Why not?"

"I grew up not believing in medication. But now I'm wondering if it was more than that." She met Esther's eyes. "I didn't trust William to tell me what to do with my body. The last thing I needed was to take orders from another man."

"I understand. What did he think you might be struggling with?" Esther asked.

"Depression and anxiety."

"Do you think that's an accurate reflection?"

Yara paused to consider. "I do feel anxious sometimes, and some days I'm depressed. But I don't know. Most of the time I just feel like I suck at being a person, that being alive is really difficult."

"Can you tell me more about this?"

Yara laughed nervously. "I feel unsafe in my own body, like it's trapped me somehow," she said, biting the inside of her cheek. "I feel like I'm constantly at war with myself, like there's something bad inside of me trying to get out." She stopped, feeling short of breath. "The feeling is so intense and all-consuming it's hard to explain clearly."

"You're doing it well," Esther said. "I'm really sorry to hear how hard everything has been for you. You've managed so much on your own all these years, and it takes a lot of strength to do that."

Yara breathed in slowly and looked back at the bridge stretched over the water. She imagined her parents standing on one of the banks, unable to cross to the other side. Mama and all her loneliness. Baba and his anger. Though they'd left Palestine in search of a better life, they'd spent their whole lives stuck in place emotionally, drowning in their unacknowledged pain, until eventually it had spilled over onto her. If she felt this bad, then how must they have felt? They'd lived their whole lives in pain, unable to find a solution, their sadness eventually becoming hers. But now she understood. Maybe she could change it before it was too late. Maybe she could stop it from happening to her daughters.

She nodded and said, "I want to fix myself. I really do."

"I want you to consider reframing that," Esther said. "There's nothing to fix. You aren't broken. You're hurting. What you need is to heal, and I can promise you I've seen many people do that and go on to lead much happier lives. Would you like that?"

"Yes," Yara said, feeling more tears spilling down her face.

"I'd like to begin this process by helping you befriend your body," Esther said. "The first step is becoming aware of the way you respond to the world around you, noticing and describing the physical sensations in your body when you're triggered. Can you try that when you go home today?"

She breathed in through her nose and exhaled slowly. "Yes. I'll try anything."

"Great. I'll schedule you for another session and see you again next week."

Yara stood up from her seat, wiping her cheeks. She wanted to throw her arms around Esther, but she just shook her hand and said, "Thank you."

45

When she heard Fadi's key in the door that evening, Yara noticed the sensations rising in her body, staring with a flinch at the sound. In the hall, she backed away in jerky steps as he moved toward her. Around her, every noise felt amplified, every light source magnified. Fadi was saying something as he followed her up the stairs, but she couldn't hear him. In her head, she'd gone over the conversation they would have, all the different ways he might react to her telling him that she'd gone to see a new therapist, that she was struggling with complex trauma. Would he be proud of her for seeing someone on her own? Relieved? She rehearsed the words while they tucked the girls into bed, her knees rubbery as she leaned in to kiss them good night.

She decided to shower with him tonight, just this once, hoping it might help relieve her nerves. In the bathroom, she closed her eyes and ran her face under the hot water. She didn't speak, but Fadi was quiet, too, seeming somehow far away. He ran a loofah across his chest, scrubbing hard, then washed his hair, staring hard at the shower tile. The moments felt like an eternity as the water roared between her ears.

Back in the bedroom, Fadi reached for his phone, and his fingers trembled as he typed. He didn't seem to notice her watching him, and the nagging feeling inside her grew. Something was really troubling him tonight, Yara thought, sensing it in his fidgety movements. But maybe this was just because she was more newly aware of the sensations in her body, and by extension, his.

She finished drying herself off, then went to the kitchen to fix their dinner plates. Filling a glass with water, she thought about her session with Esther, how it felt like she finally had an explanation for the sadness that had stained her whole life. When she returned to the room, Fadi was sitting up in bed and had opened his laptop, something he rarely did in the evenings. He wasn't wearing a shirt, and she noticed a strain in his shoulders, a clenching of his jaw muscles. Slowly, she set her dinner plate on her nightstand, but when she moved closer to him on the bed, he flinched and snapped the laptop shut.

"Is everything okay?" she said.

He set the computer on the nightstand, avoiding her eyes. "Yeah, I'm just hungry."

In bed they sat up against the headboard with their dinner plates hot in their laps. Fadi grabbed the remote and cued up a new season of *Grey's Anatomy*. Sitting there, unable to eat, she pictured herself telling him about Esther, imagining the look on his face as he set down the remote and turned toward her, his eyes glistening with compassion. But he only stared blankly ahead, absorbed in the story unfolding on the screen, sweat forming at his temples as he chewed.

"By the way, I almost forgot," Fadi said, pausing the show. "My parents are coming for dinner tomorrow."

Her heart sank. "Tomorrow? That's short notice."

"I know," he said. "But my mother invited herself and I couldn't say no. What else do you have to do?"

The comforter was bunched up around her, and she smoothed it with shaky fingers. Had Fadi made this remark any other night, she would've snapped, her hands on her hips, on the offensive. But tonight, she noticed the sensations in her body as if she was feeling them for the first time: the way her face began to harden when he looked at her; the instantaneous, nauseating rush of blood in her throat; the sudden cold sweat along her forehead, cheekbones, and nose; the tingling in her arms and legs. Her eyes stung and she closed them. She contemplated sharing what happened in her session and sobbing on his chest like a child. Instead, she told him she was tired and turned over and went to sleep in the middle of the episode, not wanting to ever wake up.

"You're not finished cooking yet?" Nadia said to Yara the next evening as soon as she came into the kitchen, eyeing the dishes on the sufra. Her bright burgundy hair was freshly dyed with red henna, and she ran her fingers through it.

Yara was pacing around the kitchen in a breathless rush, pausing only to answer her mother-in-law's questions. She had spent the day in a frenzy. After dropping the girls off in the morning, she'd returned home and wiped down all the surfaces in the kitchen, vacuumed the floors, and dusted the chandeliers. Then she'd seasoned a whole chicken with cardamom, fenugreek, and saffron before setting it on a bed of baby carrots and potatoes and putting it in the oven. It was only after she'd done pickup, rushed Mira and Jude through their homework, then taken them to soccer tryouts, that Yara was able to assemble the rest of dinner: garlic couscous, shakshuka, and cucumber salad.

"I'm almost done," Yara said, avoiding the weight of Nadia's stare. She added lemon and tahini to a bowl of diced tomatoes and cucumbers, letting all her frustration dissolve as she mixed it.

"It doesn't look like it," Nadia said.

She wished she'd told Fadi she couldn't host her in-laws. The last thing she wanted to do tonight was talk to another human being, much less Nadia. Yara didn't feel equipped to deal with her condescending tone, and all she wanted was to sit by herself and replay her session with Esther.

"You sure you don't need help?" Nadia said, rolling up her sleeves and taking a step toward her. "Here, let me—"

"No thank you," Yara said sharply. "I'm fine."

Nadia looked at her, round-eyed. "Well then."

Outside the kitchen window, Yara caught a glimpse of Mira and Jude playing catch with Fadi and Hasan. She cleared her throat and met Nadia's eyes. "Why don't you join everyone outside until dinner is ready?"

At the table, Yara hardly said a word. The chandelier was too bright and she stared blankly into her plate, twisting her fingers around her apron strings to distract herself. Around her, Fadi and his parents' voices sounded like they were coming through a tunnel. Every now and then the girls called her name, and she leaned over to refill their plates, relieved to have something to do. She was more aware of the subtleties of her surroundings: Nadia shoveling food into her mouth, Fadi shifting in his seat whenever Hasan asked him a question, her own skin burning whenever anyone looked at her. It felt like all the tension in the room was vibrating inside her as she chewed her food slowly, taking long, deep breaths.

Sitting there, Yara understood why Esther had wanted her to pay attention to her body. She'd so often felt tight and heavy, like something was pressing down on her from all sides, but she had never noticed these individual sensations clearly as they were happening. Now she could sense that they were coming from somewhere inside herself, rather than attacking her randomly from the outside. It might still be her fault, but at least she knew more about why she felt the way she did. Now she was no longer a total mystery to herself, the pain in her body no longer a puzzle to be solved.

Sometime around ten, after they'd finished dinner and drunk chai and Yara had excused herself to put the girls to bed, Nadia and Hassan finally left.

"Dinner was great tonight," Fadi said when she came back downstairs to find him standing over the pot of couscous, using a wooden spoon to take another bite. "Seriously, so good," he said, his mouth full.

"Thank you," Yara said and then went over to the sink and began washing the dishes. Eventually he brought the empty pot over to her, placing it on the pile of dishes beneath the running water.

"I don't know how you do it," he said. "It's like magic."

"Thanks," she said flatly.

He stood there for a moment, frowning, then grabbed a glass of water and headed into the bedroom. When she heard the sound of the TV, she sighed. Her face hardened as she scanned the room, seeing that the counters were still a mess. She turned off the faucet and stood in the doorway of the bedroom. "Can you help me clean up, Fadi?"

"Come on," he said without taking his eyes off the screen. "The game's on, and I'm exhausted."

She wiped her hands on her apron. "So am I."

"Well, I've been working all day."

Her lungs were now fighting for breath. "Seriously?"

He tossed the remote on the comforter, then swung his legs over the side of the bed. "All right, fine. Let's clean up."

"Come on, Fadi. That's not what I want."

"You just said you wanted me to help."

"Not like this."

He sighed, shaking his head. "Why do you always start fights for no reason?"

The harshness of this question, and the condescending way he looked at her, made her want to weep. With one hand pressed to her mouth, she said, "I went to see a new therapist yesterday."

"Really," he said, still on the edge of the bed. "That's good."

"She thinks I have some unhealed trauma."

"Trauma?"

She paused, and the silence in the room was so loud. "She thinks it's because of what happened when I was younger. You know, with my parents."

Fadi rolled his eyes. "Don't you think that's pretty dramatic?" he said. "Who do you know who didn't have a fucked-up childhood?"

She saw dismissive judgment in his expression and felt a swell of shame. "I know, but Esther said it might explain why I sometimes act the way I do when I—"

"Come on, that's not an excuse," Fadi interrupted. "Do you really think you're the only one with problems? My relationship with my father is bad enough to fill a psychology textbook, and I don't go around losing my shit. You can't just blame your parents when your life isn't going the way you want it to."

She balled her hands in fists so tight her nails could've drawn blood. "But you never acknowledge the way I feel or what I've been through."

"See? That's your problem. You think the whole world revolves around you. Your behavior has always been all over the place, Yara. That's no one's fault but your own."

"Stop it!" She could feel her jaw clenching. "I'm trying to get better, but you're not making it easy."

"Seriously? So now it's my fault?"

"That's not what I'm saying."

He stared at her. She couldn't even tell what she wanted, whether it was for him to be understanding or for her to have the ability to forgive him for being so cruel. Taking a step toward the bed, she said, "I feel completely alone."

"You act like I'm out all night getting drunk and screwing around," Fadi said, lifting himself off the mattress and stepping toward her. "I'm busting my ass so you can live like this." He waved his hands around the room. "So you can have a nice house and a fridge full of food and get fired without having to worry about it." He moved another step closer, and she inched back, pressing her body back against the doorframe. "You think I don't feel overwhelmed? I'm the one who gets the bills every month! I'm the one who pays for everything! Tell me, who's going to do that if I stay home with you and clean up the kitchen all day?"

He was walking away from her now, shaking his head. "I know I'll never make enough to support this family," she said. "But I'm not one of your children. You act like I'd fall apart if it weren't for you."

"That's what you don't seem to understand," he said, and when he met her eyes she saw disgust in his face. "You would fall apart."

At once she rushed toward the nightstand, her heart racing, and grabbed Fadi's water glass. She tightened her fingers around the glass, her hands shaking, but before she could fling it against the wall, she stopped. Breaking it wouldn't relieve the anger she felt inside.

She set the glass down.

"You're fucking insane," Fadi said as she stomped into the closet and closed the door behind her. In the darkness of the small room, she sank to her knees and curled into a tight ball, feeling the panic and shame setting in. She didn't know how long she lay there, but when she finally pulled herself off the floor, her skull ringing, the closet door was still shut.

Quietly, she peeked into the bedroom and found Fadi in bed, asleep.

The shutters were closed so tightly that no light entered the room. She climbed into bed next to him, pulled the covers over her body, and blinked into the darkness. Why did it feel like no matter how hard she tried, things would only keep getting worse? She closed her eyes and lay there, listening to her breath. Esther had validated her feelings, had even given her hope for a solution. But in one brief exchange, Fadi had been able to strip that hope away. How could she heal when the person closest to her wouldn't acknowledge her pain?

She pressed her face into her pillow and cried. What was she supposed to do? If she divorced Fadi, she would ruin her life, her daughters' lives. She knew this, had been told this since she was a child. Only now, in the middle-of-the-night quiet, she saw their future together so clearly. She would remain on this path with him, going round and round until the end of time. Getting nowhere, becoming no one.

Yara wasn't sure what her life would be like if she left Fadi, but now she felt certain what would happen if she stayed. She would spend her life under the weight of her pain, and when she couldn't bear it anymore, she would do whatever she could to set it down, even if it meant hurting the people around her. She felt her body sinking with shame at the thought. She could see the girls growing up feeling the way she had, haunted by a dull eerie presence they could never shake. For once, their future became clear to her, trapped behind the twisted glare of an evil eye, a filter of sorrow tainting everything they knew. Isn't that how she'd lived all these years, looking at the world through a distorted lens, heavy with dread, always afraid? She couldn't do that to them. In the darkness, it was all becoming very clear: perhaps the way to keep from following Mama's path was not to save her marriage but to leave it.

46

I've been thinking of leaving my husband," Yara told Esther at the beginning of their next session. She needed to voice it to someone right away so she didn't back out and change her mind.

She and Fadi hadn't spoken since their blowup, tiptoeing around each other at home, but the day before, he'd texted her a family picture they'd taken in Asheville last spring. The four of them were standing together on the porch of their rental cabin, with the blue mountains in the distance. Mira in a bright pink dress with white flowers, Jude smiling wildly at the camera to show off her missing tooth, Yara and Fadi with their arms around them, laughter on their faces. What the photo didn't reveal, but Yara remembered clearly, was the feeling inside her body. Or her jumble of thoughts, the guilt she'd been feeling about being a bad mother, the argument she'd had with Fadi earlier that day, the tension behind her face as she performed happiness. Everything in the photo was a lie, a sanitized story to make her feel better about herself.

And yet, staring at her daughters' bright faces, she was overwhelmed by a flood of tears. Even if she managed to leave, she feared she might come to regret dismantling everything she'd built with Fadi.

"It's clear that guilt has been a deciding force in your life," Esther said when Yara articulated all this. "You've spent years putting other people's needs before your own, longing for validation and approval." Yara nodded. "Is there anything else holding you back?"

"Well, the logistics of divorce, to begin with," Yara said, settling deeper into her seat.

She had never lived alone. Baba had provided for her as a child and Fadi had taken over for him when they got married. He'd been in charge of their finances since their wedding day. She felt overwhelmed by the idea of moving out on her own, earning money, and keeping a budget. Not to mention how alone she would be in the world. Baba would disown her. Fadi's parents would likely never talk to her again. Her whole community, such as it was, would see her as a failure, a disgrace.

But at least she wasn't powerless, like Mama had been. At least she had the privilege of education, at least she was born in a country that protected the rights of women and knew the basics of how to navigate, unlike her mother, with language and culture and fear acting against her.

"It seems like you have a lot to consider here," Esther said. "I know you mentioned you left your job a few months ago. Would you be able to provide for your daughters?"

"I can always find work." She shook her head, laughing quietly to herself. "Back when I was sitting with suitors for marriage, I insisted on getting a college education because I wanted to protect myself in case this ever happened. I didn't want to be like Mama, stuck in an unhealthy marriage because I couldn't support myself. I was preparing for the worst, I know, but at least I managed to do something right."

"So what's holding you back now? What are you afraid of?"

Yara felt exhausted, suddenly, by all of it. She wasn't the first woman in human history to want a divorce and find herself unequipped for life on her own, to wake up and realize that she'd spent years living in fear. But it wasn't just Baba, or her in-laws, or the difficulty of setting up a household on her own, that terrified her.

"I think what scares me most is the possibility of making the wrong decision and hurting my daughters." Yara bit her lip, feeling her eyes burn. Esther waited for her to continue. "There are so many things that can go wrong, and it's not their fault they have me for a mother instead of a normal person. What if they end up hating me for leaving their father? What if I pass my trauma on to them anyway? It's all so overwhelming when I think about it. I imagine these are the kinds of thoughts Mama had, too." She sighed. "I want to be brave and make the right choices, but it feels like no matter what I do, they'll still suffer."

Esther nodded. "Passing on unresolved trauma is a fear I hear from many patients," she said. "These are legitimate concerns, whether or not you are considering divorce. Childhood trauma runs so deep that even with the best intentions, parents can pass it to the next generation."

Yara sat very still and felt a new wave of tears spill down her cheeks. She wiped her face with the backs of her hands and dropped them back into her lap.

"I know this all sounds very frightening," Esther said. "But it is possible to break the cycle, even though it feels very difficult at the moment."

She stared down at the floor. "How do I do that?"

"You've already taken the most important step, by coming here and talking to someone," Esther said. "Being aware of how your past impacts your parenting takes tremendous courage. It means you are ready to do your own healing and work through your family's trauma. I can help you examine your past and triggers so that you don't inadvertently pass on your emotional wounds to your daughters. You won't have to do this alone."

Yara moved her hand to her ribs, feeling her heart go beat-beat-beat. How much she wanted to be better, to do things differently. But change didn't happen with a single recognition, a single step in the right direction. It was messy, courage come and gone, steps taken forward, then back. It was bravery laced with fear. She knew this, felt it so deeply within herself in this moment, that part of her knew the right answers yet another part wasn't ready to claim them.

"I know the future is scary and uncertain," Esther said. "But what about how alone you feel now? Aren't you afraid of that, too? Are you sure the alternative really is worse?"

47

Yara decided she would sell her paintings. If she planned to leave Fadi, she'd need a new source of income, and it was at least a place to start. At home, she took photos of the paintings she'd created over the past month and posted them on her Instagram. Then she set a blank canvas on the easel, dissolving her excitement and fear in the bright loops and whorls.

"These are incredible," Silas told Yara one afternoon as they stood in Josephine's kitchen. They were having lunch with Josephine, who had asked Yara to bring over a few of her paintings.

Using bold, dramatic brushstrokes, Yara had painted images from her childhood in Palestine: a terrace wrapped around a rooftop with a grape arbor, well-tended flowerpots lining the window, the leaves of an evergreen olive tree. Some days she used pencil, black chalk, and charcoal. Other days she used a palette of paints: yellows, oranges, greens, and blues. She squeezed paint from the tube directly onto the canvas, adding layers of thick, wild color. She wanted to capture the intensity of everything: wheat fields, olive bushes, flowering trees, all coated with golden sunlight.

"May I buy one?" Josephine asked.

"That's nice of you," Yara said, her face warm. "But you don't have to do that."

"Why, of course I don't have to, child," Josephine said. "But I want to own one of these."

Yara was certain her face betrayed her embarrassment. Or was it gratitude? She placed her hand against her breastbone, an expansive feeling in her chest.

"This is the one I want," Josephine said, pointing to a painting of the small village of Yaffa with a glowing moon above it. "Would you like to display a few others at my recruitment office?" she suggested. "It might help you gain some exposure."

"I'd love that," Yara said and, without thinking, leaned in to hug Josephine. "Thank you for being so kind to me."

A month had passed since she'd raised the idea of divorce with Esther, and though she'd fallen into a new routine, painting in the mornings after dropping the girls at school, she had yet to tell Fadi that she intended to leave him. Esther had encouraged her to continue journaling, too, as a way to keep "uncovering her limiting beliefs" and face her fear of confronting him. So, each evening after dinner, while Fadi watched his shows, Yara retreated to the sunroom to write. She pulled out her journal, spread it open on the table, and felt with each word she was coming closer to understanding how she had become the woman she was now. She could see how she'd been living in a box that no longer fit, her parents' stories and paradigms weighing heavily on her, and how hard it was for her to lift them off and go her own way. Had Mama ever come this close to leaving Baba? Had she hoped the fortune teller would help guide her toward a different future, a destiny not marked by misery?

Yara realized she had something her mother had not, besides her work and her education: she had support. Even if she had had to force herself to accept it, it was there now. In Esther. In Silas, in Josephine. She had friends, and between them and her new rituals of painting and writing, it was nearly enough to muster up the courage to act.

"I've been thinking about something lately," Silas told her one afternoon as they hung a new painting, of a woman picking olives, in Josephine's living room. "Ever since it occurred to me, I've been awestruck, actually."

He paused for a moment, and Yara waited, anxious to hear what he would say. Eventually he stepped back from her painting, and keeping his eyes on it, he started to narrate everything he knew about her, chapter by chapter, as though he was telling her a story about a stranger. He described how she was raised by parents who barely spoke English, in a country foreign to them. How for twelve years she went to a small, private all-girls school, sheltered from the world around her. How at home she watched her mother cook and clean, her father work and pay bills, her resistance burning in her throat. How the first time she left the house without either of her parents was to go to her first college class, "Introduction to Philosophy." How it must have felt impossible that someone like her could someday do something significant or have an impact on other people. How at nineteen she married someone after meeting him twice. How she moved here alone with the only skills she'd acquired over nineteen years: keeping a home and following the rules. How she became pregnant a couple of months later. How at twenty she was learning what it meant to be a mother when she still hadn't learned what it meant to be a person. How she still managed to stay in school and graduate college despite that. How she was caring for her girls, for Fadi, for her home, while also trying to empower herself. How she was now, what she'd once only dreamed of becoming, an artist.

"Don't you see?" Silas said when he finished. "You had so many obstacles in your way and look what you've done." He gestured at the painting, then looked at her. "That takes so much courage and strength, you know that? I'm in awe of you."

Yara said nothing. She was stunned to have someone see her this way, to be recognized like this.

"You might be the bravest person I've ever met," Silas said.

"Thank you," Yara managed, her voice cracking as tears streamed down her face. "I hadn't thought of it like that before."

48

By the end of the month, Yara had sold fourteen paintings. When she counted the money she'd earned, she couldn't believe it. It was considerably more than her monthly salary at the college. All this while doing something she enjoyed? It seemed too good to be true. She twirled her finger around the chain of her necklace, grinning, knowing: it was possible for her to go places, to find her own way.

At home that evening, as Yara simmered spiced rice in a pot, the scents of garlic and cumin all around her, a memory of Teta came to her, one she hadn't thought about in years. They were squatting in front of the taboon oven, the open fire warming their skin. As they slapped balls of dough between their palms, Teta told her another story of the nakba. "That moment was the end of our life as we knew it," she said, her voice tight. "In an instant, as if cast by a spell, our life was split into a before and after. A whole people condemned to a life of exile and rootlessness. A curse unbroken for over fifty years."

It's been over seventy years now, Teta, Yara thought. A lifetime.

She gripped the pot handle, staring down at the steam trapped beneath the lid. Her mother and grandmother had lived their lives feeling haunted by the curse of the past, and so would she if she continued on this path, her mind stuck looking backward, trapped by this old pain, unable to move forward. But she wasn't going to live like that anymore.

She removed the rice from the burner before heading upstairs to her daughters' room. From the doorway, she watched Mira and Jude building a LEGO castle on the floor and wiped away a loose tear.

"Come play with us," Mira said, and Yara smiled and took a few steps into the room.

Jude handed her a handful of blocks and said, "Can you sit next to me?"

Yara nodded and took a spot on the rug next to her. Maybe she had lost her job and ruined her marriage and lost her mother without having the chance to say goodbye, but she wouldn't fail her daughters.

For the next hour, the three of them built tall, colorful towers, laughing as they took them apart and started over. Yara sat very close to them, tracing her fingers down Mira's braid and combing through Jude's wild curls, struck by how beautiful they were. Watching them, she reminded herself to be thankful for this life, for the chance to forge a new path, show them a better way.

By the time Fadi came home, Yara was reading the girls a bedtime story. When he came to tuck them in, the girls giggled and hid under the covers. "Come on, girls, not tonight," Fadi said. He kept looking at his phone, frowning. The girls wouldn't stop laughing, even after he'd turned off the light. "I don't have time for this right now," he said sharply, stalking out of the room. "Go to sleep."

Downstairs, Fadi undressed in front of the bathroom mirror while Yara sat on the edge of the bed. His back was turned to her, but in his reflection she could see his eyebrows drawn.

"Is everything okay?" she asked.

He shook his head, unbuckling his belt. "No."

"What's wrong?"

Without looking up, he said, "I quit my job."

She stared at his reflection. "What do you mean, quit? You own the business."

"Well, I got into it with Ramy, and I gave up my half."

"You gave up your half of the business?"

He frowned, inhaling through his mouth. Something, maybe the way he was keeping his back turned to her as he spoke, made her think this wasn't the whole story.

She got up from the bed and stood in the bathroom doorway. "What happened?"

He glanced at her reflection in the mirror then looked away, slipping off his pants. "We had a disagreement about one of our accounts. I don't want to get into it. It's for the best anyway."

"I don't understand," she said, staring at him. "You've been building your business for years. Why would you just give it all up?"

"I'm ready for something new," he said, peeling his shirt off. Turning to face her at last, he said, "I thought you'd be happy. You're always complaining about how much I work. How we can't travel and all that. Maybe now we can."

"But this doesn't make any sense."

"Fuck," he said, shaking his head. "Why does everything have to make sense to you?"

She realized she was holding her breath and inhaled. "I don't know. It just doesn't feel right."

"Nothing ever feels right to you," he said.

For a moment she was quiet. Maybe nothing was wrong. Maybe this was her distorted view of the world acting up again. "I'm sorry," she finally said. "I just want to understand what happened."

"I honestly don't know what to tell you," he said, opening the shower door. He was still in his boxers, leaning inside to turn on the water. "Ramy and I got into an argument. He accused me of not working as hard as he does. But I've been so busy worrying about you and trying to be home on time so I can please you—so I lost my job. Is that what you wanted to hear?"

Yara took a step back, at a loss for words. Had he really been so preoccupied at work? Distracted by what was happening with her? "I didn't know," she finally said. "I mean, you should have told me I was causing problems for you at work."

"And then what?" Fadi tested the water to see if it was warm. "I didn't want you to think it was your fault. But it has been really hard to focus, Yara. So maybe this is for the best."

Every moment of clarity and relief she had felt from her sessions with Esther left her body in a rush. She leaned against the doorway, feeling heavy. Of course, of course, all of her dissatisfaction, her complaining, her pressure to travel. He was preoccupied with that because he cared. He did care about her.

"I'm so sorry," she whispered. "I didn't know."

"It's not the end of the world," Fadi said, frowning. "I have a good amount of money saved, and there's plenty of things I can do for work. I'll start looking around tomorrow."

Yara held her body very still, fighting the urge to cry as steam filled the room and seeped into her skin.

"Everything's going to be okay," Fadi said from behind the glass. But she knew it wasn't.

In bed, long after Fadi had fallen asleep, she stared up at the ceiling and chewed on the inside of her cheek, touching her necklace. How could she possibly leave Fadi now? It didn't matter how far she ran or how hard she tried. Bad things would always happen, and they would always be her fault. She would never get rid of the badness inside her, would always hear Mama's whisper in her ear: *Once you're cursed . . .*

YARA'S JOURNAL

"She brought a man around while you were gone," the landlord tells Baba as soon as he returns from Palestine, his suitcases not yet unpacked.

I watch them at the end of the hall, the color draining from my face. Baba tilts his head to look at me, his expression filling with something I don't fully recognize.

"Yara," he says when the landlord steps back inside his apartment and closes the door. "Come here."

I cross the hall, head down, then follow him down two flights of stairs until we are outside. The sun burns my face, and I hold my hand to block the yellow light, squinting. Above me the clouds are like streaks of white paint across a milky blue canvas.

I was so young then. Ever since that day, I'd been having nightmares where I was falling through a sky of nothingness, but the fall never seemed to end. Not even when I woke up, my body still dropping.

Baba squats down so that he is looking me in the eyes. "Did your mother bring another man around here while I was away?"

I look up at the sky. "No."

"Look at me." He brings my chin down with a finger. "Isn't it enough that your mother is a sharmouta? I don't need a liar for a daughter, too. Tell me the truth."

My eyes sting with tears, and the fist inside me tightens. I don't know if it's your dazzling smile, or the look on your face when the man is around, that makes me do it. I'm not sure if it's retaliation for all the times you wouldn't look at me, repulsed by the sight of my face, but in this moment, standing beneath the hot afternoon sun, sweat gliding down my face, I tell Baba everything I've seen.

When Baba beats you that night, he makes no effort to conceal it from us. My brothers bury their faces in my lap as we listen to the sounds from the next room. My heart balloons in my chest until I can hardly breathe. I cover my brothers' ears and hum a Fairuz melody to drown out your sobs.

"What did you expect?" you roar, your voice overpowering the music. "You threaten to kill me if I divorce you! To take my kids away! What choice do I have?"

I hum the tune a little louder, rocking back and forth gently.

"You force me to live a life I don't want! This isn't a life worth living!"

I start to sing. See how the ocean is so big? The bigness of the ocean is my love for you.

"Did you think that would make me love you?" you shout.

See how the sky is so far? The depth of the sky is my love for you.

"Tell me," you say. "Do you think that makes you a man?"

I am on my feet then, watching you and Baba through the crack in the door. "Stay in bed," I whisper to my brothers, trying to keep my voice calm. "Everything is okay. Don't worry." But my heart is a fist in my throat.

I press my face against the door, trying to make out the figures in the next room. You are lying on the kitchen floor, curled into a ball. The room is bright, and a sliver of moon is coming through the window. Suddenly Baba appears, his shadow creeping behind him. He grabs the kitchen chair, pulls it back over his shoulders, his shadow doing the same, like a gargoyle spreading its wings. You crawl back, like a tide diminishing. But Baba leans forward and slams the chair into your body, again and again, until it splinters into shards.

"It's okay, everything's okay," I tell my brothers when they hear the thud of wood against bone. "Don't worry. It's only the TV. It's a scary episode, but it'll be over soon."

49

The next few days passed in slow motion. Yara took too long getting the girls ready for school in the mornings and cooking dinner in the evenings. She dragged herself into the shower before Fadi came home so she wouldn't have to take one with him. He'd been meeting with potential partners all day, he said. Brainstorming new business ideas. But the weight of her guilt did not diminish, and she tucked the girls into bed each night without meeting their eyes so they couldn't see the failure in her face. It mortified her to think about all the ways she had hurt them. Despite how hard she'd tried to do things differently, she had given them what she'd feared: a mother who ruined everything.

She cried all the way to Esther's office for her weekly session, doubt hammering in her head. Had she been foolish to believe she had the courage to leave Fadi? To overcome the guilt and shame and start a new life for herself, free from her limiting beliefs? In the waiting room now, she tipped her head back against the sofa, blinking the wetness from her eyes.

"Yara, are you okay?" Esther said when she came out to get her.

She couldn't find the words. She just covered her face with both hands.

"Why don't you come inside?"

Somehow she managed to lift herself off the sofa and drag her immensely heavy feet across the room. Inside Esther's office, the light was too bright, the temperature too cold. Yara sank into her seat and hung her head.

"What's going on?" Esther said softly.

"I can't leave Fadi."

"Why? Did something happen?"

"He lost his job." She stared at the floor, feeling nauseated. "He said it was because of how ungrateful I've been lately, the problems I've been giving him at home." She paused, lifting her hands to her forehead and pushing her hair back. "He's worked so hard building his business with Ramy, all these years. It meant everything to him. And it's my fault he's lost it all."

"I can understand why you might feel that way," Esther said. "But what happened at Fadi's company is not your fault."

Yara shook her head. "That's not true. I'm the reason he fought with Ramy, the reason he had to give up his half of the business. Because he couldn't focus. Why couldn't I just be grateful?"

"I know this is very painful, but you're not responsible for your husband's business decisions or his behavior," Esther said.

She started to cry and covered her face with her hands. "I'm ruining his life, just like I ruined my mother's."

When Esther spoke again, her speech was slower. "Growing up the way you did, Yara, it's natural to wonder if you've brought pain to the people around you. I'm sure watching your mother suffer through an abusive marriage was very hard. But her pain wasn't your fault, either."

"You don't know that," Yara said.

"You were a child," Esther said. "You didn't cause the abuse and you couldn't have stopped it." She paused, making her voice softer. "What your father did to your mother is not your fault."

"Yes, it is." Her voice came out in a low hiss she didn't recognize. "I told my father about my mother's affair. I didn't have to. I should've tried to protect her. That's why I can't get her voice out of my head. I still talk to her sometimes. As if there's any chance she could forgive me." She paused, wiping her face. Esther pushed the box of tissues toward her across the coffee table.

"Feeling guilty is a very normal reaction," Esther said slowly. "But you were the child, and your parents were the adults. It was their responsibility to protect you, and they didn't. You have nothing—*nothing*—to blame yourself for."

In a frightened voice, Yara said: "But it was my fault, it really was." She leaned her head against the seat and stared up at the light fixture. She wanted to close her eyes and drift off into a deep sleep, into nothingness, but she continued focusing on the light until she saw spots. "When my father asked me about the affair, I betrayed her," Yara said. "She was happy, and I ruined it for her. I thought if I made a better life for myself, I wouldn't feel so guilty anymore for taking away the only happiness she ever knew. But I'm a bad person, and nothing I do will ever change that. Look at what I've done to Fadi." She blinked, new tears slipping down her face. "What's the point of being alive if I make everyone around me suffer?"

It sounded more disturbing than she'd intended, and when she finally looked down and away from the light, Esther's eyebrows were knit together. "It sounds like you're having a lot of intense feelings," she said. "Are you having any thoughts of hurting yourself?"

Yara rubbed her tongue against the roof of her mouth. She started to speak, then stopped. It felt impossible to articulate to Esther that, ever since she was a child, perhaps since her mother's curse, she didn't feel very attached to the idea of being alive. It often felt too difficult to move through the day, that all she wanted was to close her eyes and lie very still until she felt nothing. That although she had thoughts of dying, she thought about her daughters, how they would feel, how they would worry if it had been their fault.

When Yara still hadn't spoken, Esther said, "You understand that suicidal feelings aren't something to take lightly."

She stared down at her knees. "Yeah, I know."

"There are a couple of treatment options to consider," Esther said. "For starters, I would recommend we increase your sessions to twice a week. And we can talk about the option of medication, if that's something you're comfortable with. And more than anything, it's important for you to have a strong support system. Your husband needs to understand that this is serious."

Yara's sight line blurred with tears, and she closed her eyes again. In the early days of their marriage, Fadi had come home once from work to find Yara on the floor of their bedroom closet with her head in her hands. He seemed afraid to ask why she was sitting in the darkness, curled up in the fetal position, rocking back and forth and making small whimpering noises. But he got her a glass of water, pressed it to her lips. "You look thirsty," he'd said. Shortly after, when she was pregnant with Mira, she'd spent many nights in the bathroom, her head resting on the toilet seat. He bought her a neck pillow one day, handing it to her without meeting her eyes. She had wanted so much for him to say something more, but he hadn't. She wondered how he'd learned to block out people so well, perhaps as a coping mechanism for his father's criticism. Or maybe it was part of being human—you eventually learned how to protect yourself, even at the expense of connecting with someone else.

"Is there anyone else we can reach out to, besides your husband?" Esther was saying now.

"No," Yara said, sinking farther into the chair. She pushed Silas out of her mind. "No one else."

50

Fadi came home late that night, whether from job hunting or something else, Yara didn't dare ask. They barely spoke during dinner, except when Fadi mentioned that he was starting to research ideas for a new business. He reassured her again that he had plenty of savings and would have no problem opening something new. "This is good," he kept saying. "A fresh start."

Yara made a noise in her throat, unable to bring herself to ask more about their financial situation, or if Ramy had reached out to him. She couldn't bear to be reminded of what she'd done. Esther could say all she liked that it wasn't Yara's fault, but deep down, she knew better, and Fadi did, too. To her relief, he didn't seem bothered. He probably preferred this quieter version of her, guilt-ridden and ashamed, to the woman she'd been before he lost his job. But she was nothing like that woman. All she'd wanted was to feel connected to him. Now all she wanted was to feel nothing. Now she only opened her mouth to eat food that had no flavor, in front of the TV she stared at but didn't see.

That night, Yara dreamed she was back in her childhood bed, only a sliver of light coming from the window. She could hear her parents' voices in the hall. Murmurs at first, low and hard, slowly getting louder. Baba was speaking through gritted teeth. Mama was snapping back, her words fast like a whip. Yara curled up into a ball and pulled the covers over her body. She rocked back and forth, trying to drown out the noise. But the sounds echoed around her, softly at first, then louder and louder.

"Let go of me!" Mama said.

Then Baba roared, his voice like an ocean, and Yara pulled her pillow over her head. Eventually the sounds in the background dulled, because of course she had fallen asleep. Of course, she hadn't gotten up to help Mama. That was how Yara knew she was bad, why she deserved to be cursed. She had turned her back on the person she was supposed to love most.

51

The coffee shop was crowded the next day, but Yara got a corner booth by the window, looking out at the parking lot, where the asphalt glistened in the rain. People wandered in, shaking out umbrellas, or rushed out with their bags held over their heads. Others sat inside, staring at their phones, and Yara wondered how long it would be before they would look up. Their vague, distant expressions reminded her of all the time she'd spent drifting from one moment to the next, here but also far away.

She reached into her bag and pulled out her camera. She'd put it in her bag that morning without quite knowing why. As she gripped it, the metal felt cold between her fingers. She'd become so used to the lightness of a pen in her hand that the camera felt heavy now.

Without thinking, she pressed it to her face. Outside the window, the world seemed different. She twisted the lens, and the image sharpened. A woman tied the arms of her jacket across her waist as she ran across the parking lot, her face twisted in a frown. Yara snapped a picture of her before she entered the shop and stood in line, stone-faced. When she reached the cashier, she straightened her spine and adjusted her face into a smile.

For a long time, Yara sat there watching people wander in and out of the shop, not sure what she was hoping to discover. Sadness, confusion, exhaustion? Did any of them feel the way she did, disgusted by the lives they were living? Were any of them like her, ruining everything and everyone they touched?

Eventually she got in line to order another drink and glanced out the window as she waited. The rain had stopped, the fog was thinning, and slivers of the sun were shining through. She froze when she noticed a familiar man crossing the parking lot and realized it was Ramy. He entered and took a place in line right behind her, but to her relief he was looking down at his phone. She took a step forward and pretended to look inside her wallet, hoping he wouldn't notice her. But when the line began to move and she ordered her drink, she turned around, and they locked eyes.

To her surprise, Ramy smiled and tilted his chin upward in a greeting. "Yara," he said, his voice warm, putting his phone in his pocket. "Nice to see you."

She rubbed the zipper of her wallet, feeling nervous. "Nice to see you, too."

Under the bright lights of the coffee bar, she felt dizzy, but tried to seem normal.

"How are the girls?" Ramy asked after ordering his own drink.

"They're good."

"I'm glad to hear it." He nodded and looked at the floor. "Listen," he said. "I'm sorry it had to end this way between our families."

Feeling a rush of relief that he'd brought it up, Yara said, "I wanted to call you and apologize, but Fadi said I should just leave it alone. I'm so sorry for causing you trouble."

He blinked at her. "What do you mean?"

"For creating those issues for you and Fadi at work," she said. "I've been having a rough time lately, and I didn't realize it was distracting him and affecting the business until it was too late. I know how much this company means to both of you, and I'm so sorry."

He didn't seem to register her words. "What are you talking about?"

"Fadi . . . Fadi told me you were upset with his performance because of our problems at home, and that's why he gave up his half of the business."

Ramy took a step back. "Uh, I don't—" He paused, shaking his head. "This is the first I've heard of any of this."

"But Fadi said—"

He cut her off. "Fadi has been slacking off at work and jeopardizing our business, staying late to hang out, charging the business card for personal trips, even claiming reimbursement for a storage room that doesn't exist."

Her sunroom, Yara thought, staring at Ramy, disbelieving.

"A lot of shady stuff, really, but nothing that had to do with you."

His words hit her like a wave. She waited for her breath to return and finally managed, "No, no. That's not possible."

"Judging from your reaction, you don't know much about what's been going on," Ramy said. "But Fadi has been careless at work for some time now. If I were you, I'd be mindful of your finances moving forward."

She didn't remember what she said next, but she must have replied before he left the shop with his coffee. On the way back to her seat, she felt like there was something covering her face, making it impossible to breathe. Blinking into the sunlight that was now streaming in the window, she desperately tried to make sense of what Ramy had just told her, but she could not. Eventually she packed up her bag and left without touching her drink.

In her car, she picked up the phone to call Fadi, then put it down. This wasn't a conversation she could have over the phone. She needed to look him in the eye. She couldn't give him time to come up with another story, to find a way to play the victim and shift the blame back onto her. How many times had he lied to her? And why had it been so easy for her to believe him?

52

I have some great news," Fadi said as soon as he came home that night.

The girls were already asleep and Yara was sitting on the living room sofa reading a book, though she couldn't focus on the words. The warm yellow light from the table lamp was glowing faintly next to her, and she set her book down as Fadi made his way toward her. From a few feet away, she could detect the heavy scent of smoke on his skin.

"One of my old classmates is opening up a hookah lounge," Fadi said. "He asked me to go in on it as a partner. I think it's a great idea. This town needs a space like that."

Yara didn't move, just sat there looking at him. She had a terrible sense all of a sudden of what she and Fadi were capable of: he would keep covering his tracks, and she would keep pretending nothing was wrong. The thought frightened her so badly she rose from the sofa, her hands shaking.

"What's wrong?" Fadi said.

Her heart was pounding as she spoke. "I ran into Ramy at the coffee shop today."

Fadi went pale, but she couldn't interpret his expression. Shock, maybe, or fear. "What?" he said.

"He said you've been abusing your expense account and charging the company card for personal trips. Is that why you went to Vegas? You said it was for work."

Fadi shrank back in surprise, his eyes wide, though his expression seemed forced to her. "He's lying."

"Why would he lie about that?" Yara said. "And why would he tell me you'd been lying about paying for a storage room?"

"I don't know," Fadi said, his tone defensive. "He's the one having affairs behind Hadeel's back. He pushed me out because he knew I would tell her."

Very slowly, she said, "I thought you said he let you go because of me?"

Fadi shook his head. "Well, there were a lot of reasons." He began to pace the room. "He's scared I might tell his wife what I know, so he decided to ruin my reputation before I could ruin his." He gave her a wounded look. "You don't actually think I would do that?"

She stared at him.

"Are you seriously going to believe him over me?" he said.

A familiar wave of self-doubt hit her, and for a brief moment, she considered that he could be telling the truth. It was possible, of course, that Fadi had caught Ramy doing something wrong. But if that was really the case, why hadn't Fadi just told her the truth? Why had he tried to put the blame on her?

She met his eyes. "You told me it was my fault."

He frowned. "I know, and I'm sorry. But if I'd told you that he was having an affair, you might have told Hadeel." He let out a heavy sigh. "It was all too much."

I'm not even close to Hadeel, she thought. But her heart was pounding and she couldn't push the words out. Finally she said, "You should've told me the truth."

"I'm telling you the truth now," he said quietly. "I'm sorry."

Yara looked out the window, feeling numb and disoriented. She pictured Fadi's charming smile, the way his cheeks dimpled when he laughed. She replayed the years she'd spent beside him, feeling as though she was living through a silent war, one in which she was both victim and aggressor.

She swallowed. "I don't believe you."

Fadi took a step back. "What do you mean, you don't believe me? I'm telling the truth."

It felt like an eternity before she was able to respond. She'd created a life with a man she'd never actually known, someone who had never known her, not even tried to. She stared into his face, seeing every man who'd done whatever he wanted while a woman paid the price. Baba, her brothers, all of them. Then she said: "No, you're not."

"I can't believe this," Fadi said. "Are you seriously taking Ramy's side over mine?"

"You tried to make this seem like it was my fault. It had nothing to do with me!"

"I already told you, I—"

"Enough." Her voice sounded cold to her. "It doesn't matter what you say. I don't trust you anymore, and I don't think I ever did."

For a few seconds they stood looking at one another in silence.

Fadi stepped closer to her, his face tense, and reached out his hand as if to touch her. But she turned away, shaking her head as she left the room.

With the lights out, Yara lay on the living room sofa, which she'd made up with sheets and a comforter. She stared at the ceiling, the pulse in her neck throbbing as she tried to wrap her head around what she'd learned. Why had Fadi tried to blame the end of his business on her, and why had it been so easy for her to believe him? She probably would've believed him if he told her she was responsible for much worse. Her eyes filled up with tears, and she squeezed them shut.

Something in her body hardened now. Fadi had been lying. It wasn't her fault. Esther had been right to warn her about the ways guilt and shame had been steering her life, preventing her from showing compassion to herself. And if she'd been right about that, what else was she right about? Could it be that even though she never got the chance to apologize to Mama, she wasn't a bad person? She rubbed her palms against her chest, sliding the comforter off her body. Somehow a space in her heart had cracked open and a sliver of hope slipped in.

For a moment it seemed possible, finally, to forgive herself for the way things ended between her and Mama. The story she'd been telling herself arrived suddenly now: she had never stopped waiting for Mama to forgive her, even though she never could. She'd waited for Fadi to love her, too, as if that would somehow prove she wasn't an unworthy, unlovable person. She'd thought she could block out Mama's death and run away from the past, but her desperation to move on had made everything worse.

Perhaps she had never confronted the voice in her head because it had been easier to listen to it. It had been safer to sustain the belief that she was a bad person. At least then she was in control. At least then she could arrange her life so carefully that her badness didn't spill out and leak everywhere. But she could no longer live her life with this regret, paralyzed by all the words she hadn't said. It was time for her to make a choice before it was too late.

53

The next morning, on the drive to Esther's office, Yara pressed one hand flat against her chest. The hamsa charm felt cold and clammy beneath her fingers. She'd taken off the bracelet Fadi had given her and left it on their dresser. She kept one hand on the wheel and the other on her charm, staring at the passing lights and streets, the sun coming through the windows. It wasn't too late to turn around, she knew. She didn't have to do this. But she did it anyway.

In the waiting room, she stood by the window with her hands in her pockets, lightly tapping her foot against the baseboard. Outside, a dozen birds were joined together in a V shape, soaring through the clouds. Yara watched the birds spread out and come back together once before Esther opened her office door, "Yara?"

She tried to contort her mouth into a smile but couldn't. Instead, she put her head down and followed Esther into the office, taking a seat on the sofa and craning her neck at the ceiling. For a moment she stared up at the glittering white light, until she leveled her head and spoke.

"You were right. It wasn't my fault Fadi was fired." Her eyes burned with tears but she didn't touch them. "He lied to me about losing his job, when he really had to give up his business for abusing his expenses and goofing off. It had nothing to do with me. But it made me realize something."

She paused, and Esther nodded for her to continue.

"I think I've been lying to myself, too."

"How so?"

She sat upright, the words coming to her clearly now. "I've spent my whole life trying to escape this bad feeling inside me. I did everything I could to resist my memories or anything that reminded me of what a terrible person I was. And yet despite this, I knew that something was off between me and Fadi. I just assumed the wrongness I felt was coming from me, that I was the problem."

For a moment Esther waited, as though there might have been more, then she said: "It sounds like you were unable to follow your intuition, to trust yourself. Tell me more about your thoughts, how you've been dealing with them."

Yara described the voice, the whispers in her head, and the way she'd been writing about them. "There's a mental dialogue going on that never stops. It's a small voice that keeps me uncertain, insecure, afraid. A voice that always turns me against myself. Sometimes it's my mother's voice, her ideas about me. Sometimes it's simply other people's opinions of me. Other times it's my own voice. I've spent years listening to that voice, believing that everything it says is the absolute truth. It wasn't until I started writing that I noticed the incessant chatter and had a chance to step back and view it objectively. Then I started thinking, 'I am not the voice in my mind,' and then, 'what if that voice is wrong?'"

"Yes, and if it is, what would that mean for you, Yara?"

Tears slid down her face. "It would mean maybe I'm not so terrible after all, and maybe there isn't something wrong with me, and I don't deserve bad things to happen to me. It would mean that I was justified in feeling sad and alone growing up, that I deserved to be loved and cared for, that I'm not a cold, unlovable person. It would mean that I wasn't crazy for feeling that there was something off in my marriage, that the reason it's failing isn't that I'm too difficult to love. That the stories I've believed about myself for so long aren't true." She wiped her face with one hand and met Esther's eyes. "I don't want to listen to the voice in my head anymore."

"You don't have to," Esther said.

Yara turned to look out the window, her face on fire. Despite how desperately she wanted to believe Esther, the idea seemed unattainable. Even if she summoned up the courage to leave Fadi and start over, would she ever be able to work through her family trauma and heal? The change felt so massive, so difficult, especially now, when she felt so weak. "But how do I do that?"

"Forgiveness," Esther said. "We talk a lot about the importance of forgiving people who hurt us, but we hear a lot less about how to forgive ourselves, which is just as important—if not more so."

Yara shook her head. "I don't know how to do that."

Esther smiled. "You're already doing it. Talking with me honestly about the things you blame yourself for is a first step. We can work together to come up with alternative narratives for why things happened the way they did, so that you can learn new stories to tell yourself, stories that don't put the blame on you. And we can help you cultivate positive self-talk."

Yara looked down at her lap, exhaling. "I'm not sure if I can learn how to speak more kindly to myself," she said.

"It will take practice," Esther said. "But you can learn to replace the mental voice that has been a source of worry and distraction with one that is rooted in love and compassion for yourself. You'll start to remember that you are the one inside who notices the voice talking. You are not the voice of the mind—you are the one who hears it. Once you come to know this, you'll be able to pick and choose what thoughts you listen to, what you hear about yourself. You'll be able to speak to yourself as a friend would, or a loving parent. Would you like that?"

Yara closed her eyes for a moment and felt a floating sensation run through her body, a willingness to believe that everything would be okay. The feeling was so foreign to her she shivered. "Yes, I would," she said. "But there's something I need to do first."

54

Outside Esther's office building, Yara paced around her car, trying to work up the nerve. She reached for her phone, her hands shaking, and stood there looking at it until her eyes hurt. Esther was right, of course. She could learn to watch her thoughts instead of becoming lost in them, to stop using her mind as a way to hold herself together whenever she felt afraid. She knew what she had to do; she always had. But now it was time to muster up the courage to act.

Her heart pounded so hard she could hear it between her ears. She closed her eyes and thought about Mama. How young she'd been when she married Baba and moved to America, how scared and alone she must have felt becoming a mother. How she'd looked after them all day, all on her own. How she'd waited for Baba to come home each night even though she knew what would happen. How she'd curled up on the kitchen floor in her bleach-stained nightgown, how she endured all that pain and stayed with Baba even though she so badly wanted to leave, how she suffered so much, all for their sake.

If Mama could do all that, then surely Yara could do this. She pushed her hair out of her face and inhaled. Then she called Baba's number.

After four rings, his voice came on the line. "Hello?"

"I need to talk to you," Yara said.

"About what?"

She brought her hand to her throat, pressing it against her hamsa charm. "About Mama."

"What do you mean, what's there to talk about?" Baba said.

"I want to know why you treated her so badly."

"Here you go again," Baba said. "It was a long time ago. Why are you bringing this up now?"

"Because I want to know why you didn't make things right with her," Yara said. "Why didn't you apologize for the way you treated her all those years?" Her hand was clenched so tightly around her phone that her palm was throbbing. "You made it seem like she was crazy, but what about all the things you did to her? Will you ever take responsibility for it?"

"Excuse me?" Baba was shouting on the other end of the line now. "How could you say that after everything she put our family through? She dragged our names through the mud!"

"All you care about is your reputation. But what about her?"

"That's all you have in this world, your reputation," Baba said. "What else do you have?"

"Your integrity," Yara said. "Your family. The knowledge that you're living an honest life. Being true to yourself. Setting a good example for your kids. Raising them in a house filled with love." She wiped the tears from her cheek with the back of her hand. "Who cares what the world sees if you can't even stand to look at yourself?"

"I should've known you would blame me," Baba said. "You're just like your mother, putting all the burden on your husband."

"Really? Is that what Fadi says? That it's all my fault? Has he told you that he lost his business and it was his fault? That he was careless with money? Misused expense accounts? Or will you also find a way to blame me for that? You've never once cared about my happiness. Well, I'm done. I'm not doing it anymore."

"What are you saying?"

"I'm getting a divorce."

"Magnoona? Have you lost your mind?" Baba said. "Do you want to give me a stroke? I won't survive another disgrace."

"You don't have any say in the matter," Yara said.

He laughed, as though horrified. "Is this some kind of sick joke?"

"I don't deserve to live like this," she said. "And I won't."

"Ha!" Baba said. "You think you're going to feel better if you leave? You think you're going to live happily ever after? That's the bullshit this country tries to feed you. Why do you think half of them are divorced?" She opened her mouth to respond, but Baba cut her off. "You're a mother. Your children come first. What about your daughters?"

"I'm not giving them up, if that's what you're implying," she said, her chest rising and falling. "Fadi and I can share the girls' time peacefully. It's not my intention to take them from their father. I know he'll want what's best for them, too."

"What's best for them is their parents staying together," Baba said. "If you get a divorce, khalas, you'll lose them. Game over. You can't pass down our values or expect them to be Arab after a divorce. The right thing to do is to stay for your kids. Like your mother and I did."

"You still don't understand, do you?" Her fingers were shaking, and she clutched the phone harder. "Do you really think you did us a favor? What you put us through was much worse than a divorce. It's made my own life much harder."

"Your own failure has nothing to do with our marriage."

"It has *everything* to do with it. Do you really believe you did nothing wrong?"

She could hear her father's heavy breathing until he finally said, "It doesn't matter what I believe. It won't change the past and it won't bring her back."

Yara responded by ending the call, then slid into her car, her heart beating too fast, her body on fire.

Baba could not actually believe that he had played no part in Mama's suffering, could he? Was he actually cruel enough to dismiss not only Mama's pain, but hers, too? She inhaled and looked out the window. Did Baba really want her to stay in an unhappy marriage, and could he truly believe that his refusal to let Mama leave had been what was best for her?

Yara sat up in her seat now and started the engine. Through the windshield, thick clouds coated the sky, the view white like a fresh canvas. She pulled out of the parking lot and wondered what it would be like to be seen and understood by another person for once, to feel truly safe.

55

That night, Yara sat between Mira and Jude on the mattress with a book in her lap, their feet touching beneath the covers. Outside, the sky was a soft denim blue, gradually darkening as she got closer to the end of the story. They were reading about a pilot stranded in the desert who meets a young prince visiting Earth from a tiny asteroid. As Yara narrated, Jude rested her head on her shoulder and Mira leaned in and traced the outline of the illustrations with a finger. Eventually Yara softened her voice, preparing them for sleep.

She was neither happy nor sad about what she was going to do. How many nights of tucking her girls in would she lose? How would their lives turn out, how would they feel about her decision? So many questions she would have no answers to until later, perhaps when it was too late.

But she needed to do this. She would risk the chance of making a wrong turn if it meant saving them from a lifetime of pain.

Slowly both Mira and Jude closed their eyes, and she sat there for a moment, watching them. They were extraordinarily beautiful to her, so brilliant and full of life. She couldn't control much of the world, but some things were in her power: what she gave them, how she made them feel about themselves, how far she would go to keep their light blazing.

She kissed them on their foreheads and left the room quietly. Downstairs, the bathroom light looked harsh and clinical. She opened the shower door and turned the handle, peeling her clothes off as she waited for the water to warm up. As she slipped off her shirt, she caught the blue gleam of the hamsa charm in the mirror. She reached around to the back of her neck and undid the clasp, then set the necklace on the edge of the sink. The reflection of her face was the same, but the way she felt about it seemed different. She slipped inside the shower, closing her eyes as the hot water spilled over her body.

It was only when she heard the TV in the bedroom that she opened them again. She stepped out of the shower and wrapped herself in a white towel. The air smelled of her jasmine and lavender soap, and the mirror had steamed over. Quickly she dried off and pulled on an oversized T-shirt. When she entered the bedroom, Fadi was standing by his nightstand, half-undressed.

"Hey," he said without looking up. He was reading something on his phone, the screen illuminating his face, his unbuckled belt hanging from his waist.

She walked toward him, the bedroom air cold against her skin. She saw no point in waiting, she had no waiting left in her. He was still looking down at his phone when she turned off the TV and said: "I'm filing for divorce."

He looked up. "What?"

She wanted to tell him everything: That she had been in denial about her life for so long. That she'd thought if she pretended hard enough, she could convince herself she was happy. That she'd been chasing all the wrong things instead of daring to look inside herself. But she knew none of her reasons would matter to him. He wouldn't understand.

"I can't stay with you after you lied to me," she said. "I need to figure things out on my own."

Fadi looked at her, his brows scrunched together. "Couples fight all the time. People make mistakes. That's no reason for you to break up our family."

"Then maybe this is?" Yara said. "We're very different people who need different things. You're fulfilled working all day and coming home to a home-cooked meal and a television show every night. I envy how satisfied you are with our life together, really. But I want more."

"What do you mean by 'more'? You don't even have a job."

She looked at him. Her hair was still wet, dripping down her back. "This is exactly what I mean. You measure life in terms of money and career, and that's fine. I wasn't much different, so desperate to prove myself. But now I'm interested in pursuing a life that's more authentic and true. And I know that it's something I have to do on my own. I'm sorry, Fadi."

He looked at her, one hand still clutching his phone. "You can't just leave."

"Yes, I can," Yara said. "I have a choice here, and this is it."

She lifted the towel off the bathroom door, sat down on the edge of the bed, and began to dry her hair. He moved closer to her, watching her intently. "What about our girls?" he said.

"We can share custody," Yara said. "I'm not interested in dragging our family through court. We can figure it all out as peacefully as possible."

"What are you teaching them by leaving your marriage, though?" Fadi said. "To just give up when things get tough? To be quitters?"

"Have you ever thought about what we're teaching them now? We're just like our parents."

"What are you talking about? We're nothing like them."

They looked at one another, and it occurred to her that she hadn't been the only one in denial. "I know you want to believe that everything is okay between us," she said. "I've been trying to convince myself of that for a very long time, too. Deep down, I knew something was wrong. But I was terrified of admitting it to myself because it meant I'd failed, and that I'd have to give up everything I'd worked so hard for. But I can't live like this anymore." She could hear the urgency in her own voice as she went on. "We've been living a fake life. You have to see that. You must feel it, don't you?"

"Our life is fine," Fadi said as soon as she'd finished, but he looked down at his hands, not meeting her eyes anymore. "You're the one who's too blind to see it. Do you have any clue what you're going to do to our girls? And for what? What are you looking for out there? What are you expecting to find?"

She opened her mouth, then closed it.

"See? You don't even know." He looked up at her now. "You're making this huge decision without considering the consequences. It's impulsive and childish, Yara. And selfish, too."

"Maybe you're right," she finally said. "And maybe there is nothing better out there for me. I'm okay with that. I just have to stop pretending."

"You're fucking insane, you know that?"

To this, she said nothing. She rose from the bed, hung the towel on the bathroom door, lifted her pillow and the blanket from the mattress, and walked into the hall. In the living room, she stretched out on the sofa for a second night.

It's true, she thought. All this time she'd convinced herself that she was crazy, because the alternative had seemed so much worse. If she wasn't crazy, she'd have to admit that Fadi was wrong, and admitting that meant she would either have to change her life drastically or accept that she would stay with him in spite of it. But she could no longer keep lying to herself.

A few minutes later, Fadi stalked through the living room and into the kitchen. On his way back down the hall, he said, without stopping, "You'll regret this, you'll see." Then he went into the bedroom and slammed the door shut behind him.

She slipped beneath the blanket, noticing nothing as she blinked into the darkness, not the murmur of the TV from the bedroom, not the frogs creaking outside, not the hum of cicadas in the trees. She lay there and thought of a life without Fadi, mourning the loss of the only self she had ever known as an adult.

He said she'd regret it; of course he'd say that.

But he was wrong. The pain of being alone could never compare to the loneliness she felt with him. She closed her eyes, took a deep breath. This was the first real moment of her new life. Tomorrow she would call a lawyer. Then she would start looking for a place to live. She knew it would be hard on the girls at first, but they would adjust. "It's going to be okay," she whispered to herself. In the morning she would take another deep breath and begin again.

56

By August, the perennials alongside the road were bursting with color, and the sun was shining full tilt through the flowering dogwood trees. The arrival of fall bought Yara an odd feeling of renewal. This was the close of a year she was glad to see end. In a small, quiet way, she was already on the other side of it.

Yara had spent the summer looking for an apartment she could afford, and despite picking up a freelance photography job in addition to selling her paintings, it wasn't until the girls were back in school that she was finally able to find one. "I'm privileged to even be able to do this," she told herself when she started to feel down.

For most of the summer, she and Fadi slept in separate rooms and barely spoke, but she was careful to act normal around the girls, not wanting to alarm them until the divorce was official. The least she could do was give them a peaceful and carefree summer. She spent her days together with them, hanging out at the community pool, or they'd go to the park, where, on a clear day, the brilliant blue sky was cast with white clouds that drifted lazily in the gentle breeze. There, they spread a blanket on the grass and ate hummus sandwiches with cucumbers and drank cold mint lemonade.

"It is a good life," she told herself, the sun warm against her skin. "A life to be grateful for."

"Do you have any idea what you've done?" Baba said now when Yara told him that she was moving out of Fadi's house and that the divorce was really happening. "What will people say?"

"Their opinions don't matter to me," Yara said. "Please, try to understand—"

"Understand what? That you've ruined your family?"

"It's the right thing for me, and for my daughters."

"Oh, for God's sake," Baba said. "You act like you're the first person to struggle in a marriage. Whatever happened to patience and strength when things get tough? You think we didn't suffer in our lives? You think we didn't endure?"

It took a moment for Yara to absorb this. She thought about all the ways her family had suffered, how tired her father must be now. If only he had the courage to be honest with her, with himself.

"I've been enduring all along, Baba," she finally said. "And so have you. But now I want to live."

There was a long silence before Baba said, "Go live then, but don't count on me to be here."

A click on the end of the line. Her whole life she'd felt like she'd been living with two people inside her, each tugging her in different directions, but now one of them was leading the way. She had to trust that person and keep moving, despite the pain.

Now, waiting in the carpool to pick up the girls from school, Yara won-dered how Mira and Jude would feel at the news that she'd found an apartment. It had only been a few weeks, but it seemed so very long ago that she'd parked outside the girls' school all afternoon, considering how she would tell them about the divorce, terrified of all the uncertainties awaiting her—breaking their hearts, losing them, living on her own. How afraid she'd been!

But in her bedroom one night, as she was grabbing her pillow and heading to the sofa, Fadi turned off the TV. "Yara," he said as she turned to leave. She stopped, willed herself to meet his eyes. After taking a deep breath in, she said, "Can we talk about the girls?" He went on observing her a moment longer, shaking his head lightly. Finally he said, "Okay."

They discussed taking the girls to a restaurant one afternoon, a neutral place with tables outside and sunshine, to explain to them what would be happening. But Yara still wasn't sure what would be happening, at least not for the girls. Would she and Fadi be fighting in court for custody? Would he try to take them from her as punishment for what she'd done, breaking their family apart?

Fadi looked at her then, as if reading the fear in her eyes, and exhaled. "We can split the girls' time evenly. Okay?"

"Yes," Yara said, smiling way too hard. "Okay, yes." She looked at him, bursting with relief, but he turned his face away, squinting past her, toward the darkness of the inky black screen on the wall. "Thank you, Fadi," she said, saying it for herself, but also for the girls. Was that the happiest moment of her life? She was certain it was.

"What you've done takes immense courage," Esther said during one of their sessions. "We are conditioned to believe that we should feel good after making difficult decisions, but it's okay to grieve for what you've lost."

Lately she and Esther talked a lot about stories. How our culture was permeated with narratives built on an arc where struggles and conflicts resolve themselves cleanly in a final resolution. How we were naturally drawn to this story arc and the sense of completion it offered. Listening to Esther, Yara could see how she had also been telling herself a story. She would get divorced. She would go to therapy. She would embark on a journey toward recovery, and despite certain challenges, achieve personal growth. At the end of her journey, she would be cured from her problems and fully healed. She would put her past away, like it was a room whose door could be shut and locked.

But Esther was helping her see things differently. In the real world, recovery from mental illness could be a lifelong struggle, like pushing through a revolving door. Progress would be made and lost, setbacks were inevitable, and there was no finish line or picture-perfect ending. Yara had come to accept this now. To stop resisting the uncertainty. But sometimes a wave of loneliness and fear crept up on her, and the depth of the pain surprised her.

"You mentioned having thoughts in the past of not wanting to be alive," Esther said. "Do you still feel that way?"

Yara shook her head. She didn't want to hurt herself anymore, could never do that to her daughters, though there were still days when the pain was so unbearable it felt difficult to live. She said this to Esther, the words heavy on her tongue. "But I think I've come to accept these feelings as part of who I am."

It was true. This was who she was. It was like her body was an ocean, and these feelings would always come and go like the tides. The task was not to let herself be pulled away by one of the currents. The task was to accept that her insides would feel violent and tumultuous at times, and to be okay with that. To surrender.

The next morning, after Yara dropped Mira and Jude off at school, she drove back to the house she'd shared with Fadi to pack her things, feeling weightless and free.

She stood in the middle of her closet, staring at what remained to be packed. She grazed her fingers over all the clothing she'd collected during her marriage: countless blouses, sweaters, pants, dresses, and shoes, in multiple colors and styles. Items she'd barely worn but had never thought to get rid of. A royal-blue dress she'd bought for their four-year anniversary. A pair of red heels she'd hoped Fadi would find sexy. Things she'd wished would make her feel better in her own body but never had.

The next thing she knew she was on her knees, filling plastic garbage bags to their brims. Four pairs of heels. Twenty dresses. Thirteen blouses. A leopard-print jacket. She packed her suitcase with her favorite things: two cashmere sweaters, an old cardigan, a silk dress, her favorite oversized sweater. A vintage tea set with blue and white florals, tarot cards, sunflowers in a terra-cotta. A new beginning.

On the way to her apartment, she stopped by Goodwill and dropped into the donation box the garbage bags containing the rest of her things, ridding herself of everything that no longer served her.

In her empty apartment kitchen, as Yara unpacked her vintage tea set, the sun poured through the window, golden light everywhere. She was thinking about a conversation she'd had with Jude that morning before school.

Jude had been frowning more than usual lately.

"Are you okay?" Yara had asked.

"Yeah."

"Are you sure?"

Jude shrugged.

"Can I tell you something?" Yara said, scooting closer to her daughter. "I was a lot like you as a young girl. I felt things a little more deeply and struggled to express myself. I didn't notice for a long time how much I swallowed my emotions, but lately I've been learning how to manage them better."

Jude nodded.

"Our emotions are energy," Yara continued. "Energy in motion. The point is to move the emotions through and out of your body. When you don't express your emotions, when you keep your feelings inside, the energy gets trapped. So it's important to feel emotions and talk about them, because when you keep them bottled in, you start to feel sad and down and heavy."

"Is that why you paint?" Jude asked. "To move the energy out?"

"Yes," Yara said, smiling. "I think it is."

• • •

It'd been two months since she moved out. The girls spent half the time at her place, half at Fadi's. They still needed reassuring, each in their own way. On her nights with them, Yara held Mira in her arms and sang her a song, then she ran her fingers through Jude's hair, kissed her forehead, and whispered that everything would be okay, that they would always be a family.

The apartment wasn't far from Fadi's house, on the edge of the very same neighborhood, yet her surroundings seemed extraordinarily different, more vibrant somehow. A blanket of blue sky, golden light bursting among tree branches. People behind windows, talking to one another, laughing. From the outside, it might have seemed like not much had changed, but the way Yara now lived her life in moments of solitude, fully and all to herself, was completely new to her. For once, she felt like it didn't take so much effort to simply live. And that was everything.

Some days were like this, bright and free, as though she were floating in smooth water. But on other days, her old pain bubbled to the surface for reasons that were not always clear. In these moments, she sat quietly alone and retreated into herself. Then she wrote her way out, using words to stitch herself together inch by inch. Her notebook was an anchor keeping her from shifting off course. She wrote about Mama. She wrote about Teta. She wrote about the olive trees in Palestine, how they had been chopped from the roots. How, even though they'd looked dead, they were the most resilient trees and had grown back to twice their original size.

Some days language felt insufficient. The distance between what she felt and what she could communicate became a gulf. Still, each day she flipped open to a new page and brought her paintbrush to a new canvas. There were infinite opportunities for her feelings to change course, to lighten, to become comprehensible to her.

Today was Friday, for instance, and that was the day she met Silas at the coffee shop, after he'd taught his final class of the week.

"What did you bring me today?" she asked him. They were sitting together at the small round table by the window. He'd almost always brought with him a container of whatever he'd cooked for the faculty luncheon—spaghetti carbonara, risotto, apple pie.

"Carrot and Potato Gratin with Parmesan and Thyme," Silas said. "But you might not like it."

"Why not?"

He leaned forward, pushing the container toward her. "Apparently, it tastes nothing like it does on the Côte d'Azur," he said, rolling his eyes.

They laughed.

She used to think she didn't need other people. But her friendship with Silas had shown her how wrong she'd been.

Ever since she moved out, he'd shown up for her in ways she'd never experienced before. They went to the movies together or stayed in and ordered takeout. She played him all the Arabic songs Mama used to sing; he bought them tickets to see his favorite band. They took long walks around her neighborhood and took the girls to the park most weekends. She helped him pick out dresses for Olivia. He sat with her on the days when Fadi had the girls and she couldn't stop crying because she missed them so much. When she didn't have the capacity to initiate plans, he had invitations ready for her: Would she come over and help him paint his daughter's room? Could she have lunch at Josephine's house next weekend? Were they on for coffee on Friday?

"Why are you looking at me like that?" Silas was saying now.

"Oh, nothing, sorry." She shook her head, curling her fingers around her mug. "I was just thinking."

"About what?"

He looked at her, his eyes bright in the light from the window.

Quietly she said: "Sometimes I wonder how it's possible that you care more about me than my own family does."

For a few seconds he only looked at her, his eyes glassy. "I know it's hard for you to trust people after what you've been through," he said, his expression soft. "But I care about you. I do."

She rubbed her eyes with her fingertips. "I know. But it's hard not to question it sometimes. I'm sorry."

"You don't have to apologize," Silas said. "You just need time. And someone to lean on."

"But what if I'm always afraid of being let down?"

He leaned forward and placed his hands on the table. "You won't be."

She nodded, and they sat there without speaking. Yara stared out the window, watched people come and go. He cared about her. Someone cared about her, someone who didn't have any obligation to do so. Hadn't she wanted to hear those words her entire life? To love and be loved in return?

Looking down at the table now, she thought about the way she'd felt as a child when Mama wouldn't look at her, as a young mother when Baba stopped taking her calls, in recent years when Fadi turned away from her at night. The pain of those experiences was real, but so was the joy she found with Silas.

Silas was still looking at her, his expression kind and open. "Everything is going to be okay, you know that? I'm right here. You can count on me."

She reached for his hand across the table, held it. Yes, why not? To surrender to the vulnerability of love and allow ourselves to be loved by others—isn't that the most courageous act of all?

On her next night with the girls, Yara took them to a painting studio that she'd recently stumbled across downtown. Outside, the air was perfectly cool. The sun had set, and the sky was a dreamy swirl of pink and purple. Strings of flickering lights hung above them, and lively shops surrounded them on both sides. Holding hands, the three of them made their way from the car to the studio, walking slowly down the pavement.

"Can we get lights like these for our new room?" Mira said.

"Please, Mama?" Jude said. "They're so pretty."

Yara smiled. "Sure. That would be nice."

At first, Yara hadn't wanted to give up any of her time with them—she'd never spent a second away from them, outside of school. But getting a divorce didn't mean that she had given up being their mother, she could see that now. If anything, she felt more alive when she was with them, more available, and they saw a better version of her than before. On nights like this, Yara wondered how Mama's life would've turned out had she gotten the chance to find a better version of herself. She would never know the answer, of course, but at least she had the chance to be a better mother now.

Inside the studio, they washed their hands, slipped on aprons, and headed to their seats. Yara sat between Mira and Jude. People filtered in around them. They greeted the instructor, a cheery Asian American woman with a silky black bob, then took their places around the paint-splattered tables. Paper plates with gobs of paint were distributed at each station, next to canvases with outlines of the evening's painting leaning on small easels.

The evening's image was a portrait of Frida Kahlo, a reproduction that stood in the center of the room. Yara had chosen to bring the girls tonight for this particular reason, hoping they would have fun making a self-portrait of their own.

Every seat was filled by the time the class started. At the front of the room, the instructor held up the reproduction and explained how Frida Kahlo had taken up painting to cope with isolation. "Her ability to express so many emotions in her paintings is one of the gifts she gave humanity," the instructor said.

Jude turned and looked up at Yara, and the two of them shared a smile.

Mira stared at the painting with her mouth open, seemingly mesmerized. Sitting between them, Yara felt herself expand. She blinked hard, trying to keep her tears back. But the painting, and her daughters' reactions to it, moved her. She spent the rest of the evening feeling weightless, floating in a strange state of wonder. How was it possible for an image to move her this way? Frida might never have anticipated that her work could speak to a girl like Yara, yet it did.

"I want to help other people," she'd told Esther during a session earlier that week. "I want to be a voice for Palestinians and open up doors for other underrepresented groups and historically marginalized people. I want to make people feel seen."

"How will you do that?" Esther had asked.

But it wasn't until she walked out of the art studio with her girls into the perfect fall evening that Yara knew exactly how she would. Her whole life, she'd believed that relatability would never be granted to someone like her. But even though her experiences could never speak for everyone, they would speak for some people, women like her who were searching for themselves in the art around them, women whose experiences needed to be legitimized. She could create a space for people to feel represented, a space that made visible the presence of people of color in the art world. Maybe that was enough.

Later that night, after they'd hung their finished paintings in their new bedroom, Mira asked her, "Can we go again?"

"How about something better?" Yara said.

"Like what?"

"What if we open our own art studio?"

She didn't know how or when, but she could see it in her mind, as vivid as a painting. A space that inspired creativity and healing with a focus on art created by people of color. A space where she could feature her own work while fostering a diverse community of designers, photographers, painters, sculptors, and their families. A space that would lift up the voices of individuals from historically underrepresented communities. She closed her eyes and painted this dream in her mind, one brushstroke after another, then she described it aloud for the girls, the two of them listening with rapt attention, as if this were the best story their mother had ever told them.

YARA'S JOURNAL

"Where did you get your necklace?" I ask you one afternoon.

This is a memory I keep returning to lately, holding it like a warm cup of mint chai in my hands on a rainy day.

We are in our Brooklyn apartment, rolling grape leaves at the kitchen table. Outside, trains rumble in the distance and the sun tucks itself behind the London plane trees, a yellow sliver of light coming through the open window. Across from me, you are smiling, your fingers shining with olive oil. You are slumped forward in your seat, as though trying to disappear, as though apologizing for something, but my question has actually made you smile.

It's been years since what I'd done, telling Baba everything, when you spent your days suddenly moody, your sadness like a gas in the room, poisoning our every breath. But sitting together that afternoon, cupping rice between our fingers and arranging it neatly on leaves, a faint breeze coming through the open window, I know, even now, that this is a moment I would want to hold on to, maybe keep forever, just like the shimmering gold chain that hangs from your neck.

I want to reach out and touch it, but I'm afraid the magic will break and the darkness that seems to stand beside you lately will return. Instead, I ask you about the necklace.

"I never told you?" you say.

"No."

A faint strip of sun is splayed across your chest, and the charm shines like a treasure.

"My mother gave it to me before I moved to America," you say. "Your grandmother was a very superstitious woman, you know. Have I ever told you about the time she sewed a hamsa bead around the handle of my oud, hoping to protect me from the envy of our neighbors?"

I shake my head. "No."

"Well, she was convinced that my voice was beautiful enough to . . ."

Listening to my mother speak, I picture Teta sitting around the table with us, rolling the leaves into fingerlike shapes before slipping them into the pot. I imagine her laughing as you share the story. Teta saying, "I was only looking out for you." And you retorting, "I know you meant well."

I wipe sweat from my upper lip, watching as you place a mound of rice on a grape leaf. "Can I wear your necklace one day?"

You sit back, wipe your fingers on a wet rag. Your glance, as you look down at your chest and then back at me, hardens. "Why do you want it?"

"What if I need it one day? To protect myself."

Something passes over your face—discomfort, maybe. Or fear. "You don't need a charm for protection," you say.

"I don't?"

Your eyes well up and you don't respond.

"Will you protect me, then?" I ask.

You shake your head, touching the end of the wet rag. In a near whisper you say, "I'm sorry, habibti, but I'm afraid I can't."

As you pick up another spoonful of rice, I can feel my face burn beneath the harsh kitchen light. In the sudden silence, while we continue to roll the leaves, you say quietly, "I'm afraid I can't teach you the things you need because I haven't learned them myself. My mother couldn't teach me because she'd never learned either and . . ." You pause, your face crumpling. "That will always be my biggest regret. Not knowing how to protect you. Instead, I only know what it is to be cursed."

That moment when you look down into your lap, discreetly wiping tears from your eyes—I have an urge to put my arms around you, but I can't move.

"I'm sorry," you say. "I wish I could go back and do things differently." You

pause for a moment, then look at me. "But I know you will. I can see it in your eyes, ya binti. In those deep, dark eyes of yours, there is so much goodness ahead. I feel it."

"Really?"

You nod, a faint smile brightening your face. "One day you'll do things better than we did. Inshallah you will."

ACKNOWLEDGMENTS

Thank you: firstly to you, my dear reader, for taking the time to read our stories; to Julia Kardon for her early support of my writing, and for always offering wisdom and guidance; to Emily Griffin, whose thoughtful, detailed feedback helped shape and complete the novel, and for being so incredibly kind and lovely to work with; to Erin Wicks, who was with this novel long before I had finished writing it, and whose conversation and guidance contributed substantially to its development; to Maya Baran, the marketing directors, production editor, and everyone who has worked on the publication, distribution, or sale of this book: I owe a great debt of gratitude to you; to Lauren Tamaki, for creating a strikingly bold and powerful cover—the most beautiful I've ever seen; to Hannah Popal, for being my first reader and offering wise advice; to Kate Milliken, whose excellent feedback helped me see what was good in the novel, and how it could be better; to the librarians at Braswell Memorial Library, for their help and support over the years; to my family, particularly my sisters, for their unconditional love and friendship; to Brandon's family, and to Mallory, for showing me endless love; to my children, Reyann and Isah, for being the light of my life and greatest source of joy—every word I write is striving to make your world a better place; and to Brandon, hayati, for everything.

ABOUT THE AUTHOR

ETAF RUM was born and raised in Brooklyn, New York, by Palestinian immigrants. She lives in North Carolina with her two children and owns a coffee shop and bookstore called Books and Beans. Her first novel, *A Woman Is No Man*, was a *New York Times* bestseller and a *Today* show host Jenna Bush Hager's Read With Jenna book club pick.